PURSUIT
of
Innocence

BETHANY ROSA

GALLATIN PUBLISHING

THE *pursuit* SERIES

Pursuit of Innocence

Holidate Pursuit

Dangerous Pursuit

Pursuit of Love (mid-2025)

PURSUIT *of* Innocence

Prologue

Lily

My head is pounding. *Crap.* I don't remember how I got home last night. Did I let myself get that out of control? Reluctantly, I peel my eyes open and immediately notice this isn't my bed. I have no idea where I am. When I move to sit up, I'm stopped by a tug on my ankle. I lift the covers to see a rope around it. *What the hell is going on?* Questions flood my mind as I start to panic.

"Good morning, sleepyhead" comes a voice from the doorway. *Wait…* I recognize that voice. He enters completely. *Oh my God.* "You should learn to control your drinking, Lily. It's a terrible habit. However, you're not entirely at fault. There may have been a little something slipped into your drink last night," he mockingly says as he sits in a chair by the bed.

"Why am I here and tied to the bed? What's going on? What happened?" I'm so confused. I have no memory of how I got here.

"I'm sure you have a lot of questions. All in due time, which we have plenty of now that we're finally together."

"You're scaring me. Will you please tell me what's happening? What do you want?" Panic has officially set in.

"I want it all, Lily. I want what's mine."

1

NO SHORTAGE OF PRICKS

One month earlier
Lily

THE WALK HOME FROM WORK TONIGHT SEEMS TO TAKE FOREVER. I'm exhausted after another grueling week between work and school. What is it about Fridays that seem to drag on? Probably because I'm forced to endure Brad, my pervy boss, all day. Classes are only three days a week, so I get the privilege of working in the office all day on Wednesdays and Fridays.

I'm relieved to be walking in my front door and am instantly greeted by Ebony, the black Persian cat we adopted, weaving around my legs. She was given up because she was too affectionate. Who does that?

"Hey, how was work today?" Cici asks from the kitchen. I can see she's already opening a bottle of wine.

My best friend, Cici, graciously lets me share her apartment for way less than what I should be paying. Rentals around Balboa Park aren't cheap, but Cici's family owns the building, so it affords more generosity. It was a battle getting her to accept even the little I do pay. With her knowledge of my crazy past and her family taking me in when my dad abandoned me at fifteen, her empathy runs deep and charity over the top.

Setting my stuff down, I pick up Ebony. "Oh, thrilling as always. I don't know why I haven't started looking for something else yet."

"If I hear you say that one more time before you do it, I'll start sending out résumés for you. What happened today?" Cici hands me my wine while I sit at the breakfast bar and situate Ebony on my lap.

"You know how I've told you Brad is weird sometimes? He had me work in his office today instead of the reception area because he said he needed me to take notes for him, which I barely even did. It was so uncomfortable. Not only did I run out of work but I couldn't start on my homework like normal because he was sitting right there watching me. Ugh, it gave me the creeps."

She points her finger at me and begins her lecture. "Lily, I'm telling you, something's wrong with that prick. You've had this feeling for too long to ignore anymore. At least start looking at what else is out there. Why don't you do that when you get bored instead of homework next time?"

I take a big sip before answering. "I can't look for a new job at my current job, Cici. He could catch me, and I can't afford to get fired."

"You know I have your back no matter what. If it's a matter of your safety, I'll cover you anytime."

I shake my head. "I won't do that. Thanks to you and your family, I've supported myself this long. I'm not taking any more help than I've already had to. Anyway, all I need to do is get through the next few months, and I'm on my way to better things. Once I graduate, I'll be able to get my foot in the door at a bigger, more prestigious marketing firm and finally start making enough money to do more than get by."

She slams her hand down on the counter. "Ugh, it's so frustrating that you have no support in situations like this. Your loser dad will never step up, so let me be your family, and if you need help, that's what family's for."

"I know and thank you. That means a lot. Now, no more about me. How was your day?" Cici will push and push until I give in. I've become an expert at redirecting.

"Wait until you hear this. I found out that Layla broke up with Braden! I finally have a chance at him!" She squeals and claps her hands.

I laugh and give her a high five. "Well, if there's anyone who can make him forget about his girlfriend of, what, three years? It would be you."

Cici is the classic California girl with thick long blonde hair, sparkling blue eyes and a fantastic body thanks to the gym. She's also the most genuine person on the planet. The only reason no one has snatched her up yet is because she's as picky as they come and doesn't have a monogamous bone in her body. I'm the opposite, with my auburn hair, olive skin and wide hazel eyes. Boring and basic, but attractive in the girl next door kind of way. At least I have a decent body thanks to my lack of a car and low budget. I walk to everything within a couple of miles and run whenever I can find the time. My diet consists of basic home-cooked meals with no room for indulgences unless Cici's buying.

The biggest difference between us is my experience with men. The closest thing I've had to a boyfriend was a kiss in the closet in fifth grade. Okay, that's exaggerating, but not by much. There just hasn't been time since being on my own at fifteen and having to work my butt off ever since. It doesn't leave much time for dating. I've gotten so good at putting off the not interested vibe that my approachability level has become nonexistent. Not to mention, the only two guys I've kissed since the closet incident left me with no desire to work on that issue.

"To celebrate my new pursuit, I've decided we're heading out to a new dance club that's all the rage, and it sounds like you need it after the day you had." She raises her glass to clink with mine.

Instead, I leave her hanging. "Oh, Cici, I don't think I'm up for it. You know I'm not very fun at those places, and I'll end up holding you back more than anything." She rolls her eyes at me and takes a drink. I can already tell her mind is made up; there's no way I'm winning this argument. She's too damn good at persuasion when she digs her heels in.

Pouring more wine into our glasses, she gives me her speech. "Listen, Lily, you need to get out more. It won't kill you to let loose for one night. You know, one of these days, you need to lose your V-card or at least explore a little further than a make-out session with someone who doesn't know what he's doing. Then you'll see what all the fuss is about. That won't happen if you stay home all the time and don't put yourself out there. Let's go for it tonight, get tipsy and see what happens."

"I am not going to get drunk and have—"

She holds her hand up, palm facing me. "I'm not saying you should give it up tonight. I know you better than that. I'm just suggesting you loosen up and be open to the possibility of more. Someone's out there for you, but you need to give them a chance. Regardless, you deserve to have fun now and then, so get ready. We're leaving in an hour." She sticks her tongue out and walks off with her wine.

An hour later, I'm putting my glass away when Cici walks in and stops dead in her tracks. "Whoa, you are not going out to the hottest club in San Diego dressed like you're going to the office. Follow me." She turns around without another word, leaving me staring down at myself.

How are black slacks and a nice tank top considered going to the office? Okay, I can see her point on the slacks, but I would only wear this tank with a jacket to work. Most importantly, I put wedges on instead of flats. These are way different from my work shoes. Sighing, I tread down the hallway to her room.

"I think it's fine. I don't want to give the wrong message anyway." Cici's already standing in her closet and tossing things onto the bed. I can see from here there's nothing I'm comfortable with. Luckily, we're similar in size other than my average chest in comparison to her voluptuous one. Most of her clothes fit me, but that doesn't mean I'd wear most of them. Everything in her overflowing closet is trendy and expensive thanks to her trust fund, but her style and mine are like our looks, night and day. However, I do borrow something for an event now and then since nice dresses are out of my budget.

She scowls at me. "Lily, stop it. Just because you dress hot doesn't mean you have to screw anyone. It just makes guys notice you more, and that's step one to meeting the man of your dreams. You have to stop hiding behind your wardrobe. You're gorgeous and you need to own it. What are you afraid of?"

Instead of answering, I go through the stack of clothes, pick two reasonable options and hold them up. Of course, she grabs two more and pulls me into the adjoining bathroom.

"Come on, you're trying all four, and then I'm giving you a smoky eye. Lily is coming out to play!" She winks at me as I groan.

Thirty minutes later, we're pulling up in the Uber, and I must admit, I'm feeling pretty damn sexy with the final look from my stylist for the evening. Exiting onto the sidewalk, I head toward the end of the line, but Cici grabs my arm and pulls me to the VIP entrance. She gives the bouncer our names. He lifts his clipboard to check the list and steps aside, motioning us in. The club is already packed. Opposite the dance floor, there's a bar the length of the building. Separating them is an enormous staircase lit with in-floor blue lighting leading to the second level, where a balcony looms over the lower level. The club is dark, with just enough strobes and motion lighting to see throughout. The music is pumping, and it already feels stuffy. It's going to be a long night.

I lean in to Cici. "How did you get us on the list?"

"My brother knows one of the owners, and he got a table for all of us tonight. I forgot to tell you that Jackson and Braden are meeting us here. Oh look, there they are." She points up to the balcony, where you can see the tables through the glass railing.

There he is. Jackson Soloman. The one guy I can't seem to keep from thinking about, wishing I was good enough for. I've been in love with him since Cici and I became friends during freshman year of high school and I went over to her house for the first time. It was an instant crush. Her older brother by three years, and the hottest boy I had ever seen. If there's one guy who makes me want to do more than make out, it's him. The problem is, I don't think he's ever considered me as anything other than his little sister's annoying friend. Why are they even joining us anyway?

Cici starts climbing the stairs, and I pull her arm to stop her. "Why are they here? We never go out together."

"Well, I wanted to get us into the club without waiting in a line we might never get through, and voilà, here we are. I begged Jackson to get us on the VIP list with his connection, and luckily for me he made joining us a condition. Like I'd say no to spending time with Braden, duh. Now come on, let's have some fun." She resumes up the stairs, giving me no choice but to follow.

We walk to where Jackson and Braden are sitting, drinks already on the table with a bottle on ice. Jackson looks amazing, and instantly my insecurities come out in full force. "Hey, ladies, looking good!" Braden says, looking us up and down as we take our seats. "Anyone ready to join me in getting shit-faced tonight and drowning our sorrows?" He lifts his drink in salute and takes a big gulp.

"You'll have to excuse Braden. He's on a mission to forget 'she who must not be named,' and alcohol is the poison of choice," Jackson explains, looking at Braden with concern. "It's why we came tonight." Well, that explains that.

"I can't join you in drowning sorrows, Braden, but I'll join you in getting hammered," Cici happily agrees. I know how excited she is that he's finally free of Layla, but I hope she's not setting herself up for disappointment. "What are you guys drinking tonight?" she asks.

"Only the best for a breakup—tequila, tonic and lime. Would you ladies care for one?" He lifts the bottle from the ice, ready to fill two more glasses.

Cici pushes her glass toward him as I shake my head. "No thanks. I'll start with prosecco." Thank goodness Cici told me the drinks are on them tonight. Otherwise, I'd be stuck with cheap beer.

Jackson waves the waitress over, and I order while Braden makes Cici her drink. "Hey, Jackson, thanks for getting us in tonight. That was nice of you." I'm awkwardly trying to pull the dress down past my upper thigh. Cici insisted I wear this short, dark blue, curve-hugging dress, telling me, "It makes your chest pop and your legs go on forever." She's full of it, but sometimes you have to agree to get her mouth to stop moving.

"This one"—Jackson pats Cici on the head—"was relentless. She wouldn't take no for an answer and said it was the only thing she would ask of me until next year."

"No way! Cici wouldn't accept no? I find that so hard to believe!" I say sarcastically, putting my hand over my chest.

"Yep, you know Cici—when she wants something, she gets it. If only we could all be like that." He contemplates for a moment before he slaps Braden on the back. "It happened to be perfect timing since someone here needed a bit of a distraction."

"Dude, this is great. Look at that dance floor and all it has to offer. If this can't cure a broken heart, I don't know what will. Thanks for getting us out tonight, Cici. I, for one, am grateful. Cheers!" He holds his glass up, and we all follow, toasting to Cici. She's blushing like crazy of course. Good for her that she has her chance. Maybe one day I'll get mine.

"Who's ready to join me on the dance floor?" Braden asks right after we all take a sip. This level has another dance floor, so we don't have to go far.

"Oh, me for sure! Come on, Lily, let's go." Cici tugs my arm as she gets up. Pulling out of her grasp, I quickly down my glass of prosecco, then rush to catch up.

It's packed. Everybody is glistening with sweat and bumping into one another. I try my best to keep from touching anyone and stay within our small circle, but soon Braden has two girls surrounding him, separating us, and Cici has a couple of guys vying for her attention as well. Suddenly, I feel someone behind me, and I turn around to see a guy smiling, tilting his head in question. I smile back shyly, reminding myself what Cici said. Just because I put myself out there doesn't mean I have to sleep with anyone. I dance with a few inches between us for a while, but he's slowly closing the distance. The guy is good-looking and smells great, but he isn't the one I want to be with. This is the problem being here with Jackson—he's all I think about. *Ugh.*

Suddenly, Mr. Smooth Move's hands are on either side of my hips, holding me close. I can feel his package against my stomach. *Gross.* I try to pull back a bit, but he's holding me tight. He leans his head toward my neck, and I push him, forcing him to release me. After breaking free, I decide to leave the dance floor for another drink. Cici seems happy with both guys grinding on her, so I leave her alone.

I return to the table and find Jackson talking with a beautiful blonde. It doesn't surprise me; there's never a shortage of gorgeous women throwing themselves at him, and he's usually not batting them away. Jackson is dreamy with his bodyguard physique. He's worked hard in the gym habitually since his high school football days. He also inherited the family genes of blond hair, blue eyes and a face that makes you want to stare at it for days—something I had to train myself not to do early on. He's a model for all women's wet dreams.

I notice a full glass of prosecco waiting for me in place of my empty one. "Thanks for the drink," I say, taking a large sip.

"Sure, figured you may need it after fending off that jackass out there." He motions behind me, and I turn to see he has a perfect view of the dance floor. I notice Cici is still going strong, but I swear it's two different guys now.

I turn back. "It was fine. He just got a little ahead of himself. I don't know why guys always assume anything goes on the dance floor." Although, judging by the girl hanging on Jackson's every word with obvious lust, the assumptions probably aren't far off.

"Well, I'm in an anything-goes kind of mood if you'd like to join me out there…," Blondie says seductively while pouting up at Jackson, proving my thoughts correct.

"Not yet, babe. I'm here as moral support for my buddy and might need to carry him out later. Here he comes now," he says, looking behind me.

"I guess I'll leave you to it then. Come find me if you change your mind," Bombshell purrs before she kisses Jackson on the cheek and saunters off, blatantly strutting her ass. Ugh, I'm internally rolling my eyes.

Cici joins us at the same time Braden makes it back. "Why did you come back to the table? It's not as fun out there without you." She pouts.

"It looked like you were having plenty of fun from what I saw, so don't even try to guilt trip me. I left 'cause some prick started getting too handsy. Perfect timing to get another drink anyway." I show her my glass and take another sip.

Cici doesn't let me off that easily. "The guy dancing with you looked pretty cute. Maybe you should've let him be a little handsy or at least had him buy you a drink," she says, wagging her eyebrows.

"Luckily, Jackson already had another one waiting. Besides, there's no way I'm letting some creep put his hands all over me just because we're dancing. He didn't even ask my name," I say incredulously.

Braden, who's succeeded in drinking enough to forget his problems, decides to chime in about mine. "That's not how it works out there, babe—names are for later. I think little virgin Lily is just scared to get her feet wet. Maybe you should give it another shot. Cici can show you how it's done." The shock on my face is apparent. It's not a secret that my virgin status is well-known among everyone present, but that's just a low blow, and what makes it even worse is Jackson practically spits his beer out laughing. *Great, just great.*

"I guess there's no shortage of pricks here tonight," I rant, looking at Braden and Jackson.

Deciding I've had enough fun for one night, I lean in to hug my best friend. "You know what, I think I'm just going to head out. I'm tired after this week. You stay and enjoy yourself, and I'll text you when I make it home." I quickly turn around, grab my purse and run down the stairs before Cici can protest.

I'm halfway down when I hit a wall. A solid, warm wall that smells dreadfully sinful. Before I have time to process, two firm hands are on my shoulders to steady me. "Hey, watch where you're going" comes the deepest, sexiest voice imaginable, which would be incredibly hot if the words spoken were anything other than rude and demanding. Looking up, which is crazy, considering I'm one step higher, I freeze as my eyes land on a dark, handsome god of a man who looks like he wants to commit murder. What is it with me and jerks tonight?

His eyes get bigger, and his brows furrow as soon as my shocked gaze meets his. He has short black hair that's longer on the top and styled perfectly. His menacing eyebrows are folded downward from scowling at me. The dark scruff that shadows his face is so sexy, trimmed razor straight, accentuating his perfectly chiseled jaw. Mentally slapping myself, I apologize.

"Crap, I'm so sorry. I didn't see you there." He doesn't release his hold.

"That's because your head was down. Your eyes should be looking forward." His voice is hard and demanding.

Flustered and—I reluctantly admit—slightly turned on by his strong, firm grip and penetrating stare, I stand there frozen in place. After what seems like minutes but I'm sure is only seconds, I snap out of it and apologize again. "Sorry, I'll watch where I'm going from now on." The words rush out as I pull away to leave, this time keeping my head up. I think I hear him say something else behind me, but I don't stop. Running into one of the hottest guys I've seen in a while should've been the highlight of my night. Instead, I'm more irritated. Do all good-looking men have a license to be an ass, or what?

Once I'm outside the club, I decide to take the bus. An Uber alone is too expensive and an indulgence I don't need. Luckily, it's perfect timing; the rain has let up, and my app says it's only a few blocks to the stop and five minutes until it arrives. Friday night in downtown San Diego is busy, so I'm not worried about being alone, but just to be safe, I have my phone ready to push the emergency button because you never know. Once I reach the bus stop, I sit on the empty bench, and suddenly, a nervousness creeps over me, accompanied by a feeling of being watched. My instincts tell me to do what any intelligent person would do. I look down at my phone, then bring it to my ear to answer an imaginary call. Because who can kidnap you when you're talking with someone on the phone, right? I'm relieved to see the bus pulling up a few seconds later and quickly rise to hop on.

Arriving home safe and sound, I text Cici good night, get ready for bed and finally crawl under the covers with Ebony snuggled up to me. My mind immediately starts reflecting on the night. God, I'm honestly so sick of being a virgin. It never fails to come up. I'm sick of guys being pricks too. Sometimes I wish I could meet someone who finally does it for me other than Jackson. And what was with that jerk on the way out? That's the problem with gorgeous men. They're pompous, domineering bastards who think women will drop their panties and do anything they want. I close my eyes and try to focus my mind on positive things. After what seems like forever tossing and turning, trying to wrangle my thoughts, sleep finally overcomes me.

Waking up Saturday morning, I'm just as irritated as the night before and decide my positive thinking didn't do me any good. But a good cup of coffee may do the trick. I don't usually indulge in morning lattes, but I think I deserve it after enduring the crap from yesterday and last night. I throw on joggers and a shirt, put my hair in a messy bun and head out the door. My favorite coffee spot is only a few blocks away. No Starbucks for this girl. One, it's ridiculously priced, and two, I don't like their coffee. I'm not sure what all the fuss is about unless you want insanely sweet, fattening drinks that come in a size no ordinary human being should be consuming. Nope, a regular nonfat latte will do while supporting a local business.

The elevator doors open into the lobby, where Jackson is waiting to get on. Great, just what I needed. "Good morning," I say as I step out. Jackson also lives in the building because why wouldn't he? Their family owns a ton of real estate in San Diego, but this is their best residential building.

He holds the door open and faces me. "Morning, Lils. Hey, sorry about last night. Braden was drunk and acting like an ass. He didn't mean any harm, and I shouldn't have laughed."

"Yeah, well, I should be used to the teasing by now, but sometimes it gets old. Thanks for apologizing, though. So… are you just getting home? Must've been quite the night." Shit, I'm cringing inside. Why did I even ask that? It's obvious since he's wearing the same clothes from last night. Apparently, I like punishing myself.

He looks at me sheepishly. "Yeah, I guess it was."

"Well, good for you then. See you later, Jackson." I wave goodbye, turn around and walk outside. Wow, if that isn't the writing on the wall. I need to get over him in a bad way.

The sun is finally shining after three days of rain, and it's a balmy sixty degrees this morning. Nice enough to enjoy the walk down the street, and after a couple of blocks, I'm starting to feel better. A little vitamin D goes a long way. I get my coffee and start the trek back, soaking up the sun.

Walking in, I see Cici making her own cup of coffee. "Sorry, Cici, I didn't expect to see you up until this afternoon, or I would have grabbed you something."

"That's okay. It ended up being a way earlier night than expected since someone decided to get blackout drunk so early. I left with Jackson to help wrangle Braden into the Uber. I don't know why he's so upset about this breakup; she was such a bitch."

"Well, three years is a long time no matter what. And yeah, he was wasted all right. I can't believe he had the nerve to call me out and be a jerk about it." My anger returns in full force.

"You know people say things they don't mean when they're drunk. It was a dick move though. I bet he'll apologize today if he even remembers it. How was your Uber ride home?" she asks.

I look down at my coffee guiltily. "I ended up taking the bus. The stop was just a couple blocks down, and the bus wasn't far away. It all worked out," I spit out quickly, already seeing the look of disapproval on her face.

"Lily! You know that's not a good idea at night by yourself. I could've ordered your Uber from my phone, silly. No wonder it took so long to hear you made it home. Jackson was driving me crazy, asking every five minutes if I got your text."

"That's weird. Why would he care? I figured he didn't even notice I left." I'm shocked he even gave me a second thought. And this is my problem—I hear one thing about Jackson, and I'm hooked.

"You know him, he's a worrywart, always thinking the worst. And of course he noticed. You're my best friend and important to me. So, what are you doing today and the rest of the weekend?" she asks.

"Right now, a run to clear my head. Then I'm staying in until I get my final project done that's due this week. It's 80 percent of my grade, and even though I've pretty much nailed it, I want to add some finishing touches. And most importantly, I need to catch up on my sleep." Story of my life.

2

LOOKING GOOD

Lily

THE REST OF THE WEEKEND WAS WELL SPENT FINISHING THE AD campaign for my final project and catching up on my sleep. In fact, for a Monday morning, I wake up feeling so great that I put extra effort into choosing my outfit. Usually, I throw on whatever is clean and comfortable, but today I find something that makes me look as good as I feel. I end up with a black pencil skirt, blue silk blouse and a pair of rarely worn short heels to give me a boost. I even apply the barest amount of makeup. Mascara, blush and a hint of lip stain. My favorite jewelry completes the look.

I'm happy as I walk into Professor Milton's class despite my already sore feet from the heels. It takes a moment to spot Kevin before taking the seat beside him. He gives an appraising smile, looking me up and down. "Wow, Lily, looking good. What were you up to this weekend?"

Kevin is one of my favorite people. Fun to talk to and always eager to hear about my boring life. We only see each other outside school to grab a coffee or a quick bite after class. Although we've been in most of the same courses for almost four years, we never seem to connect otherwise. "Friday night, I tried that new club everyone's talking about downtown.

Cici's brother, Jackson, has a connection with one of the owners and got us on a list. It's quite the place. What about you? Anything fun?"

"That sounds awesome. Nothing exciting for me, so you can tell me all about your night when I buy you coffee after class." He winks at me.

"I won't pass up the coffee, but you may be disappointed when you hear about my boring night." I roll my eyes. Kevin is always offering to buy me coffee. He knows a lot about my life since we've been friends for so long and I enjoy his company. He's easy on the eyes with dirty blond hair that hangs over his forehead. He reminds me of a surfer. I'm pretty sure it's one of his pastimes. He's fun, easygoing and always out for a good time. If there had been any free time in my life, we could've had some good times ourselves. He's given it his best effort over the years, but it was never in the cards for me, and I made it clear early on. Now, I've known him too long to think of him as anything other than a friend.

"I'll be the judge of that, and anyway, you could never disappoint me, Lily," he says right before Professor Milton starts his lecture.

We're sitting in the café sipping our coffee and eating the chocolate-strawberry croissants Kevin insisted on as I tell him about the club. Another reason I adore him is that he knows exactly how to butter me up.

"So, who did you go with? Meet anyone cool?" He's fishing. By now, he should know my answer will never be any different.

I roll my eyes. "No, I didn't meet anyone worth discussing. Cici and I met Jackson and Braden there. It was cool being on the list and bypassing the line."

"Oh, so you went with Jackson. How was that?"

He knows about my not-so-secret crush. "Also not worth discussing. Running into him the next morning still in his clothes from Friday is your sign, or really, it should be mine. Anyway, tell me how your ad campaign project is going. Are you ready to turn it in this week?"

"Sorry, Lily, I know the feeling. But yeah, I finished it. A couple more tweaks to make and it should be good. How about you?"

"I worked on it a ton this weekend putting together my finishing touches. I'll keep tweaking it until it's due to make sure it's perfect."

"Seriously, Lily, everything you do is perfect. I'm sure you'll ace it as always. I bet you'll get scooped up by some bigwig firm as soon as you graduate."

And this is another reason I love Kevin; he's constantly telling me how great I am. Who wouldn't love someone like that?

After coffee, my next two Monday classes fly by, and before I know it, I'm headed to work. The heavy weight returns to my shoulders. I know Cici is right and I should be looking for a new job, but I'm so close to the next phase in my life that I need to wait it out. Only a few more months until I have my degree and can apply for a full-time position at a firm with growth potential. Not a no-name advertising company like the one I'm at now that has no major corporate clients and is comfortable with its lack of growth. My résumé will look much better if I stay with the same company and show that I'm loyal, not someone who moves around a lot. I've already been here for three years, and not only have I been their receptionist, bookkeeper and office manager but I also get to help with campaigns and put together pitches. It's more experience than I could have gotten with any other job. It would be perfect if it didn't come with a creep for a boss. I can get through this if I keep the end goal in mind.

I sit down at my desk to see what appointments are on the schedule for the day or if Brad has given me any other tasks to do. As I wait for it to boot up, Brad enters the reception area from his office in the back. He leans his hip on the side of my desk, looking not so subtly down to where the top buttons of my blouse are open, revealing a hint of my barely there cleavage. Shoot, I should have buttoned one more on the way here, but it's too late, and doing so now would make it awkward. I greet him, trying to get his focus off my chest. "Hi, Brad, I was just opening the calendar to see the schedule for this week. Anything you need done right away?"

"You look lovely today, Lily. Perfect, considering we have an important client coming in this afternoon. The CEO and CFO of a prominent corporation acquiring one of the companies in our portfolio want to review the account. We need to impress them so they'll keep the account here instead of taking it to their in-house marketing department. I want to show them how well we've done and can continue to do. There's a lot of money on the line."

"Oh, which account is it? I'll get to work and put some things together for you." *Spit it out so you can go and stop hovering over me.*

"That's why I'm here. They want everyone involved to sign a non-disclosure agreement to prevent word of the acquisition from leaking before it's finalized. The document is in your inbox, so if you print, sign and bring it to my office, we can go over who you'll be greeting and what I need you to prepare. I'll see you in my office in five minutes." He walks off without another word.

Hmmm, interesting. Most companies we work with are insignificant since we're a small-scale marketing firm. However, we do have a couple more well-known businesses who have been with us since conception and stayed during their ride to success. It must be one of those accounts if an NDA is required. Or it's the company doing the takeover who wants it kept discreet. I'm excited to find out. This could be good for my career if I'm involved and establish a relationship or at least make connections with the executives coming in.

Stepping into Brad's office with a notebook, pen and signed NDA, he takes a moment to look me up and down now that I'm in full view. While I feel good dressing up today and confident in my looks, it's scum like Brad who make me want to stick to slacks and oversized sweaters. *Seriously, buddy, not gonna happen.* Stepping up to his desk, I hand over the nondisclosure. "All right, what's the plan?"

Sebastian

My brother and I are being driven to our next meeting while going over strategy. "Why are we even wasting time with this? You know our in-house team can more than handle another account."

Looking at me with exasperation, Eli answers, "This firm has been doing the marketing for the company since inception, so it would be nice to get their perspective on the direction the campaign has taken as well as any future plans. It's also a good idea to play nice before ripping it out of their hands, so when we do, they may be more cooperative with our team in handing everything over… promptly."

I'm less patient than Eli and hate schmoozing. I like to get to the point without unnecessary pleasantries—one of the many differences between my twin brother and me. We're fraternal twins, so while I took after our father, he is the complete opposite and inherited not only our mother's soft looks but her calmness and charisma. We both had good genes in the looks department, but where he's handsome in a charming way, I have our father's hard Italian look with dark features and an intimidating physique. It goes well with the no-bullshit attitude that makes people fear my attention.

"They've signed the NDA? We don't need word slipping out, fucking up the deal before it's done." Not only are we wasting our time, but we're jeopardizing a leak about the acquisition before it's finalized. While I realize due diligence is necessary, this meeting is a risk that could've waited until the takeover was complete.

"Yes, Sebastian, all the i's are dotted and the t's crossed. You know I wouldn't endanger the deal, and anyway, it will be finalized by the end of the week. I don't see them pulling out at the homestretch. Not to mention, the office we're visiting includes a total of two people. When Jim said they had a small firm handling their marketing, he wasn't kidding. I don't even know how they've been able to handle it up to this point."

"I'm going to guess with sheer luck along with the fact that the business could probably succeed with no marketing due to its product alone. When the papers are signed and our people get their hands on this, it will go next level. We just need to make sure we're ready," I say as we pull up to the curb.

"Which is exactly why we're here. Thanks for making my point, brother." He pats me on the back before he exits.

Following him out, I look at the building in front of me. The place is tiny. It reminds me of a ma-and-pa marketing firm that still uses a fax machine. Different from the caliber I expected. Loyalty is one of the problems with the company we're acquiring. Too much devotion can make you stagnant and unable to propel yourself to the next level. If you're afraid to ruffle feathers and piss a few people off along the road to success, you won't get very far, and this is an excellent example of that. There's no way we're not bringing the marketing to our people who probably run circles around these guys.

I open the door for my brother to enter, him being more approachable, and follow behind. There's a small lobby area with two chairs on each side of the door we came through. In front of us is the reception desk with a wall behind it, shielding our view of the rest of the office. My brother moves to the side to introduce us, and my gaze lands on the receptionist. *What the fuck?*

Schooling my features immediately, I realize I've seen her before. Just this last Friday when she plowed into me while rushing out of the club. She would've knocked me down had I not seen her coming. Her deer-in-the-headlights reaction was amusing. I frustratingly haven't been able to forget her and her huge brown eyes. She was exquisite in that sinful blue dress, and when she spoke, her voice was like honey, smooth and sweet. If I hadn't been so stunned by my reaction, I would've stopped her from fleeing and taken her upstairs for a good time. I'd tried to call out to her, but it was too late.

Today she's dressed more conservatively, but it doesn't diminish the instant attraction I have. Her eyes still hold the same intrigue from that night, even before moving in my direction. I've never been this instantly drawn to a woman before; it's unnerving.

Eli holds his hand out to shake. "Hi, Miss—" He looks down at the nameplate on her desk. "—Thompson. Eli and Sebastian Dubree. We're here for our three o'clock meeting with Brad Smith."

Her eyes go wide as soon as she makes eye contact with me. Obviously, the recognition is mutual. I lean in to shake her hand, crushing it in my firm grip. "Miss Thompson," I acknowledge curtly, surprised by the strength she returns.

After a few seconds of stunned silence, she seems to snap out of it, shaking her head. "Please call me Lily. Let me show you to the conference room, and I'll inform Brad of your arrival." Yep, there's that voice I can't get out of my head.

She stands nervously, more than likely remembering my boorish attitude from Friday. I observe her as she leads us back. Once again, I'm captivated. She doesn't have the "in your face" kind of beauty I'm typically attracted to. She's natural and subtle, with a look of innocence. Her thick brown hair falls in waves past her shoulders, and I can't help imagining myself gripping it while I taste that luscious neck. The way her blouse is open just enough to show the barest mound of cleavage is fucking sexy. There's a hint at what's hiding underneath instead of revealing too much like most women. I can't help but notice her firm ass, accentuated by the pencil skirt she's wearing. It's a perfect fit for the palm of my hand, and my dick starts to stiffen at the thought. This is not my usual reaction to the average woman. Still, there's just something I can't quite pinpoint drawing me in.

"Can I get you something to drink while you wait? Coffee, tea, water?" she asks as we take our seats.

"Coffee, black," I demand gruffly, frustrated by my fascination with her. I'm not someone who gets easily distracted from matters at hand.

Her eyes go wide.

Eli looks at me like I just kicked his dog. "I'll take water, please. Thank you, Lily," he practically purrs, trying to counter my rudeness. Like I said, I'm not one for pleasantries and won't start now. She leaves the room, closing the door on her way out. "Jesus, Sebastian, think you could act like a decent human being on occasion? You scared the shit out of the poor girl."

"Don't worry, the poor girl already knows I'm an ass. She's the one I told you about on Friday, who barreled into me on the stairs." Eli was upstairs that night, waiting for me to join him, and I immediately told him about my run-in on the way up. She made quite an impact on me.

"You're shitting me. That's her? You made her sound like a bombshell, dude. I mean, she's definitely not lacking in the looks department—just not what I expected from your description. What a coincidence."

"Yeah, no kidding. What are the odds? Doesn't it seem a little too coincidental?" My brain is starting to fire. Her being at our club right before this meeting is bringing out my suspicious nature. They had to sign the nondisclosure agreement, but those didn't arrive until this afternoon.

"Seriously, Seb, out of all the people to be worried about, these two are not worth your time. They have nothing to gain by leaking the deal."

"Don't be naïve, Eli. They stand to lose what's probably their biggest client with this acquisition, so I'd say that's a big motivation." I stare pointedly at him.

He sighs in frustration when the door opens with Lily carrying our drinks. She sets Eli's water down, then bends slightly to place the coffee before me. I catch a whiff of her scent, vanilla with a hint of something I can't identify, and again, blood rushes to my cock. What is it about this damn woman? I decide to ruffle her feathers a little since that's what she's doing to me. And I don't like to be ruffled.

"So, you were certainly in a hurry to leave Friday night. Care to explain why?" I can tell my question takes her off guard. I'm sure she wasn't expecting me to bring up the elephant in the room. Good, let's see her squirm a bit.

"Oh, I thought that was you," she states coyly as if I missed the immediate recognition written all over her face. "Sorry for almost knocking you down. I was just tired and frustrated at my friend for being a jerk. He said something out of line. I shouldn't have reacted so hastily. Again, I apologize." She's rambling.

"Yes, you've done that quite a bit already. May I ask what was said?"

"No, it's not even worth repeating." She trails off as Mr. Smith walks through the door. "I'll just grab my notepad and be back in," she says before scrambling to leave the room.

Again, I focus on that tight round ass that I can't seem to take my eyes off. Interesting that she refused to answer my question. I'll have to press later to see if I can get it out of her. She intrigues me and I have no idea why. What the hell is going on? I don't indulge in conversation with women. I fuck them. What makes her different? The lack of an answer is aggravating.

Her boss makes his introduction. It's obvious he overheard our conversation by his curt tone. How much, I'm unsure. Sitting down, we dive right in, with my brother and I opposite Lily and her boss. Lily is obviously more than a receptionist. During the meeting, she not only takes notes but goes through the entire campaign to date. She seems to know more than Brad on most topics. Interesting. I wonder what her role is exactly. My fascination with this woman deepens with every passing minute.

Also apparent is that Brad is a total pervert. On more than one occasion, he brushes her shoulder inappropriately, making her tense up each time. He also can't keep his eyes from wandering to her chest whenever she speaks. It's one thing for me to ogle her from across the table and quite another for her boss to be doing so. It makes me wonder what else she's forced to contend with from the slimeball.

I've already concluded that his sales pitch is for nothing. There's no way I want this sleaze involved with any company in our portfolio. *Although…* The insensible side of me comes up with a different idea. Keeping these two involved would be a great excuse to get close to her and weasel my way in. Into her bed of course.

"Thank you both for your time today. We appreciate you bringing us up to speed on the account and reviewing your proposal for the future. We'll consider it as we wait for the finalization of the merger. As you know, your discretion is paramount to keep rumors from spreading and causing employee uncertainty. We want as smooth of a transition as possible," Eli states in closing and stands, extending his hand to Brad, then Lily.

I do the same. However, when I get to Lily, I can't help but caress her unbelievably soft skin with my thumb. I pause, keeping hold as I look her in the eye. "I realize you just signed the nondisclosure agreement this afternoon, but I want to clarify that any information leaked from today on, or prior, about the merger taking place, including anything about our involvement, will be in direct violation of the rules to that document and be punishable. Is that clear?" Oh, the ways I'd like to punish her are endless.

She immediately yanks her hand from my grip and glares at me. "Yes, Mr. Dubree, I know what an NDA is and its parameters. I don't need you to remind me that a breach of contract is punishable by law. I'm more than capable of following the rules, as I have no intention of ever mentioning your name again."

"Is that so?" I can't repress the smug grin from appearing at her petulance, and since I did goad her, I'll let it slide—this time. My brother, knowing me so well, refrains from commenting.

Brad, however, is beside himself. "Mr. Dubree, rest assured you have our utmost confidentiality, mine, as well as Miss Thompson's. We both"— he looks pointedly at Lily—"look forward to a future relationship."

Still focused on Lily, I respond with the only words that come to mind with the mention of a future relationship. "As do I. Lily, please see us out." It's a demand rather than a request, causing what is fast becoming my favorite look of shock to appear. I hold my arm out, gesturing for her to proceed. She propels forward, and I can't help but place my hand on the small of her back as I join her, a slight smile curving my lips. I can feel her small frame through the thin silk blouse, the warmth of her body making me want to explore other areas. I can already tell she won't be escaping my mind anytime soon.

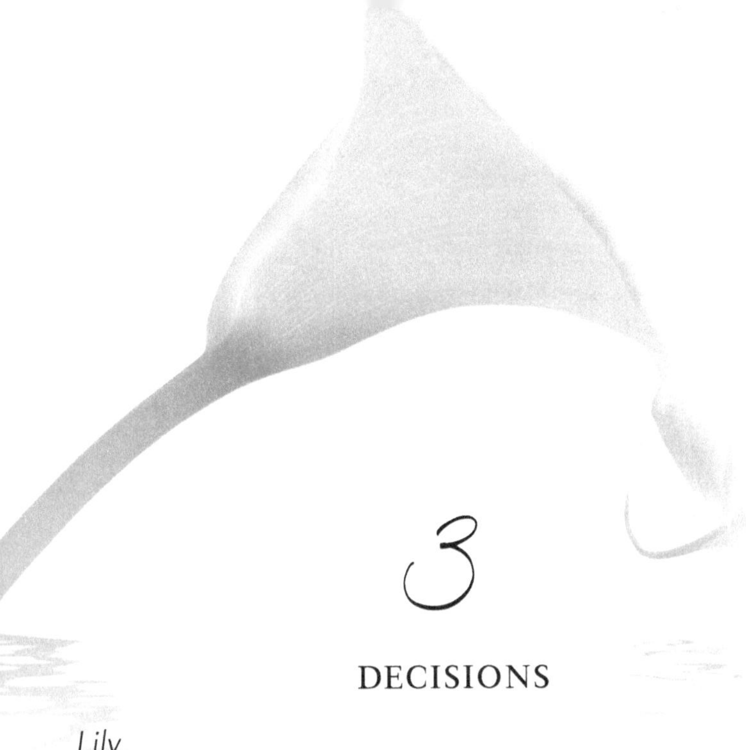

3

DECISIONS

Lily

WHAT THE HELL IS HAPPENING? SEBASTIAN'S HAND ON MY BACK feels good. Too good. Why is my body reacting to this jerk? My brain should certainly be telling it otherwise. He's been a total douche ever since walking into the office—really since our first encounter on Friday. I have no idea why he's making me walk them out. Probably to torture me some more.

Outside, Eli shakes my hand again. "It was nice to meet you, Lily. I'm glad I got to put a face to the story from Friday. I do hope I get to see more of you. I'll wait for you in the car, Seb." *Hmmm, so Sebastian told him about our encounter.*

Time to ditch the asshole. "Well, it was interesting meeting you officially. If you'll excuse me, I need to get back to work." I turn toward the door, but he grabs my hand. Yet again, my traitorous body reacts to his touch. It's so unfair.

"No, I don't excuse you. I'd like to see you this evening."

What the actual F? "Um, no. I barely have time for people I like, so I'm certainly not wasting any time on someone I despise."

"Despise is a strong word and quite improbable after only knowing me barely an hour. So here's what I propose, you grant me one evening in order to make a proper assessment. Then, if you still insist, I'll leave you alone."

"As much as I would love to prove my judgment isn't premature, it's simply unprofessional. Nor do I have the time as I said. I go to school and work all week, barely completing my homework. Thanks for the offer, but it won't be happening. Good luck with your merger." Again, I turn to leave, and yet again, he stops me, wrapping his arm around my waist, which makes my body go up in flames. By the look on his face, the calm facade is fading, and I get a glimpse of the impatient man I recognized from Saturday.

Tightening his grip, he speaks in a deep, commanding tone, causing my core to tingle in an unfamiliar way. "This will happen one way or another, but if you insist on making me work for it, so be it. Enjoy your week, Lily. I'll be in touch." And with that, he releases me, walking to his car without another word. Could this guy be any more pompous? Who does he think he is, other than one of the wealthiest, most successful men in San Diego, or for that matter, probably the entire state of California? Dang it, how did I end up on his radar? My stupid emotions, that's how. I wish I could rewind and not react like I did on Friday. Then I wouldn't have run out, right into the arms of Mr. Asshole. Ugh. If only my body would catch up to my mind because I'm fairly certain my panties are damp as I walk back into the office.

As soon as I sit down, Brad arrives, grabbing the back of my chair and spinning it around to face him. Unless I look up, his crotch is all I can see. *Gross.* "What was that about? Do you two know each other, or were you just unbelievably rude to a client we're trying to win over?"

"Sorry, Brad. I ran into him at a club as I was rushing out last weekend. He was just some jerk I didn't give another thought to. Then he was rude again the whole time he was here, and I snapped at the end. But I didn't know who he was before today."

"Well, he happens to be one of the most influential CEOs in the country, so if he acts like a jerk, he has a right to. I won't tolerate that behavior again. And what's with you escorting them out? Anything I should be aware of?" He's a little nastier as he says this last part.

"Nothing of concern. He asked to see me tonight, which is highly unprofessional. Secondly, I don't have the time or desire to accept his offer, so I turned him down." Thinking the conversation over, I swivel back to my computer. Apparently, it's not. Again, he turns my chair toward him. I'm surrounded by asshats today who seem to think they can keep pulling me in whatever direction they want.

"He asked you out on a date and you declined? What were you thinking? This could be the key to keeping the account. Call and tell him you changed your mind." He starts grabbing for the phone.

"No, I'm not whoring myself out for an account. Honestly, I don't have time to go out with the guy, and besides, I really don't like him. He's a jerk. It's not happening." I'm fuming at his request. This is just another instance that proves what a weasel Brad is.

"I don't think I made myself clear. Your job is on the line here. If we lose this account, which happens to be one of our largest, our income will take a direct hit and your position may be eliminated. So, I'd think hard about your decision because a lot is riding on it." He practically spits on my face he's so furious.

"Hmmm…." I place my finger on the corner of my mouth and look up as if pondering. "Yep, still a no. If I should start looking for another job, let me know. Until then, I'm getting back to work for the rest of the day." This time I turn my chair and start typing immediately, ignoring him as he practically stomps toward his office.

Sebastian

"Okay, what just happened? I could see your wheels spinning the entire meeting, and it was not on the topic at hand." As soon as I enter the car, Eli starts the inquisition.

I rub a hand over my face in exasperation as the driver pulls away from the curb. "I don't know, man. I can't make sense of it. I told you on Friday about my reaction to her and how I regretted letting her walk away. Then, when I saw her sitting there after we walked in? Fuuuck, something about that girl makes me want her. It's pissing me off."

"Well, I hate to break it to you, buddy, but you royally screwed that up. I know you were trying to dig out her motives for being at the club. But, dude, between before, during and after the meeting, I don't think you could have been more of a dick. I'm surprised she didn't tell you to go fuck yourself before you made it out the door."

"Thanks for the unnecessary observation. Don't worry, she gave me the 'go fuck yourself' right before I came to the car. This attraction to her is driving me crazy, so it's tough keeping my attitude in check. Jesus, Eli, this is the only girl who isn't dropping her panties for me. It's infuriating to want someone who doesn't reciprocate. I'm not sure how to handle it."

"I have a solution. How about we go to the club tonight and find someone to take your mind off her? I don't know what's gotten into you, but you need to clear your head. By the way, did you notice Brad couldn't keep his eyes off her, or should I say her chest? What a scumbag. I can't wait to tell him we're yanking the account." I did notice, in fact, and it made me see red.

I better broach the subject sooner rather than later, I think as the car approaches our building. "I want to talk to you about that. Let's head upstairs, pour a drink and discuss what my wheels are turning about. I'd like to run something by you." He gives me a look that says he knows this conversation won't make him happy.

Exiting the car, we go up to the thirty-fourth floor of the One America Plaza building, home of Dubree Enterprises. We occupy the top two floors of the tallest building downtown. We make it to my office without running into anyone since it's just after six. We run a tight ship but make our employees leave the building by six unless prior approval is granted. We believe everyone needs downtime to be productive during working hours. It's one of the key elements to our successful transition as CEO and CFO after our dad passed away two years ago. We instated that along with other game-changing policies by being young, fresh and forward-thinking.

Barely out of graduate school, we had no choice but to step up to run the conglomerate our dad had spent his whole life creating. It was one of the largest in the US, with businesses spanning the globe. My brother and I both inherited Dad's eye for a good investment. Between that and the top-notch education and natural intuition that always seems to steer us right, we've made an already successful business into one that surpasses all competition.

At the bar I pour us two glasses of port; one of the habits we kept from our travels abroad. I hand one to Eli, who is already sitting on the couch in front of the floor-to-ceiling windows looking out over the San Diego skyline with the bay in the background.

"All right, Sebastian, tell me what's going on in that head of yours so we can get out of here and let off some steam," Eli says before taking a sip.

"Initially, I couldn't wait to take this account from that pathetic loser and bring it over, but then I had an epiphany. Suppose we kept it there for a short transition period. It's a convenient way to justify my presence. Eventually, she'll give in. There's also her worthless boss and blatant advances. We should be keeping an eye on that." I pause to take a drink, savoring the flavor. That all sounded much better in my head.

I know it's selfish to use the situation to my advantage. And it goes entirely against my earlier argument, but it's an opportunity I simply can't pass up. It won't be forever—only until she's hooked. Once she caves, I can take it from there. Besides, I saw her physical reaction to my touch, and when her mind catches up, I won't need an excuse to see her.

Eli is silent for longer than I can handle. "Eli, give me something here. What are you thinking?"

"I'm thinking there's no 'we' in this equation. It's all you, bro. Honestly, this is the first time in history I've seen you make a decision with your dick instead of your head. But hey, we all make idiotic decisions occasionally, and since it won't make or break the bank, I'm gonna roll with it and have fun watching the fallout." He smiles and raises his glass in salute.

"Thanks for the vote of confidence, buddy. I appreciate it. So, you're cool if we ride it out for a while? When I have her in my clutches, we can pull the account over." I want to make sure we're on the same page.

"Wow, you really are fucked in the head over this girl. Like I said, it's not a deal breaker, so sure, have at her. I really am going to enjoy the show. Now that that's settled, let's get our asses to the club."

Lily

"Cici, he's horrible! I didn't even think to tell you about running into him on my way out that night. I had no idea who he was other than some jerk with no people skills." I take another big gulp of my wine. I sent an SOS to Cici from the trolley on my way home, so she had drinks and a char-cuterie board waiting for me. That's why we're best friends and have been for the last seven years. We always have each other's backs.

"Okay, let me get this straight…" She's on her computer stalking Sebastian Dubree online. This is the third article and third glass of wine. We've scrolled through three pages of photos, proving that Sebastian is a total man whore. He has different women in every picture—not one showing up twice—and no mention of any relationships.

"Actually, hold that thought. Get this, their dad died only two years ago, and both brothers, twins by the way, had to step in to run the company. Oh wow, their mom died from a brain aneurysm two years before their dad. But it doesn't say how their dad died. Oh my gosh, they were only twenty-five when they took over the company and have grown it every year since. Pretty impressive but sad." She doesn't stop. "Okay, so where were we? Oh yeah. You literally ran into one of the hottest guys in the world on the way out last Friday and neglected to tell me about it. Uh-uh-uh." She holds up a finger to stop me from interrupting.

I was only going to remind her that he was a pompous ass that night and not worth mentioning. I mean, yes, he does happen to be incredibly hot, with his thick jet-black hair, blue eyes to get lost in, a chiseled jaw with the perfect amount of stubble that screams authority and lips I swear were made for kissing. Ahh, what am I thinking? *Get your head out of the gutter, Lily, and focus on the problem.* Three glasses of wine might not be helping.

All this research is a double-edged sword. On one hand, it proves what a player he is, but on the other? Wow. To take over that huge busi-ness at such a young age and do so well. It's remarkable and shows he has a good head on his shoulders… when it comes to business that is.

"So then, the same hottie just shows up in your office two days later and you turn him down for a date, get your job threatened if you don't go out with said hottie, yet you still refuse. Does that sound right?" She sips her wine, awaiting my response.

"Yes, other than you're leaving out the important parts, like where he's a completely arrogant, pompous, controlling, sexy asshole!" I slam my hand over my mouth. "Shit, I didn't mean sexy. Yes, he's sexy, but that's not the point. There's no way I'm going out with someone like that, and anyway, he didn't ask me on a date. He told me he wanted to *see* me. That could mean anything. He probably wants to get laid and call it good, according to his track record. Or, since I'm not the supermodel he's used to banging, he just wants to irritate me even more. He probably gets off making other people miserable."

"Well, I think you're certifiable that you're willing to lose your job rather than go *see*"—she air quotes the word—"the sexiest man alive. But hey, who am I to judge? I'm only your best friend in the entire world who would never steer you wrong. Your boss is a creep and we've always known that, so I'm okay with the 'losing your job' part but screw him and his demand. Do this for yourself. Maybe the guy was having a bad night on Friday. And maybe he was just stressed over this meeting and wasn't his charming self, but I'm sure if you went out with him, you'd see the real Sebastian. This could be your chance to finally get past first base with someone who will show you what you've been missing. This is your chance, Lily!" She's highly animated and my head is starting to hurt.

"Ugh, I have class tomorrow, and you're too much for me. I love you, Cici, and yes, you are my sister, my best friend, and you usually know what's best. But this time, I'll agree to disagree." I hug her good night and head to my room.

Plugging in my phone as I crawl into bed, I notice a missed text from an unknown number.

> Unknown: Good evening, Lily. Did you rethink your decision yet? I'm waiting for the correct answer.

Crap, who is this? There are only two options, and neither should be texting me.

> Me: Who is this?

> Unknown: The man who makes your panties wet, your blood boil and is eagerly looking forward to your company.

> Me: Sebastian? How did you get my number?

I program him into my phone immediately.

> Arrogant A: You wrote it on your NDA. But I would have found it regardless.

Me: I won't be "seeing" you and stop saying things like that. You do not make my panties wet.

Arrogant A: Would you like me to prove it? I'd be happy to stop by. Your address is listed as well.

Me: OMG, no! You'd just be disappointed anyway. Now stop texting me. I have school tomorrow.

Arrogant A: You could never disappoint me, Lily. Sweet dreams.

Oh God, what have I gotten myself into?

4

STRATEGY

Lily

MY BODY DIDN'T GET THE MEMO ABOUT NOT LIKING SEBASTIAN because I wake up abruptly, panting from the heavy make-out session I was having with none other than said asshole in my dream. Damn that man and double damn that I woke up. I was about to get past first base. I may as well do it in my dreams since it will never happen in real life. So this is what sexual frustration feels like? Huh. I don't like it.

Just the barest hint of daybreak peers through the window. When I sit up, it doesn't go unnoticed that I'm soaked. That infuriating, pompous man happens to be right about making me wet. My body needs a swift kick in the ass, and that's precisely what I'll give it. I throw on some running gear and quietly make my way out.

Six miles later, I huff back into my building, thinking I've done a great job at punishment since my legs are about to give out. There, that should use up all the pent-up energy my body has—no more unwanted thoughts, subconsciously or otherwise.

"Hey, Lils, looks like you had quite the run. Are you okay?" I hear as I'm bent over, trying to catch my breath.

Standing, I turn to see Jackson looking mighty fine on his way to the gym. I can only respond in pants. "Yeah, just need to catch my breath. I might've been too aggressive this morning." I just hope it works. Although, with Jackson standing there, his broad shoulders showcased with muscles for miles, I may need to go for another lap.

"Well, take it easy." He takes a step toward the exit and stops. "Hey, you're not still upset about Friday, are you?"

Not this again. "No, Jackson, I'm not. I shouldn't have reacted that way. It was just a long week. Having that hanging over my head in those situations is irritating, so maybe I'm just as frustrated with myself as I am with the comment. I'm fine. Really. Please don't give it any more thought." I hope this puts him at ease because I can see the conflict in his eyes, and I don't want to talk about it more.

"Good, and Lily? Don't feel bad. Any guy would kill for your innocence." He actually winks before walking off.

Another lap it is.

Sebastian

Waking this morning, I firmly resolve to get Lily into bed. Her defiance will make this that much more exciting. It'll create enough mental foreplay that by the time I succeed, I'll probably combust on the spot. I'm unsure what prompted my text last night, but the game has begun. She consumed my thoughts the entire time at the club, so much so that no other woman could dissuade me. What makes this girl tick, and how am I going to conquer her? The chase could be what this is about. I've never had anyone turn me down before. Hell, why would they? I was endowed with looks made for magazine covers, which I've been on, and my skills in the bedroom are no secret. The internet can vouch for that.

Any female would jump at the chance to be with me. Not only for the fantastic romp in the bedroom but they all want their chance to be the one woman who can make me fall in love. Little do they know it's impossible. I saw what that shit does to a man and the mayhem resulting. There are only a handful of people who know how my father died. And even fewer who know what he ultimately died from. A fucking broken heart.

We were the picture-perfect family with two parents who loved each other so fiercely, it was embarrassing to be their kid sometimes with all the PDA. Our mom was the most patient, hands-on, loving parent on the planet while our dad was the leader we all respected. The perfect amount of strictness, high expectations, and no doubt about his love for us. Until the day he took it all away.

While at university, on my way home after screwing the cheer captain all night, I got the call. My dad and Eli were already on the line waiting for me. My dad's hoarse voice immediately indicated something was wrong. The words out of his mouth will haunt me forever. "Boys, your mother's gone. Pack up. The jet's waiting to bring you home."

We all changed that day, but no one more than Dad. He became a shadow of himself. He tried to appear strong, but everyone, especially my brother and me, could see the decline happening. Instead of getting better with time, he deteriorated. Eventually, the board was concerned. Hell, we all were, but there wasn't a lot Eli or I could do while finishing our master's. Upon our return, however, we saw the shell of a man he'd become. Little did we know that my dad, the ultimate businessman, had been making significant preparations while we were gone. Two years after Mom left us, Dad joined her of his own accord. He chose to follow her to the afterlife rather than stay with us.

That is what love does to you, and why I'll never be a part of it.

Lily

Brad isn't happy I haven't changed my mind about Sebastian's offer, so needless to say, work is unpleasant with his snippy attitude. The good news though? He won't be in on Friday, so I'll have a day in the office alone. Now there's something to look forward to. He's also impatiently waiting for a decision from Dubree Enterprises, which is making him antsy. I can't imagine they would leave the marketing in the hands of a small company, and Brad is delusional thinking we have a chance. All this results in a reprieve from him today because he's so cranky that he's sulking in his office, and before I know it, I'm headed home.

On my way, I have a weird feeling I'm being watched, like the night at the club. It's unnerving. Thankfully, my apartment is close to the office with plenty of people in the area, especially as I get closer to Balboa Park. But once again, I pull my phone out and put it to my ear for a fake conversation. I could call someone, but I'm probably being a head case, and no one is following. Nevertheless, I speed up and sigh in relief as I head into the building.

I'm snuggled up on the couch in jammies, doing homework with Ebony on my lap, when Cici walks in. Her social calendar is insane, and I never know when she'll be in or out. I don't know how she does it between school, her parents' company and her many flings. It's too much for me to keep up with. "Hey, Cici, what's wrong?" She looks upset.

Joining me, she flops on the couch, causing Ebony to skitter away. "Ugh, my fricking parents decided I need to start taking on more responsibilities since I'm almost finished with school—and not just the cushy, easy ones. I had to drive around for miles doing site inspections at each of our properties, and I didn't even make it to all of them. I'm exhausted. They say I have to know everything from the ground up if I want to take over. Uh, hello? What if I don't want to take over? Did they even consider there may be something different I'd like to do with my life?"

"Oh, that sounds like a lot. You're lucky to have your future mapped out and a career right after graduation, but I'm sure your parents would understand if you change your mind and want to do something else. They're so awesome." They really are. The fact they took in their daughter's best friend to live with them during high school is proof of that. Who else would allow some kid who came out of nowhere to move in and then feed them until graduation?

"Yeah, we'll see. And I shouldn't be complaining anyway, duh. I have it pretty darn good compared to most. Anyway, tell me about your day. Did you change your mind about Sebastian yet?" She smirks at me.

"Not you too. You sound like my boss without the douchey comments. I'm not changing my mind. Brad was so pissy today after telling him the same thing, but the good news is he's out all day on Friday, so I'll have the office to myself. Also, I'm finally done with that huge project I've been working on all year. I turn it in on Thursday." I'm proud of my swift change of subject and internally cross my fingers that she drops the whole Sebastian thing.

She claps excitedly and reaches out for a high five, genuinely happy for me. "Yay! I'm so glad that's over with. You've been crazy for months! Let's celebrate this Saturday. You deserve it after all the time you spent stressing. We should give the club another chance since it was ruined last week by a certain someone. Pleaaaase?" She puts her hands together before her chest like she's praying.

I must really love her. "Fine, I'll give it one more chance, but can we just wait in line instead of using Jackson so it's only us?"

Typical Cici claps her hands in excitement once again. "I'll make sure it's only us, but I'm still gonna ask Jackson to get us on the list. I hate waiting in lines, and there's no point in having connections if you don't use them. I'll make sure he knows we're having a girls' night though. Like you said, he doesn't usually join us for things anyway. I think he only did that because of Braden."

Later, when I crawl into bed, I'm already stressing about going out this weekend. I wish I could be more confident and comfortable in social situations like Cici. I loosen up after a couple cocktails, but I can't ever seem to shake my awkwardness around strangers. I'm googling tips to portray more confidence when a text comes in.

Arrogant A: Do you have a different answer for me tonight?

Me: You need to stop texting me. My answer won't change.

Arrogant A: We'll see about that. How was your day?

Me: Seriously, you're asking about my day? My boss is sulking for turning you down, so I'll at least extend my thanks for that.

Arrogant A: Are you being facetious right now?

Me: Not at all. It makes time at the office more bearable when he ignores me.

Arrogant A: Glad I could be of service. But how is it unpleasant otherwise?

Me: Just the typical sexist, egotistical, inappropriate male boss. I'm sure you're familiar. Something tells me you have all that going for you and some.

Arrogant A: I may have some of those traits, but inappropriateness to my employees is not one of them. Do I need to step in?

Me: Um, that's a definite no. I can take care of myself, thank you. Furthermore, it's not your concern.

Arrogant A: For some reason I've yet to figure out, you've become my concern.

Me: Don't bother figuring it out, simply unconcern yourself. Good night, Sebastian.

Arrogant A: Good night, Lily. Sweet dreams.

5

VIRGIN

Sebastian

I FEEL GREAT. AFTER GOING TO BED LAST NIGHT WITH A PLAN FIRMLY in place, I'm prepared for execution. It's brilliant and will help solve the boss situation while giving me a reason to see her more regularly. I'm an absolute genius. Lily should appreciate the sly way I step in to help and be eager to express her thanks. My dick gets hard thinking about how she can show her gratitude.

I walk into the drab office ten minutes early in anticipation of speaking with Lily before the meeting I set up with Brad earlier this morning. "Good morning, Lily. It's good to see you. Did you sleep well last night?" I greet her with a smile, taking in all her beauty as she glares at me.

"Don't bother with the pleasantries. Why are you here?"

Feisty, I like it. "Is that any way to welcome your guest? I should hope you have better manners than that. I'm here to meet with Brad. I would've assumed he informed you."

"That's not what I mean. This better not have anything to do with our conversation last night. I need this job. You can't come in here causing problems." She's whisper shouting at me. Why am I turned on right now with her blatant disrespect? That is the question of the hour.

I scowl at her as I speak, lowering my voice. "I would never put your job in jeopardy. I don't run a multibillion-dollar company by being ignorant, so stop making assumptions and show me to the conference room." Judging by the shock on her face, that may have come out a little harsh, but damn if this girl doesn't get under my skin. Her lack of confidence in me is insulting. How dare she insinuate that I would sabotage her?

She stands immediately. "Certainly, Mr. Dubree, right this way." My dick twitches at her aggression and what I'd like to be doing to that fine ass to show her what happens when she misbehaves. Too bad she's not wearing another low-cut shirt and something to show off her beautiful back end. She's much more conservative today. It makes me want to get her alone, strip her down and see what's waiting for me underneath. "Would you like coffee, Mr. Dubree? I made a fresh pot just for you. Black, right?" If I'm not mistaken, I swear I hear her say, "Just like your soul," under her breath. Oh, I do like her, she's just asking for it.

"Why yes, I'd love some. And please, call me Sebastian. Aren't we past formalities?"

"Never," she states as she walks out the door. I find myself grinning ear to ear as I rearrange my dick, relieving the pressure. Bantering with her is much more fun than I could have imagined. I don't tolerate insolent behavior, but it will be worth the wait when I finally bend her over my knee. And if I'm honest, her spirit impresses me.

Lily

Ahhhh! I'm screaming inside. The literal nerve of that man. Absolutely arrogant and, damn it, so fricking gorgeous. I hate that I want to punch him and throw myself at him at the same time. It's infuriating. For the second day in a row, I woke up sexually frustrated after not getting any further in my fricking dream. Not to mention, I was wet again. Texting Sebastian has got to stop. I can't keep having him be the last thing I think about right before bed.

I'm gripping the edge of the countertop in the small kitchen area, trying to calm myself and do breathing exercises, when Brad walks in. He puts his hand on my lower back, asking if everything is okay. *Please, not today.* His advances are the last thing I need right now. "I'm fine, just tired is all. I didn't sleep well." I immediately move away from him and fill a mug with coffee.

"Well, there are a variety of cures for that." Seriously, I'm going to lose it. That was a blatant innuendo. *Gross.* "I assume you haven't had a change of heart regarding Sebastian?" He scowls at me.

"No, I haven't and won't. Did he mention why he wanted to meet this morning?" I try to sound nonchalant.

"No, just that he wanted to discuss a few more items," he says as he steps back.

Crap and double crap. If this has anything to do with that stupid conversation we had last night, I will lose it. He can't ride in here on his white horse and make problems for me because he thinks I need saving. I can't afford to have Brad let me go just yet. Accusing him of sexual harassment, especially telling an important client, is not a great way to keep my job. *Okay, Lily, take a deep breath, calm down and focus.* Sebastian said he wouldn't jeopardize my job. He could just want to go over some ideas. That's highly improbable but not impossible, right? It was sweet of him to want to help with Brad, but on the other hand, hello? I've made it this far just fine on my own; I don't need some knight in shining armor to save me.

"See you in the conference room." Brad grabs the coffee I just poured and walks out. *Really?* I look up to the ceiling and breathe deeply. Am I being punished for something? Deciding I could use some caffeine myself, I grab two more mugs and fill them.

Entering just as they finish their greeting, I place the coffee in front of Sebastian. He pulls out the chair next to him. "Sit." Fine. At least I won't have to stare at his condescending face the whole time, and not to mention, I won't be next to Brad.

"So, Mr. Dubree. Sebastian. May I call you Sebastian?" Brad kicks off the meeting.

"Mr. Dubree will be fine." Wow, if looks could kill. Between the cold stare Sebastian is giving my boss and the contempt directed back toward him, this meeting is definitely off to a bad start.

"All right, Mr. Dubree, what can I help you with today? You were very insistent we meet as soon as possible." I'm starting to sweat, literally. Holding my breath, I pray while waiting for Sebastian to respond.

"My brother and I discussed the ramifications of your proposal to leave the marketing here. We generally don't subcontract any portion of our business dealings and wouldn't be comfortable with that situation. However, you made some good points regarding the growth achieved with your campaign to date and some impressive ideas for the future, so a compromise may be in order."

"I appreciate that, Mr. Dubree, and I'm intrigued," Brad practically purrs. Cue internal eye roll. What a kiss ass.

"I see that Miss Thompson here is a valuable asset to your company and very involved in the project." Oh shit, where is this going? "We also noted the size of your office makes it possible to be without someone posted in the reception area at all times. In that case, what I propose to be a win-win situation is for Miss Thompson to spend part of her working hours with our marketing team in the Dubree offices, reviewing past strategies and collaborating on the implementation of our ideas moving forward. We're considering a full rebrand once the merger is complete, which will be a huge undertaking. We'll need all hands on deck." I'm staring at him now in shock. Is he for real? I sip my coffee to keep myself from bursting out in protest. I wasn't prepared for this scenario.

"So let me get this straight, I would be loaning out an employee on my payroll to your marketing department? I don't see how that's to my benefit." Score one for Brad.

"We would be happy to absorb her salary for any hours spent in our office. Let me remind you, Mr. Smith, if we do transfer the account completely to our staff, you will be losing a significant client, which I'm sure you're aware of, correct?" *Really? Do they realize I'm still sitting right here in the same room?*

"Excuse me for interrupting, but as the topic at hand concerns me, and since I happen to be present, in case you didn't notice, shouldn't I have a say in the matter?" I can't keep the sarcasm from slipping out. It's one of my weaknesses, but a great way to deal with anger, especially when what I want to say would most likely get me fired.

They both start to answer at once. "Not really, since…," Brad starts.

"Please…" Sebastian makes a gesture with his hand.

"While you may be right about the office doing fine without someone up front and about my knowledge of this account, I hardly think it necessary to be on-site to work with your team. You might not be aware,

Mr. Dubree, but in this day and age, there are a multitude of platforms for videoconferencing. And when Brad is away from the office, like this coming Friday for example, I need to be here." *Take that, Mr. Smarty Pants.*

"He's right, though, that a rebranding would take a lot more effort and would certainly benefit from an alliance between our offices, which would also allow us to remain involved," Brad says encouragingly. Score retracted.

Sebastian's ego would never ask for outside assistance. This is a total play to get what he wants, and that's me. All Brad is thinking about are the dollar signs. Alleviating some of his payroll while still earning the commission. "This is a great compromise for now, don't you think?" Brad prods. I think I want to reach across the table and pour my coffee on his lap.

"Well, it seems you two have it all worked out, so it doesn't matter what I think." I know I'm acting like a petulant child, but damn if I wasn't already being treated like one.

"I'm glad we agree then," Sebastian states while smiling. The smug little weasel.

Sebastian

Lily's reaction is not as expected. I don't understand why she's fighting this when she told me last night how her boss behaves in the office. Where is the sign of relief I was expecting? Her stubbornness is aggravating me; it's time to step up my game. "In order to proceed, I'm proposing Lily accompany me to my office following our meeting to get acquainted with the team. We can finalize a schedule that works for both of us after they have a chance to strategize and estimate the amount of time required to finish the project. Is that acceptable to you?"

Her boss, eager to acquiesce, gives his immediate consent, but Lily unsurprisingly interjects with another argument. "I can't just be forced to change where I go to work at the drop of a hat. I use public transportation to commute, and this is close enough to my apartment to walk. It would be a huge inconvenience for me with your downtown location and rob me of the little free time I use for homework. It's simply not feasible."

"Point well made. I understand your concern and there's a simple solution. We at Dubree Enterprises have a car and driver for employee use when the situation warrants. This scenario applies of course, so it would be available to you. Not only after work but on days you have school, it can pick you up and bring you to our office. It will be at your service. Does that assuage your concern?" There is no argument I won't counter. She's delusional if she thinks she'll win this battle.

She's speechless. I can see as she tries to formulate her next argument and the moment she realizes she's lost. Her defeat is palpable as she says, "Well then, I guess that's settled whether I like it or not. I'll gather my things and the necessary files to review with your staff and meet you in the lobby." She smiles oh so sardonically. I can't wait to be alone with this infuriating woman. I've been rock-hard the entire damn meeting, and the anticipation is killing me.

Brad seems pleased as we shake hands after Lily leaves the conference room. I decide to part ways with one final thought. "While I'm sure this arrangement will benefit all involved, let me remind you that Miss Thompson is your employee. When present, she will be treated respectfully, meaning your hands will never touch her again. Your eyes will remain focused strictly above her neck, and your conversation will be limited to work. Is that understood?" The venom in my voice is clear, my threat unspoken. He may be pissing himself as he nods in agreement. Problem solved.

Lily is at her desk when I walk around the corner, her anger palpable. "Shall we?" I motion her forward like I did Monday, powerless from placing my hand on her back once she passes. It feels so much more intimate than it should; my dick seems to agree.

I lead Lily to the town car and climb in after her. When the door closes, I press a button to raise the soundproof blackened barrier between us and the driver. She immediately freezes, looking ready to flee. "Is something wrong, Lily?" My voice slithers like a snake, ready to strike.

She hesitates briefly before I see the defiance in her eyes as she turns to me. "Why are you doing this? I made it clear I won't go on a date with you. Is this the plan to get your way?"

That fire is sexy as fuck. "I didn't say anything about a date. I said I wanted to see you. And I always get my way. Did you not Google me and figure that out already?" I move closer to her and rest my hand on her thigh. I immediately feel her warmth and the way she tenses. I'm unsure if it's from intimidation or arousal. I'm assuming a little of both.

"You confirmed my assumption then, so let me save you the trouble.

I'm a virgin. I won't just be another notch on your belt. So you can stop this game now because your end goal will not be happening." She pushes my hand off her thigh and turns toward the window. "Are you done now?"

I'm speechless as I adjust the huge ass bulge in my pants. What the hell have I gotten myself into, and where the hell do I go from here? I'm literally at a loss. I don't fuck virgins. Primarily because there's no such thing in my world, plus my tastes are too rough to be anywhere near one. Yet here I am. *Motherfucker.*

Lily

That certainly shut him up. I could see where he was going with this. It was better to rip the Band-Aid off than let him keep manipulating his way in. I'm irritated by how much I liked the feel of his hand on my leg but push the thought aside. I refuse to get derailed. It's not that I don't want to find someone to take the next step with, but it certainly won't be the playboy of the year, nor will it be until I'm financially independent in my full-time career. I'm expecting him to order the car to return any second. Wouldn't that be an answer to all my prayers, not to mention hilarious. It's amusing to see him sit there and sweat as if I told him there was a tarantula on his head.

After a few minutes, he finally snaps out of it and rotates toward me. "How is that possible? You're beautiful, smart and almost twenty-two years old. Are you not into men?"

"Seriously? You have got to be kidding me. Just because I haven't put out for jerks like you, that must mean I'm not into guys? Unreal. Not that it's any of your business, but I just haven't had time to date, and I'm not going to give it up for the sake of getting it out of the way."

Seeing he's still on edge, I try a different approach. "Relax. Let's pretend you weren't only trying to get in my pants and just move on. I'll still hand over all the information we have to date along with any plans for future campaigns to your team, and we can go our separate ways. I'll tell Brad your department insisted they had it under control and declined any help. No harm done." I think he may be having a heart attack. "It's not a disease. You can't catch it, I swear." I roll my eyes.

"What do you mean you haven't had time to date? For the last five-plus years? You're in your fourth year of college, so maybe you've been busy, but what about during high school?" He literally cannot comprehend this atrocity. Who knew it would be such a hot topic? This day keeps getting better.

"Listen, I'm sure your ego will eventually recover from my lack of interest. Go to any bar after you drop me off, and you'll have no problem finding some bimbo to restore it."

"Let's get one thing straight, your lack of interest is not the problem, sweetheart. You're plenty interested, and don't bother pretending otherwise. The problem is, I'm too much to handle with your lack of experience. And I certainly don't do romance, which is what someone like yourself requires. How about for now, we finish out today, and afterward, you can return to your boring little bubble, and I'll enjoy restoring my ego like you said."

What a serious jerk. I'm not even going to respond to his egotistical speech. Did I mention he's full of himself? If I ever question my decision not to give my innocence up to some random guy, all I need to do is remember Sebastian.

Sebastian

"Dude, what's going on with you? You got exactly what you wanted today, yet you're in the pissiest mood ever. You're bringing me down, man. Wait. Don't tell me your charm didn't work?" Eli's sitting across the table from me at one of the trendy downtown bars not too far from our condo building. I haven't come clean with him yet about the bombshell dropped on the way to the office this afternoon. I'm still reeling and trying to process what bothers me about the whole thing. Like she said, we'll forget it and move on, and I'll satiate my thirst with someone else. Except that's the problem. Now I don't want anyone else; I want her.

"She's a virgin," I announce. Eli, taking a sip of beer, spits it across the table.

"You've got to be kidding me. The one woman you go head over heels for, and she ends up being a goddamn virgin? Man, what are the odds?" He's fucking laughing now, and I'm growing more irritated by the second.

"I did not go head over heels for her. I wanted her in my bed, end of story."

"Really? Because I've never seen you change our business practices to get a woman in bed before," he says mockingly.

"I haven't needed to. Women don't turn me down—until now apparently. I don't know if I should let this go or let my dick decide and step up my game." I'm lying to Eli and myself, trying to blame it solely on my dick.

"I'm your brother, so I'm allowed to say this. You are way too hardcore in the bedroom to be with someone like her. And that isn't meant as a challenge. That's meant to stop you from damaging her." He's right. It's why my mind is at war, but I'm not ready to give up. This would be so much easier if she didn't intrigue me, but damn it, she does. Eli stands. "Now, let's hit up those ladies at the bar, and then we can reevaluate this situation tomorrow—if you still need to."

I get up from the table but call it a night instead of heading to the bar. "No, you go ahead without me. I'm gonna head home and crash. I need to sleep this day off. See you tomorrow." I decide to walk the few blocks home and get some fresh air. Pulling my phone out to check my messages, I see the thread with Lily. *Why not?*

> Me: What had you so busy all those years that you forgot to date?

There's still no response when I walk into my condo. Could she be asleep already? I give it a few more minutes while I get ready for bed. Maybe she's thinking about how to answer. I'm sure it's not her favorite topic.

> Me: No good answer for me?

> Lily: I thought we decided to end the pretenses and move on. Can't you just leave me alone?

> Me: Apparently not. So?

> Lily: Remember the part about it being none of your business? That still stands.

> Me: It will be easier if you answer the question. I know where you live, remember?

Lily: Okay, you're certifiable. Not that it's any of your business, but my dad left when I was 15, and I worked to support myself. I had no time and more important things to worry about than dating.

Whoa, I'm not sure how to respond. That's some heavy shit and not something to address through a text conversation. Her tenacity impresses me. There's more than meets the eye to this girl.

Me: So, you've never had a boyfriend?

Lily: Of course I have.

Me: And?

Lily: And you're infuriating. You know that, right?

Me: Answer the question.

Lily: There wasn't a specific question in there.

Me: Don't be coy. You've had boyfriends, so why did you never have sex?

Lily: Wow, you're so subtle.

Me: Subtle's my middle name. Now quit avoiding the answer.

Lily: Only because I can tell you won't be able to sleep until you find out how I can still be a virgin and live to talk about it, I'll divulge. I've been with a few different guys, but nothing made me want to go further. As I said, I don't have time for much between work and school. That's it. Satisfied now?

Me: Not until you are. Good night, Lily, and as always, sweet dreams.

Unbelievable. Been with a few guys but no interest? My mind has been going full speed all night, and now that I know it has nothing to do with saving her virtue or any propriety bullshit, my resolve strengthens. She just wasn't turned on enough. Shit, what that isn't doing to my ego and the need to prove I can spark her desire. Not to mention, my cock seems to love the idea. The pressure that's been building all day needs significant relief. It just so happens I have the picture-perfect image of a tight ass in a pencil skirt and the vision of when I bend her over my desk to uncover those beautiful round cheeks. How satisfied I'll be when they're pink and flushed after I deliver the spanking she deserves for her defiance. I may have just set a record for the fastest jerk-off in history. I'm a goner.

6

STUBBORN

Lily

I SWEAR THIS IS PART OF HIS PLAN—TEXT ME EVERY NIGHT BEFORE bed and make sure he's at the forefront of my mind so my dreams are filled with him. I can't take this frustration anymore. I mean, yes, I can admit our kissing in my dreams is damn good, but then to wake up every time right before he's about to go further is killing me. *Ugh!* And what was with the last text he sent? Not until I'm satisfied? Way to put my mind in the gutter before falling asleep.

Needless to say, I'm not in the best of moods walking into class this morning, and damn it, I should be in a great mood today. I'm turning in the most important project of my entire college education, which I've spent months agonizing over. And now, he's robbed me of my happiness. Screw all that crap about no one being responsible for your feelings but yourself. I'm blaming Sebastian.

I sit down forcefully next to Kevin. "Bad morning, huh?" he says, nudging me with his shoulder.

"More like a bad week. TGTF. It literally can't come soon enough."

"What's got you in such a mood? Normally, you're like a cool cucumber. Nothing can get past that skin of yours. Anything I can help with?" *Be my fake boyfriend?*

"I wish, but no, something just came up at work. It'll pass, and anyway, I think I solved the problem, so hopefully my mood is temporary. Hey, are you ready to turn in your project today? I'm so relieved to be handing mine over. I can't wait to go home and not think about it for the first time all year." *Now if only I could stop thinking about a certain someone.*

"Yeah, me too. It's as ready as it'll ever be at this point. Any celebration plans?"

"Cici talked me into trying that club again, so we're going on Saturday. Girls only this time. I'm looking forward to it, especially after this crazy week." Really, I am. I've decided to step out of my box this weekend and try a new version of Lily. I'm testing out some self-confidence tips I looked up. We'll see how they work.

"Nice. Well, I won't interfere with your night, but after you told me about it on Monday, a few of my buddies wanted to check it out this weekend. Maybe you could save a dance for me?"

"Yeah, for sure. I'm glad you're going. You'll probably love it."

"Yeah, me too, especially now that I'll know the hottest chick there." Leave it to Kevin to lighten my mood.

Brad was anxious to hear about my meeting with the Dubree team. It went better than expected. The marketing division felt like a separate business with its own reception area, conference rooms and offices. With the number of companies Dubree Enterprises consists of, it makes sense to do all their marketing in-house. It's one floor below the executive team but just as nice. I know this because we also toured the executive level where he introduced me to his secretary. He didn't show me his office, though, leaving the door closed as we moved on. He's done trying to get me alone at this point.

After dropping the virgin bomb in the car, all conversation between Sebastian and I ceased unless it was business-related, which was much easier to deal with. The staff accepted me with ease and were all friendly and excited about the information provided. I would have liked working there if it wasn't for Sebastian and his ulterior motive. It's too bad it's not an option now. I can even admit it would have been nice to ogle Sebastian occasionally. Just because he's a cocky bastard doesn't mean he's not fun to look at.

My story to Brad, though, was only half true. After sharing about the meeting and informing him of their office dynamics, I set up the exit strategy by telling him the department was a well-oiled machine and they were still deciding whether to collaborate. I told him they planned to revisit it on Monday and get back to us. When he began to freak out over the possibility of them saying no, I cut him off, making it clear no decision had been made and we should wait for their answer and go from there. After arguing with me again about going out with Sebastian, he gave up and sulked in his office the rest of the day, which made my afternoon considerably more pleasant than usual.

When I crawl into bed that night, it's with a massive weight lifted from my shoulders. Having my project turned in and out of my hands is euphoric while putting the Sebastian issue to bed, pun intended, is a relief. I took a rare night off from homework to relax. Cici and I shared a bottle of wine while starting another *Twilight* marathon as a mini celebration. She even ordered our favorite Thai takeout from down the street.

I have three things to look forward to tomorrow. I get to sleep in since I start work an hour later than usual along with a whole day without Brad in the office. And last but not least, Fridays are always something to look forward to. I'm just about to doze off when I hear my phone ding.

Sebastian

I couldn't get Lily out of my head all day, and Eli wouldn't let up on the jabs, which put me in a fucking mood. To top it off, we had our monthly board meeting with China tonight, which didn't finish as quickly as I'd hoped and ended up delaying my new favorite ritual of texting Lily, sending me over the edge.

She wouldn't discuss a schedule with me yesterday, as if the decision was already made to part ways. Then she refused to let me accompany her home, so I had no opportunity to set her straight. She is hands down the most stubborn woman I've ever encountered. If she thinks I'll leave her alone just because of her innocence, she's in for a surprise.

Me: Sorry I'm late tonight. Meetings. How was your day?

Lily: Seriously? I was almost asleep. I'm sure your "meetings" were very "important." (Eye roll.)

Me: Are you insinuating something?

Lily: I can only imagine what type of "meetings" occur at this hour.

Me: The type with associates from China. Difficult to conduct those during regular business hours. No need to be jealous.

Lily: Absolutely zero jealousy. Can we stop this charade? It makes things complicated with Brad.

Me: In what way? If he was inappropriate, let me know, and I'll fucking handle him.

Lily: Down boy. He was better today in that regard now that I think about it.

Me: I certainly hope so after my visit yesterday.

Lily: Wait, did you say something when I specifically told you not to?!

Me: I clarified what appropriate workplace behavior looks like and what it does not. Enlighten me then. What is more complicated?

Lily: Damn it, Sebastian, I told you I could handle it. You don't listen at all. Ugh, mind your own business.

Me: I can and will handle anything I deem necessary. Now explain the problem, Lily.

Lily: You're annoying in case I haven't told you. He just got antsy when I alluded that it likely won't be necessary for me to work in your office. Can you just yank the account so things can go back to normal?

So, she thinks that's how this is going, huh? She is sorely mistaken thinking she's getting off that easy.

> Me: Have I not made myself clear? You will be working in our office. But just to clarify. You would rather return to normal, as in going to work every day and being harassed by your boss?

> Lily: Who do you think you are? You cannot just come into my life and tell me what to do. What is this really about? I already told you, you're not getting me into bed, so why are you still wasting your time? I'm sure you have plenty of women in your upper-class circle who would be happy to "see" you.

> Me: Are you intimidated by the fact that I have money? Is that the problem?

> Lily: Your complete package is the problem. The fact that our worlds are eons apart doesn't help, but don't answer a question with a question. What are you hoping to gain from this situation if you're not getting me under you?

> Me: That's an excellent question. Should we get to the bottom of it over dinner tomorrow?

> Lily: Oh, so now you want to take me "out"? In your dreams. Good night, Sebastian.

> Me: I do much more than that in my dreams, sweetheart. Good night, Lily, and sweet dreams to you.

Damn it, I've either lost my touch or don't know how to handle an ordinary woman who's not trying to get something out of me. Have I seriously only surrounded myself with fake women all these years? Of course I have, because anything else would have been too much work, like now. The file I received on Lily today clarified a lot. My background checks are thorough. There's more to her than initially meets the eye. I'm impressed by the perseverance she's displayed over the years. That she didn't go in a bad direction after being emancipated at such a vulnerable age but took the high road instead speaks to her inner strength and determination. The apparent struggles she's had to deal with and the fortitude displayed prove that her stubbornness has served her well, until now. She's met her match.

I'm still determining my next move. If I didn't have the merger tomorrow, I'd have planned to visit her office. It would've been perfect with Brad out all day. Then, Eli will want to go out and celebrate tomorrow night, so I'll have to bide my time and figure something else out. Eli's not on board with my fascination, if that's even what you call this. Being the womanizer he is and knowing my inclinations in the bedroom, he thinks I'm a fool for considering something with her. I'd say he was right, but I can't seem to convince myself.

Lily

Dang it, we were right there this time, the hottest so far. Maybe I do need to go out with Sebastian and get him out of my system. Prove he doesn't live up to my dreams. Gah, no. I need to go to that club tomorrow night, pretend I'm not frigid and inexperienced and hard-core make out with some rando on the dance floor. There, that's exactly what I need. Cici will be ecstatic to hear my plan and play my stylist again.

Throwing off the covers, I make my way into the kitchen, where Cici's already getting her morning fix. "Morning. Last night was so fun. I needed it."

"It was. I can't believe how long it's been since our last *Twilight* marathon. Let's do it sooner next time. We have the last two to watch anyway."

"We could always finish them tonight?" I ask while I make my coffee.

"I can't. Hot date and all that. Not sure if I'll even come home. I have high hopes for this one." She giggles.

"Oh my gosh, Cici, you're terrible. Well, good luck, I guess, and be safe! Oh, and you'll be happy to hear that I'm actually excited about tomorrow night. We're still on, right?"

"Definitely, I can't wait. I'm glad I don't have to drag you kicking and screaming this time." I roll my eyes. "Why the change of heart?"

"It's time I take your advice and let my guard down a bit, maybe pick a random guy to make out with on the dance floor. Want to help me get ready and make me irresistible?"

"Who are you, and what did you do with my best friend? Seriously? Of course! You'll be the hottest one there when I'm done with you! Yay,

I'm so excited!" She's jumping up and down clapping. Only Cici could get this worked up about a makeover and a night of debauchery.

Getting ready for work isn't a chore this morning, knowing I have the office to myself. I decide to dress up since Brad won't be ogling me over my shoulder the whole time. It's so messed up that I have to consider that while planning my outfit. However, I might not have to worry about it anymore if Sebastian did threaten Brad.

Unbelievable, the nerve of that man, thinking he can say or do anything he wants. His money and power don't impress me like they do Brad. Sebastian can kiss my rear end. I'm curious what'll happen once the merger is complete this afternoon. Will he be done with this fixation and move on? I have a feeling that won't be happening and may be lying if I said that's what I want. I've gotten used to the nightly texts and banter. I'm even starting to look forward to them.

Heading out, I see Jackson in the elevator. "Hey, Jackson, happy Friday." He looks so good dressed in his slim jeans and button-down. Not to mention what the smell of his cologne invading the small space is doing to my senses.

"Hi, Lils. You're chipper this morning. What's got you in such a good mood?" I notice his eyes stray from my face and wander down over the rest of me, making me do a little happy dance inside. But I quickly remind myself that he's not used to seeing me dress any way other than conservatively, and it has nothing to do with him checking me out. Why would he when he has plenty more attractive women to choose from?

"Just that I have the office to myself all day, and it's Friday. Cici and I are going out tomorrow to celebrate a big project I turned in. I think she was going to pull your strings again to hook us up at the club from last weekend." Our conversation continues as we head through the lobby.

"She already did, and I got your names on the list, no problem. My friend owes me for some information I gave him about a property we have ties to. Cici told me it was girls' night, so don't get mad if you happen to see Braden and me there. We'll leave you alone, I promise. He just wanted to go again and hopefully remember it this time. I swear, we'll act like we don't even know you." He raises his hand in a scout's honor.

Laughing, I respond, "Thanks for letting me know. Yeah, I definitely don't want a repeat of last week, but it's fine. I'll at least say hi if I see you. It's a big place, so who knows? Well, I've got to get to the office. I'll see you later." I start walking away when Jackson stops me seconds later.

"Hey, Lily, wait. Why don't I give you a ride? I'm headed in that direction anyway. I need to visit one of our buildings in the area. Come on, my car's in the garage." He doesn't give me a chance to respond, but then, I certainly wouldn't decline the opportunity to spend time with Jackson. Why is he being so nice? For the first time I can recall, he puts his hand on my lower back to guide me, giving me butterflies.

Right before we head down the stairs from the sidewalk, I see a familiar car drive by slowly. It makes me pause for a second, but I'm so engrossed in Jackson that I dismiss it. Oh well, if they needed something, they would have pulled over.

Sebastian

After another night of self-satisfaction I resolve to make my next move, even though I haven't worked out what it is yet. I'll see how today goes and how much Eli wants to celebrate tonight and decide from there. I may have to find someone to satiate myself with for a distraction, but right now, the thought is as unappealing as nails on a chalkboard.

As soon as I arrive at the office, all hell is breaking loose. Apparently, there's an issue with the paperwork. *Are you fucking kidding me?* How much are we paying the idiots in our legal department to review this shit? I'm beyond pissed when I walk into Eli's office.

"What the hell, man? I thought this was solid. Do I need to be worried?" Eli looks up as I bark at him.

"Good morning to you too, Seb. Yeah, I slept great. How about you?"

He knows exactly how to push my buttons. "Who needs to be fired? I mean it, Eli, what's going on? And since you asked, I slept like shit because I can't seem to get a certain girl out of my head. I don't need this crap today, so talk to me."

"It's a simple matter of legal jargon and nothing you need to stress over. I know we were all set for it to happen this afternoon, but it's not a deal breaker and already rescheduled for next week. It's certainly not ruining my day. Worry about what you're doing with your female situation so you can return to behaving like the semi-normal human being I know you're capable of."

I run my hands through my hair. "Shit, is it too early for a drink? Seriously, I'm losing it. Lily's driving me crazy with her complete lack of interest. I don't understand this pull I have toward her at all. It came out of nowhere, and it's killing me, man."

"I hate to add fuel to the fire, but Lily showed up on our VIP list tomorrow night. She's best friends with Jackson's sister. He's the guy I told you about that I met at poker. He recently gave me some inside property information regarding our acquisition. In return, I add him and his friends to our VIP list when he calls."

"Wait, are they together then?" That could explain a lot.

"It doesn't sound like it. He asked for separate tables."

Thank God for some good news. My next move was conveniently handed to me. "Thanks for giving me the heads-up. I was going to head over to her office today since the fucking merger is delayed, but I'll take some time to cool off and wait until tomorrow night. You know we're going, right?"

"I figured that. I told Jackson we'd meet, have drinks and introduce you two. Do you want to go to the shooting range after work then? Maybe it'll help you blow off some steam. You need it since you won't take my advice and get laid."

"Sure. Get me when you're ready, and damn it, keep me posted on this. If anything else comes up, I expect to hear about it right away. Otherwise, those fuckers better avoid me if they hope to keep their jobs." I leave his office and head into mine, slamming the door behind me.

The wise decision is not to visit Lily in my foul mood, but maybe I can make a play to soften her up for tomorrow. I find a florist close to her office and place a call, making sure they deliver flowers during the lunch hour. Then I order a few different things from my favorite deli to be delivered. Game on.

Lily

This day is turning out great. I had enough Jackson fantasies to dream about through the morning. The short car ride over was my happy place. I was still intoxicated by his smell while walking into the office. And not dealing with Brad today is fantastic. I've been able to get ahead on my work for next week and could end up with time to finish my homework and free up the weekend.

The front door opens, and a guy walks up to the desk with three brown paper bags. "Delivery from HUB," he says, placing them on the desk.

"Sorry, I think you have the wrong office. I didn't order anything, and I'm the only one in today."

He looks at the ticket. "This is the address I have. Lily Thompson?"

"Oh. Well, that's me, but who ordered it?"

"The ticket doesn't say. It looks like someone treated you. There are quite a few things here to choose from, so enjoy. Have a good weekend," he says and walks out.

I start opening the bags one by one. There's a salad, a cup of soup and two different sandwiches. *What the heck?* This is a lot of food for one person. The last bag is the best, with a bottle of chilled white wine. Okay, well, Brad would never do anything like this, right? I wonder if Jackson did, knowing I would be in the office alone today. That would make the most sense, but why would he go to all this trouble? I'm still contemplating as the front door opens again. This time with a huge floral delivery. *Oh my gosh.*

"Good afternoon. I have a delivery for Lily Thompson."

"Uh, that's me."

"Great, just sign here please. So cute, lilies for Lily. I love it. Enjoy your day!"

"Yeah, you too. Thanks," I reply as I pull the card out.

Lily,
I hope your dreams were as sweet as mine last night.
Enjoy your peaceful day in the office.
I've provided a few things from my favorite deli
since you won't be able to leave the office.
Until we meet again…

Sebastian

Oh. My. God. Sebastian? This is all him? I think I'm hyperventilating. He sent me lilies, food and wine. What am I supposed to make of that? I thought he would be preoccupied with his merger all day. How did he make time for this? More importantly, why? He knows I won't put out, so does he think I'm stupid enough to believe he's just being nice? I don't know what to think anymore, except that I can't get involved with someone like Sebastian. He's out of my league in so many ways. I'd be a fool if I went out with him, right? Not to mention, completely embarrass myself with my lack of experience. There's just no way. I need to put a stop to this.

When I got home, I had the second sandwich for dinner along with the soup and—*oopsy*—the whole bottle of wine. So I'm fully prepared to set him straight when his text arrives tonight.

> Persistent:How was your day alone in the office? I'm sorry I missed it.

> Me:I received quite the spread, along with a beautiful flower arrangement, thank you. The food was delicious, and I may have enjoyed the wine too much.

> Persistent:I'm glad to hear that.

> Me:Wait, why are you texting me right now? Aren't you supposed to be celebrating?

> Persistent:Unfortunately, it was postponed until next week. Paperwork issues. The good news is we have more time to muddle through the marketing. I'll email Brad an expected schedule for next week.

> Me:No, Sebastian, this needs to stop. You and I both know it

can't go anywhere, and I don't want to play games. You may think it's fun, but you're wasting your time.

Persistent:Any exciting plans for the weekend?

Me:You're seriously a piece of work. Did you read what I just wrote?

Persistent:I did, and I'm ignoring it. So, what's on the agenda for the weekend?

Me:You drive me crazy.

Persistent:Good. Plans?

Me:Busy with Cici, headed dancing. How about you? Any bimbos on the schedule?

Persistent:Only the innocent ones for me these days. My taste has recently changed.

Me:I find that hard to believe. You can't paint a black house white overnight.

Persistent:I beg to differ. With proper determination, you certainly can. You'd be amazed at what I can do when I put my mind to something.

Me:And you would be amazed how not interested I am. Good night, Sebastian.

Persistent:I can't wait to prove you wrong about that, sweetheart. Good night and sweet dreams, Lily.

7

SIREN

Lily

L AST NIGHT WAS A MESS. MY DREAMS KEPT GOING BACK AND FORTH between Jackson and Sebastian, and I can't decide which was better. I've always had vivid and memorable dreams, but never this frequent or with such a consistent topic. My body may be trying to tell me something. The good news is that tonight, I plan to listen—well, partially that is.

I have butterflies in my stomach thinking about what's in store. I'm glad Jackson will be there again. I should move on, but I wouldn't have to if he finally noticed me. Giving Sebastian a firm reason to drop his pursuit would also be nice. If I were with someone else, he wouldn't have a choice. I may have a chance at catching Jackson's eye after Cici works her magic on me tonight.

I'm in the kitchen making coffee when Cici comes through the front door. "I'm guessing your night was successful?" I ask while raising my eyebrows and smirking.

"More than. The date was amazing and then got even better after ending up at his place. God, it was so good, Lily. Ugh, I wish we could talk about all the juicy details. Obviously, I know we can. It's just not the same since you can't relate. And you know I don't mean that in a bad way.

I just can't wait to gossip about all this stuff together. Speaking of which, are you still gung ho about tonight?"

"I am. I woke up more determined than ever. It'll be hard to make it through the day, I'm so excited. You'll have to give me some encouragement and be patient, but you're about to see a whole new Lily tonight. Are you ready to do your most intense makeover yet?" I'm counting on her quite a bit for this. I need to be transformed into someone who looks the part to go with the confidence I'll be faking. Who knows, maybe she'll do so well, I won't have to pretend as much.

"Seriously? I've been waiting for this moment forever. You know you've unleashed a lion, and there's no taking it back. You're going to give me free rein with full cooperation. Capisce?"

"You're kind of scaring me, but all right, I'm game. What time should we start? I'm going to study and go for a jog to keep busy. You, missy, better take a nap." I'm not mentioning that my studying is not the school kind....

"Happy to comply. Let's make a night of it and go to dinner before the club, my treat. Then, you'll be primed and ready to get your groove on. How about we start at six? It'll be plenty of time for hair and makeup and trying a few dresses. Sound good?" She's already making her way down the hall. I'm positive sleeping wasn't part of her night at all.

"I'll be showered and ready to start. Sleep well. I'll be as quiet as a mouse. Love you, Cici." I blow her a kiss before she closes the door to her room.

After pushing myself a few miles around Balboa Park, I settle down to look up various kissing techniques and ideas to put the right signals out there. Hopefully, after tonight, I'll have some more experience. I'm determined to find a hot guy to set my sights on.

Sebastian

Trying to keep from obsessing about seeing Lily tonight will be impossible if I have nothing to distract myself. Having a twin who happens to be your best friend, does anything you ask and lives a few doors down is convenient. I call Eli bright and early to tell him I need a distraction.

"Hey, let's take the boat out today. I need something to do. The wind is perfect. What do you think?"

"Dude, what the hell time is it? I know you may be on a sabbatical from sex, but I am most certainly not and had quite a few rounds last night." It's apparent I woke him.

"Rub it in, why don't you. Fine, I'll let you sleep a couple more hours while I go to the gym, but then you're getting your ass up. Sailing?"

"Sounds good. Wake me up when you're ready." He's off the line before I can say another word.

This will give me another opportunity to blow off steam. And it's nice to spend some time in the gym. I don't always make it as often as I'd like with my schedule.

The anticipation for tonight is killing me. I'm still deciding which direction to take, whether to make my presence known immediately or observe for a while and approach her later in the evening. I'm leaning toward the second option, thinking it may be good to watch and see what she's like when uninhibited.

All I know is I can't wait to make my next move and see what happens. She must have some interest in me. Otherwise, why would she engage in texting me? Not to mention her body's reaction to the few times I was lucky enough to put my hands on her. Now, I need to get past the barrier she's put up and get her to stop denying her attraction toward me.

Sailing with Eli today will be a good distraction. Plus, I haven't gotten out as much as I'd like, with this acquisition taking so much time. Growing up, our dad taught us how to sail from an early age, and it's become second nature. Although, I took to it a little more than Eli because of his endless need for more stimulation. For me, it's a distraction, putting my mind at ease. To focus on the simplicity of the wind taking you in any direction. It does wonders. Hopefully, it does the trick today.

I should have known better. Eli and I ended up talking about the situation the entire time. Deciding how I should proceed while scrutinizing all possible outcomes. It stems from our business minds and the constant need to analyze everything. Maybe since it works so well professionally, it will have the same effect on a personal level. I can't see this not going my way with how determined I am. Although what it is I want exactly, I'm still unsure.

I've never pursued a woman until now. Lily intrigues me. Her self-perseverance and drive are impressive. I want to see what makes her tick and what made her that way to the point of sacrificing relationships. I want to penetrate her walls and discover what she's hiding inside them. I don't know where I'm going with this, flying by the seat of my pants for once in my life. The question is, how has this girl gotten under my skin already?

Eli and I arrived at the club early. Not only to work but I needed to check with management regarding table assignments in the VIP section to verify my instructions were followed. Unbeknownst to Lily and her friend, they have a reserved table waiting for them, and their tab is on the house. I've strategically placed our table far enough away to be inconspicuous but still in the perfect position to keep my eyes on her, whether seated or on the dance floor. The maître d' will hopefully do his job correctly and make sure Lily is seated in the chair I specified. I'm positive she's still unaware I own the club. If she did, she'd probably have gone elsewhere.

Eli's friends arrive as the place begins to fill, so we head out to join them. I already hung my jacket on the chair I planned to occupy earlier, covering all my bases. After Eli makes introductions I decide to take advantage of the situation.

"So, Jackson, I hear your sister is roommates with Lily?" I ask casually once our drinks are delivered.

"She is. You know Lily?" I hear something I don't like in the tone of his question.

"We've recently become acquainted through the company she works for. So, how long have you known her?" Maybe I can learn more about her.

"I sort of grew up with her. She moved in with my family when she was a freshman in high school. Crazy story, but her dad just left her to fend for herself. Cici and Lily were already best friends, and since my parents adored her, they took her in."

Well, shit. It's clear as day that the fucker's in love with her. "That's heavy. So you're like siblings?" Might as well screw with him.

"I wouldn't say that. I was a senior and went to college the next year, so I didn't have much time at home with her. I see her quite a bit now, though, since we live in the same building. She's great, and Cici and her are thick as thieves."

Jackson's friend Braden chimes in at this point. "Boy is that the truth. I pissed off Lily last week, and Cici hasn't talked to me since."

Hmmm, interesting. Could that be the incident that ran her out of the club? "What did you do to piss her off?"

"Oh man, I was already drunk off my ass, and in my defense, I was trying to drown myself fresh out of a breakup. I probably shouldn't say, and don't repeat this, but I made some jackass comment about her being a prude with some guy on the dance floor. The worst part is, he may have been a jerk, but I was the bigger one." He looks remorseful, but I don't care. I want to kick his ass for upsetting Lily.

"That must be why she was running out. She slammed into me on the stairs last weekend." Now it all makes sense. I should be thanking Braden for pissing her off, or she might never have run into me. However, is that something I'm thankful for? Fuck, who knows at this point, but I'll find out soon.

I'm distracted from the conversation when I spot Lily and her friend Cici being led to their table. This is not the Lily I'm used to. This one is a siren calling to every male in the place. Her hair is pulled to one side with a clip, exposing her smooth, kissable neck. Her long brown locks are loosely curled, cascading over her left shoulder. The dress she wears tonight puts the one from last week to shame. The black shimmer hugs her curves and stops just above midthigh, showcasing her long legs, begging for attention. It has a full sleeve on one side, but the fabric angles down, skimming right over her cleavage, wrapping tightly around her body to leave her right shoulder and arm completely bare. From the top mound of her breast to her bare shoulder, up her gorgeous neck, her skin is begging to be licked and sucked. Holy shit, I'm screwed, and now, uncomfortably rock-hard.

$\mathcal{8}$

CONFESSION

Lily

AFTER TWO HOURS OF PRIMPING AND TWO GLASSES OF WINE AT dinner, I feel amazing, not to mention already a little buzzed. Why I haven't let Cici make me over before this is beyond me. She really is my fairy godmother, making me feel sexier than ever. That word hasn't ever been used to describe me. I planned to feign my confidence tonight, but the great thing is, I don't think I need to.

Once we exit the Uber and give our names to the doorman, which I'll admit I'm super thankful for, he calls someone to escort us. We're greeted by the maître d', who states he'll assist us throughout the evening and informs us that our tab is on the house. Cici and I look at each other and raise our eyebrows in surprise. Wow, I didn't know Jackson had this much pull.

We're being led to the VIP section, and as we follow our host, I can't help but remember the last time I was on these stairs. Running into Sebastian made quite an impression—and not a good one. However, I can't forget the fantastic smell that overtook my senses and the firm grip on my shoulders that burned into my skin. It's too bad his arrogant attitude continues to outweigh any positives. I shake my head to snap out of any more thoughts regarding Sebastian. We arrive at the table, and the maître d' pulls out our chairs, points to the waitress who will serve us and reiterates that our tab is on the house. He finishes by bowing in retreat. *Okay then.*

Cici turns to me immediately. "What the actual? Can you believe this? Our drinks weren't on the house last time. How'd we get so lucky? I bet Jackson and Braden felt so bad for ruining your night last weekend that they're paying for everything. Way to take one for the team." She puts her hand up to high five me.

I reciprocate because, heck yeah, I'll take one for the team for a night of free drinks. The waitress arrives and we each order a cosmo. She also says someone will watch our table whenever we want to dance. Wow, I never knew that VIP came with so many perks.

"Okay, let's scope out the floor while we sip on our drinks and see if we spot any prospects. Then we can head over and get our groove on. What do you think?" Cici's making sure I follow through on my commitment to make out with someone before I leave.

I look toward the dance floor. "Agreed. It's packed tonight. There better be someone worthy of my lips out there."

"Lips? You're supposed to get a little more than that. I didn't get you this dolled up just to kiss. We picked that dress for easy boob action, so get your head in the game, Lily. I need first base at least." Oh boy, she's taking her role as my coach seriously.

Our drinks are delivered while we're engrossed in watching the dance floor and going over options. There are plenty of hot guys to choose from. All of a sudden, I spot Kevin. I remember him saying he'd be here. Perfect. I'll start there, then make my way further in. "Hey, that's my friend Kevin from school. Let's go say hi." I point him out to Cici.

"That's Kevin? He's super cute. You should make out with him tonight."

"Ewww, I can't. I don't think of him that way. We've been friends too long. Come on, let's go. I'll introduce you, and you can make out with him." She winks at me, enthusiastically agreeing.

We signal to the waitress and let her know we're heading out. After taking one more sip of our drinks, we get up as our "guard" arrives. I lead us to Kevin, who immediately wraps me in a bear hug, lifting me off my feet and swinging me around.

"Holy shit, Lily, you look hot as hell. Where have you been hiding all these years? I wondered if I'd see you with this place being so huge. I'm glad you found me." I can tell he's tipsy. I hear the slur in his speech.

"Me too. What do you think, do you like it?" I pull out of his embrace and move to the music while we talk.

"I like it a lot. And the club is pretty great too." He winks at me.

He's acting interested and dancing closer than I'd like, especially since I'm hoping to attract someone else's interest. Kevin is good-looking, and any girl would love his attention, but I'm not attracted to him that way, and I made that clear from day one when he hinted at asking me out. I made sure he knew I wasn't interested in dating but that I'd love to have another friend. He seemed to take it well, and we've been close ever since.

I need to redirect his focus. "Let me introduce you to my friend Cici, the one I always talk about. Cici, this is Kevin, the friend I told you about from school."

"Nice to meet you, Kevin. If Lily had said how good-looking you were, I'd have made her introduce us sooner." Oh, she's good.

"Hi, Cici, glad to put a face to the name. I'm happy to hear Lily's talked about me outside of school." Oh boy, Cici better make a move fast. This is going in the wrong direction.

Sebastian

I watch Lily and her friend make their way to the dance floor. I'm glad I put someone on security detail for them. I wanted her to feel comfortable to let loose and not worry about things like leaving her drink unattended. Although, now that I've seen what she looks like tonight, I want to scoop her up and drag her sexy ass out of here so no one else can ogle her. It's killing me to watch every male out there staring her down. She's oblivious to them, except for the one she approached on the dance floor. *Who the hell is that?*

"Hey, isn't that Lily and I'm assuming your sister, Cici?" I bring everyone's attention to the ladies.

Jackson responds. "Yeah, that's them. But holy shit, Lils looks hot as fuck. Man, she doesn't usually dress like that. I wonder who the guy is? I can tell from here she's uncomfortable, and he seems to have missed the memo. I promised I wouldn't get in the way of girls' night, or I'd step in."

Oh yeah, he has it bad for her. Lils? What the fuck. They have nicknames for each other? Is he one of the boyfriends she mentioned?

Eli observes the two ladies with a strange look I can't pinpoint. Hopefully, I don't piss him off with the next thing to come out of my mouth. "Eli and I made no such promises, so maybe we should offer our services. What do you say, bro?" He looks at me, knowing exactly what my aim is, along with something else. If I didn't know any better, I'd say trepidation, but that doesn't make sense.

"Sure, let's go." He gets up, and I follow him to the edge of the dance floor. It looks like Lily is trying to encourage the guy toward Cici. From what I'm observing, it isn't working. Let's see if I can help with that.

Coming up from behind, I grab her hips and move with her. She stiffens immediately as I watch the douchebag take in my presence behind her. I hold firm, preventing her from turning around, then lean down. "Hey, sweetheart, you look delectable this evening. Shall we pick up where we left off and put your theory of not being interested in me to the test?"

I feel her sharp intake of breath. The blood rushes to my cock upon seeing her lips mouth my name. The way her body relaxes as soon as she realizes it's me makes me want to wrap her in my arms and haul her off. Her scent is intoxicating, and having her hips in my grasp is bliss. My mouth waters, and I know I'm not making it through the night without tasting her.

I glance over to Eli and Cici, who I haven't met yet, and see they're already in conversation. I also notice that surfer dude is quite put out by my presence, which is precisely my intention.

"Would you like to introduce me to your friends?" I ask loudly, standing up to my full height behind her while keeping my hold, staking my claim.

She's reluctant, I can tell, but makes the introductions nonetheless. "Kevin, this is Sebastian and his brother, Eli. They're associates from work. Kevin is a friend from school, and this is my best friend, Cici, who's also my roommate. It's such a coincidence we all ended up here tonight," she says with sarcasm. I'm sure she assumes I went to every nightclub in the city until I found her. Which I would have had to do if I weren't aware she'd be at mine.

"Well, not really a coincidence. Eli and I recently opened this club. It's the fun part of our business." I squeeze her hips. She's already tried to finagle herself out of my hold, but I'm not having it. She does manage to turn her upper body slightly and look up at me in shock.

Cici pipes in at that point. "Well, it's nice to meet you *both*." It doesn't go unnoticed when she accentuates the word "both." "And I'm assuming we have you to thank for our comped evening and table security? Because we really appreciate it." I smile in response. She exaggerates her gratitude for Lily's benefit, made apparent by the look she shoots in Lily's direction. *Hmmm.* It appears Cici's in favor of her best friend seeing me. Interesting. I figured I'd be dealing with an overprotective best friend. Good to know that won't be the case.

"I'm happy to see you outside of school, Lily. You look amazing." Kevin leans in to kiss Lily's cheek, and I feel her go rigid, confirming she's uncomfortable with him. Pulling back, he addresses everyone. "Nice to meet you all. I'm going to head back to my friends now. I'll see you in class on Monday." He makes his departure. One down.

I've still not released her, but once he's out of sight, she puts more strength into her body and twists around. "What the heck was that? You can't just come over and act like we're together. I wanted to hook up with him later, but now you've completely scared him away." I can't help but smirk at her. "And you just did that on purpose, didn't you? Ugh!"

God, she's fucking adorable and sexy as hell when she's all hot and bothered. I can't wait until I'm able to get her alone.

Lily

Sebastian looks down at me with a cocky grin on his face. "Well, I certainly achieved my desired effect. And sure, I could tell you were waiting for him to scoop you up and carry you off the dance floor. It was so apparent in your body language. Sorry if I ruined some big plans for later. But hey, I can stand in if you'd like."

"Absolutely not. I was hoping to get hit on by someone else. Now you've made it look like I'm with you. Also, what's with not telling me about owning this place? You already knew I would be here when we were texting last night, didn't you?" *Oh shoot.* I turn to Cici, remembering she's within earshot. I haven't told her about the texting.

"What's this about last night? Lily, have you been keeping secrets?"

Before I can answer, she turns her attention to Sebastian. "And just so you know, Sebastian, Lily *was* intending—" I elbow Cici hard before she can finish what she was saying. That is the last thing I need Sebastian to know. I already told him I have no time for men, so my intentions tonight wouldn't help my case.

I level a glare at Sebastian and finish the sentence for her. "I was intending to have some fun and dance with a ton of different guys." I turn back to Cici. "I haven't been keeping anything from you. It just wasn't worth mentioning that Sebastian feels it necessary to obnoxiously text me every evening. I promise to fill you in later, but what do you think about going somewhere else since this place is so crowded?" I'm hoping she gets the message and agrees. This is not going as planned. I'm not getting anywhere between Kevin trying to escape the friend zone and Sebastian coming in like a caveman.

"Nonsense, our drinks are paid for, we're already here, and there are two dance floors of eligible bachelors, right, boys?" Cici responds, grinning at Sebastian and Eli.

"Absolutely, and it looks like there are two willing bachelors right here, am I right, Sebastian?" Eli says pointedly to his brother. Oh boy, he's obviously in on this.

"Definitely. For now, though, why don't you ladies return to your table, enjoy another round on us and look around? Let us know if we can be of service. In the meantime, we'll rejoin our friends and check in with you later. Does that work for you, Lily?" Sebastian finally says something I agree with.

I roll my eyes, which I can tell irritates him. Good. "I think that sounds like a great idea. It was nice to see you again, Eli. Come on, Cici." I yank her away a little more aggressively than I should.

"Lily, what the heck is going on? You better fess up, girlfriend, and I mean it." She's looking at me like I stole her favorite coffee mug as we sit at our table.

"Don't be mad at me. I just didn't want to make a big deal about it. It's been a long week." Damn it, I didn't want to have to talk about this. I know she'll just try to convince me to give him a chance, and I don't know if my resolve is strong enough to hold out much longer. It seriously felt so good to have his hands on me so possessively. Not to mention the heat radiating from his body. And when he leaned in close to speak, oh my God, my brain short-circuited. From his sultry voice, intoxicating smell and the bulge I felt from the back, I was melting like butter. Obviously, attraction is not the problem. It's the wide gap in our social standing, his blatant arrogance and overbearing personality.

"We need a fresh drink for this convo," I say as I down the last sip of my cosmo and signal to the waitress for another round. "So, you already know he tried to get me to see him after that first meeting, and you also know I turned him down. What I haven't told you is that he's been texting me every night before bed." Her eyes go wide. Then she smirks as I continue. "They're all short conversations but always flirty with a ton of suggestive comments." Our drinks arrive, and I take a sip to give myself a break before explaining the rest.

"I can't believe you haven't told me all this. Why are you not going for him? He's even hotter in person than in pictures! What am I missing here?"

"What you're missing is that on Wednesday he demanded a last-minute meeting with Brad, insisting I work part-time with his marketing team *in* his office. He didn't even talk to me beforehand. Then he made me go with him afterward to meet the staff. Yeah right. I'm sure it was only to get me alone because, during the car ride, he made another attempt to get me to go out with him, this time making it clear he only wanted me in his bed. I snapped. I told him it wasn't going to happen. And to bring the point home, I told him I was a virgin." I take a big sip of my cocktail.

"YOU WHAT? Lily, that's something you keep in your back pocket. Not just blurt out before you've even gone out with the guy." She's holding a hand over her face in exasperation.

"I disagree. He should know up front so he can stop wasting his time trying to win me over only to get me under him. I figured he'd give up if he knew. At the time, his only goal was to have sex with me. But it backfired because now he seems more determined than ever. I don't know what to do, Cici." I'm exasperated. Finally, I earn a look of sympathy. It's about time.

"I'd say sorry, but you realize you have one of the hottest bachelors in history trying to get in your pants. If it were anyone else, they'd be tripping over themselves to accept." I'm giving her the death stare. "I'm not saying you should sleep with the guy, but why not find out if any of the stories are true? I bet it would be the best kiss of your life, something you could brag to your kids about someday."

That gets a laugh out of me, and I feel a little lighter. The second martini going down so quickly may also have something to do with it. I'm glad I finally fessed up to Cici. "I should also mention he sent me lunch and a beautiful bouquet of lilies to the office yesterday."

"Oh geez, girl, you're digging yourself deeper. Give the guy a chance already."

"Or we can look around and stick to the plan to find my conquest tonight." I point to the dance floor. "How about you pick someone out while I go to the bathroom, and when I get back, you can show me who I'm going for."

I head toward the bathroom before she can say another word. Of course, with my luck tonight, I'm halfway there when I run into Eli and Sebastian's table. Their "friends" happen to be none other than Jackson and Braden. Seriously, what are the chances? That must be the connection to the VIP list.

Dang it, why did I tell Jackson I'd say hi? I should have taken him up on acting like we didn't know each other. Oh well, putting my big girl pants on, I walk right up to their table as if I haven't a care in the world. *That's right*, I remind myself, *confident Lily is out tonight*. "Hey, guys. Jackson, I told you I'd say hi if I saw you, so here I am. I didn't put two and two together, but it makes sense now, the VIP list thing. Have you all known each other long?"

Jackson answers. "Eli and I met through poker a while back, but this is the first time we've all gotten together. I'm glad you stopped. You look amazing, Lily. I told you I'd let you girls have your night, but it was hard not to join in when I spotted you out there." He looks like he means it.

Okay, serious swoon. I need to let Cici dress me more often apparently. "Thanks, Jackson. Also, thanks for respecting our night, but you don't have to be a stranger. Good to see you guys. I need to get back to Cici, so I'll leave you to it."

Walking away, I try strutting my stuff like the girl hitting on Jackson last week. We'll see if I have what it takes. I would give anything for Jackson to be the guy I make out with tonight. I don't think I would stop at just making out if it were him. Oh God, who am I kidding? He's not suddenly into me because he's seen me look hot for once.

Luckily, there's no line for the bathroom, giving me time to freshen up. A few steps out, someone grabs me, pulling me around the corner. I panic, trying to get free, but he's strong, and I can't yell with the hand clamped over my mouth. His smell registers, and it's familiar. When he whispers in my ear, I freeze and stop struggling.

9

UNINTERESTED

Sebastian

COULD SEE IT THE MOMENT SHE LOOKED AT JACKSON. DAMN IT ALL to hell. The attraction is mutual. Her infatuation is written all over her face. That's an issue; one I plan to take care of. How have they not hooked up already? Is it because Cici's their sister and best friend, or are they just plain blind? I wonder if Cici knows they're secretly pining for each other. Well, it doesn't matter now because Jackson's too late. He just doesn't know it yet. And I just got the perfect opportunity handed to me by Lily herself, who's headed toward the bathrooms, not her table.

"Hey, guys, I'm gonna head to the bathroom. If you're gone when I get back, I'll see you on the dance floor." Eli smirks at me like he knows exactly what I'm up to.

I approach the exit to the ladies' room, conveniently located next to a hallway leading to the offices. I maneuver the roped barrier enough to slip through the side but still keep it obvious that the area is off-limits. Then, I stand and wait, hidden in the shadows. As soon as she starts to pass, I grab her. Luckily for me, no one is going in or out at the time, and all staff, including the bouncers, know me and won't interfere if they happen to catch it. She's struggling, of course, while I drag her around the corner. As soon as we're out of sight down the darkened hallway, I pull her body to mine, still covering her mouth from screaming. Standing with my back up against the wall, I whisper in her ear.

"Sweetheart, it's me. I didn't see another way to get you alone." She stills as soon as she hears my voice. "I'm going to remove my hand now."

I bring it down and flip us, pinning her back against the wall with my body holding her firmly in place. I cage my arms around her, giving her no way out. She has both hands on my chest, applying enough pressure to make her feel like she's keeping me at bay while bringing out the animal in me with her resistance. She's stunning in all her fury. I want to ravage her, but I need to be careful.

"What do you think you're doing?"

"I told you last night I plan to prove that you are, in fact, interested in me. Are you ready for your test?"

"Sebastian, seriously, no. What is your fascination with me anyway? It's not like I have anything you haven't had before. I don't understand why you're bothering."

"I don't either. All I know is you've mesmerized me. And you have everything I've never had: innocence, drive, spirit and so much more that intrigues me. So, I'll decide if I should bother with you." I press my hips into her as she swallows her desire, stunned into silence.

"I know what my cock wants me to do." I give her ass a squeeze. "I'm pretty sure your body agrees. Your brain just needs to catch up." I need to rile her up to distract her before I make my next move.

"Are you kidding me right now? You literally just kidnapped me from the bathroom. You're delusional if you think I want you. Stockholm syndrome doesn't set in that quick."

I tip my head back and laugh. She's priceless. "I love your feistiness. Although you need to take some self-defense classes because if what I just saw is all you've got for fight in you, you're in trouble. And, Lily, if I were to kidnap you, I would take you somewhere much farther away than a dark corner of my club. There are more appropriate places for everything I want to do to your body." Her mouth goes wide, and oh boy, does that make my dick pulse. I'm sure she felt it. I'm already beyond rock-hard with lust for this woman.

"You're not taking me anywhere. And you caught me by surprise. I wasn't prepared to put up a fight."

"So your next kidnapper is going to warn you before they attack?" I laugh and can't help but continue to poke fun at her.

"Ha, so you admit you kidnapped me. You just said when my *next* kidnapper, which means that's what you are."

"Lily, I'm going to kiss you now because it's the only way to shut you up."

Lily

"Wait, no, you can't—" But that's all I get out as he cuts me off. In record time, he grabs my wrists, pins them above my head, and pushes his lips to mine. My brain takes a moment to register what's happening, but when it does, I melt into him. His lips are warm. Soft but demanding. A moan sneaks from my throat. I lose myself, with no time to stress or worry about my actions, because he completely takes control. His initial strike was forceful and hurried, but now he slows, easing the pressure. It's as if he's savoring every touch of our lips, kissing and retracting while occasionally nipping my bottom lip.

"You don't know how many times I've imagined this over the last week. Nothing came close to the real thing. You are pure heaven." All I can do is pant in response to his words.

His tongue tentatively grazes my lips, seeking entry. I whimper in need, realizing how badly I want to meet his tongue with my own. So I open to him, giving access to explore completely, allowing me to do the same. One hand moves down to wrap tightly around the back of my neck and pull me into him forcefully as our mouths feast on one another. I feel his hard bulge as he pushes me against the wall. There's an unfamiliar, pleasant sensation in my core, and I find myself hungry for more.

As if reading my mind, he brings his hand around to skim his fingertips over my collarbone, then down to the mound of my breast, where he hesitates for just a moment before lightly dragging the back of his fingers over my nipple, causing it to harden. I mewl in response and push my chest into him. He grabs my breast entirely and squeezes. It's his turn to moan, or rather, growl.

"You are so fucking hot, Lily. Can you feel how hard I am for you?" He grinds his hips into me while kneading my breast through my dress. He kisses the corner of my mouth, and then his lips are on my neck, lighting my body on fire. When he shifts his attention to below my ear, sucking and licking in the most delicious way imaginable, I feel wetness pool in my panties. That's when I realize I'm grinding into him, straining against his hold on my wrists that are still secured above my head.

Suddenly, my chest feels the cool air of the club as he pulls my dress down, making my nipple rock-hard. He cups my breast in his palm and runs his thumb over my tight bud. I'm a goner. "Oh God. Mmmm," I mumble in ecstasy as he squeezes and leans down to run his tongue over my nipple.

"Fuck me," he growls out slowly as he kisses his way back toward my mouth. "I love your lips." He kisses the corner of them. "Your moans." He kisses the other corner. "Your tits." He pinches my nipple hard, then caresses it, making me suck in a breath while feeling a fresh wave of cream in my panties. "This is just a taste of what I want to do to you, Lily. For now, it'll have to be enough." Right then, he pulls my dress back up, brings my arms down and takes a step back while reaching in to adjust the massive bulge in his pants. "I'd say you passed the test. Would you like to tell me how uninterested you are now?" he asks right before he walks away, leaving me with my mouth agape.

"Tell me what happened. You're scaring me, Lily. Did someone hurt you?" We're in the Uber on the way home, and Cici's still waiting for me to talk to her. In a daze, I somehow made it back to our table, only to tell Cici I wanted to leave.

I'm still in shock and waiting for my libido to return to its cage. What have I gotten myself into? And what the hell was I thinking? Anyone could have walked by. The problem is I *wasn't* thinking. My brain must have short-circuited. I probably would have let Sebastian keep going in the heat of my desire, which scares the crap out of me. And why did he have to ruin it with his damn cockiness at the end? I guess I shouldn't be surprised.

I drop my head in my hands and garble, "Seb—"

Cici pulls my hands away from my face. "Let's try that again because I didn't catch one word you said."

I exhale before spitting out, "Sebastian and I made out right before I returned to the table."

"Oh my gosh, I knew that was going to happen! I want to hear all about it!" She's ecstatic, bouncing up and down with a gigantic smile.

I lean my head back and close my eyes, remembering. "It was amazing. I don't think any other kiss will compare. It wasn't just a kiss, Cici. It was a total, full-on consumption of my senses." I look at her. "He's very talented, which makes sense with his extensive experience, right?" I say the last part vehemently, then pause the conversation until we exit the Uber and go inside. She knows I want privacy to tell her the rest.

"Okay, spill," she demands as soon as we make it to the kitchen for some much-needed water.

I tell her, in detail, every moment, from when he grabbed me to when he lowered my dress. Her eyes go from saucers to dreamy as I get further into the story, and then I pause for water before confessing the part where he walked away.

"Holy shit, Lily, that's hot! Way to go, girl. So what's the problem? Why did you run out after?"

"Because he just stopped, made some cocky-ass comment, then walked away. He left me standing there like it was nothing. The nerve. It's exactly why I didn't agree to see him in the first place. Regardless of his sweet words, which are probably all bullshit, he's only after one thing. I need more than kisses in dark corners, only to feel humiliated after." And that's the crux of it. I feel weak and foolish for letting him get the best of me, damn it. He said all those things about what he liked about me, and I caved. I should know better. I wasn't enough for my own dad to want to stick around; how would some guy see those things in a week?

She comes in to hug me, and I lose it. "Oh, sweetie, I'm sorry you feel like that. Don't think that way. How about you look at it from a different angle? It sounds like you got exactly what you hoped for. He got your juices flowing, gave you the best kiss of your life and a delicious taste of second base. Now you can go out there and find your dream man who wants more than a one-night stand. And you can look forward to it now since you know how amazing it feels, right?" Thank God she can talk me off a ledge.

"Ugh, you're right. You always know how to make me feel better, Cici. Thank you. Your perspective is way better. And truthfully, I am looking forward to more because, holy shit, that was hot." We giggle as she hugs me again before we both turn in for the night.

Sebastian

Fuck. I couldn't walk away fast enough. Heading back to the table, I quickly retreat with the excuse of forgetting something at the office. The questioning look from Eli doesn't go unnoticed, but that will have to wait. I need to get the hell away from this place before I do something stupid and go back for more. This time, it's me rushing down the stairs for a hasty exit to where my driver is waiting out back. "Home," I bark as soon as I enter the car.

That was hands down the hottest, most intense make-out session I've had, and that's saying a lot. I don't generally "make out," but how else was I supposed to start? Normally, I skip all that and plunge right into whatever woman I'm using to get off. Then, her reaction was off the fucking charts, making that shit more enticing than most of the things I've done with anyone else. She responded to my every touch, bite, pinch and caress with the most delectable sounds. Put that with how she ground into me, begging for more, and fuck, it was incredible. *She* is fucking incredible.

It took everything I had to stop when I did and even more self-control not to change my mind. I was two seconds from reaching under her dress to feel how wet she was for me. God, just thinking about her untouched pussy makes the need to relieve the pressure from my dick unbearable, and if I had more than one minute to my doorstep, I wouldn't hesitate to do it. As it is, you can bet that's the plan as soon as I make it to my bedroom.

After taking care of the problem twice—once immediately and once more in the shower—I crawl into bed. I'm still so wound up that I could go for round three, but my dick may fall off at that point. I'm contemplating my text to Lily, unsure where to start, when my phone rings. I knew this was coming. I may as well get it over with.

"Hey, Eli."

"Dude, what the hell happened? Because I know you didn't leave something at the office. I could see hunger written all over your face, and I'm not talking about food." Yeah, we tend to read each other like books. Twin thing? Maybe. Or that we're the closest people in each other's lives and barely go a day without seeing the other.

"I cornered Lily and kissed her. We made out like goddamn teenagers, Sebastian style. It was hot, dude, like over the top. If I didn't leave right then, I would've gone back for more, and you know I can't with her." I groan in frustration.

"Huh, I'm surprised. After seeing how pissed she was on the dance floor, it didn't seem like she wanted anything to do with you. How did it happen?"

"I took her by surprise outside of the bathroom. She fought it. But it went fast and furious when I finally kissed her to stop arguing. I couldn't get enough, and neither could she. We were on fire, and I still can't put the damn thing out. That's how fucking amazing it was."

"That was the plan. I'm glad it went well for you, man. So, now what?"

"That's the million-dollar question right there. Fuck, I can't ruin her. What the hell am I thinking? Don't even consider answering that, jackass." I could hear him snickering as soon as the question slipped out.

"I don't know what to tell you, bro, but if it was that explosive, maybe there's more to her than meets the eye. She's a nice girl, though, so don't fuck it up. Determine how far you want to take this before you get too deep and be smart about it. Can we do it over lunch tomorrow if you need to talk some more? I'm beat."

"Yeah, okay, talk tomorrow. Thanks, man."

Time for my nightly text and to get some answers.

Me: So tell me what's going on between you and Jackson.

I see the dots moving, but no text is appearing. She doesn't know how to answer.

Me: Cat got your tongue? Oh wait… that was me.

Lily: I just can't believe that's the first thing you texted.

Me: I could see you ogling him the minute you walked up to our table. Is he one of the boyfriends you mentioned?

Lily: It's none of your business. Why, jealous?

Me: I want to know if I should be worried about the fact you live in the same building as him.

Lily: Worried about what? It's not like I'm off limits. We kissed. Big deal. If I want to hook up with Jackson I can, maybe even Kevin if I feel like it. Aren't you the king of hookups?

Me: So you're going from innocent little Lily to working your way around? If that's the case, let me get you primed and ready. May as well learn how to please a man from an expert.

Lily: Fuck you, Sebastian. Leave me alone. I'm done playing your games.

Me: We'll see about that. Sweet dreams, siren.

Shit. I didn't mean for that to end badly, but damn she pushes my buttons. I wish I could convince myself to leave her alone like she asked. Instead, I think I'm just getting started.

10

UP FOR GRABS

Lily

AFTER NURSING MY PRIDE ALL DAY YESTERDAY FROM THE KISS fiasco, along with successfully refraining from responding to Sebastian's relentless texts last night, I wake feeling better and ready to tackle a new week. School isn't nearly as stressful as it had been now that it's nearing graduation, and to top it all off, I'm relieved that work will return to normal now. As crappy as working with Brad is, I know what to expect and can look for something else in just a couple more months.

As I arrive on campus, it hits me suddenly that I'll see Kevin in a minute, and I can't help but wonder if it will be awkward. He made some comments on Saturday that implied he was into me a lot more than I was aware of, but I love our friendship the way it is, and I'd hate to ruin it. Spotting him as I walk into class, I don't hesitate to sit beside him. *Please, please don't be weird.*

"Happy Monday! It was fun seeing you this weekend. I still can't get over how great you looked." Not terrible, but let's deflect.

"Oh yeah, well, you weren't too shabby yourself. My friend Cici certainly thought so." I smile at him and smirk.

"Nice, well maybe you'll have to set us up sometime. She was a looker, and if she's your friend, she must be awesome. So, what's up with you and the Sebastian guy? He was all over you." Shit, I wasn't expecting the conversation to go this direction, and I'm not sure how to answer that. Thankfully, Professor Milton walks in and greets the class, halting my reply.

"Good morning, class. Before we begin, I have an update regarding your final projects turned in last week. I reviewed all of them over the weekend and decided to submit one outstanding campaign from our class to the American Advertising Awards of San Diego. Lily Thompson, will you please stand?" *Oh my gosh.* I stand timidly, not totally registering his words. "Congratulations, your project will be entered for the Addy Award in the student-integrated campaign category." Seriously? Did I just hear that correctly? The students clap, and Kevin beams at me while patting me on the back. I look around stunned and smile as the impact of what Professor Milton said finally hits me. That will get my name in front of a lot of people in the industry, whether I win the award or not. Just by being submitted, it will be seen by the entire committee responsible for viewing all the submissions.

He continues, "In accordance with the rules, you'll need to submit a three-minute video of your sales pitch to accompany the entry. I'd like you to prepare something to present to the class on Thursday. We'll have a video camera set up to record your presentation. Do you think you can be ready by then?"

I don't even think twice, knowing what a massive opportunity this is, and answer immediately. "Yes, I'll be ready. Thank you, Professor Milton."

"You deserve it, Lily. Great job. See me after class and I'll give you more details. All right, class, let's get to work."

I'm still shocked as I walk out of the classroom after speaking with the professor. It's a pretty big deal if I win, and after hearing his enthusiasm about my project, I can't help but get excited. After rounding the corner outside the professor's office, Kevin pushes off the wall. He's been waiting for me.

"Lily, how'd it go?" he asks as he gets in step with me.

"Good, I still can't believe it. Hopefully, my sales pitch goes well. He gave me a couple examples to work from, so it should be easy."

"If anyone can pull it off, it's you. Let me know if you need any help." We get to the crossroads where we go in different directions.

"Thanks, Kevin, I appreciate it. I'll let you know. Otherwise, I'll see you Thursday. Have a good week," I say as I start to head off.

He starts talking, though, before I make it a few feet. "Hey, so I have to ask, are you and Sebastian a thing?" Oh crap, not this again. Maybe it's a good idea to just go with it, so he doesn't get his hopes up about me. *Ooh, brilliant.* At least Sebastian will be good for something.

"Sort of, we're still just seeing where things go. So we might be?" I shrug at him.

"Good to know. I wanted to see if you were up for grabs, but I'm obviously too late. You snooze, you lose, right?" He chuckles.

"To be honest, I can't say I'm sorry. Our friendship means a lot to me, and it would suck to mess it up, so it's probably for the best. But seriously, if you want me to set you up with Cici sometime, let me know. I think you guys would hit it off."

"I'll think about it. Good luck with your pitch. I can't wait to see it on Thursday. See ya, Lily." He walks away looking a little down in the dumps. Ugh, what in the world? When it rains, it pours.

"Hey, Brad, do you have anything for me today?" It's another day in the office with Brad. *Yippee!*

"Lily. How did everything go on Friday? Any word from Dubree yet?" I assume they would contact him directly, so I don't know why he's asking me.

"No, nothing further since I visited the office, but like I said, they might not need our help. Friday went well. It was quiet, with just a couple calls from clients asking about this and that. I took care of everything."

"Great, I knew you'd hold the fort down. I wish Dubree would at least give me an idea of their thoughts. The silence is killing me."

"Well, I wouldn't hold your breath; companies like that don't care about anyone but themselves. They could string us along forever. Also, the acquisition was delayed by a week, so I'm sure they're busy. We might not hear anything until next week." I hope he lets it go for a while. I don't want to rehash this every day.

"I'd like you to call them first thing Friday if there's still no word. You'll have better luck getting through since you're the one he's trying to date. Let them know we'd like to have a plan by Monday. Would it kill you to go out with the guy just once?" Did he seriously bring this up again? And now he's using me to get in touch with them. *Great, just freaking great.*

"Brad, I'm not having this conversation again. My decision was made. I'm not going to whore myself out for you." Seriously, the nerve of this man.

"I didn't say anything about sleeping with the guy, although I'm sure that wouldn't hurt." I give him the deadliest look I can manage. He holds up his hand. "Kidding, I'm kidding. Okay, just call on Friday and we'll go from there. Until then, I've put together a list of potential clients. I'd like you to spend this week researching their current marketing and sales data to see if there's a pitch opportunity for any of them. Once you've determined a few, report back, and we'll make a game plan. If we do lose this account, we need to be prepared. That's all for now."

There went my good mood for the rest of the day. At least I don't have to think about it until Friday. Thank God for small miracles. Wait until I tell Cici about Brad's douchebag comments. Although maybe I shouldn't; she'll just lecture me about quitting again. I repeat my mantra for the rest of the day. *Two more months. Two more months.*

Sebastian

Lily didn't respond at all to my texts last evening. I thought she would have cooled down after having a day to get over it. My comments were rude and probably out of hand, but she baited me with thoughts of her getting with those two assholes. Now that I've had a taste of her, I'm not letting her go so easily. Hopefully, after another day to calm down, she's ready to be finished with this tantrum she's throwing.

> Me: Feeling better today?

> Me: Still feeling sore about my comment, I see. You know you baited me, right? I just want to know what's going on between you and Jackson. I'm not one to share, Lily.

Me: Damn it, Lily, you give me the blue balls from hell, and now the silent treatment. Come on, can you honestly deny there's something between us? Let's explore the possibility. I can't forget the feel of you grinding on me. I'd like to show you how good it can be when you give in to what your body wants. And trust me, baby, your body wants this.

Me: Just consider it. It's all I've thought about for the past two days now. Good night, Lily. Sweet dreams.

Damn this woman. Am I going to keep acting like a goddamn fool, or am I going to do something about it? Why am I letting her get under my skin like this after one kiss? These questions and more have been plaguing my mind. I've never had a woman blatantly ignore me. It's unacceptable and I need to handle it.

11

DON'T IGNORE ME

Lily

'M DISORIENTED AS I WAKE UP. IT TAKES A FEW MINUTES TO REMEMBER it's Wednesday. I feel like I've been on cruise control since Saturday. I trudge from home to school, to work and home again while still getting that damn creepy feeling like someone's following me sometimes. Maybe my dad got into trouble again, and the bad guys are coming after me now. I laugh at myself. Cici's made me watch too many crime shows.

What's really been bothering me, though, and taking up way too much of my brain cells is that I'm mad I allowed myself to get this invested in Sebastian already and that I actually considered going out with him. With all his efforts last week and texting me every night, he's done a number on my psyche, not to mention the kiss that rocked my world. I feel like such a fool and wish I could just look at what happened the way Cici told me to, but for some reason, I can't. It could have to do with my lack of experience in this department. Oh, who am I kidding? It has everything to do with that.

I've managed not to respond to his texts for the past three nights, and it wasn't easy, considering his persistence. He asked over and over again what was going on between me and Jackson. He told me how our kiss gave him blue balls in various ways, my favorite one being, "They were the size of Violet in Willy Wonka, and they may never recover." That one made me giggle. I am now aware of numerous things he'd like to do to me. What scares me are the butterflies I get from each description. He gave up each night after about five texts in a row. And let me tell you, the fighter in me so wanted to reply, but I held back, knowing it would only prolong the situation, which is starting to ebb.

I'm feeling decent, with a little more pep in my step as I head into the office. I go straight to my desk in the reception area to put my purse away before heading back to grab a cup of coffee. As I pass the conference room, I do a double take. *What the* …? There's Brad in a meeting with none other than the man of my nightmares. Okay, they may resemble a different type of dream, but right now, that's what I'm calling them.

I walk straight in with no hesitation. "Good morning! What did I miss?" I am seething inside, so the fact that I made the question sound as jovial as it did is an absolute effing miracle.

Brad looks over with a smile on his face. "Ah, Lily, glad you're here. We were discussing the details of your work schedule at Mr. Dubree's office and finalizing the terms. Would you like to join us?"

Did I say seething? I think the correct term is murderous.

"It's interesting that you're having this conversation without my presence since it directly involves me. When was the meeting scheduled, and why was I unaware?"

Sebastian looks at me at that point with a devious grin on his face and takes over from there. "I took the liberty of calling Brad as I was headed into the office this morning and asked if I could stop by to discuss the particulars so we could proceed. Since we needed to decide the logistics regarding your salary, I felt it unnecessary to waste your time until that part was settled. I assumed we would finish with those details and be ready to move on to your schedule when you arrived. And here you are, just in time."

Did he just wink at me? The nerve of this man to just waltz in here and make arrangements behind my back. "I was under the impression that your marketing department felt they had it under control and didn't need my input or assistance."

"I'm sorry if they gave that impression, Miss Thompson. Perhaps you misunderstood. They are more than capable of driving a new campaign. Still, we feel your expertise concerning this account will be invaluable to the success of the overall outcome. As such, we would like you in our office to work alongside the team for the duration it will take for a complete rebranding. Can you be on board with that?"

Crap, put me on the spot why don't you. Why can't I be as quick on my toes as Sebastian? He combated all my concerns during the last meeting, so I have no legitimate argument. Damn him. "You haven't left me much choice, so I suppose I'll have to be, won't I? What's the plan then? Have you two already talked about what days I'll be here versus there? I suppose, with the company car I was so graciously offered to use, it doesn't matter, but it would be nice to be included in the conversation." Could I be any snarkier? But he should know how underhanded this was. This is his way of getting back at me for ignoring him for three days; I know it.

Brad is smiling, knowing he gets the best of both worlds. He doesn't have to pay me while I work in their offices yet still earns the commission for being part of the marketing campaign. Little does he know, as soon as Sebastian gets his fill of me or gives up trying, he'll ship me right back here and yank the account.

Sebastian doesn't give him a chance to talk. He continues to command the conversation. "I agree you should be involved. So far, Brad has laid out your current schedule. I'd like to make the following proposal: we would have one full day and one half day, splitting time equally for now. I would like your Fridays and half-day Mondays to be in our office. We can begin there and play it by ear whether we need to adjust. As promised, the company car will be scheduled to pick you up on Mondays from campus and from your residence on Friday mornings and take you home at the conclusion of each day. Is this arrangement acceptable to you?"

He's all business, and I'm rendered speechless at the unexpected admiration I feel for his speaking skills and commanding nature. Not to mention how sexy it is. I end up staring at him in awed silence.

"Unless you have another suggestion," he adds when I don't reply.

Get a grip, Lily. You do not find this man sexy. Okay, who am I kidding? He is sex on a stick, but his egotistical attitude cancels that out. "Um, no, I think that sounds fine." I almost forgot. "Will I still qualify for health coverage, even though I won't technically be working here for the required thirty hours per week?" I definitely can't let that detail go unaddressed. I've been taking care of that responsibility since my dad left me high and dry.

"I'm sure Brad feels this is the best strategy for all involved and will make no changes to your health care coverage. Isn't that right?" He looks to Brad, who only nods in agreement before Sebastian continues. "Are we in agreement then and ready to start this Friday? I can have the car waiting for you at 8:00 a.m. Our office hours begin at eight thirty." I look at Brad to see his reaction, and it occurs to me that he's been reticent since greeting me upon entering. I can't help but wonder what Sebastian must've said to make him this complacent. Brad has no comment, just dips his head in acquiescence.

Damn, I can't come up with anything good to avoid the situation. If he hadn't blindsided me, I'm sure I could've thought of something. "I guess I'll see you at the office Friday morning then. Anything else I should be aware of, like dress code, check-in requirements, et cetera? I don't want any surprises come Friday morning." Although his staff was friendly and seemed accepting of me, this is an entirely different environment than I'm used to, and I don't want to make a fool of myself on day one.

"What I've seen you in thus far has been adequate, and you'll be directed where to go upon arrival and given a full introduction to our offices and staff." I nod in acknowledgment.

"If there's nothing further, I'll leave you both to your day. Lily, I look forward to having you on Friday." Oh my God, did he just make an innuendo, or is my mind in the gutter?

He shakes hands with Brad. "Thank you again for seeing me on such short notice." Then, he turns to me. "Lily, see me out?"

Do I have a choice? "Uh, sure." And in pure Sebastian style, he gestures for me to lead the way. What is happening? I haven't seen him since Saturday, and holy hell, the memory of that kiss is killing me. What I wouldn't do to feel his hands on me again… *Ugh, NO, Lily. Get a fricking grip, and remember, this infuriating man is not the one you've been holding out for.* This is so not good. How will I see him all the time and be able to keep him at bay? I can already feel the cracks in my resolve.

We make it to the front door, and even though I open it for him, he places his hand above my head to hold it, motioning for me to proceed. "I'd like a minute of your time," he says as he leads me to his car. "Please join me for a moment, and I'll be on my way." He opens the back door and motions me in. Hesitating briefly, I get in.

He climbs in behind me, informing the driver to give him a few minutes. Sebastian raises the privacy glass and moves like lightning as soon as it's up. Reaching his hand out, he grabs the back of my neck and pulls me to him with force, his mouth devouring mine—fierce and probing, like he's starving for a taste of me. Apparently, I am too, as I match his ferocity. His other arm wraps around my waist and pulls me on top of him, and I go willingly, my legs straddling his torso while we ravage each other. There is nothing soft or slow about this.

He pulls away and looks at me intently. "You think you can ignore me? Think again. I've wanted nothing else but this since Saturday." He grips my hair and pulls my head back to reveal my neck. He consumes me while the hand wrapped around my waist pulls me tight against his groin. I moan loudly, his grunt of approval turning me on even more. "I know you feel it too, damn it. Don't lie to me."

"Yes… ahh… so good," I manage in between moans, accidentally fessing up. However, my actions speak louder than words as I grab his hair in a death grip, grinding on his huge, firm bulge. I did lie, though, because "good" is not even close to the right word for what I'm feeling right now. Oh my God, I almost can't take it.

"Good girl. That's it, baby, ride me. Feel what you do to me."

Suddenly, my senses come rushing back, and I realize what I'm doing and who I'm with. Pulling back quickly, I jump off his lap. "Shit, Sebastian, I can't do this. We can't do this. I'm going to be working with you and… wait, no, I'm going to be working *for* you. You're my fricking boss for Christ's sake." I try to smooth my hair and right myself before exiting. "There's obviously attraction between us, but it has to end here. This can't happen again. I'm sorry. I'll see you at the office on Friday." I rush out of the car and try to walk back into the office calmly. Yeah, right. There is nothing calm about me.

Sebastian

I can't believe she just walked out. This girl is maddening. I've once again ended up with my dick throbbing and in need of relief. After signaling the driver to go, I decide to take care of it. There's no way I can show up to the office like this, and it's not going away anytime soon. Not with her smell still permeating the car. All it takes as I unbuckle my pants and pull out my cock is the memory of Lily's moans and how her body responded to my touch, grinding her pussy on me while I tasted her sweetness. After twenty strokes at most, I'm a goner, gripping hard, imagining myself filling her up with my seed. Fuck. She's my goddamn kryptonite. This will happen, or I'll die trying. Time to step up my game.

On a mission, I head straight to Eli's office, walk past his secretary and barge in without knocking. "Update me. Are we closing tomorrow or what?"

"You need to work on your greeting skills, man. What's gotten your day off to such a great start?" I stare at him, unblinking, until I get an answer to my question. "Yes, we're signing the deal at nine tomorrow. It'll be finalized before five and go public Friday morning. Now that that's out of the way, what's up, buttercup? I assume you aren't just arriving to the office at ten because you overslept, so tell me where you've been and what or who I need to thank for your lovely ass mood today."

I sit down roughly on one of the sofa chairs and exhale a sigh of frustration. "Well, I just finished myself off after another steamy encounter with Lily. There was no way I could step into the office with what I had going on. This girl is killing me, dude. I need to get her under me and out of my system already."

"Hey, I thought we talked about this. You can't just one and done her like that, so get your head on straight. Why were you with her this morning anyway?"

"She's been ignoring me since Saturday night, not responding to my texts, so I took matters into my own hands and paid a visit to her boss this morning. She starts with our team Friday and will be here Monday afternoons as well."

Eli stares at me with raised eyebrows in that way of his that says, *I know what you're doing, and you're crazy.* I wish I knew what I was doing and could counter that sentiment, but he's right. I am crazy when it comes to Lily. "That doesn't explain why you're so riled up. What happened after said meeting, and how did things get steamy?"

"Lily came in midway, spitting mad that we were discussing it without her. Not only does her boldness impress me but it turns me the hell on, and after tasting her last week, I decided it was time for another. I had Lily accompany me to the car on the pretense of talking and instead pulled her straight into my lap for a repeat of Saturday. The attraction is mutual, Eli. This electricity between us is undeniable. I'm not doing her any favors by leaving her alone, dude. She wants me just as much as I want her—she just won't admit it."

"That still doesn't explain your foul mood, so it didn't end well, I take it?"

"She panicked and jumped off me, saying we couldn't do that again, that I was her boss and shit. I don't give a damn. I want this woman like I've never wanted another. There's something about her." I can't believe that crap just came from my mouth.

"Well, if that's the case, and you're insistent on pursuing her, then let me offer some advice." I nod. "Ask her on a proper date. I know you're unfamiliar with the concept, but it's something women appreciate before getting intimate with someone."

I stand up and start toward the door. "That's rich coming from the guy who has a different girl, sometimes multiple, every weekend. But duly noted. I'm glad to learn my brother's an expert with the ladies." He's laughing as I exit, so I give him the finger on the way out.

I decide to stop at my secretary's desk. "Good morning, Lucy. Please make a reservation for two at Stake on Coronado for dinner this Saturday and book a dock slip at the Coronado Yacht Club for an overnight stay." Just because I like to give Eli shit doesn't mean he isn't on to something.

"Yes, Mr. Dubree. Is there a special occasion to make note of?" I can hear the curiosity there, hoping for more details. This is out of character for me; she knows I don't do the date thing. Why go through the bullshit unless there's a business event I have to appear at? And the only reason I allow a woman to accompany me to those is to keep others at bay. When I want to get laid, I get laid; there's no need for pretenses.

"No, that'll be all. Thank you, Lucy."

I guess we'll see if Eli is correct soon enough. Now for the tough part, getting her to accept.

Me: Thank you for speaking with me this morning.

Lily: Is that what we're calling it?

Me: Oh good, you're done ignoring me. Wise choice before I had to get creative.

Lily: Showing up at my office unannounced was pretty creative. You certainly know how to get your way.

Me: If that were true, you wouldn't have left the car this morning. You should stop resisting this.

Lily: There is no "this." "This" can only end one way, and that's with one of us on the receiving end of disappointment. I'd like to ensure it isn't me.

Me: I certainly haven't been disappointed, and there won't be any on your end either if you'd just give in. We'll continue this conversation in person. Good night, sweetheart, and sweet dreams.

Lily: I know how your conversations go, Sebastian, not happening. Good night.

I laugh as I put my phone down for the night and think about how much I look forward to our next encounter, which leads me to take care of myself for the second time today.

12

GET IN THE CAR

Lily

THE DAY I'VE BEEN DREADING IS HERE, AND I'M A NERVOUS wreck—even more so than giving my presentation in class yesterday, which went perfectly. The thought of seeing Sebastian again gives me butterflies. I'm owning up to the fact that there's some serious chemistry between us, and while I'm not thrilled to be the object of his affection, I can at least admit that I don't mind the results so far. Although I'm getting frustrated that my dreams continue to leave me aching for more every morning. His suggestive texts every night aren't helping.

My alarm goes off early this morning, so I have more time to prepare for the day. I'd love to say it's only to impress the polished staff and fit into their posh atmosphere, but I'd be lying if I said it had nothing to do with wanting to look good for Sebastian. What is happening to me? I don't remember the last time I tried to impress a guy. Even with Jackson, it's never something I think about since we've always been around each other.

Now here I am, raiding Cici's closet after doing just a touch more with my makeup, and damn it, I actually curled my hair. I'm pitiful. Cici's in her bathroom getting ready as I walk into her room. "Good morning, sunshine. Mind if I borrow something sleek to wear today? I have to work at Dubree Enterprises, and I don't want to look paltry next to those people."

"Of course not, help yourself." She turns around. "Whoa, girlfriend, you look great. This wouldn't have anything to do with a certain someone, would it?" I've kept her up to date on everything that's happened since she caught me red-handed keeping things from her.

"Maybe, but it doesn't mean anything. I just want to step it up since I'll be on his turf. I feel inadequate already, so I figure if I can make myself look a little more refined, it may help my bundle of nerves. It certainly doesn't help that he told me he's looking forward to seeing me today. He makes me nervous," I tell her honestly.

"Here, let me help you pick something to knock his socks off. And, sweetie, you know he's already into you even in your basic Brad attire, so anything extra will only make him crazy. You better be ready for that." She holds up a dark blue, formfitting, V-neck dress that stops above the knees. It's sexy and professional at the same time. It's perfect and she's well aware blue is my color.

"That's perfect, Cici, thanks. And yes, I'm ready. I think I'm getting used to his attention a little too much." She gives me the biggest smile ever.

"I knew this was going somewhere. I could see the heat pouring off both of you while you were arguing on the dance floor that night. Yay! Have fun today!" She claps her hands excitedly. "I can't wait to hear all about it. I have nothing tonight, so let's grab dinner and you can fill me in." She's incorrigible.

I'm already grateful for the car waiting at the curb since I wore my tall heels to go with the dress. I must say, I look pretty damn good for a workday, and I'll definitely hold my own alongside his staff. As I walk out the lobby doors onto the sidewalk, I practically run right into Jackson.

"Hey, Lily… wow!" He takes a step back to look me up and down. "You look amazing. What's the occasion?" I can tell he just came from the gym, and his bulging muscles and sweaty shirt distract me from my answer. God, he is so hot.

"Um… actually… I… I'm just headed to work." As I manage to get the full sentence out, the back door of the town car opens, and Sebastian appears. What the heck? I'm stunned as he stands at the car, holding the door open, looking sexy as hell in his tailored suit.

"Good morning, Lily, Jackson. Lily, are you ready to go?" Oh boy, he does not sound pleased; this should be fun.

"When did you start working for Dubree Enterprises?" Apparently, Sebastian's demeanor rolled right off Jackson since he feels having a conversation right now is okay.

"Well, I'm temporarily working part-time with his marketing department. I still have my normal job and go into Dubree a couple days a week."

"Lily." One word, a demand. That's all it takes.

"Sorry, Jackson, I better go."

"Yeah, okay, let's catch up later." He leans in to kiss me goodbye on the cheek. What the heck?

I turn toward the car, and if looks could kill, I'm not sure which of us would be dead, Jackson or myself—maybe both? I stop in front of Sebastian. "What are you doing here?"

"Get. In. The. Car."

"Well, not if you're going to be cranky about it. I can find my own ride."

"Lily, you have two seconds to plant yourself down on that seat, or I will do it for you. And you look so lovely today. I would hate to muss you up, or would I?"

"You're insane, you know that?" I say as I lower myself into the car. Sebastian follows and slams the door closed. The privacy screen is already up.

"What the hell was that about? You refused to answer my question before and ignored me for three days instead. I will ask you one last time. What is going on between you and Jackson? And Lily, don't you dare say nothing. It won't go well. Trust me when I say I would love a reason to bend you over my lap and spank your ass until it becomes the most beautiful shade of pink."

Did he just say what I think he did? And am I seriously turned on by that absurdity? I want to say something snarky in return, but I think he's serious because he looks like he's about to combust. Maybe I shouldn't stoke the fire. "You're not going to like this, but nothing is going on." Okay, I couldn't resist, but I quickly hold my hand up and continue before he can say or do anything. "You also won't like hearing that I've had a crush on Jackson practically my whole life and still do. However, he's never given me the time of day or seen me as anything other than his sister's best friend, so I'll repeat: nothing is going on. Happy now, Mr. Grumpy Pants?"

"That didn't look to me like he sees you as his sister's best friend, and I think you're oblivious to the effect you have on the opposite sex, which worries me. Are you really that naïve?"

"Oh, so we're going there again, are we? I've already told you I agree that I'm too inexperienced for you. Can you let up on the whole naïve thing already? What are you doing here anyway? I thought I would just see you at the office."

"Damn, woman, you infuriate me. I'm not referring to your lack of experience. I'm referring to your blatant blind eye to men's attraction toward you and what trouble you can get into if you're not careful."

"Jackson would never hurt me, and you're delusional in thinking there's any reciprocated interest. Furthermore, I'm not a complete idiot and wouldn't let myself be taken advantage of. I've made it this far in life just fine, thank you. Ugh, this conversation is pointless." I throw my hands up in frustration.

"You're right. It is." The next moment, his hand wraps around my neck, pulling me in firmly, and his lips crash to mine. I feel the other hand grab onto my leg with his thumb pressing into my inner thigh. Holy shit, his grip is so high that the pressure creates an almost painful ache at my core. A moan escapes as my mouth opens and our tongues clash. A few seconds, or minutes later, I'm unsure which, he pulls away and sits back in his seat; a huff of frustration leaving his mouth.

"I can't control myself around you, Lily. You're like a drug I want more of. I don't know how to handle this." He runs his hand through his perfect head of black hair and messes it up in the most delicious way.

I look down shyly. "Apparently, I have the same problem because I'm not normally this…" I wave my hand in a circular motion, unsure of what I'm trying to say. "Way," I finish vaguely, not able to think of anything better.

"You mean insanely turned on?" He looks at me with a smirk on his face.

"Ugh." I put my face in my hands in embarrassment.

Sebastian

She's adorable. Insufferable but endearing, and I'm not nearly ready for our time to end, but unfortunately, the car pulls up to the curb in front of our building. I reach over and tilt her head up, moving a strand of hair from her face. "You happen to be saved from any more ravaging since we're here. To be continued, as they say. Let's get you settled with the team, and I'll grab you for lunch so you can fill me in on the morning." I open the door and grab Lily's hand to help her from the car, releasing it as soon as she stands. My goal is to display a professional relationship for appearance's sake, which unfortunately prevents me from placing my hand on her back as we walk. My desire to constantly be touching her is insatiable.

After what seems like the longest elevator ride in history, I reintroduce Lily to the marketing department and give instructions to Bob, the division head, for a tour and office briefing. I head straight to Eli's office next.

"She's here. I went with the driver to pick her up this morning, and that prick Jackson was talking to her outside their lobby. I don't like the obvious infatuation he has."

"Good morning to you as well, Sebastian. I thought you were going to work on your greeting skills."

"You mentioned it. I didn't say I would. What should I do about this Jackson situation? You're friends with the guy."

"I would say acquaintances, maybe business contacts. I don't know about friends. Regardless, it seems she's fair game at this point, bro, so you better step up your game." He laughs like this is the most fun he's had in a while.

Damn, when was the last time I acted like a lovesick teenager? Not since I was fifteen and horny as hell, that's when. "I'm trying to. I have a date planned for tomorrow night, if I can get her to go. Also, now that we finally closed yesterday, the celebration party at my place is next Saturday.

I'll add her to the guest list." I'm hoping to talk her into the date at lunch today.

"Well, good luck with that. Keep me posted and let me know if you need anything for the party. I'll get my guest list over to Lucy this afternoon."

"She's got it handled, but I'll tell her to expect your list. Are we on for the shooting range again tonight? I could use the release." Boy, could I ever.

"Yeah, come get me at my place after you bring her home. You know you're pathetic, right?" He smirks at me.

"Yeah, I know, shut up already." I walk out, head to my office and stop at Lucy's desk.

"Are all the arrangements made for tomorrow night?" I ask as I reach her desk.

"Yes, Mr. Dubree, I got the boat slip you requested and reservations for seven thirty at Stake. Did you need anything else?"

"Thanks, Lucy. I assume you have everything under control for the party next Saturday. Eli will get you his guest list this afternoon so you can cross-check it with mine. I'd also like you to add Lily Thompson, our new hire in marketing, to the list."

"Certainly, is that everything?"

"For now." I walk into my office and count down the minutes until noon.

When it finally arrives, I head over to escort Lily to lunch. Before anyone sees me, I watch her interacting with the team through the conference room windows. She's magnificent. Her confidence is refreshing to see when she's in her element. The easy way she interacts with the others spikes my attraction to her differently than the physical one that seems to constantly consume me. It's when I see her hunched over Jordan, pointing to something they're discussing and oblivious to his gaze on her chest, that I realize it's time to stop gawking and step in. I swear she's going to be the death of me.

"Good afternoon," I say, walking in. The entire room stiffens slightly, which is the normal reaction to my presence among the staff. All except for Lily, who stands up slowly, turning to face me. She forces a smile on her face. "Are you ready for lunch?" I ask her.

"Sure. Let me grab my purse and meet you at the elevator." She walks away, and I enjoy the view of her fine ass on the way out. I turn around to catch a glimpse of anyone else doing the same, and sure enough, there's Jordan, his eyes glued. My throat clears, followed by a glare that hopefully ends any thoughts he has about her.

I wait for Lily at the elevator and push the button upon seeing her approach, silently praying that no one else shows up for the ride down. Luckily, we're still alone when it arrives. I usher her inside and push lobby, followed quickly by the door close button. I don't suppose we'll get lucky enough to be alone for all thirty-three floors on the way down, so I don't waste time shoving her up against the wall and pinning her in place with my body as soon as the doors shut. I frame her face with my hands and meet her mouth with my own; she reacts immediately, melting in my arms, and returns the kiss enthusiastically. We get ten floors until I feel the elevator slow down. I step aside just in time for the doors to open.

I lean down, whispering in her ear, "You don't know how many times I've imagined doing that today." My hand finds hers, gently caressing it until we reach the ground level.

"What do you feel like for lunch?" I ask as we walk to the car and get in.

"I'm okay with whatever. As long as it's not Mexican."

"Good to know. Blake, can you take us to Sab Lai? I hope you like Thai. It's the best in town and only a few blocks away in the Gas Lamp District." My driver raises the screen this time. By now, he's probably clued in that there's more here than the typical employee-employer relationship.

"I do. It's one of my favorites. So, do you take all your new hires to lunch?" she asks in jest.

"Only the ones I'm trying to date."

"You do this often, then. Oh wait, you don't date. You're a one-and-done kind of guy." Ah, the feistiness I've come to look forward to.

"Exactly, so I guess you could say you're my first… pursuit, that is. See, we each have firsts to give each other." The look on her face is priceless. I think I just stunned her into silence, but alas, I should know better.

"Oh no, you can give me all the firsts you want, but you won't be getting mine."

"I intend to claim them all, Lily. Whether you've come to that realization is irrelevant because I plan to start soon."

Lily

Little does he know, he already has. Thankfully, he wasn't fully aware of the extent of my inexperience. How embarrassing is it that I hadn't even made it to second base until last week? I'm glad to see the car slowly pull to the side and park before I can come up with an appropriate response because I have nothing other than the now-familiar feeling of lust he instills in me with his words. He walks me to the door with his hand on my back, and right before entering, slides it lower, giving my ass a squeeze. I glance up at him in shock while he gives me the most panty-dropping mischievous grin. Seriously, this man is eye candy to the extreme, and when you add a sexy smile to his face, it's positively dangerous. I don't understand how I'm even on his radar. I'm doomed.

After we've been seated and receive our drinks, he dives straight into business. "So how was your morning? Do you feel like you have a contribution to make and agree that you're not here just because I want you? To be here, that is." He winks at me, which makes me roll my eyes and smirk in return. His flirting is kind of cute.

"Well, like you said, it's only been a few hours, but yes, they're all very nice and receptive to what I bring to the table. Obviously, your people have way more experience than I do, especially since I'm still months from graduation. But as you said, I've been involved with this account for the last few years, so I know what's worked and what hasn't, and they seem interested in my input. So, besides the fact you're using this to your advantage, I do think I'm an asset for now. The question is how long my assistance will be needed, and honestly, I don't see it as a long-term thing. Your staff is more than capable of taking this in a new direction without my help." There, point made. He needs to know that I'm not fooled and that I know there's only one reason I'm here—for his benefit.

"I'm glad to hear they're treating you well. As for your experience, I've hired plenty of employees right out of college, specifically for that fact. Recent graduates tend to be fresh, come with new ideas and, most importantly, are moldable with no preconceived notions. So, for you to think you're at a disadvantage to anyone else in my office is all in your head. I may have ulterior motives that I've made specifically clear, but I wouldn't bring you in only to get what I want if there were no other benefits. You're poised, articulate and aren't afraid to speak to a room full of people. You're just as qualified as anyone else, if not more so."

Okay then. His tone was more than adamant on that topic. Although flattered, one thing sticks out. "Regarding ulterior motives, you haven't been exactly clear. You originally wanted me in your bed. Is that still your only goal? Because that doesn't work for me."

He reaches for my hand and holds it, his thumb caressing while he proceeds. "I'll be honest, I'm not sure what my goal is exactly, but I know I can't seem to get enough of you. I want more time to explore both your mind and body. When I'm with you, I crave more; when I'm not, I simply crave you." He leans in close and quietly says the next part. "I've pleasured myself more in the last two weeks than in the last five years combined, all to images of you in my head. So, I might not know my end goal, but I'm willing to explore options to get what I want, which is ultimately you." He looks me straight in the eyes, deadpan. Holy shit, Batman, is it hot in here?

I pull my hand from his and sit back just to get some distance. I'm not sure what to do with that information, and I'm saved yet again with the waiter delivering our meals. This man keeps rendering me speechless, and I'm not equipped to handle his level of intensity. I need Cici with an intercom in my ear listening in, feeding me lines.

Instead of responding, I dig my fork into my pad thai. "I'm starving."

He chuckles. "I am too."

Even though I'm focused on my plate, I can tell by the sultry tone of his voice he's not talking about the food. I look up, and sure enough, he's made no move toward his plate but instead is staring right at me. Oh, he is so out of my league. I don't know what I'm thinking even *entertaining* the idea of being with him. Is he full of lines, or is he sincerely implying he wants more than just a romp in the hay?

"I have a proposal for you, and I'm asking you not to give me a knee-jerk reaction but hear me out. Think about it and keep an open mind. Are you willing to do that?" He finally starts in on his meal and gives me a minute to answer.

"I'm willing to listen." After he scowls at me, I add to my answer. "And I will keep an open mind and consider your proposal before answering."

"Good girl." Why do those words coming from Sebastian's mouth make my stomach flutter? Something's seriously wrong with me. "I'd like to take you sailing tomorrow afternoon and dock at Coronado Island for dinner." He sees the immediate look of hesitation on my face and keeps going. "I want to share a different version of myself than what you've encountered. I can be more than just a playboy or the bossy CEO who scares everyone in my vicinity. Again, I can't tell you exactly where I want this to go, but I know I'd like more time getting to know each other. Will you give me this chance to show you I can be a gentleman… at times?"

"Wow… okay…. Hmmm." After a few seconds, I bob my head and take another bite of my food to give myself something to do with my mouth instead of talking. Part of me wants to say yes, but the more sensible part is holding back. Nothing good can ultimately come out of this, I'm sure. Either say no and cut my losses now or give in and risk the heartbreak.

He's being uncharacteristically patient while I'm considering my answer. If I didn't know any better, I'd say he was nervous, but I know something as trivial as a date with me does not make a guy like Sebastian Dubree nervous. In fact, I'm sure if I decided to walk away right now, he'd have another girl on his arm by tomorrow who's probably way more suited for him.

Okay, what would Cici do? That's easy; she'd say quit being a baby and go for it.

What do you have to lose? she'd ask.

Oh, only my virtue, I'd reply.

Ugh, enough internal monologue. I need to decide already. "Yes. All right, I'll go."

The smile that lights up his face is sort of adorable and solidifies my answer. I think I may be in over my head already.

Sebastian

I somehow managed to keep my hands off Lily for the entire ride back to the office. As soon as we get up to our floor, we head in separate directions, and I go straight to Lucy's desk. "Can you arrange to have an evening dress and shoes for my companion waiting on the boat? No budget. Also, arrange a loan for the evening of a necklace and earrings to accompany it from Tiffany's. Please have everything delivered by one o'clock in the afternoon tomorrow."

"Sure thing. What size should I plan for?" she asks with somewhat of a smirk. Shit, I didn't think about that. I look down at her body. This time she definitely smirks. "Would you like me to stand so you can get an idea?"

I scowl in frustration. "Yes, please." I can't believe I'm in this position. I've always treated my secretary professionally. Dating staff is way too close to home. "She's a couple inches taller than you and has a slightly smaller frame but not by much. Will that cover it?" *God, please don't ask me about chest size.*

She sits back down to take notes, then looks up expectantly. "And what size shoes?"

Crap. "Let me get back to you." I go into my office and shut the door with a little more force than needed.

Since when has dating become so difficult? This is ridiculous. I pick up the phone and dial the marketing department. The secretary picks up. "This is Mr. Dubree. I need to speak with Lily Thompson."

"Certainly, Mr. Dubree. Hold one moment, please."

After about one minute, Lily comes on the line. "Sebastian?" she whispers.

"The one and only. I forgot to ask you before leaving what shoe size you are. I have a strict policy for proper boat shoes to prevent scuffing the deck. The marina will provide a pair and have them waiting; they just need to know what size to deliver." Smooth.

"Oh, seven and a half. And, uh, what should I wear then? With dinner after, I'm not sure how to dress," she asks shyly.

"How about casually for boating. I'm sure you'll look amazing in whatever you choose. Enjoy the rest of your day, Lily. I'll see you around five to accompany you home."

"You don't need to do that, Sebastian, I'm fully capable of handling myself," she says defiantly.

"I'm aware. See you at five." I hang up before she can respond. I imagine her look of frustration in my head and smile to myself.

That went well. I inform Lucy of her shoe size and add a pair of Dockers to the request. Where there's a will, there's a way. Mission accomplished.

I arrive at the marketing department to collect Lily right at five. We're not as fortunate this time in having the elevator to ourselves for the ride down, understandable since it happens to be when most people leave for the day. The car ride will have to do. However, I don't even have a chance to make a move, as Lily lays into me immediately.

"You do realize if you keep escorting me around, taking me to lunch, collecting me at the end of the day and having the secretary track me down for a call from 'Mr. Dubree' that people are going to start talking. In fact, they probably already have. I don't want to become the office slut, Sebastian. I know this is only temporary but still." She's spitting mad.

Her feistiness probably shouldn't be having this effect on me, but shit, my dick has a mind of its own and becomes stiff at the sight of her getting all worked up. "You're right, and I'm sorry if I put you in an uncomfortable position." Oh, that statement conjures all sorts of filthy images. It takes every ounce of restraint I have not to smirk at this moment. "I thought I was merely helping a new employee on her first day, but I can see how my actions could be misconstrued."

"Misconstrued? Do you escort any other of your new hires around? And it's not misconstrued since you are, in fact, trying to get in my pants. This isn't a good idea, Sebastian. Maybe we need to rethink my involvement here or not do this date thing."

That's it; I can't resist her for another second. I lay her down on the seat, crushing her with my torso as I grip her head and smash my lips to hers. Thankfully, I already had the privacy screen up. She instantly matches my intensity as I ravage her mouth. Her immediate response encourages me even more. My hand travels down and grips her ass as I grind my pelvis into her. I bunch her dress up just to feel the luscious bottom curve of her bare ass cheek with my fingers. Her skin is made from pure silk. I'm not sure how much time passes, but I feel the car slowing before it comes to a stop.

I breathe into her neck and slowly release my grip, then gently pull her up with me to a sitting position. While she's trying to compose herself and slow her breathing, I use her distraction as an opportunity. "I'll be here to pick you up at two tomorrow afternoon. We'll sail around the bay for a couple hours before we dock for dinner." Opening the door, I grab her hand to help her from the car, but before releasing it, I bring it to my lips and give it a lingering kiss. "Until tomorrow."

Me: I'm looking forward to our date.

Lily: You distracted me from finishing our conversation in the car. We shouldn't be doing this.

Me: You already said yes, there's no going back.

Lily: You are the most frustrating man on the planet.

Me: Says the most stubborn woman in the universe.

Lily: Good night, Sebastian. I'll see you tomorrow.

Me: Good girl. Sweet dreams, Lily.

Lily: You distracted me from finishing our conversation in the car. We shouldn't be doing this.

Me: You already said yes, there's no going back.

Lily: You are the most frustrating man on the planet.

13

FIRSTS

Lily

I WAKE UP WITH A TOUCH OF EXCITEMENT AND A WHOLE BUNCH OF butterflies for my date with Sebastian this afternoon. I can't deny he makes me feel things. I mean, who wouldn't? He's one of the hottest guys on the planet, every girl's image of tall, dark and handsome. Just his kissing alone would make any woman give in. But I'm not any woman; I'm a girl with no clue what she's doing or gotten herself into. Not to mention that he makes me feel amazing while simultaneously frustrating me beyond belief. I'm still not sure which emotion is winning, but maybe today will shed more light on the subject. I'm either going to end up doing something I could regret later, or I'll run for the hills screaming.

After dinner last night with Cici, where I filled her in on my entire day, there's no possibility she'd let me get out of this. I'm pretty sure she's already fallen for the idea of Sebastian and me together. She swooned multiple times during the retelling. When we got home, she helped me pick out an outfit that could transition to dinner, although he forgot to mention where we'd be eating, so hopefully it works.

Finishing my morning coffee while working on homework, I decide it's time to go for a jog. As luck would have it, I run into Jackson on my way out. It's not like we never run into each other—we've lived in the same building for years—but it seems much more frequent recently. Or maybe it only feels that way because previously, we would just wave or say hi, but now he seems to notice me more. Could Sebastian be right about Jackson being interested?

"Morning, Lily. Having a good weekend?" He looks like he's just coming in from the gym. At least I didn't catch him slinking in from another overnighter.

"Hey, yeah, it's going good so far. Cici and I had dinner last night at our favorite sushi place. How about you?" Seriously, he never had these conversations with me before. I wish I was more relaxed around him, but I'm always nervous.

Jackson replies, "Nice. I just took it easy on a Friday night for once. It was a long week. Maybe, if you're around tonight, we could get together for a drink or something."

Did I just hear him correctly? I'm shocked and must take too long to answer because he adds sheepishly, "We could see if Cici and Braden want to join."

I snap out of it. "Oh, uh, I have another commitment tonight. I'm sorry. Otherwise, I definitely would've taken you up on that." *Shoot, too eager?*

"Oh, well, in that case, I'll take a rain check. See you later, Lils. Enjoy your run," he says as he heads into the lobby.

I stand there for a moment or two in disbelief. Did the object of my infatuation seriously just ask me on a date after years of pining for him to no avail? If I weren't already outside, ready to run, I'd need to sit down for a minute. As it is, I shake it off and head out.

By the time I return, the shock hasn't worn off. I'm still as stumped as before. Cici's gone when I return, so I head straight for the shower. Drying off, I put my robe on, grab another cup of coffee, find Ebony to snuggle with and plant myself on the couch to get a grip on my feelings. After getting nowhere and still just as confused, I glance at the time. Crap, I have less than an hour. Setting my thoughts aside for now, I rush up to get ready.

Sebastian

I've just exited the car in front of Lily's building as she walks out the door. She's beautiful. I meet her halfway and catch a glimpse of Jackson behind her, just inside the lobby, about to exit. *Perfect.*

"Hello, beautiful, you look amazing as always." I grab Lily's hand, pull her to me and stroke her cheek, giving her a soft, sensual kiss.

When I pull away, she looks up at me with lust and says breathily, "Well, hello to you too."

I can see in my peripheral vision that Jackson is frozen behind the glass lobby doors, which tells me he saw precisely what I intended. Keeping hold of Lily's hand, I lead her to the waiting car and usher her in, preventing her from turning around. A few seconds later, we're on our way.

"I'm glad you decided to come," I say as I hold her hand and caress it, loving the feel of her soft skin.

"You didn't give me a chance to change my mind, even though every bone in my body tells me this is headed toward disaster." She keeps her head down, focused on our joined hands rather than making eye contact.

I gently grip her chin and lift her face toward mine. "Why not just for today, you let your fear go and see where we end up. If you still think it's a bad idea after this, I'll *consider* backing down." I smirk at her and lean in to give her a chaste kiss.

"Well, I'm already here, so you have the day to make your case. I just want you to be prepared for this not to go any further."

"Let me worry about what I'm prepared for, sweetheart. Now get over here." I pull her toward me and give her a proper welcome. There's no denying the passion we have. I'd say that's a pretty good foundation to start from. It still confounds me that with as much sensuality as she exudes, no one else has tapped into it. I suppose I should just be thankful and leave it at that.

We arrive at the marina a few minutes later. It's difficult for us to peel away from each other, but somehow, we manage. We walk hand in hand down the dock toward my pride and joy. I've never brought a woman out sailing before and never even considered having anyone other than Eli aboard my boat. It's always been my escape from the outside world, not something to share with anyone. I'm still perplexed at the spell she has on me that makes me want to share it with her.

"That's your boat? It's ginormous!" she says in awe as I stop in front of my slip. I love the gorgeous smile on her face as she takes it in.

"If you get excited over big things, baby, I can show you something later that will blow your mind."

"Ugh, you're terrible. When you said you were taking me sailing, I wasn't picturing anything close to this. Can you manage this yourself or is there a captain, because I don't know a thing about boats."

I can't help but chuckle. "Call me Captain for the day, and you'll know everything you need to by the end of it."

She whacks me in the ribs for that one. "You are full of it today. Seriously, Sebastian, can you handle this thing by yourself?"

"I can sail it myself, baby, don't worry." I kiss her forehead before helping her aboard, handing her the boat shoes and settling her in the cockpit as I ensure everything's in order and get things ready. I talk as I work. "Eli and I have been sailing since we were toddlers. It was one of my dad's few passions outside of work, and he passed it onto me. Eli still goes out occasionally, but mostly it's just me and the ocean out here. It's where I can lose myself and just be in the moment. Since my dad passed away, I haven't had anyone other than Eli come out with me." I want her to understand the significance of her being here.

"Like anyone? *Ever*?" I love the look of shock on her face.

"As in, this is the first time I've shared this with another human being apart from my brother. So, we can add that to our list of firsts we're bestowing upon each other," I say jokingly and smirk to lighten the mood.

"I suppose if we were keeping a list, we could. It would certainly be a good one to put down. But we're not. It wouldn't be fair since, well… hello? My life experience so far has been school, work and a few night-clubs; yours is… extra. More importantly, you should get it through that thick skull of yours that the first you're *trying* to get out of me won't make the list." She crosses her arms over her chest in defiance. I love how cute she is when she pouts.

"I suppose we'll see about that, but we'll call it an impasse for now. Come on, I'll give you the tour." I take her hand and lead her downstairs.

Lily

Wow. Just wow is all I can think of as Sebastian leads me through the space below deck. It's huge. It has a washer and dryer for crying out loud. There are two bedrooms, each with its *own* bathroom, and I'm pretty sure the master bed is bigger than a king. The main sitting area, "saloon," seems massive and contains the kitchen, "galley," as well. I had no idea there was that much space on the inside of one of these, or that boats came with their own language.

I can tell as he gives me the tour that he's very proud and excited to show me. I learned that this is the second boat he's owned himself. He purchased it specifically to captain alone but still big enough that both he and Eli could be comfortable going out on multiday voyages. The boat's name is *Veni, Vidi, Vici,* which means "I came, I saw, I conquered." Fitting for a man like Sebastian. I feel like that's also his motto regarding me.

Once the tour is over, he settles me down in the cockpit while the dockhands untie us, and he motors slowly out of the marina. As we go, we chat about what it was like learning to sail as a young boy. He tells me about his brother and how close they are. He points out different things around us as we go and tries to explain what he's doing and why. However, that may be a lost cause. I don't think I'll ever remember what side starboard and port are or which side of the red or green buoy you're supposed to be on.

As soon as we're in the open water, he raises the sails. I'm mesmerized watching him. He takes it very seriously and moves so methodically, it's like an art. I can't keep my eyes from watching his every move. That and his muscles are sexy as hell. He obviously spends a fair amount of time in the gym. I never really noticed how built he is, but he's delicious.

After everything's in order and "on course," he motions for me to join him at the helm. He positions me in front of him, places my hands on the wheel and holds them there. His body is flush against mine, arms around me. I like it more than I should.

"How are you doing? Are you warm enough? Queasy at all?" he asks with genuine concern.

"I'm perfect, thank you. You know your stuff out here. I guess you'd have to since you own a boat like this. It's crazy that you can do it all yourself. You make it look effortless," I say in awe because it genuinely blows my mind.

"It's second nature to me, so it's easy, but I'll take your praise since you're yelling at me most of the time." He laughs.

"I am not, and when I am, it's because you deserve it."

"I'm glad I brought you out here, Lily, to share this experience with you." I think he may have just made a crack in my wall. He moves my hair to one side and leans down. I feel him caress my neck with his nose like he's breathing me in. He gently kisses me several times before I feel his tongue graze my skin. It sends heat to my core immediately. Then he begins to suck the back of my neck below my ear, and my knees, honest to God, almost cave in. Thank goodness I have something to hold on to.

My breath is heavy as I say his name. "Sebastian."

He raises his head to see we're on course, then turns mine back to kiss him. No arguments here. I won't ever admit it, but I think I could kiss him for days and not tire of it. I love how good it feels. I'm also starting to crave the sensations I keep getting in other areas of my body. Too soon, he pulls away and says it's time to tack. *Hmmm.*

I sit down out of the way and just watch, infatuated with his ability to handle this huge vessel. And just thinking those words instantly makes me wonder about his other huge vessel and how good he may be with that as well. *Oh my God, Lily, get a grip!* I'm internally chastising myself. He's messing with my head. Those type of thoughts are so not like me.

"Sit tight for a minute. I need to grab something out of the galley," he says after completing the tack, which I now know is a turn in the other direction.

"Wait, what about the boat? Do you need me to steer it?" I ask, panicking.

He chuckles as he responds. "No, sweetheart, it's on cruise for a bit. Keep your eyes open, but I already made sure we're clear. I'll be right back."

I'm not gonna lie, as soon as he leaves, I'm a nervous wreck. Luckily, he's gone for under five minutes, and I can breathe easy when his head pops out of the cabin. He returns with champagne, two flutes and a tray of chocolate-covered strawberries. This man is killing me. He's really making a dent in my resolve. I don't know if I'm okay with where my thoughts are headed.

"Wow, you planned ahead," I say, impressed.

"You have no idea," he says cryptically. I'm not sure what to think about that.

He sets it all on the table, checks our surroundings and joins me after ensuring we're still on track. "I hope you like champagne. I figured we could toast to our first date."

"Getting a little ahead of yourself, aren't you? I was coming into this thinking it would be our only date. But yes, I love bubbly." I laugh as I answer.

He opens the champagne, then fills our glasses as he responds. "I'm going to be honest. I have every intention of pursuing you unless you convince me with absolute certainty you're not interested. And what comes out of your mouth versus what your body tells me are two very different things. I'll be taking orders from the latter." He hands me a glass of champagne, and I'm unsure how to respond, so I don't.

He raises his glass. "Cheers, Lily, to seeing where this goes and enjoying the ride. I'm looking forward to showing you how enjoyable it can be." We toast, and I take a sip of the most amazing champagne I've ever had.

"Open up." Sebastian brings a strawberry to my mouth.

"Mmmm. This is so good." He's staring at me with pure lust in his eyes.

"Let me have a taste, sweetheart." I'm barely able to swallow it down before his mouth is on mine, plunging his tongue in. A minute later, he pulls back.

"You're right. It is delicious," he says, then winks at me. Crap, what is this man doing to me?

"Drink up, sweetheart. I need to tend the boat again." He leans over and kisses my forehead. I'm so screwed.

Sebastian

Having Lily here with me is more than I could've hoped for. Seeing her awe and fascination is endearing. I love that this is a new experience for her, and she's seeing a part of me no one else has. I want to share more firsts with her. And what's crazy is I'm not only thinking of the ultimate first but more experiences like this. Seeing the delight on her face and her gorgeous smile today is what I genuinely want more of.

We continue sailing, talking and drinking champagne for the next hour before reaching the point to head into the Coronado Marina. The sails are furled and Lily's standing at the helm in front of me while we motor in slowly. We're just about there as I lean down to nibble her ear. "I have a surprise for you once we're docked." She doesn't respond, too caught up in what I'm doing with my mouth on her neck. I can tell her body wants more from how she's pushing back into me, and by the time we're pulling into the slip, the hard-on I'm sporting is impossible to hide.

Once we're secure, I bring Lily downstairs to the master cabin. Moving her toward the bed, I have her sit and close her eyes. I open the closet, hang the dress on the door, then set the shoes on the ground. I keep the jewelry in my hand for the last reveal. "All right, beautiful, open your eyes."

She looks at me, then sees the dress and shoes. Her eyes widen at the signature red bottoms. "What's going on? What are those for?"

"Well, I intentionally didn't mention where we were going to dinner so you wouldn't bring something else to wear. We're going to a nice restaurant where our boating clothes probably wouldn't suffice, so I took the liberty of providing something for you." I open the box with the matching necklace and earrings. "The dress and shoes are yours to keep, but I have these on loan for the night to accompany. I hope you like it all."

"Wow, I don't know what to say. I can't believe you did this…. I mean, it's way too much. Those shoes cost more than one month's rent. There's no way I can wear those or any of this. I'll ruin something. And what if I lose an earring? I just can't." She looks panicked.

"Lily, it would make me very happy if you would accept these gifts. You won't lose an earring. I'll watch them all night for you if I must. And consider the dress and shoes a peace offering for strong-arming you into being here. How does that sound? This is my treat, so indulge me. I know you brought a few things in your purse to freshen up with. I'll grab it and leave you to get ready. My suit is in the other cabin, where I'll change, and I'll meet you in the saloon. Can you be ready in thirty minutes?"

"I can, but I'm only wearing it tonight, I'm not keeping anything." Always defiant.

"We'll talk about keeping things later." I set the jewelry on the counter and go get her bag. Bringing it in, I place it next to her, then wrap my hand around her neck and use my thumb to lift her chin. I lean down and slowly brush my lips against hers. What I wouldn't give to lay her down on this bed and take her right now. I whisper against her mouth, "See you soon, sweetheart." Standing back up, it takes everything to force myself to walk away instead of giving in to my desire.

I'm waiting on the sofa in the saloon for Lily to finish, wondering what the hell I'm doing. I'm worried I may be unable to convince her to stay overnight and unsure how to approach it. Then that leads me to think about how far I can take this with her if she does stay and at what pace. If she was any other woman, I'd already be balls deep in her. But if she was any other woman, she wouldn't be here, in my space, carving a path through the forest of my heart.

When I hear the door to the master cabin, I stand, ready to go to her, but the moment she appears, I freeze. She's breathtaking. Gorgeous, sophisticated and fucking sexy as hell.

"Lily." I clear my throat before I can get words out. "You render me speechless. You're stunning." The designer dress hugs her curves and widens slightly once past her hips. It has a slit to her upper thigh, showing most of her incredible leg, and a plunging neckline going further than it probably should. Her hair is up in an elegant twist, revealing her gorgeous neck that I can't stop staring at, ready to devour.

She looks down shyly, mumbling, "I'm sure this dress and shoes can make anyone look like a million bucks."

I'm to her in four strides, grasping her jaw, bringing her eyes to mine. "Did you not hear me correctly? I said *you* look stunning. Not the dress. Not the shoes. *You.* Understand?" She nods as much as she can with the grip I still have on her. I kiss her quickly on the lips. "I don't want to hear you discount yourself again. You're beautiful, and nothing should make you feel otherwise. Is that clear?" She nods her head again. "I want to hear it, Lily, out loud."

"Yes. There," she huffs out.

"Tell me what you heard me say."

She rolls her eyes. "That I'm beautiful and nothing should make me feel like I'm not."

"Good girl." She rolls her eyes again. "However, you've rolled your eyes at me twice now. One of these days, I'll show you what happens when you do that, but for now…" Before she can argue and dig herself deeper, I lean down and give her the greeting she deserves for looking so delicious.

Lily

What the hell? I'm about to give him a piece of my mind, but before I can get the words out, his mouth is pressed to mine, his tongue plunging inside. Immediately, I respond like it's second nature to me, matching his ferocity with my own. Once again, we lose ourselves to the passion between us that only seems to grow stronger each time. I've forgotten why I was upset by the time he pulls away. I want to continue, but we have to go.

"If I allow myself any more, we might not make it out of here, and I would hate to squander the chance to have your beautiful presence on my arm. Give me your heels so you can make it up the stairs and off the boat in one piece." He's so incredibly bossy about everything. Instead of arguing, I just take them off and hand them over. He climbs up, then reaches for my hand to help me. I can't say I mind having him constantly touching me. His hands are so masculine and always so warm; I love them.

As soon as my head pops out, I see what we've been missing. "Oh my gosh, look at the sunset! It's beautiful. We're just in time to see the end of it." He wraps his arm around my waist as we take a minute to admire it.

"Next time, we'll have to go for an evening sail. There's nothing like it." He turns and kisses the top of my head—everything he says and does seems to make my heart flutter. I don't know whether to be happy for going on this date and getting to know Sebastian or mad for giving in and setting myself up for disappointment. But one thing's for sure: I'm already too deep to surface.

He helps me from the boat and refuses to hand my shoes over until we're on solid ground, which I suppose is a good idea. I'd hate to get a heel stuck between the planks and break it off. There's a golf cart waiting to take us to dinner. He holds my hand on the way, and I'm fairly certain he's held one of my hands or been wrapped around me since I came out of the cabin. It's like he won't let go, and honestly, I don't want him to.

14

SCARED

Lily

ONCE WE ENTER THE RESTAURANT, I REALIZE WHY HE GOT THE dress and heels, although he did go a little overboard, pun intended. I don't think anything nice enough exists in my closet. We're led to a booth meant for four with a bench on either side. I'm directed to sit while the waiter places our menus on the table. I expect Sebastian to sit across from me, but instead he waits until the waiter moves and joins me, so we're side by side, our hips touching, his hand resting on my leg.

"I hope you don't mind. I can't seem to keep my hands off you," he whispers in my ear and squeezes my leg, which does all sorts of things to my insides.

"Not at all. I like having your hands on me."

"Oh, baby, you really shouldn't say things like that while we're in public. I don't know whether I want to use that as a challenge or carry you out of here so I can put my hands everywhere." He's whispering in my ear, moving his hand further toward my heat, making me clench in anticipation.

Thank goodness the waiter comes to take our drink requests, or we may have skipped dinner. After ensuring I like red wine, Sebastian chooses a bottle for us. He then proceeds to ask questions about what foods I like.

After a short conversation, he says he'd like to order for me. Am I that easy to read? Does he know I'd choose the cheapest thing on the menu if I order for myself?

Instead of arguing, I simply agree. "I guess so, just don't overdo it. I'm thinking that's something you do quite often, and I don't want to waste food, especially with these prices. I'd be happy with soup. And maybe dessert, because can you pass up a peanut butter mousse bar?" I add, smiling up at him.

"Of course not, although I had better ideas for dessert." He's been casually stroking my leg, but this time, when he goes higher, his hand dips toward my center and squeezes. Holy shit, my core clenches of its own accord. I'm in so much trouble. He leans in, whispering so no one hears. "I can feel your response, and you have no idea what that does to me, Lily. I'm going mad thinking about everything I want to do to you."

I'm saved by the waiter again, this time with the wine I'm beginning to desperately need. I can't seem to form words. All I'm thinking about is where I want his hand. I've never experienced this level of desire. Damn it, why does it have to be while we're in a restaurant? That's probably good, because if we were still on the boat, I know where I'd be—under Sebastian on that massive bed.

After Sebastian tastes the wine, the waiter pours a glass for each of us. During this whole encounter, he continues to caress my leg and squeeze now and then while giving his full attention to the waiter. I think he gives our food order, but I'm too focused on what's happening under the table to pay attention to anything. Once the waiter leaves, he lifts his glass, motioning for me to grab mine as well.

"Your turn, beautiful. What would you like to toast to this time?"

Really? I'm supposed to think of something when the only things in my brain are thoughts of a sexual nature. "Um, well, I'm finding it hard to think at the moment." He chuckles but doesn't remove his hand, just stops moving it.

"Cheers to not falling and making an ass out of myself in the Louboutins." He laughs at that. "And cheers to not ripping each other's heads off today." I give him a big smile.

He's still chuckling as we clink our glasses. "I'll toast to that." We each take a sip, and he keeps going. "And I agree, it's a great thing you didn't fall and twist your ankle. I would hate to have taken you to the hospital. I have too many plans for us."

"Really, what are we doing after this?" I ask curiously.

"After dinner, I'll let you in on the rest of the evening. For now, I'd like to learn about you. Your childhood, your parents, do you have siblings? I want to know everything."

Oh boy, really? I didn't see this type of conversation happening with Sebastian. He doesn't strike me as someone who cares about the person they're with, just what they'll be doing after. He keeps surprising me. I'm not sure if I want him knowing all the sordid details of my childhood, so instead of going deep, I hit the surface. My surface is still not your average story, so it's probably enough. After going over the very basics of my dad leaving me and my mom's early abandonment from her alcoholism, I change the subject quickly. We talk about school, work, and a lot about Cici and living with her family. He asks a lot of questions, some of which I avoid answering by changing the topic, and shockingly, he allows it. Understandably, he's curious about me living with Jackson back in the day since I already confessed I have a crush on him.

We're so caught up in conversation that I barely notice a gorgeous woman stop at our table. "Sebastian, hi. I thought that was you over here. My goodness, it's been a long time. Since attending the Jewel Ball together last year, in fact. It's great to see you. How have you been?" Wow, if this is the type of woman Sebastian is used to, perfectly put together and confident, then what is he doing with me?

"I'm good, Gretta. Yes, it has been a while. And I trust things are good for you as well?" He seems polite but short at the same time.

"Couldn't be better. Hi. I'm Gretta Johansen, and you are?" She holds her hand out to shake.

"*She* is none of your business." He answers before I can say anything and gives the hand he's been holding under the table a squeeze, not giving me the option to reach out.

"Well. We should get together again soon. I remember we had such a *good* time." Did she just hit on my date? Not to mention the reference to the "good time" they had. I stiffen immediately. Sebastian, sensing my unease, brings my hand to the top of the table, making a show of it.

"I don't do seconds, Gretta. I made that clear already," he says with venom in his voice. I could almost feel sorry for the woman if she hadn't insulted me with this entire conversation.

"Oh, okay then. If you change your mind, you know where to find me." She looks at me again, probably trying to figure out what he's doing with someone so plain, before walking away.

He speaks immediately. "I am truly sorry about that. She was completely out of line, and there will be consequences for her behavior, I guarantee you." He caresses my hand with his thumb as he talks.

"So you dated her?"

"I told you. I don't date. Various women accompany me when I attend events to prevent others from making advances. And yes, the evening ends satisfying each other's needs, a bonus for being my 'date.' But that is where the night concludes and we go our separate ways. I've been up front with you and won't pretend to be anything other than who I am, which I'm sure you've learned about on the internet. I won't apologize for my past." There's no reason to be angry at what I already knew about him, but I'm still uneasy.

"I'm aware of your reputation with women. It's not that," I say quietly, looking down.

He moves my chin up to look at him. "Then tell me what's bothering you. I can tell you're upset."

"She was beautiful, Sebastian. I can tell she's affluent and poised, and I just don't understand what we're doing here. Why are you trying to spend time with me when I'm not even your type?"

"And what type is that? Unbelievably fake and full of herself, because that's all that woman was. Lily, we wouldn't be here if I thought you were anything other than spectacular. You are a natural beauty in every way. You're just going to have to trust me on that. As to what we're doing here, I've been completely honest, but I'll repeat: I don't know what I'm doing. It's no secret my original intention was to get you in my bed, but now? I'm not sure. This is new territory, and I'm taking it one moment at a time. I'm incredibly attracted to you, but I also enjoy your company. Is that enough for now?"

"I think so. I'm sorry I keep questioning you. She just really threw me off."

"You have nothing to be sorry for. I wish I could erase that whole encounter from our night, but please don't let her get to you. She is nothing to me." He brings his hand to the back of my neck and pulls me in for a kiss, right here, in front of the whole dining room. Before we get carried away, the waiter clears his throat, interrupting with dinner. Probably for the best so we don't make a scene.

As soon as he leaves, I tell Sebastian it's his turn to share. It's only fair since I did. He ends up surprising me when he talks about how great his childhood was and how loving both his parents were. When I think of ultrarich families, I always imagine the children being ignored, but I couldn't have been more wrong in this case.

I do catch a slight edge to his voice when he mentions his dad, which makes me think there's more to the story. He said it was hard on all three of them when his mom died. But when I asked how he lost his dad, his guard came up, and he immediately ended the conversation, telling me he doesn't discuss it with anyone.

Sebastian and his brother have always been close, considering each other best friends. They went to the same college and now live in the same building. Each one takes after the other parent, so maybe that's why they get along so well. Their parents seemed to, from the sound of it.

The waiter comes to clear our plates. Dinner turned out to be amazing. It was the best meal I've had in ages, and having Sebastian choose for me made it even better. I probably would have just ordered a salad, but scallops may be my new favorite.

Now that we've finished eating, I feel the wine making me fuzzy and realize it's probably time for some water. I'm not drunk, but I know I can't lose my head around Sebastian, or I may lose something else. Since we each had turns divulging our history, I remind him he's supposed to tell me what's next on the agenda.

"Okay. But keep an open mind. I could call my driver to pick us up, which I will do if you'd like, or we could enjoy this night to the fullest. I thought it would be nice if we returned to the boat, watched the stars with a nightcap and stay overnight. We could have a delicious brunch here in the morning, then sail back after. It's amazing to sleep on the water and feel the boat sway. What do you think?"

Oh God, oh God, oh God. I think I may start hyperventilating. I stopped hearing anything he said after the words "stay overnight." Did he just ask me to sleep with him? Oh shit.

"Lily, breathe. I'm not trying to get anything out of you other than more time. We've been doing our fair share of kissing, which I plan to do more of, but we don't have to go further or do anything you don't want. I simply want to lie next to you… hold you. You have the power here, Lily, we only go as far as you want." He's turned toward me; his hand is still doing those magical things under the table, and now his other hand caresses my neck.

This waiter has excellent timing bringing our dessert. But he doesn't take as long as I'd like, leaving us alone too soon. I'm still in shock—not just because of his request but because of how much I want to say yes and the fear of what will happen if I do.

"I'm scared," I blurt. His hands still abruptly, and he starts to retreat. I stop him by grabbing them and holding them in place. "Not of you. It's myself that worries me. I'm already feeling things I never have, desires I'm unfamiliar with. I'm afraid of making a decision I'm not ready for." That's one way to do it, just spit it out.

"Lily, I don't want you to be uncomfortable. You know who I am and what I've done, and you're well aware of what I want to do with you. But I'll be perfectly clear, I won't do anything until you're ready, and if I need to be the one to put the brakes on at some point, then I will." He stares right into my eyes, right into my soul. The battle was over before it began. There's no way I could've said no, not to the man sitting here in front of me, showing me how much more he is than the man he shows the world.

"Thank you. I need you to be the one to keep a clear head because I'm not sure I can. If you can promise me that, then I'll stay." I see him release the breath he'd been holding. He grabs my hand and kisses my knuckles.

"I give you my word. I won't let you do anything you'll regret later. Allow me to take the lead and trust I'll do the right thing. You won't be disappointed, I promise." He takes my breath away. I want to trust him more than anything and allow myself to enjoy the moment.

I take a deep breath. "Let's do this then. Should we have our dessert here or take it back to the boat?" Geez, I'm internally slapping myself.

"Oh, Lily, what am I going to do with you?" He chuckles, kisses my head, then signals for the waiter. "I think dessert on the boat sounds delicious."

Oh boy....

Sebastian

"Here, hold this." I hand Lily the box of dessert. The golf cart driver just let us off in front of the dock. She takes the box, and I bend, lifting her into my arms bridal style.

"Sebastian! What are you doing?" she shrieks.

"Well, now you won't have to walk barefoot the whole way, and I get the pleasure of having you in my arms." I kiss her forehead.

"Ugh, you're crazy."

"Crazy good or crazy bad?" I ask.

"Hmmm, undecided. I'll get back to you on that."

"How about I ask you again tomorrow morning?" I laugh.

She slaps the hand holding her legs. "Hey, that's not funny. You better be joking."

"Just because we're not going to have sex doesn't mean other things can't be good, sweetheart."

"Sebastian..."

"I told you to let me take the lead. Do you trust me?" We're at the boat, and I've stopped, holding her in my arms while she stares at me in contemplation.

"Yes."

I kiss her forehead again. "Good girl." Then I touch my lips to hers and can't help myself from the groan that escapes as she pulls the back of my hair and takes the lead this time in deepening the kiss. She undoes me. It's going to take everything in me tonight to keep my head on straight.

After getting her situated in the cockpit, I grab forks, two glasses and a bottle of port to go with it. Hopefully, it'll do the trick to settle her nerves since I can tell they set in as soon as we made it back.

Upon my return, I hand her the blanket I grabbed at the last minute. "Here, baby, wrap this around your shoulders. It's cooled off." Setting everything down, I sit and pull her onto my lap. "I grabbed a port to go with dessert. I think you'll enjoy it. It's become somewhat of a favorite of mine after a trip to Portugal last year." I proceed to open the bottle and begin filling our glasses. "How are the stars tonight?" I ask while I finish up and hand her one.

"They're amazing. It's so peaceful. I like the sound the masts make when the boats rock. Whatever clangs inside. It's sort of soothing. I can see why you like to spend time out here." I'm crazy for this woman. She's not the only one who's scared, just the only one brave enough to admit it.

"I love that you noticed that. I've never considered it something I liked the sound of until now." I kiss her nose.

"It's your turn to make the toast. What will it be this time?" She reminds me.

"Ah, that's right. Let me think about this one…. Cheers to you saying yes to spending the night in my arms… and telling me how crazy good I am tomorrow morning." I wink at her and clink my glass to hers. "Drink up, buttercup. It's going to be a long night."

She takes a sip of her port and surprisingly doesn't comment. I think she may be at a loss for words at this point. "So what do you think, do you like it?" I ask, hoping she does.

"Mmmm, it's good, so sweet, like a dessert. Is this what you had in mind when you said other things?" she says teasingly.

"Are you trying to bait me, sweetheart? Because I'm pretty sure you know exactly what I meant." I take the glass from her hand and set it down. "Here, let me give you a sample." Then I grab the back of her neck and pull her mouth to mine. She doesn't even hesitate.

This girl is mine. She wants me as much as I want her. I won't take advantage of that knowledge, though, which I will remind myself of throughout the night. We get lost in the kiss, our tongues dancing together, wanting more and fighting for it with wild abandon. I reach through the slit of her dress, loving the feel of her skin as I continue moving my hand toward her ass. She's leaning into me so I'm able to grab her ass cheek and squeeze, pulling a moan from her lips. I need more of her. I move my mouth down her jaw to her neck and continue ravaging her. I want to taste every inch of her tonight.

"Ah, that feels so good," she says between heavy breaths.

I fist her hair in my hand and pull her back as I continue down, past her neck, to her chest. I pull her dress down to finally get my mouth on those perfect tits teasing me all night. *Thank you to whoever designed this dress to be worn braless.* I bring one breast into my mouth and suck hard. Her nipple is a perfect bud I can't help but nip at.

"Oh my God, Sebastian!" she exclaims as her hips buck. I need her naked.

Removing my mouth from her breast with a pop, I pull her dress back up and breathe in her neck, inhaling her luscious scent. Extracting myself reluctantly, I stand and reach for her hand. "Come on, sweetheart. I think it's time to go inside so I can make you more comfortable."

15

INADEQUATE

Lily

'M SO INCREDIBLY TURNED ON RIGHT NOW IT SCARES THE CRAP out of me. I'm just hoping that Sebastian will hold up his end of the bargain and put the brakes on when he needs to. "Okay," I say tentatively.

Taking my hand, he leads me down the stairs into the main cabin bedroom. He pulls me around so I'm standing in front of him with my back against his front, his arm around my waist. He kisses the back of my neck, the sensitive spot right below my ear that makes my knees weak and breathing heavy. All too soon, he stops and whispers in my ear, "Lily, I'm going to take your dress off now—only your dress. I want you bare for me, to caress every inch of your body, to devour you with my mouth and make you crazy with desire. Say the word at any point, and I'll stop." He doesn't wait for an answer.

His hand goes to the base of my neck where the zipper is, and his lips softly touch the skin above it. Then I feel his hand lower, pulling it down little by little, kissing my back along the way. With every kiss, I melt a little more. Once he reaches the end, his hands come up to my shoulders and slide the dress down slowly, giving me goose bumps along the way, until I'm naked from the waist up.

He stops there for now, and once again I feel his lips on the back of my neck as he begins to suck and lick. My knees go weak, and his arm wraps around my waist to support me with his hand splayed on my stomach while his other hand kneads my breast.

"God, Lily, you feel so good," he says between kisses.

I'm surprised I don't feel as awkward as I expected being naked in front of a man. It could be because I'm facing away and don't have his eyes on me. I wonder if he did that on purpose. Or it could be that I can't think much about anything with all these new sensations and how good it feels to have his hands and mouth all over me.

I miss his lips on mine. "Sebastian, I want to kiss you."

"Anything, baby." He turns me around—his arm around my lower back and his other around my neck—then looks down. "God, Lily, you're gorgeous." He brings my mouth to his and consumes me completely. My dress is still around my waist, but he reaches inside to grab my ass and pull my hips into him. Oh God, I can feel his hardness pressing into me. My hands are tangled in his hair, holding him tight as we devour each other. I can't seem to get enough.

He pulls back slightly. "Climb up on the bed, sweetheart. Lie back and let me look at you for a minute." He pushes my dress over my hips, and it falls to the floor, pooling around my feet.

My shyness sets in, and I look down, not wanting to make eye contact. He doesn't allow it.

He places both hands around my neck and pushes my chin up with his thumbs. "Do you remember what I said earlier?" I nod. "Then why are you embarrassed?" He caresses my jaw with his thumbs.

"I've never been naked in front of anyone," I admit shyly. I want him to understand why I'm uncomfortable.

"Wait, what? You told me you'd been with a couple different guys," he says incredulously as I feel his hands stiffen like he's trying to maintain control.

"I said I'd had a couple boyfriends that I did stuff with. I didn't say what we did. It was none of your business at the time."

"Well, it's my business now, so what *stuff* did you do?" He doesn't sound pleased. I'm not sure whether this is going to go in my favor or not. Oh well, here goes…

"We made out, French-kissed—that's it. Happy now? Are you sure you still want to do this because I can go." I start to back away, but he's having none of it.

"Stop." That's all he says as he pulls me against him and lifts me up on his pelvis, making me gasp. His hands grip my ass as he holds me up, then sits on the bed with me straddling him. This feels so weird. I'm practically naked while he's fully clothed. His hardness is right *there*, where if we didn't have clothes on, he'd pretty much be inside me.

He places a hand on each side of my head and looks into my eyes. "You are fucking perfect, and knowing I'm the only man to lay eyes on this beautiful work of art is the biggest turn-on in the world. Knowing I'm the first to touch you is enough to bring me to my knees. And knowing you allowed me to makes me want to ensure this will be the best night of your life. Do you trust me to do that?"

"I do. But can you be strong enough for both of us not to go too far? Because I don't think I am." I want this man so bad right now it hurts.

"I can be for you." He kisses me passionately, and within seconds, my hands are gripping his hair, grinding on top of him. His bulge rubs against my clit, giving me the most incredible sensation down there. He's got one hand around my neck and one on my breast, teasing the nipple. He grabs my hair, pulling my head back to suck my neck.

"Ahh." I moan out loud.

He leans my torso back, supporting my back with his arm, and brings my breast into his mouth, sucking it hard. The angle makes his shaft press into me even more. I feel an ache down there now. It's not bad but unfamiliar. I grind harder, back and forth, chasing the feeling. My breathing is getting faster when Sebastian suddenly pulls away and brings me back to him.

"Hey, baby, we need to chill for a minute. I know where you're headed, and I want to be the one to bring you there, so let's get you comfortable, okay?" He lifts me, crawls on the bed like I weigh nothing and lays me down on the pillows hovering over top of me. "I want to give you what you were chasing back there, okay?"

"Okay… what are you going to do?"

Sebastian

Fuck me. I want this girl so bad in every way that I'm literally in pain from my throbbing cock. The amount of restraint I'm having to use is insane but so worth it. I'll never know how I got so lucky to have this innocent beauty before me.

He answers, looking me straight in the eyes. "Well, sweetheart, I'm going to kiss the hell out of you. Then, I'm going to touch every inch of your body—and I mean *every* inch—until I penetrate that tight little pussy of yours with my fingers, and it squeezes me so hard, you'll be screaming my name in pleasure. How does that sound?"

Once the shock passes and her eyes return to normal, she quietly responds, "I'm not sure, but I think it sounds nice." I'm absolutely enchanted by her perfect innocence.

"I can guarantee it'll be a hell of a lot more than nice." I bring my head down and kiss her mouth softly. Just lips—her plump, luscious lips that feel so good against mine. So good that I bite the bottom one still swollen from ravishing just minutes ago. Everything I do to this girl makes her respond in a way that drives me wild: her moans, her pants, her thrusts. I can't get enough. I keep wanting to push the next button and see her reaction. It's a dangerous slope, but damn, she's so fucking responsive.

I move to her side so my free hand can roam her body. I wasn't lying earlier when I said she was a work of art. She's perfect. Perfect tits that fit in the palm of my hand. Perfect hips to grab onto when I'm finally able to plunge deep inside her. And that perfect ass. Honest to God, this girl was made for me. I fondle both breasts, switching back and forth between them as I deepen our kiss. She tries to grab my shoulder to turn her body to the side flush against me, but I stop her. This is my show, and I have just the solution.

"Do you trust me?" She nods. Fuck, she kills me. I sit up and loosen my tie, removing it. I've been too preoccupied with her to worry about taking anything of mine off. Rising to my knees, I grab her wrists and tie them together. "Is this okay?"

She nods in response. "Words, Lily."

"Yes, it's okay."

"Good girl. These stay here, understand?" I say, bringing her arms up over her head.

"Yes, but what if I want to touch you?" I start unbuttoning my shirt as she stares at me intently, wide-eyed.

"You don't get to, not this time. This time, you just feel." I slide my shirt off but leave my pants on because every barrier will help keep me under control, and I need all the help I can get right now.

"Fuck, Lily, you're perfect, you know that? Tonight's for you, baby. Only you." I crawl back over her, wasting no time working her up. Moving my lips straight from her mouth to her neck and then down to her breasts, all while feeling every inch of her with my hands and grinding into her with my pelvis. The feel of her silky skin against my torso is killing me. I want my whole body to feel her softness, but I know it's too soon for that.

She's doing pretty good keeping her hands in place, almost bringing them down a couple of times but stopping herself. She's panting hard, writhing in lust, and I feel like the luckiest man alive to have her under me right now. Once I've thoroughly riled her up, I move to the side of her and prop myself up on one arm. She closes her eyes in ecstasy as I slowly caress down her stomach to her thighs and push her legs apart slightly, one at a time. I come close to her sweet spot, just teasing her until my fingers softly graze her clit as they pass over her panties. I palm her mound and squeeze, pushing slightly with my fingers over her opening, giving her a taste of pressure as she bucks into my hand. Christ, she's soaking; I can feel it through the fabric.

"Sebastian," she whines. She wants this so fucking bad.

Instead of making her wait any longer, I bring my hand up slightly and reach inside her panties. *Oh, fuck me.* She feels divine. I can tell she's trimmed but not bare. I tease her clit with my fingers for a minute, watching in awe as she continues to squeeze her eyes closed and buck her hips every time I touch the right spot. I apply a little more pressure.

"Oh God, please. Sebastian, I need…" She opens her eyes and looks at me, pleading.

"You need my fingers in that tight little pussy of yours is what you need, sweetheart. Are you ready for that?" She nods quickly in answer. "Are you sure that's what you want, Lily?"

"Yes, Sebastian, ugh, just…" I forcefully grab the back of her head and plunge into her mouth with my own before she can finish that thought. My hand moves farther, and I probe her tiny hole with my finger. It's slick with her juices, and I use them to circle her opening, causing her to moan into my mouth. I give the slightest push to see how she reacts, and she bucks, wanting it. I go in.

Fuuuuck. It's so tight. She takes me greedily, thrusting forward, begging for more, so I give it to her. I push in as far as I can, then repeat that a couple of times until she cries out.

"More," she begs. She doesn't have to ask twice.

"Oh, baby, I've got so much more for you." I pull out and, this time, use two fingers. I don't go slow this time. She moans in ecstasy as I retract and push in repeatedly, increasing the tempo as I go. I'm devouring her neck now so she can release the sounds I love. I'm drowning in her pussy that's tight as fuck while sucking and licking her nipple when I know it's time. So I do exactly what she needs to bring it home. I find the sweet spot deep inside and curl my fingers, pushing in as hard as possible. And that's all it takes as she comes unglued.

"Sebastian, oh my God, oh my God. Ahhhh." She screams out. I keep it up, moving deep inside, watching her beautiful climax while milking it out of her. Only when I feel she's spent do I still my hand before gently withdrawing.

"That was the sexiest fucking thing I've ever seen," I say as soon as she blinks her eyes open. I undo the tie that binds her hands, massaging her wrists as I wait for her to come back down to earth.

Lily

Wow. Did that just happen? When the pleasure ebbs and I come down from whatever madness that was, the panic sets in. Oh God, I don't know how to act. I'm so embarrassed right now. I just let him touch me and… finger me. I didn't do anything to him or give him any pleasure in return. I'm pretty sure that's not how this works.

"Lily, what's going on in your pretty little head right now? Why do you look panicked?" He brushes my hair from the side of my face and caresses me up and down as he waits for an answer.

"I don't know. I think I'm just really overwhelmed at the moment. I didn't know what to expect, and that whole"—I wave my hand around in a circle down there—"feeling came out of nowhere and freaked me out, but then it just burst. It was incredible, and I didn't do anything for you, and I'm sure that's not how this is supposed to go, and I'm just feeling really inadequate right about now." I spit it all out as fast as possible while staring straight at the ceiling. I can't bring myself to look over.

"Wait, back up. What do you mean 'that feeling'? You mean the orgasm I just pulled out of you? Was it that much more intense than when you do it yourself?"

"Do we have to talk about this? I'm fine. It just took me by surprise is all. Sorry, I shouldn't have confessed all that." Shit, maybe I can distract him. I turn toward him and start feeling the skin on his chest, and now that I'm not distracted by lust, *wow*. This is a beautiful, very chiseled chest. I start roaming it with my hands.

He stops me, placing his hand over mine, and speaks more intensely. "Lily, answer me. What about that scared you? I don't like that word in your vocabulary when there should only be pleasure."

A groan escapes before I answer. "Ugh, why do you make me tell you these things?" I pause as he stares me down menacingly. "I don't touch myself, okay? I was scared because I thought something was wrong until I didn't. I've never had an orgasm. Ugh, this is so humiliating." Sighing in frustration, I bury my face in his chest so he can't see me, and holy shit, he smells fantastic.

"Wait, that was your first orgasm ever?" I'm seriously not repeating it, but I nod as I stay buried, enjoying the smell of this delicious man. "Holy shit, whatever did I do to deserve you?" He kisses the top of my head.

He continues to caress up and down my back as he talks. "Let me enlighten you then on how this works. I just pleasured you because pleasuring you, pleasures me. There are no rules, Lily. You don't have to do anything to reciprocate, and if that's what I wanted, I'd have led you in that direction. For now, I'm satisfied, baby. I got exactly what I was aiming for. You are the farthest thing from inadequate there is. Watching you climax was the highlight of my evening, and trust me, I can't wait to see it again. Maybe I should make you pleasure yourself right now so I can watch." He rubs his hand down my head and kisses the top again as he squeezes my ass. His suggestion causes a reaction in me that I'm a little ashamed of.

"Can we stop talking about this now? I'd like to survive the night without dying of mortification, and you're not making me do anything, remember?" He chuckles and the sound vibrates in his chest, causing me to kiss it since I'm nuzzled here. He's just so sexy. I can't believe I'm almost completely naked in his arms. Thank God he left my panties on; I don't think I could handle that level of vulnerability. All of a sudden, I shiver. "Can we get under the covers now? I'm lying here almost fully naked, and you still have clothes on, plus it's a little chilly."

"Sure, sweetheart, but only because you're cold. Come here." He rolls me on top of him, and I squeal. After moving the covers out of the way, he rolls us back but stays on top of me, covering me with his body.

"Your innocence is sexy as hell, and you have nothing to be embarrassed about. Not your thoughts…" He kisses me on my temple. "Feelings…" He moves to the other temple. "Reactions…" Now, my cheek. "Your experience, or should I say lack thereof…" He smiles and kisses me on the tip of my nose. "And certainly not your nakedness." He lowers and takes a nipple in his mouth, licking it quickly before coming back up. "Your body is worthy of worship, and I intend to do just that… but after that mind-blowing orgasm I gave you, it's break time. Let me get comfortable, and I'll join you in a minute." He kisses my lips tenderly and retreats, pulling the covers over my nakedness before leaving me to process everything for a few minutes.

That was amazing. I had no idea any of that could feel like… *that*. It did pinch a little when he added the second finger, which makes me blush thinking about. Then, whatever he did after that. Oh my God, remembering it makes me ache for more. I stretch out, reaching my arms above my head, pushing my legs out as far as possible, and get the giddiest smile. Wow, Sebastian is really good at… everything so far. I think I'd like going further, especially if he takes control.

I didn't know what to think when he tied my hands together, but in hindsight, I love that he took responsibility for me. It was nice not to worry about what I should do and simply focus on what was being done. There wasn't one moment where I panicked if I was doing something right or wrong, which made it all easier and I'm assuming more enjoyable, but I have nothing to compare it to. I admit, he not only lived up to the dreams I've been having but surpassed them by a landslide.

Sebastian

Holy shit, I'm so thankful I left my pants on because my cock has been screaming for me to sink into her from the minute we hit that bed. Watching Lily come undone was indeed the highlight of my night, but the part where I told her I was satisfied mainly came from my brain and not my dick. I'm glad I didn't take it out in front of her tonight, especially now that I know she hasn't even seen one. Shit, I would have scared the crap out of her. I made the right decision in making this night about her, but fuck if I don't need to release this tension right the fuck now.

Closing the door to the cabin, I head into the en suite bathroom, closing that door as well. I don't want to risk her hearing. It would kill me to give her any sense of guilt if she were to hear. Quickly removing my pants, my hand grips my engorged head not wasting any time giving myself the release so desperately needed. Closing my eyes, I picture Lily in the height of her orgasm from only moments ago, and not only do I come fast, releasing into the sink, but more intensely than expected from a self-administered hand job. Staying quiet was tough as I imagined myself going back to finish inside of her. I'd be up for number two if I didn't need to get back. Instead, I rinse away the evidence, clean up and arrange myself in my boxer briefs. She'll see plenty even with only these on.

I stop in the galley on the way back. "I come bearing gifts. Figured we can't let the dessert you insisted on go to waste, even though I think mine was way better," I say as I walk into the room with a glass of port and the dessert we never made it to, setting it down on the table beside her. I see her blush from my statement. Or it may be the result of seeing my body on display in my boxer briefs. They don't leave much to the imagination. My dick is a thing to behold when it's hard, so I've been told, but even when it's not, I'm not a small man.

"I wouldn't want to make your ego any bigger by agreeing with that statement, so I'll refrain from commenting. I'm glad you brought dessert with you, though, because it's all I've been able to think about since we've been back." She says this with the most serious look she can muster, then giggles.

"Oh, I'll give you something to think about, you little minx." I whip the covers back and crawl on the bed, grabbing her and flipping her over my thighs so she's face down with her ass in a perfect position as I smack it hard enough to make her yelp.

"Sebastian, what the?" My hand holding her down won't let her maneuver away.

"Now, what was it you've been thinking about?" I say as I caress her beautiful ass cheeks.

"The peanut butter bar you didn't let me have." If I didn't know any better, I'd say she was trying to egg me on. *Smack!* I bring my hand down again, harder this time.

"Sebastian, seriously…" Once more, I caress her cheeks and catch the slightest hitch in her backside, asking for more.

"Let's try that again, baby. I know from that climax you had your mind was definitely occupied with other things. Now, be a good girl and tell me what you've really been thinking about since we've been down here." My hand dips down, grazing her opening with my fingers. Holy shit, she's so fucking wet.

She lets out the slightest moan before answering. "Well, I might've been distracted at times, but I just couldn't seem to…" *SMACK!*

"Ahhhh. Sebastian." That was unquestionably a cry of pure lust, evident by the moan that followed. I can see the slightest pink print on her cheek from where I smacked the hardest this time, making my dick come to attention. My fingers return to her core feeling her slickness. She whimpers, begging for more.

"What have you been thinking about, baby? How good I make you feel? What you want me to do to you?" I put the slightest pressure on her opening but don't breach it.

"Yes. It's all I can think about. Please, Sebastian."

"That's my girl." I plunge my fingers in hard and flick back and forth inside. She comes in less than a minute. Screaming her pleasure while clamping around my fingers, making them feel like they're in a vise.

"Fuck, Lily, you're so goddamn responsive." I caress her back and ass as she recovers. "I can't wait to show you all the ways I can pleasure you. You're irresistible." Well, she'll get a good look at what I'm packing now and probably already a good feel of it, seeing as how she's on my lap. Slowly I retract my fingers and give her ass another stroke or two before turning her over. I cradle her shoulders in my arm and lift her mouth to mine, cupping her face. I fucking love how sexy she is. Our kiss is slow and sensual, but before it gets out of hand again, I lift her back up against the pillows.

After a minute of silence, she says, "Um, so I'm not sure what to say after that."

"How about something like 'wow, Sebastian, it just keeps getting better and better. I can't wait for more,'" I tease her, smiling.

She smacks my arm but laughs nonetheless. "You're incorrigible. Just put some covers over that thing and hand me the dessert."

"This thing, huh?" I repeat but do as she asks by bringing the covers over our laps. I hand her the dessert and take a sip of port before passing it over. She has a small taste and gives it back. "You know this thing has a name," I tease.

"Really? Please do tell so I can address it appropriately next time," she says sarcastically, making me tip my head back in laughter.

"I love hearing you say next time, baby. Nothing better could have slipped from your mouth." I lean over to kiss her blushing cheek. "On a serious note, what did you think of what we just did? Did you like it?" This could be a defining moment as to how far I can go with her and what direction I should take.

"Um, which part did *we* do? I distinctly remember only *you* doing things to *me*," she says coyly as she feeds me a bite of dessert.

"Mmm, that is good, although I still think mine was better." I wink at her and offer another sip of port. "I'm more interested in the part where I spanked your ass since the latter half I already know you enjoyed."

"Hmmm, I'm not sure how to answer that. Initially, it shocked the heck out of me and made me feel awkward, wrong even. But as you did it again and then again, well… by then, it made me feel other things. I ended up looking forward to the next one, wanting it. I'm not sure how I feel about that honestly. It seems like something I should be against."

"Good answer and thank you for being honest. All your feelings are correct, and that's what makes it erotic. To give someone else power over you is a gift and shouldn't be given without trust, nor should it be taken without respect. Pain can be sensual in the right context. I'm glad you recognize the part of you that wanted more. I look forward to exploring that with you if you let me."

"I don't think I'm ready to commit to more of anything yet. I'm not ready to think past tonight and what happens from here or what comes next. I've decided the best course of action right now is to live in the moment because if I start thinking, I'll start overthinking, and you likely won't get the answers you want. Everything about you and this situation makes me nervous. I won't deny our sexual chemistry, but I'm just not part of your world, and I can't imagine you're interested in anything more than sexual satisfaction before getting bored and moving on to the next. That's just not for me. I've loved tonight but won't do it again without the relationship component." She's been fidgeting with the covers while making her point, avoiding eye contact.

The dessert has been set aside, along with the glass of port, so there's nothing in the way as I scoot down in the bed and give her a tug to join me. She gets comfortable on my chest as I shut the light off before wrapping my arm around her and caressing her back. I don't think I'll ever get my fill of her silk-like skin. "I love that you're so honest and open with me. I know what you need, Lily, and I can't make any promises. The last thing I'll say before we get some sleep is not only are you the first woman ever to step foot on my boat but you're also the first I've taken on an actual date and now, the first to sleep in my bed."

I can feel her tense with that knowledge, probably shocked at my admission. To lighten the mood, I add, "Hey, I think I may have you beat on our list of firsts now, so maybe we should work on adding another of yours tomorrow." Before she responds, I kiss her head. "Sweet dreams, sweetheart. I know mine will be."

16

I MAKE THE RULES

Lily

"He spanked you? Wowza, did you like it?" Cici asks during my detailed account of the previous night. We decided to go to our favorite Sunday brunch spot down the street since I came home early this morning. My date ended up getting cut short when Sebastian got a call from the office with an issue to deal with bright and early. You'd think that wouldn't happen on a Sunday, but when you're CEO of a major corporation with multiple businesses in your portfolio, there are no days off.

"I hate admitting this out loud, and if you ever speak of this to anyone, I'll deny it, but yeah, I did. Just thinking about it makes me crazy." I put my hands over my face and squeal.

She claps and squeals along with me. "I'm so excited to be talking about this with you! I swear, I've been waiting for this day forever. Oh, Lily, I'm so glad you had such a good experience. If that's a sign of what's to come, then holy cow, Batman! Okay, keep going. What happened next?"

"Well, we did talk more before going to sleep. I told him I wasn't sure if I could keep being with him just for sex, and don't you dare give me that look, Cici, you know I'm not that way. This last part's crazy and you won't believe it. I told you I was the first woman he'd brought out sailing, but then he said I'm the only woman he's taken on a date, and are you ready for this?" Keeping her in suspense, I take a drink of my mimosa. Thank goodness they're bottomless because we've been here for over two hours.

"Freaking spit it out already!" she insists.

"He's never slept with a woman before until last night, as in slept overnight. Cici, it was so romantic. It's sickening how perfect he was. But I know better. I do. There's no way he can suddenly change from the world's biggest playboy to someone interested in dating. Right?" I ask her, which is stupid because I'm sure she's team Sebastian right now. She probably has the T-shirt being made as we speak.

"It's probably too early to tell, but at least he's being honest about not knowing what he's doing. He could just feed you a bunch of bullshit about everything instead, right?" She certainly knows how to twist things in a positive light; I'll give her that.

"But that could be exactly what he's doing. I guess I still don't trust him at this point. Maybe he believes he's pursuing me with good intentions, but what if it's not in his DNA and I end up getting hurt? I just need to be careful, Cici, that's all."

"I know, sweetie. I'm just excited for you to have this amazing guy chasing after you. Okay, so what happened next?"

"Well, you pretty much know the rest. He got that phone call this morning, and his driver picked us up right away. According to one side of the conversation, Sebastian was pissed about whatever was happening. Hearing him in business mode is kind of scary when he's angry but sexy at the same time. He was upset about not having the morning we planned but incredibly sweet about it. He completely turned off his anger when he hung up. And to top it off, I enjoyed an extended goodbye in the car with one last parting gift. It was so unexpected… all just from grinding on him, Cici. No joke, it was the best one yet because I think he orgasmed too, if that's possible. He took charge by grabbing my hips and moving me over him. I didn't have to do anything but let him take over. It was amazing." We both swoon together at that point.

"Seriously, Lily, you just might be the luckiest girl in the world right now. I never thought I'd say this about your sex life, but I'm kinda jealous." We both crack up, causing heads to turn our way, but we're too in the moment and a few too many drinks in to care.

As we head into our building after getting our money's worth and then some of the bottomless mimosas, we're stopped by Jackson in the lobby, who looks like he's headed out to the gym. "Hey, ladies, what are you two coming back from?"

We both can't help the giggles that escape as Cici tells him we just spent the last three hours at brunch. They'd put a time limit on that bottomless stuff if they were smart.

"Now it's nap time. Lily didn't get much sleep last night," she says as she raises her eyebrows up and down giggling again. "Right, Lily?"

I elbow her, probably harder than necessary, but what the heck? "I actually did sleep, well in fact, but after twenty thousand mimosas, a nap sounds great."

"It sounds like you're having a fun morning, that's for sure. I think a nap for both of you is a good idea. Can I talk to you before you head up, Lily?" Jackson asks, catching me off guard.

"Jackson, leave the girl alone. I was just kidding around about her night. She's an adult. She doesn't need you hovering over her." *Oh my God, Cici, shut up already.* Could this get any more awkward?

"Got it, but it's not about that, don't worry," he responds.

"Well, what is it then?" she asks with a pouty expression.

"Damn it, Cici, can I just talk to Lily for a minute? Alone?" His patience with his sister has left the building.

"Geez, don't get your panties in a bunch. All right, I'm going. It's not like she's not coming upstairs and spilling whatever you talk about anyway, but okay, Mr. Secretive."

I can't help but giggle at the sibling squabble and that she's right.

"See you in a minute, Lily. If I'm not already passed out, that is," she says as she walks into the elevator.

Jackson turns to me, grabbing behind his neck like he's unsure or embarrassed. "Hey, I wanted to hold you to that rain check for drinks, but I guess I should ask whether last night was serious." Whoa. Am I that drunk? I pinch myself to double-check if I'm still coherent. Ouch, yep, still functioning. Shit, what do I say?

"I get it if I'm too late. You don't have to feel bad. I just, well, I never tried before because I didn't know what Cici would think, and I thought it could be weird since we sort of grew up together, and I wasn't sure how you'd feel about that. But screw it, I don't want to regret never trying." He's serious. This isn't just some fluke.

"Um, well, I would say last night isn't serious yet. It's only been one date, so it can't be, right? I guess it doesn't hurt to have a drink together no matter what since we've been friends forever. Although I think I've met my quota for the day, so…" I laugh at how true it is in more ways than one.

"Yeah, you're probably right. How about we go for happy hour after work tomorrow? I'll pick you up from your office. Sound like a plan?"

"Um, yeah. Oh shoot, I'll be at Dubree Enterprises tomorrow." Oh boy, this isn't good.

"That's perfect. We can go somewhere on the waterfront. I'll be there at five. I'm looking forward to it." He leans down and kisses me on the cheek before making his way out, leaving me frozen.

What did I just do? And why now? Oh God, Cici's going to freak out. I know it. And I can't even think about Sebastian's reaction if he was to find out. All these thoughts are swirling around in my head as I make my way up.

I was wrong. Her reaction to my conversation with Jackson is much worse. "YOU WHAT? What the hell, Lily? What the actual hell are you thinking?" Freaking out was definitely an understatement.

"Listen, I'm sorry. I know this is awkward being your brother and all, but I have to fess up. I've had a crush on him for years but was too afraid to say anything. And it sounds like he might've been on the same page, maybe not for years like me, but for a while I think."

"That's not what I'm upset about! I'm not stupid, Lily. I've known that forever. I never brought it up because, yuck, he's my brother. No, I'm pissed because you finally met someone who gives you butterflies, is a nice guy and didn't fuck around in pursuing you the way my idiot of a brother did, and now you're just throwing that out the window?"

"I'm not throwing anything out the window. Since when did this thing with Sebastian become exclusive? We didn't set any expectations. In fact, he was very specific about not knowing what he's capable of, so why would I pass up a chance with the guy I've been hung up on for years?” My frustration may be getting the best of me at this point. I probably didn't need to yell that last part.

“Be real, you can't be hung up on someone you've never even talked to.”

That's it, I can't keep the tears from coming. As soon as she sees them, she throws her arms around me.

“God, I'm such a bitch. I'm sorry. You've spent plenty of time with him over the years to know him as well as I do, so that wasn't fair. I just want what's best for you, and while I love my brother, I'm worried you'll ruin your chance with this amazing guy who's already doing a pretty good job at rocking your world.” She's rubbing my back, trying to console me. How did I end up like this? Oh yeah, bottomless mimosas. Bad idea.

In between sniffles, I try to make sense of everything out loud. “No, I'm sorry. I know you're just looking out for me. And honestly, I don't have a clue what I'm doing. You, of all people, know that. Navigating the dating world isn't something I've experienced, let alone with two men at once. What am I thinking, Cici? I should at least see if there could be something between Jackson and me or if it's only in my head. And yes, I'm having a good time with Sebastian. I like him. Too much. But that's the problem. Even you can admit it's risky dating someone with his track record. Isn't it fair that I protect myself from falling too fast and getting hurt? You should understand better than anyone that going on one date or even being sexual with someone doesn't imply exclusivity, am I right?” Please say I am, please, please, please. I don't think I can follow through without Cici's approval. As crazy as that sounds, she's my rock, and I trust her. If she insists going out with Jackson is the wrong thing to do, then I'll have no choice but to cancel.

“You're right. It doesn't mean you're exclusive. But just hearing your stories about Sebastian and even meeting him at the club, I can tell how possessive he is. You better know this won't go well. Going out for drinks isn't a big deal to most, but I'm positive it'll be a huge deal to Sebastian. If it's worth the fallout to you, then you should go. You can't be infatuated with Jackson while starting something with another guy, anyway. So you should find out if you're really into him or put it to rest once and for all and move on. Now let's go sleep these damn mimosas off and remind each other not to order bottomless ever again."

Amen to that.

Sebastian

"Jesus, dude, what is going on with you?" Eli asks. We just hung up our conference call with one of our shipping companies that's having issues at the international border.

"I'm pissed that we had to deal with this on a Sunday."

"Since when do you give a shit about what day of the week it is? We've never had days off, Sebastian. What's gotten into you? Does this have to do with Lily? Wait, you went on your date last night. How'd it go? I'm guessing like shit based on your attitude." He has the nerve to chuckle at that.

"Quite the opposite." I smile. "It went exactly according to plan. I'm probably pissy this morning—" I look at my watch. "—because I'm supposed to be setting sail about now to return from Coronado, where Lily and I stayed last night on the boat," I say smugly.

"Fuck, man, did you finally get laid?" I don't remember when I last wanted to punch my brother, but I'm close.

"No, Eli, I didn't. I thought you were the one to remind me not to fuck with this girl, which means taking her virginity on the first date would have been uncouth, am I right?"

"Wait, that means you spent all night with a woman you weren't banging? Dude, who are you, and what have you done with my brother?" He's laughing now, the fucker.

"Don't be such a prick, man. I took your advice, went on a date and gave her a taste of what I can do for her."

"Elaborate, you can't leave me hanging now."

"Let's just say I have hands of magic. She's honest to God the most responsive woman I've ever been with. Her body reacts to everything I do in spades. I probably shouldn't be telling you this, but last night was her first orgasm. It was hands down the sexiest thing I've ever seen."

"Christ. She's way more inexperienced than I thought. Boy, did she pick the wrong son of a bitch to start with. Tell me you're not going down the wrong path with her, man," he says seriously. What's his deal? He barely even knows Lily, for fuck's sake.

"What's your deal? So what if I am? She loved everything about last night, three orgasms worth by the time I dropped her off this morning, including one immediately after being spanked. She even enjoyed having her hands tied. Dude, I'm telling you, she's a natural submissive in the bedroom." Not so much out of it, but we can work on that. Just talking about all this makes the blood start pumping down there. Especially the part I don't divulge, where I ended up coming just from rubbing her over my cock. I can't wait to get her in my clutches again.

"Sounds like you have it all worked out then, except the part where you've never seen the same woman twice. Do you know where you're going with this, and is she on the same page? I'm just saying, she's waited this long, I'm pretty sure she wasn't saving herself to give it up to a guy who's not looking for anything serious."

I don't remember Eli ever being the voice of reason, and it's starting to grate on my nerves. "What's your problem, man? When did it become your concern how I treat a woman? You've never given two shits."

"I don't know. It's different this time. I met the girl and she's nice. I'd hate for you to do something you can't take back. Not to mention the publicity nightmare something like this could cause. You brought her into our company, Sebastian, there could be ramifications if you fuck this up."

"So that's what this is about, the company's reputation? Don't worry, she signed the NDA before we even stepped foot in her office. It didn't only cover that particular transaction. It applies to all interactions with us and our company with no exception or expiration. If it'll make you feel better, I'll remind her." What the fuck? Since when did Eli become the responsible one? There's got to be something else going on.

"Might not be a bad idea, other than I don't think that would earn you any brownie points. I'm sure she won't run to the media anyway, but the paparazzi are everywhere. I just want you to have a clear head about this going forward and stop only thinking with your dick. Sorry, bro, I am happy for you. It's good to see you finally into someone. Who knows, maybe I'm just jealous she's stealing your time away." He chuckles.

Could that be why he's behaving this way? Shit, it would make sense since we usually hang pretty regularly. "Well, in that case, what the hell are we doing sitting in the office still? Let's get the fuck out of here and do something. Instead of having the boat transported back, why don't we head over and do it ourselves? Stay out for a while, yeah?"

We're in the car heading over to Coronado while Eli's busy texting some chick he's had on the hook, giving me time to contemplate. I can't stop thinking about her. That may be what concerns me the most. I won't end up like my dad. Eli's already noticing how hung up on her I am. I can't allow feelings to get involved. This is purely sexual for me—I need to remember that and keep my head on straight. I just wish she wasn't so damn appealing. She brings things to the surface I'm not looking for. I've never wanted to spend time with a woman for anything other than sex until now. I'm truly fucked.

After distracting myself all day with Eli, I find myself alone again with only one thing on my mind. Her. We parted this morning with no plan in place to see each other again. I'll see her in the office tomorrow afternoon, but not in the way I want to. It could be… but she made it clear not to make it awkward for her at work. Screw that, I can do whatever I want; it's my goddamn company. Since when do I give two fucks what people think? Apparently, since I started caring what Lily thinks, which means it's time to set some rules. Rule number one: I make the rules, not her.

The fact that I'm wishing Lily was here with me as I crawl into bed has me pausing. Where the fuck did that come from? I've never had anyone in my bed. I swear she's just an itch I need to scratch. At least, that's what I tell myself.

> Me: I hope you enjoyed the rest of your day.
>
> Lily: Cici and I had too many mimosas at brunch, so I slept most of it. But it was fun while it lasted.
>
> Me: I'm glad you had a good time. Sorry again for having to cut our time short. I'm looking forward to seeing you tomorrow.
>
> Lily: That's right, I'll be in your office tomorrow afternoon.

Me: Forgotten so soon? I must not have made the impression I thought then.

Lily: And what impression is that?

Me: The one where you can't stop thinking about the next time you'll see me.

Lily: Hmmm, I'd say that's a bit presumptuous.

Me: Not after the three orgasms you've had in the last 24 hours.

Lily: Touché. Looking forward to seeing you tomorrow. Good night, Sebastian.

Me: That's what I thought. Sweet dreams, Lily. Until tomorrow…

17

MATURE ADULTS

Lily

SCHOOL WAS RELATIVELY UNEVENTFUL. I WOULD LOVE THE REST of the day to go that way, but as I make my way to the town car waiting at the end of the sidewalk, I have a hard time believing that will be the case. I'm surprised not to see Sebastian holding the door open but the driver this time. Honestly, the disappointment that follows creates a sliver of fear. I don't want to be the girl who gets that invested so soon.

"Blake, right?" He nods. "Thanks for the ride."

"My pleasure, Miss Thompson. Mr. Dubree sends his regard and was sorry not to be here, but he left something for you inside."

As soon as I step in, I see a brown paper bag with a card stapled to it. Tearing the envelope open, I see his distinct monogram and read the handwritten note.

Lily,

Unfortunately, I couldn't leave the office this afternoon as planned. Please enjoy the lunch provided. I look forward to escorting you home this evening. I'll meet you at the elevators promptly at five. Until then, sweetheart…

Sebastian

My heart is racing, and not in a good way. I was hoping to avoid this today, but that ship just sailed. Opening the bag, I see my favorite Thai dish waiting for me. I may as well fuel up because this is going to be one tough afternoon. I make quick work of my meal and put the contents back into the bag as the car arrives at the office. My heart is thudding as I make it to the marketing department and set my things down.

I check in with the team to see if anything new came up, otherwise I'll just keep plugging away on the assignment I was already tasked with. I'm stalling the inevitable. When I return to my desk, I decide the best course of action is to get it over with. Maybe he'll be so busy he won't ask questions. Here goes nothing.

> Me: Thank you so much for the yummy lunch. Sorry you couldn't join me. Unfortunately, I have plans after work and won't be taking a ride home.
>
> Bossy: I'm glad you enjoyed lunch. What plans?
>
> Me: Meeting a friend for drinks after work.
>
> Bossy: Cici? Mind if I join?
>
> Me: No, someone else, sorry.
>
> Bossy: Is there something you're not telling me?
>
> Me: No.
>
> Bossy: Who are you meeting?
>
> Me: It doesn't matter who. I just won't be available.
>
> Bossy: The hell it doesn't. Answer the question, Lily.
>
> Me: Jackson asked me to meet him for a drink after work.

Oh God, he's not responding. Is that a good sign? Bad? Crap, what the heck was I thinking? I should have postponed Jackson until tomorrow. Something tells me Sebastian would've found out no matter when it was though. Maybe he's ruminating on it a bit, trying to see reason?

> Bossy: You have precisely two minutes to make it to my office right the fuck now, or I'm coming over to drag you here myself.

Me: I don't think that's wise.

Bossy: Don't test me, Lily. The clock is ticking.

Oh no. Can I make it there that quick? I don't think he's kidding about coming to get me. Standing abruptly, I hurry as fast as possible without making a scene, politely smiling along the way while my insides shake in fear. I make it to his office in record time. His secretary sees me approach and smiles politely. "Head on in. Mr. Dubree is expecting you." *Great.*

I open the door reluctantly and step inside his office for the first time. It's massive. His desk is facing me from the farthest end with floor-to-ceiling windows along the whole wall behind it as well as the whole wall to the right. The view is spectacular. On the left wall is an elegant mini bar and door leading to something, maybe a bathroom? In the middle of the room is a couch across from two sofa chairs with a table in between. There are also two wingback chairs in front of his desk.

"Shut the door." Oh boy, he is undeniably angry. I close the door apprehensively. "Come here," he demands menacingly.

"Can we talk about this like mature adults?" I ask with a tremor in my voice.

"You want to talk about it? Which part? The one where you're going out with another man the day after I got you off on top of my dick, or the part where you weren't going to tell me?" Hm, when he puts it like that…. Maybe silence would be a good thing here.

"Already done talking, I see. Smart girl. I thought I told you to come here." He is not taking it easy on me.

"I'm thinking that wouldn't be the smartest move at the moment." He stands immediately. I hold up a hand. "All right, all right, no need to get upset."

"Oh, Lily, I was way past upset as of—" He looks at his watch. "—five minutes ago." I stop in front of his desk as he stares impatiently, pointing to the spot between the desk and where he sits. I slowly walk around and stop.

"Turn around and bend over the desk." My eyebrows raise in shock. "Now." He's not messing around. What the hell have I gotten myself into? I do as instructed, propping my upper body on my elbows, staring at the door. I'm starting to wonder if coming here was the best decision. Doesn't the saying go, ask for forgiveness, not permission?

I feel his hand on my back, pushing me down so my upper body lies flat over the desk, with my cheek against the wood. "So, you want to discuss this like mature adults?"

"Uh… yes?" I reply while he sits back down. His hand touches behind my knee and travels up until he reaches the hem of my skirt, where his thumb skims underneath the material that hugs my legs. My heart is racing again, this time in anticipation. God, how can he make me tremble in fear one second and lust the next?

"I'm telling you now, this is not for your pleasure. I'm doing this because you apparently don't understand the meaning of the word communication. So, maybe this will help remind you. Are you going to take your punishment like a good girl?" Oh God, I'm dripping. How is this not for pleasure?

"Yes." He slowly raises my skirt. The string from my panties doesn't cover any part of my backside.

"Tell me, Lily, did you enjoy our *date* this weekend?" He touches my bare ass, and it feels delicious. I'm having a hard time focusing right now.

"Yes" is all I manage. *SMACK!* Ow, that was harder than he started with the other night.

"Yes, what?" he asks, caressing the spot he spanked.

"Yes, I really enjoyed our date." I'm panting as he continues rubbing my bare cheeks.

"I'm glad to hear you *really* enjoyed it. Do you remember how many times I made you come?" My face is beet red, I'm sure of it.

"Three," I squeak. *SMACK!* Oh fuck.

"Three, what?" he asks, stroking the sting until it's gone.

"I had three orgasms."

"And did I give you the impression that that would be our only date?" Where is he going with this?

"No." *SMACK!* Ahhhh. Oh boy, he's serious. I try to rise, but his hand on my back prevents me from moving.

"No what, Lily?" He continues to massage the sting away.

"No, you didn't make me think it would be our only date."

"Then tell me." *SMACK!* "Why." *SMACK!* "You thought." *SMACK!* "It would be okay." *SMACK!* "To go out." *SMACK!* "With another man."

SMACK! "Right after." *SMACK!* He went from cheek to cheek, each one firmer than the last.

"Sebastian!" I'm panting and squirming under his hold, partly from the pain and—I must be crazy—partly because I'm turned on. I can feel the wetness pooling. "I don't know."

"You don't know." He continues to caress my ass, turning the pain into pure arousal. "Do you like him?"

"I don't know." It's the only answer I can give.

"You don't know." He dips his hand between my cheeks and lowers it, grazing my opening. I moan this time and push my ass into his hand.

Sebastian

Goddammit. Why am I reacting this way? Who cares if she wants to see another man? But just thinking about it makes my anger rise even more. What the fuck, I don't do relationships, so why should I expect exclusivity from her? Finding out about her plan for "drinks" after work knocked the wind out of me. I need to get myself under control.

I reach down to see if she's enjoyed her punishment as much as I did. Fuuuck, she's soaking and so turned on, apparent from how she presses into my hand. Seeing her bent over my desk, ass on display, at my mercy, makes my dick ache. What I wouldn't give to plunge into her and prove who this pussy belongs to.

Standing up, I lean over to whisper in her ear. "Should I remind you just how much you enjoyed our date?" I ask her seductively as I continue to stroke her clit. I can't resist pleasuring her; selfishly I love seeing her come undone.

"Yes, please," she pleads.

SMACK! Fuck, I love the feel of her skin, warm from my slaps. I love seeing the pink come to the surface. Damn, my dick can't take much more. Before I can ask her again, she corrects her answer.

"Yes, I want you to remind me. Please, Sebastian," she moans.

"Good girl. You're learning." I caress her ass once more before I lower my hand and plunge two fingers in, immediately making her squeal and try to rise, but she can't with me lying over her. I move my fingers inside her, rubbing her sweet spot, going back and forth between thrusting and flicking right where I know will cause the dam to burst. "Tell me you want this, baby." I curl my fingers deep inside.

"Yes! I want this. God, Sebastian, please don't stop." She's begging.

I won't make her wait any longer. I wrap her hair around my fist, yanking her head to the side, and nip her neck while thrusting deeper and faster. I can feel her orgasm right on the edge, and when I use my thumb to put the slightest amount of pressure on her tight little asshole and bite down with my teeth, she bursts, screaming louder than ever before. It's nice to finally use my soundproof office for something other than yelling at people.

"Your orgasms belong to me and only me." Fuck, what am I saying?

Slowly I withdraw my hand and caress her probably sore ass while kissing her neck as she comes down. Her breathing is rapid, and I can feel her pulse hammering against my lips. Instead of standing immediately, I slide down her body and give each of her ass cheeks a few soft kisses. I'm pretty sure I hear the faintest moan escape from her mouth. This woman is insatiable and so fucking amazing.

My dick can't take the pressure from my crouched position, forcing me to stand and adjust. I need inside this woman. Soon. I pull her skirt back down and bring her into my lap as I sit. She's pretty much Jell-O at this point and pliable as fuck. "Was that a good reminder, sweetheart?"

"Oh my God, yes. That was… intense. I thought I was going to pass out." I laugh at that as she keeps going. "Um, Sebastian? I can feel you under me. Aren't you needing to be satisfied too?" she asks shyly.

"We'll worry about me another time. For now, I want to finish our mature conversation. Tell me why you agreed to go out with Jackson, baby. I need to know where your head's at." So I can figure out what the fuck to do about it.

"I don't know. He caught me off guard. It was after our bottomless mimosas, and I'd like to use that as an excuse, but honestly, I can't. You already knew about my infatuation with him, and after Cici and I talked it over, we decided I shouldn't start something with one person while I'm stuck on another. So we thought it would be a good thing to put it to rest." She's fidgeting with her nails as she talks, not wanting to make eye contact.

"Look at me, Lily." I wait until her gaze reaches mine to continue. "What if it doesn't go that way? What if you don't want to put it to rest?"

I brace myself for the answer while I stare into her eyes, getting lost in her vulnerability.

"I don't know…," she whispers, and I can see her eyes start to water. *Fuck.*

I pull her close to my chest and hold her, never wanting to let go. But as far as mature conversations go, she's right. She can't get any deeper into this, whatever this is, while she's hung up on someone else. Jackson had years to make his move, and he waits until she starts seeing someone. Fucking asshole. Well, he's too goddamn late… except he isn't. Because her *infatuation* seems to run deeper than I thought.

"Well, unfortunately, you've already started something with someone else. But you're right. As much as I hate to admit it, you need to figure out what you want before whatever we're doing here goes any further. I don't do relationships, Lily, and as much as I want to tell you I'll do more, I can't because it's never happened. Having said that, I'm intrigued enough to see where this goes, but only if you're all in. I know that's not fair when I give no such promise in return, but I'm all sorts of fucked up, Lily. I've been against serious relationships too long to change overnight. And maybe you're right about not painting a black house white, but I was willing to give it my best effort." I kiss her head and give her time to soak it all in.

"So where does that leave us?"

"I think that's up to you. If you can't let that part of you go, we should stop here. Because, Lily, if we keep going down this path, let me be clear: I will have you fully, whether exclusive or not. And if you're still unsure which of us you want, you'll regret that. I don't want to hurt you, do you understand?"

"I think so. It sounds like a breakup, except we weren't together to begin with, right?" She sits up straight and moves to stand.

My arms tighten around her, preventing her retreat, not ready to let go. "And that's the problem right there. I'm sorry, Lily. I wish I could offer you more, but I guess you were right all along. I'll cherish the firsts you bestowed, and I'm glad to have shared a few of my own. Now come here for a proper goodbye, sweetheart." I'm praying to whoever's listening that it will only be temporary, but I know better than to hold my breath.

Cupping her cheek, I pull her lips to mine and kiss her like it's our last, because it just may be.

18

ANOTHER FIRST DATE

Lily

TRUDGING THROUGH THE REST OF MY DAY WAS DIFFICULT. FINDING out Sebastian is done with me now rather than later is probably good. But knowing it may have been the last time we'll be together is depressing. I let myself get too attached too quickly, which was what I was afraid of. As I try to focus on work, I keep repeating to myself how this is probably for the best. I almost believe it by the time I pack up for the day.

"Lily. I was wondering if we'd bump into each other one of these days. How are things going in the marketing division?" I practically run into Eli as I turn the corner for the elevators.

"Hi, Mr. Dubree. Good, things are good. I think it's a valuable partnership so far." I'm not sure what he knows about Sebastian and me, and it feels awkward. I'm probably not making the best impression, that's for sure.

"Just Eli is fine. I'm glad to hear that. So, anything I should be aware of regarding the other project you're involved in? Sebastian seemed pretty on edge this afternoon, to put it mildly. It'd be nice to know what I'm stepping into." He smirks at me.

If I'm not imagining things, I think he just asked about what happened today. "Um, well, I'm meeting my friend Jackson for drinks after work. He's probably waiting downstairs. I let Sebastian know I wouldn't need a ride home because of it, so, uh, he decided the project had gone far enough, and we won't need to be working together anymore." Thank goodness no one else is around to listen to this awkward conversation or pick up on anything.

"Ah, I see. That's too bad. I've never seen him more excited over any other project before. I wish there was more time to see it through. Maybe you can circle back at some point and make sure you explored all possibilities." He winks at me and continues down the hallway, leaving me motionless.

It takes a minute to come to and start toward the elevator again. I can't stop analyzing everything Eli just said and the implications he was making. God, this is so complicated. Why did Jackson have to wait until now to ask me out? I mean, I'm glad he did… right? Suddenly, I'm not so sure what I think anymore. Since when have I ever questioned my feelings for him? Apparently, since a certain someone weaseled their way into my life, or should I say bed. Well, it doesn't matter now; by going out with Jackson, Sebastian made it clear I was closing the door to him.

I step out of the elevators into the lobby of the One America building and pause, all thoughts of Sebastian leaving my mind as I look straight ahead to see Jackson. He looks incredible in a white button-down shirt and tailored pants that fit him perfectly, accentuating his muscular physique. Our eyes meet, and he gives me the most adorable smile.

"Hey, gorgeous, these are for you." He kisses me on the cheek and hands me flowers.

"Thank you. They're beautiful, but you didn't have to bring me flowers."

"I know I didn't, but I want my intention clear. This isn't just two friends meeting for drinks after work," he says pointedly as he leads us out of the lobby.

"Oh, well, I gathered that, but I'm glad you clarified. So where are we headed?" I ask curiously.

"I figured we could leave those in the car and walk one block to the Harbor Rooftop. They have great cocktails, and we can probably catch the sunset if we stay long enough." He opens the door to his Range Rover and places my flowers on the front seat. "I think they should be okay in there for a couple hours until we get home."

After locking up, he grabs my hand as we walk. "Is this okay?" he asks shyly. This is so different from any other time we've spent together. It's like we've never been around each other or something. I think we're both feeling awkward.

"Of course. Are you feeling as weird about this as I am?" I ask with a grin on my face. I figure the best course of action is to address the elephant in the room.

He chuckles and lets out a deep breath. "Yeah, it does feel awkward. I'm hoping it's just nerves. I've thought about this for so damn long, and now I don't know how to act. God, it's not like we haven't been around each other. I don't know why this should be any different." He squeezes my hand and stops us right outside the entrance to finish our conversation.

"You're right, and I'm feeling the same way, so how about this? Why don't we pretend we've never met and start over." I hold out my hand and say, "Hi, I'm Lily Thompson. It's nice to meet you."

He shakes my hand. "Hi, Jackson Soloman. Thanks for meeting me tonight. Shall we?" He sticks his elbow out to escort me, and I curl my hand around his massive bicep as he leads me inside.

Two cocktails and a few appetizers later, we've gotten past the awkwardness and reach a comfortable stage in the night where we no longer pretend to be strangers. Looking back, I think it was an excellent place to start. It revealed how much we honestly didn't know about each other, even with all the time we've spent together. We talked about everything from our jobs and school to reminiscing over the past and a few funnier moments we've shared. Like the time he had a bunch of friends over, and they thought having a pepper-eating contest was a good idea. With Jackson's competitive nature, he just had to show everyone up, only to overdo it and puke on his girlfriend at the time. She broke up with him on the spot. I did fess up about that being my favorite part. I never liked her, or any of his girlfriends for that matter.

"So, how long have you seen me as somebody other than your little sister's annoying friend?" I ask, curious.

"Ever since I saw you in a swimsuit." He laughs. "You've got an exceptional body, and hey, I'm a guy. But seriously, when I got home from college and you were a freshman at SDSU, I realized how mature you were compared to the rest of us, and it hit me that you're the kind of girl I want to be with, you know? It's hard to explain. I knew how innocent you were, though, and didn't want to corrupt you. So I watched you over the years, seeing who you were with and for how long, waiting for you to become more interested in dating. But it never seemed like the right time with you being so busy."

"What made you decide to ask me out finally?" I'm trying to figure out the "why now" factor and decide to take the direct approach.

"God, I hate admitting this, but I saw how that Sebastian guy looked at you at the club the other night, and then I was there when he picked you up on Saturday for an obvious date. It struck me that if I didn't make my move, I could lose my chance forever and have to live with the what-if. So here we are. I'm glad I wasn't too late." He reaches for my hand, caressing my fingers while pulling me closer.

Leaning in seductively, he says, "Lily, I'd like to explore the possibility of us if you're willing. I've waited so long to reach out and take your hand." He caresses my fingers. "To touch your skin." He reaches out and cups my cheek. "And feel your lips on mine." He leans over and kisses me softly. I'm so caught up in his words—words I never thought I'd hear from him—that I can barely focus. But once I do, my mouth responds, matching his need with my own, like we've both been waiting for this moment forever. I suppose we have.

We pull apart and stare at each other in shock or awe, maybe both. I can't help but wonder what he's thinking while hoping he can't see the conflict I'm feeling. I came here to see this through and find out if what I've felt all these years is real or just a childhood crush with no merit. But seriously, who am I? I just kissed someone other than Sebastian hours after he made me come. Which is honestly ridiculous to feel guilty about, considering that the man has been with an unimaginable number of women and admitted he doesn't do relationships.

"Wow, Lily, you don't know how many times I've imagined that. My imagination didn't do it justice. I'm really kicking myself for not asking you out sooner, trust me. How are you feeling?" He's still holding my hand, and our knees are touching now, as we've scooted closer on the couch.

Shaking myself from my wayward thoughts and feeling guilty about where my head is, I contemplate my answer. "I think I'm in shock. I've had a crush on you forever but gave up hope. I never thought we'd be sitting here, let alone kissing, so I'm trying to process. I wanted this for so long, and now that I'm here, my thoughts are all over the place." I take a sip of my drink as an excuse to look away.

"That's understandable. I'm sorry if I kissed you too soon. I couldn't resist. The last thing I want is for you to feel pressured, so please be honest, even if you realize this isn't what you expected and don't want to see me as anything other than a friend. Of course, I'll be devastated." He puts his hand to his heart exaggeratingly, making me laugh. "But, Lily, the ball's in your court. I'd like to take you out on another date, but I'll give you some time to process, like you said."

"Thank you, Jackson. That means a lot. It is a little overwhelming, but I promise I won't take too long to figure it out. Is that okay?" What's going on with me? I'm fighting this internal battle with myself and don't know if it's from guilt or real feelings I may have for someone else. Ugh, this cannot be happening.

"Of course it is, Lils. I just want you to be happy. Now, let's enjoy this amazing sunset we stayed long enough to see." He lifts his glass and motions for me to grab mine. "Cheers to finally testing the waters together." We clink our glasses, take a sip and sit back to watch the sunset.

I'm glad he's still holding my hand on the way to the car, keeping a measure of closeness between us. It feels so right in this moment and yet wrong at the same time. Maybe a few days to settle my thoughts would be good before giving it another shot, and maybe not on the heels of seeing Sebastian earlier that day. Just having a game plan makes me feel better and less guilty.

I've been relaxed for the last part of our night and the ride home. It's weird that we're going to the same place. It's not, of course, because we've lived in the same building forever, but it gives a whole new meaning to the concept of walking me in. We laugh at the irony as we exit the car.

When we enter the elevator, the air is charged. He's still holding my hand, which I've learned is his thing, and I feel him tug me to him as the doors close, crashing his mouth to mine. It's way more intense than in the bar. It's hungry and insistent like he wants to savor every last drop in case he doesn't get the chance again. And frankly, I do the same for the exact same reason. It's everything I imagined, making me moan into his mouth and grip his hair tightly. As he pushes me against the elevator wall, we hear the ding as the doors slide open to my floor.

"Shit, Lily, I'm sorry. I don't know what came over me. Well, I do, but I still should've shown a little restraint. It's hard to control myself after wanting you for so long. Fuck, I hope you're not upset." He's holding the door open and running his hand through his hair, clearly distraught.

"Jackson, it's okay. I would've stopped you if I wanted to. I… liked it. You have nothing to be sorry for." He visibly relaxes and sighs in relief. I lean up and kiss him on the cheek. "Thanks again for the flowers. I had the perfect time tonight, thank you." I wave and say good night as the doors close.

My mind goes a hundred miles a minute while I'm getting ready for bed. I'm so mentally exhausted when I crawl under the covers that I hope sleep will come sooner rather than later. Usually, I'd go over everything with Cici and have her help me sort through this mess in my head, but I'm so glad she's out late tonight. I can't handle any more judging from either of us. We made plans for Tuesday to have dinner and catch up. She's been seeing someone who's been keeping her quite busy lately.

I hear my phone chime with a text and immediately get butterflies, wondering what Sebastian has to say tonight.

> Jackson: I just want to say good night. I had a great time tonight. Reach out when you're ready for date number two. I'll try not to bother you in the meantime.

> Lily: Me too. I'll be in touch. I won't make you wait too long. Good night.

I don't know what's more disturbing, the fact I'm not jumping for joy over Jackson texting me, or that I'm sad it wasn't Sebastian.

Sebastian

What the actual fuck. I can't believe I tortured myself watching the scene in the lobby until they walked away hand in hand. I was tempted to have the damn car towed to be spiteful but didn't want to make things difficult for Lily. I was so close to walking out the door and following them. How pathetic can I get? Pathetic enough that I already have a security company doing that for me with a full report in the morning.

"Hey, earth to Sebastian, are you ready to go?" The tone in Eli's voice snaps me out of my thoughts. Either he's stood there for longer than I realized, or he already tried to get my attention. It could be both, for all I'm aware.

"Yeah, I'm coming." I grab my suit coat, and we head out. Going straight to the club tonight is exactly what I need to distract me. Even though it's still considered work and takes more time than expected, the diversion from our more stressful day job is appreciated. Our decision to hire a general manager for the more mundane parts of the operation was a godsend; now we get a little more play than work where the club is concerned.

"I heard Lily has a hot date tonight. You must not have made quite the impression you thought."

"Shut the fuck up unless you want a fist to your face. How did you hear about it? Talked to your new BFF Jackson, did you?" Fuck that guy.

"Nope, talked to the woman of the hour myself. Sounds like you're done with that, then?"

"I'm giving her space to get her head clear. I don't share, so it's up to her to decide who she wants." I'm already sick of this conversation.

"Ah, you're giving her to this other guy after you primed her for him." He chuckles, setting my blood on fire.

I have him in a headlock at record speed. "I said shut the fuck up, and I meant it." I give him another squeeze and push him away from me. I've never resorted to violence with my brother, fuck.

"Well, at least I know how you really feel. Dude, you're just gonna sit back and take it? That's not the Sebastian I know. Since when do you let anything go you clearly want?" He's baiting me; I know it. I'm not one to give in to pressure; he should know better.

"I clearly don't want her bad enough. Jesus, Eli, it was just the chase. I got enough to satisfy my curiosity. She was never mine to let go of." This conversation is giving me a headache.

"Well, that's too bad. I thought you'd finally met your match. I guess you're looking forward to jumping back in and checking out the selection tonight, huh?" Fuck him for calling me on my bullshit.

Relieved to be pulling up to the club, I say nothing as I leave the car while it rolls to a stop. I stride in the back door, not waiting for Eli, and head to the back offices. Passing the corridor, I'm reminded of that heated kiss with Lily, and anger surges to the surface again. Maybe I do need a distraction.

After having dinner while addressing any current issues with our GM before opening, Eli and I settle into our usual booth in the VIP section, which gives us a visual of most of the club.

"What do you think of those two hotties over there in fuck me dresses? Mind if I call them over?" Eli's trying to call my bluff from our earlier conversation, but it won't work. I already decided a distraction is exactly what I need.

"I think that's an excellent idea. Go ahead." He calls the nearest bouncer over, who knows our routine by now and can handle our request.

Minutes later, he's escorting the two women to our table. They look at each other before deciding which of us to sit next to, communicating in silence.

"Good evening, ladies. We saw you standing there and couldn't pass up the chance to introduce ourselves to the most beautiful women in the house tonight. I'm Eli, and this is my brother, Sebastian." That's my brother, the smooth talker, always the one to schmooze. I just don't have it in me.

"I'm glad you invited us over. I'm Genevieve and this is Anna." The girl next to Eli makes the introduction.

The waitress comes to take their order. "Two cosmos, please." Really? That's what Lily was drinking, fuck me.

"Are you looking for more than conversation tonight or what?" I ask the chick next to me, ready to get this charade over.

"I could be persuaded," she says demurely. That response alone tells me talking is not on her agenda for the evening.

I grab her hair and pull her head back, diving straight to her neck. "Don't be shy, show me what you're hungry for." She doesn't waste any time after that and leans into me, her hands going straight to the bulge in my pants. Her skin isn't as soft as Lily's, and her perfume is too heavy. I can't complain about her hands roaming over my dick, ready to get inside my pants, but I wish it were Lily's hands instead. God, what the fuck am I doing? I sit up and shove her away. "On second thought, I think I'm too full. Eli, they're all yours. Enjoy your drinks, ladies." I stand up and make my way out. Tomorrow morning's report from security can't come soon enough.

19

UNDECIDED

Sebastian

"WHAT DO YOU MEAN THERE WERE ONLY TWO THINGS TO BE concerned about? There should have been none. Get to the point."

I listen as Lily's security detail elaborates, giving me the rundown of her date last night. Thinking about it makes me cringe, and I probably should have stayed in the dark regarding their kiss.

"I caught someone inconspicuously taking photos of them at the bar. I obtained the camera and deleted the pictures, but you should know there were photos of the two of you from Saturday after your dinner, exiting the dock in the morning and exiting the car when you dropped her off at her place. Can't guarantee those haven't gone out, but I deleted them all."

"Fuck! How did anyone know we were there? This is bullshit. Did they say who tipped them off? Is there any indication if the photos have already gone out?" I'm livid; there was no one other than Lucy and Eli who knew of my plans.

"Said some woman called in anonymously, and no, she wasn't forthcoming about the pictures since she was pissed I deleted them.

Noticed something else that may be a concern. There was another male keeping tabs on the couple. He followed them from here and stayed all night. Sat hidden in the corner but kept his eye on them. Not sure of his purpose; he just watched. I couldn't get a good photo from where I was." He hands me the phone.

It's too grainy to make out the details; it could be anyone. "All right, you did good. Follow up with the pictures from our date. Find who has them and kill whatever story they're putting together. I'll do whatever it takes to keep her out of the press. Due to this new development regarding the possible stalker, I'd like someone to monitor her moving forward. Not round the clock. Maybe from noon to when she's in for the evening. I want any paparazzi handled and an eye on the stalker situation. If he's spotted again, I want a good picture next time. Clear?"

"Clear, sir. I'll have someone assigned by this afternoon."

"Good."

What the hell am I doing? I shouldn't concern myself with her. I was clear we were done unless she could free herself from Jackson. It's evident at this point that's not happening. So why am I putting resources toward her when I shouldn't give a damn? The problem is I do give a damn.

It's also not her fault she got photographed with me, goddammit. Why did I think I could slip under the radar for once? The press eats up anything I do outside of business, especially when it involves a woman. I know better but was too caught up to think straight and consider the repercussions. Then there's this stalker. Fuck, it's none of my business what's going on, but hell if I'm going to let some scumbag mess with her when I have the resources to take care of it.

"Sir, your nine o'clock is here," Lucy pipes in over the intercom.

"Send him in." I have a standing therapy appointment thanks to my dad and the preparations he made before offing himself. As part of the requirement to receive our inheritance and the reins to this company, Eli and I were forced to schedule regular therapy sessions for five years. Oddly enough, it's something I look forward to now. An hour to bitch about everything to some guy who can't legally divulge any of my secrets. Who wouldn't love that? Maybe he can help shed some light on this fucked up situation I'm in.

Lily

"So how did your date go with Jackson?" Kevin asks as soon as I sit down. I told him about it on Monday because I was so stressed. "I still can't believe you went out with him when you had a guy like Sebastian on the hook."

"You know about my crush. I had to see if it was real or not. Otherwise, I'd always wonder." I love being able to talk to Kevin about all this.

"I can relate to that. So, was it all you hoped for?"

"Undecided. Yes, if I hadn't met Sebastian, it would have been exactly what I wanted, but now, I'm not sure. I'm so frustrated." I sigh, exasperated.

"I'm guessing two is enough to handle at the moment, or would you want to add a third into the mix?" He smiles and raises his eyebrows at me.

"Ha, ha, not funny. We talked about this. I like being able to tell you things. Isn't it nice being comfortable enough to have these types of conversations together? Also, I thought you were open to me setting you up with Cici?" Why do I have to keep explaining this?

"I was until I realized you weren't too deep with anyone else. What if our friendship means we'd be great together? Would you give it one chance?" I see the hope in his eyes, and it's killing me. It wouldn't be right to lead him on, though. It's better to extinguish those thoughts now. It'll have to wait until after class since the professor just started.

This gives me time to think of the best way to say no and make it final this time without hurting his feelings if that's possible. I already told him I was seeing where things go with Sebastian, only to turn around and go on a date with Jackson. It looks bad, but honestly, I've been talking about Jackson with him for years, so he knew I'd been pining over the guy. Kevin's sweet, fun and laid-back, but he's not the one for me. I wish I could like him that way; it would've made this all so much easier if we were already dating before I got myself into this mess, but I was never attracted to him like that. Maybe I just need to say it like it is and hope our years of easy friendship can survive.

As soon as we exit the classroom, I pull him aside. "Kevin, I'm sorry, but I don't think of you romantically. I can't see us as anything other than friends, and I don't think it's the timing, so please don't get your hopes up or be mad at yourself for not asking sooner. I can't help who it is I'm attracted to. Are you okay with being friends with me, or does that not work for you? I'd hate to lose our friendship, but I would understand." We can't keep dancing around the issue. I just need to stop it, and if I lose him in the process, I'll have to come to terms with that.

"I'd have you as my friend any day over nothing. Just don't expect me to give up completely. I'll ease up, though, I promise. Good luck with your love triangle, I guess, and for what it's worth, I think Jackson's a dick, and I don't even know the guy." He laughs, making me laugh.

"Thanks, Kevin. I'll keep that in mind. And for what it's worth, I'm sorry. I'll see you Thursday, okay?" I walk away with a weight lifted from my shoulders. That ended better than expected. Now let's hope it stays that way.

"Lily, can you come here for a minute?" I hear Brad call from his office. Going back and forth from the massive offices of Dubree Enterprises to our tiny office is weird. I prefer the larger environment. I can't wait to start applying to bigger ad agencies, and if I had that award under my belt, there would be plenty of opportunity.

"Hey, Brad, what's up?" I say, stepping in. I notice how plain it is in here after being in Sebastian's massive, richly decorated office. Brad furnished the place on a budget. If he's happy being his own boss and earning an income to satisfy him, that's his prerogative. I certainly want bigger and better things, a less sleazy boss being one of them, which I'm reminded of as he looks me over from head to toe, shaking himself before finally settling on my eyes.

"How is the research going with that list of companies I gave you?"

"Good. If it's okay, I'd like to finish organizing my notes for the rest of the day and present you with the data and recommendations tomorrow. Was that all?" I ask hopefully.

"Actually, no. You received an invitation to the appreciation party the Dubrees are hosting to celebrate their acquisition." He says this with obvious suspicion.

"Oh wow, that's… unexpected."

"Yeah, apparently, it's at Sebastian Dubree's personal penthouse, which is an anomaly. I also received one a few days ago, so that's how I knew what it was. Any reason you'd be receiving your own invite and not just included in with the office?" He hands me the envelope, and I see it is addressed directly to me.

"No, other than I work for them a couple of days a week, so maybe they added me to their employee list." I'm not about to disclose any information regarding my interactions with Sebastian outside of work. It's none of Brad's business, not to mention nonexistent anymore.

"That could be. In any case, I'll see you there. Please remember this is a work event and to handle yourself appropriately," he says, giving me a stern look.

"Of course, I wouldn't think of doing otherwise." I turn and leave his office, fuming.

The nerve of that man treating me like a child. And to assume I would behave anything other than professional. I've never given any indication otherwise to the pig. If anything, I should be lecturing *him* on how to behave around other people, women especially. *Dick.*

I'm relieved to be home and praise the Lord when Cici hands me a glass of wine as soon as I hit the stool in the kitchen. Ebony jumps onto my lap like she knows I've had a rough day. Some unconditional love is exactly what I need.

"Thanks, girlfriend. This is a much-appreciated welcome after the day I've had." I take a sip of wine and sigh.

"Well, I still haven't heard about your date with Jackson or how Sebastian reacted, so where do you want to start? I ordered takeout since I had a feeling this was going to be a long night with a lot of wine involved."

"God, I love you. Why can't we just be lesbian lovers and run away together?" I say dreamily.

"Because I like dick way too much, and you will too when you finally get some. But if you want to visit the sister-wife scenario sometime in the future, I may be willing to give that a try," she says with the most deadpan face ever, making me crack up.

Taking a deep breath, I'm finally able to speak. "Oh, I needed that. You always know how to lighten my mood. All right, so—"

On and on the night went, and by the end, I was drunk, exhausted and relieved to spill it all, getting the best advice in return.

20

WITHDRAWAL

Lily

MY NERVES ARE SHOT AGAIN THIS MORNING. I HOPED BY NOW I'd be somewhat back to normal, especially after I rocked the presentation to Brad yesterday. But having a second date with Jackson tonight, a full day in the Dubree offices tomorrow and the party at Sebastian's this weekend looming over me, I'm more of a mess than ever. Not to mention, I have to get through school today, where I'll find out if my campaign project received the award and if Kevin and I are still friends after shutting down any hope he had of us going out. When did my life get so complicated, and where is the rewind button?

"Hi, Kevin, how's it going?" I say as if nothing is amiss. Nothing like ripping the Band-Aid off.

"Hey, Lily. Well, it'd be a lot better if this girl I like would go out with me, but you're here now, so I'll survive." He gives me one of his signature grins and nudges me with his shoulder as I smirk back.

Not a terrible response, with a glimpse of the old Kevin, but we're not there yet. Maybe in a couple weeks, he'll forget all about it. "I'm so nervous to find out about the award today. I know it's a boon just to be entered, but can you imagine the doors this could open if I won?" I decided a change of subject is in order.

"Lily, you're the best marketing student in the program, hands down. There's no way it's not yours."

Professor Milton walks in and begins his lecture. I hoped he'd get it out of the way at the beginning of class, but he's obviously waiting until the end. It's killing me to think he might be procrastinating having to deliver bad news. Ugh, could he go on any longer…

"All right, class, listen up. I've received the results of the competition for the Addy Award. Miss Thompson, will you please stand?" He wouldn't ask me to stand if I didn't win, right?

"It is with the utmost…" He draws out the word and pauses. Why did he make me stand? This is so embarrassing to lose in front of everyone. "Honor to inform you that your senior campaign project has won the American Advertising Awards student division." The room erupts in applause, and Kevin beams at me with an "I told you so" look. "See me after class and I'll give you details for the gala. You're expected to attend and receive the award in person. You're allowed one guest. Congratulations, Lily, it is well deserved."

Wow, just wow. I can't believe I did it. At least now I know all that time spent on the project while everyone gave me shit for working so hard was worth it. I turn to Kevin and see his genuine happiness for me; instinctually, we hug each other. It doesn't feel like anything other than congratulations. "Kevin, oh my gosh, I did it!" Pulling apart, I keep talking. "I get to take someone to the awards gala. Will you come with me?" I ask before thinking about the repercussions. But he's been with me every step of the way, and it makes sense for him to be there when I accept the award.

"Of course. I wouldn't miss it for the world. I knew you'd win, Lily. You're amazing." He gives me another hug, but this time, he doesn't retract right away, and I'm immediately rethinking my impulsive decision. What have I done?

Before I head home from the office, I decide to let Brad know about my win. "So, I have some good news. I found out today I won an Addy Award.

In the student project division," I add quickly, not wanting Brad to think I submitted something behind his back.

"That's great news! Congratulations, Lily. Will you be attending the gala then? It's next week, isn't it?"

"Yeah. Apparently, I have to attend to be presented with the award. Were you going as well?" Shoot, at least I'll have Kevin with me. He'll protect me from the sleazeball.

"Yes, it's been on my calendar for quite a while now. I go every year. I'm thrilled someone from the company will be receiving an award; that's wonderful!" He seems to think this will benefit him; I should set him straight on that now.

"I'm a winner in the student division, so recognition will go to me as a student of the marketing program at SDSU. Unfortunately, it won't say anything about where I work unless they have some sort of bio they put in the program." I wouldn't give Brad any recognition, regardless.

"I see. It will still be nice to have as a conversation piece throughout the night. Way to go, Lily. Are you prepared for the Dubrees' party this weekend?"

"As ready as I'll ever be. I don't know what to expect, but my invite allowed a guest, so I'm bringing my roommate, Cici. How about you?"

"Mine didn't specify, and there's no one I have in mind anyway, so I'm sure I'll see you there." What does that mean? I hope he's not planning to hang around me all night, yuck.

"All right, I'll see you Saturday since I work at Dubree all day tomorrow." Which I'm dreading…

"Yeah, about that. Has there been any talk of what the future holds for the account? Do they plan to continue this arrangement or use us for their gain and then yank it?" he says snippily.

"I'm pretty sure it gains them nothing by paying my wages when they already have a more than competent staff. We're the ones to gain from this by them not taking the account from day one. But, to answer your question, no. They've not said anything, and I don't know what they're planning. I'd recommend speaking with one of the Dubrees directly if you want answers."

"I'll wait and see how this plays out a bit longer. No sense stirring the pot when it seems to be working just fine. Especially when our focus should be on the new prospects you outlined. I'll have a game plan for you next week. I'm looking forward to seeing you Saturday." I hate how he says that, like he's implying we're meeting up. *Less than two months, less than two months, less than two months* is my mantra on the way out of the office.

Jackson's walking me to my door after dinner. I'm not sure what the protocol is when your date's sister is your roommate, but I'm sure it isn't to invite him in—not that I'd do that anyway. "Thanks for dinner tonight. It was delicious," I say quietly, feeling awkward for the first time.

"I'd say the company was better than the dinner. I'm glad you decided to see me again. I really like you, Lily," he says as he reaches up, cups my face and pulls me in. He pauses briefly, an inch apart, then closes the distance and kisses me passionately. It's more intense than the other night. There's more feeling in it. Instinctively, I match his intensity and wrap my arms around him; at the same time, my mind is at war, telling me I shouldn't be doing this.

He pulls away suddenly with heavy breaths and pure lust in his eyes. "I want to invite you over. I don't want this to end, and I'm pretty sure my sister will kick my ass if I give any more of a show outside her door." He smirks and caresses my cheek with his thumb.

I hesitate, thinking. I've wanted to be in this exact situation for so long, and now that I'm here, it's not as easy as I expected. The conflict running through my mind is driving me crazy. That I'm sitting here comparing this kiss to the fire I feel from Sebastian is a clear sign I'm not in the right headspace for anything more.

"I'm sorry, Jackson. I don't think that's a good idea. This is hard for me to say, but I'm still not sure what I want. It wouldn't be fair for either of us to go further when my thoughts are all over the place and not right here in the moment. I've wanted this forever, and now I'm so confused. God, I feel terrible," I say, bringing my hands up to cover my face.

"Hey," he says, pulling them away and looking into my eyes, "you shouldn't have to apologize. I did this. I'm the dipshit that waited too long and made this more complicated than it should've been, and for that, I'm sorry. I'm willing to wait, Lily, as long as it takes. You don't need to feel bad. Don't give up on me, okay?" He couldn't be any sweeter, making me doubt my decision.

"Okay," I respond.

He gives me one of his sexy smiles and leans in to kiss me chastely. "Good night, Lily. I'll see you later." Then he turns and walks away.

"You had to make out right in front of our door, gross," Cici says as soon as I walk in.

"Maybe you should mind your own business instead of being a Peeping Tom," I say smugly.

"Ugh, just tell me how the date went, although, from the goodbye kiss, I'd say pretty good."

I slump down on the couch opposite her. "It was great. Everything is so natural between us…. It's almost too easy."

"Oh, you mean you don't argue every couple minutes like you do with Sebastian? Yeah, I could see how that would be pretty boring."

I throw the pillow at her. "Shut up. I thought you were on team Sebastian. What I mean is, we already know so much about each other that there isn't much to talk about. There's always stuff like work and school, but the newness isn't there. And when he kissed me tonight, I was comparing him to Sebastian the whole time. How terrible is that?"

"I would say that you're accomplishing exactly what you were trying to. Maybe this 'crush' you've had on my brother is just that, a childhood crush with no real substance. Who would you rather masturbate to, Jackson or Sebastian? There's your answer." While I laugh, she smiles and sips her wine like it's the best advice in the world.

"God, you're awful, and we're not having that conversation. But speaking of Sebastian, you know I work in his office all day tomorrow, and then we have his party Saturday night. Meaning you're going to help me dress for the next couple of days, right?" I ask hopefully.

"You bet your ass I am. We're going to make that man weep. I can't believe he's gone all week without talking to you. There's no way he's done. I'd bet money this is killing him."

"I wish I could agree, but I'm pretty sure that's not the case. He made his feelings clear. He doesn't do relationships and won't put up with my indecision, leaving us nowhere. I bet if he knew I'd kissed Jackson a few times, he wouldn't even care. Either way, I still want him to see what he's missing out on with his hasty decision." I waggle my brows.

"Heck yeah, you do. I'll have something set out in the morning for you and then let's get ready together on Saturday, and I'll do your makeup again."

"Sounds good. I'm so excited you're going with me. Love you, girl. Night," I say, getting up and heading to my room, dreading the terrible night of sleep I'm sure to get with all this turmoil.

As I lay in bed, my head is filled with comparisons between Jackson and Sebastian, the guilt about not feeling more excited about Jackson and the sadness I feel about losing my chance with someone I didn't realize I had. The more I go over the past few weeks, the more it becomes clear. I'm head over heels for Sebastian. He definitely started out with less than virtuous intentions, but he's shown a different side of himself. The night of our date, I learned more about Sebastian and who he was than I ever knew about Jackson in all the years we've been friends. He makes me feel things I've never felt—not just physical, but more. It scares the crap out of me. I've shut out relationships from sheer determination to succeed in life, but what if I can have both?

Part of me is disappointed that I didn't feel the connection with Jackson I was hoping for, but another part of me is excited. No matter what happens with Sebastian, at least I can let my fantasy go and move on from my old infatuation. I love Jackson, but not in the way I should for a relationship. I just hope we can maintain our friendship after exploring other possibilities.

The question now is whether I've realized all this too late, and that's what keeps me tossing and turning all night.

Sebastian

Fucking hell, this has been a long week. Not only have I not texted her but not seeing her is killing me. What was I thinking when insisting on Mondays and Fridays? That gives me three whole days in between without her. I've never had this feeling of withdrawal before. Ever. And after making my thoughts clear on the matter, I can't even seek her out in the office tomorrow. What the hell have I done?

After hearing from security about her second date with Asshole tonight, I'm more consumed than ever by thoughts of her. I can't stop my anger from boiling to the surface whenever I imagine his hands on what's mine. It infuriates me that they live in the same building and there's no way of knowing whether their date ended at the elevator or I'm missing the final details. Restraining myself from texting her has been one of the most challenging decisions I've made in a while, and even more so is the follow-through on that decision. I've lost count of how many times I grabbed my phone tonight to text her, only to see if she'd respond or if she's otherwise occupied. Son of a bitch, being this helpless is driving me to the brink. I need to regain control of the situation, and that's all there is to it.

I formulate a plan and call Eli to set it in motion. "Hey, man, what's up?" He answers on the second ring, a sure sign I wasn't interrupting anything.

"I'm thinking you should set up a meeting with the marketing department tomorrow, so we can get an update on their progress with the new campaign." I'm all business as I make the suggestion.

"Hmm. Don't you think it's too soon? And why don't you just schedule a meeting yourself?" I'm not fooling him, but I keep up the charade anyway.

"I think it would be nice to present something at the party, to give people an idea of our vision for the new acquisition. I've been hovering over the progress and a fresh assessment from you would encourage the team. I'll be there, but I want you to lead the meeting," I say in a purely professional manner.

"I see. So, you're telling me your hands are tied with Lily, and you have no other option than use me to get to her?" he quips.

Fucker. "Just set up the damn meeting, Eli. I'll see you tomorrow." I hear him laughing as I hang up the call.

And tomorrow can't come soon enough. I stroke my cock for the hundredth time this week while thoughts of what I'd like to do when I come face to face with Lily again run through my mind.

21

UNTIL TOMORROW

Sebastian

"WILL YOU BE ACCOMPANYING ME TO TRANSPORT MISS Thompson this morning?" my driver, Blake, inquires as he holds the door open.

"No, I won't. Nor will I be this evening. You can return to the office for me after she's home safely," I answer gruffly.

"Certainly, sir."

It pains me not to be able to take advantage of her during the drive either to or from the office today, but I need to see this through if I want her as eager for me tomorrow night as I am for her. I can't cave to my desire now, not when I'm so close to the final prize.

When I reach my office, I call security to hand deliver the report regarding last night's date. I don't want anyone else seeing it—certainly not my secretary, who will wonder why I'm stalking our new marketing hire. "I want to know everything: where they went, how long they were there, if he touched her and how many times. I'd like it within the hour." I hang up without another word.

My secretary chimes in forty-five minutes later. "Mr. Burns is here to see you, sir. He said you're expecting him?"

"Send him in."

He comes straight to my desk, setting a manila folder before me. "Good morning, sir. Everything you requested, along with any information worth mentioning."

"Such as?" I ask curtly. I'm so riled up that I can't manage pleasantry. Apparently one date wasn't enough for them.

"We noted a man from her place of employment watching them leave the premises. He stayed inside the building but kept a close eye until they pulled away. It seemed more than just curious, but I could be wrong, sir."

"Trust your instincts, rarely do they lead you astray. Anything else? Stalker or photographers?"

"No, not this time. It seems this… outing was off the radar." Clever catch, not using the word date.

"That's good news. I'll review the report and contact you if I have questions. Dismissed."

"Thank you, sir." He leaves, shutting the door behind him.

Pulling the report out, I hesitate, almost afraid to look. Right on top are the pictures of them and I immediately see red. A kiss outside her office, holding her hand in front of the restaurant, another kiss in his SUV. That one's hard to make out, but I see her hair fanning over her face and his hand gripping her head as they meet over the console. I want to wring his neck as soon as I get the chance. I've seen enough. The only thing not in here is what I'm desperate to know, and that's what happened after. If he touched what's mine, I'll not only wring his neck; I won't let go.

"What?" I bark, answering a call from Eli.

"Dude, how many times is it going to take? A simple hello or hey, bro, what's up, will do. Especially when you ask me a favor, and I'm calling to give you details." Great, he's in one of his lecturing moods.

"Good morning, cocksucker. Now give me the details, or I'll bring Lucy to take notes for you during the meeting." My secretary has the hots for Eli in a bad way. I probably should have taken care of it ages ago or moved her to another department, but it's hilarious to watch him squirm whenever she's around.

"Yeah, you would do that, wouldn't you? Seriously, you're a douchebag. You're lucky I love you, or I'd tell you to fuck off. But, since I do, I stopped by marketing on my way in and scheduled a team meeting for three. I told them we'd like something to present at the party and gave them enough time to prepare. You'll just have to wait a little longer, baby brother. And fair warning, she looks delectable today, so you may want to tame the beast before walking in."

"Why don't you keep your thoughts about how good she looks to yourself, or better yet, stop thinking about her at all. I have enough of her admirers to deal with already," I say in exasperation.

He picks up on it immediately. "Is her boss still giving her problems?" he asks, concerned.

"It sounds like it. There's also a potential stalker. Someone followed them on their date Monday, sat in the corner and watched them all night. It could've been her boss, but the picture was too grainy. No one was spotted on last night's date, so maybe it was a fluke, but I'm not leaving anything to chance."

"If Lily had a date last night, it wasn't with you. So that's number two with Jackson. I assume that's the reason for the foul mood you've been in, along with the change of heart?" Shit, leave it to Eli to pick up on that so quick.

"It's her last date with the prick, so it doesn't matter. Her time to decide is up," I state matter-of-factly.

"Does Lily know that?"

"She will soon. I'll see you at three," I say, ending the call before hearing any more lecturing from my older brother by eighteen way too long minutes that I will never hear the end of.

Damn it, he's right again. I need to get myself under control before this meeting. Arranging to see her this afternoon satisfies my selfish desire to lay eyes on her, but I'm hoping being in the same room as me will bring some of her desires to the surface. Her body naturally reacts to me, and there's no way she won't be affected. Conveniently, it's just in time for tomorrow night.

Lily

After arriving this morning, Eli came in to tell us we're presenting our proposal for the rebranding to him and Sebastian this afternoon. They want something for the party tomorrow. A little more heads-up would've been nice. He knows this is a big ask and instructed us to order lunch on the company card to give more time to prepare while we work through lunch.

This must mean they're through with me. Sebastian wasn't kidding when he said he was done with whatever we had. He probably doesn't even want to waste his time today, but he can't just send me away, so we're speeding things up instead. It makes sense. It's just a bitter pill to swallow and makes the crack in my heart open that much more. It's been a rough week. I feel like my brain didn't get the memo that we weren't a couple because I've been missing him and his texts way more than I thought possible. I know what I want now, but I wish I'd known before making such a colossal mistake. Now it's too late.

"Crazy that we're presenting today, huh?" Jordan and I are sitting next to each other in the conference room, putting the finishing touches on a few of the slides and checking for grammatical or formatting errors. The others are in the front of the room, running through the presentation one final time. Luckily, we had most of it done before Eli dropped the bomb this morning, but we all scrambled to get it put together.

"Yeah, hard to believe we're to this point already. I feel like I just got here, and now it's almost time for me to leave," I say wistfully.

"What do you mean 'leave'? Why would you do that?" He leans in closer. They must not have been informed about me being temporary. That's weird.

"I was brought over to help with the transition and give any insight into past performance with previous campaigns. Now that you all have a new campaign and are ready to move forward, there's no point having me. I'll return to my other office since my job here is done."

"What job is that?" I freeze as soon as I hear his deep voice. I see Jordan's eyes widen right before he turns back toward his computer, leaving me to fend for myself.

I slowly turn around and see Sebastian looking as handsome as ever. My insides quiver at the sight of him. I want to pull him aside and tell him the truth about my feelings, but it would be pointless, obviously, from how he glares at me. "Uh, I was just explaining to Jordan that now that we've reached this point in the campaign, my role here is done."

"Your role here is done when I say it is and not a minute sooner. Is that clear?"

"Crystal… sir," I answer with a little more sass than intended, but he doesn't need to be so harsh to me in front of everyone. I feel Jordan's knee nudge me under the table, probably trying to tell me not to poke the bear. It doesn't go unnoticed by Sebastian, who's looking down at our laps at how close we are. His eyes travel up to where our arms touch. We were comparing screens, asking questions about each slide. Jordan must register Sebastian's gaze and notice the venom in his eyes because he quickly moves his chair by at least a foot.

Eli arrives at that moment. "All right, I see I'm the last one here. Are we ready to begin?" Smiling, unaware of the tension he walked into, his cheery presence immediately lightens the mood.

That is until Sebastian takes the chair next to me. "Let's proceed. I have somewhere else I need to be," he says instantly upon sitting.

Eli looks at me apologetically. Oh, he has no idea. Just having Sebastian beside me is complete torture. Is he doing this on purpose, just to rub it in? God, what a jerk. I fared better than expected throughout the week not having to see him. But now, having him mere inches from me, breathing in his scent… it's excruciating.

I end up hyper-focused on the man sitting next to me and the regret I'm feeling rather than the presentation, which I've memorized by now, and only become aware that the meeting is over when I hear my name.

"What?" I ask absently.

"I said I'd like a word." Dang it, of course he would. "Follow me," he orders before stepping out of the room. I see Jordan out of the corner of my eye, scared for me by the looks of it. Then I see Eli with the slightest smirk, so slight that if you weren't clued into the situation, you'd have no idea. "Now!" barks Sebastian, obviously out of patience. Who am I kidding? He never had any to begin with.

Deciding not to anger him further, I hurry into the smaller conference room, where he closes the door behind me. I notice he leaves the blinds open, probably so everyone gets a good look at my humiliation from being yelled at for God knows what.

"What do you think you're doing, blatantly flirting with one of your coworkers in front of the entire staff?" he demands.

"What are you talking about?" I ask in shock.

"I saw you with Jordan. I saw how close you two were, practically on each other's laps. That behavior will not be tolerated in the workplace." He crosses his arms over his chest and stares at me in anger. Is he serious right now?

"We weren't flirting. We were leaning in to see each other's screens, reviewing the presentation again and looking for errors. There's nothing going on between Jordan and me. We're just friends." I can't believe I'm defending this nonsense right now.

"Since you seem blind to men's infatuation, I'll clue you in. Jordan would like to be more than friends, so watch yourself and maybe try to dress a little more conservatively in the office," he says authoritatively while his gaze moves up and down my body.

He did not. "You're not only a complete ass but seriously delusional. I'm done with this conversation and would like to go back to work now if you have nothing more important to say than comment on my wardrobe." There's no Jordan here to nudge me under the table, so digging myself deeper seems to be the road I'm taking.

"You'll be attending the party tomorrow night, correct?" I didn't see this coming. At this point, I don't even want to go, but Cici would be devastated, so I guess it may be a good time to probe if I'm even still welcome at the damn thing.

"I was planning on going, but only if the invitation is still applicable. My feelings won't be hurt if you'd like to rescind it." Absolute lie.

"Please enlighten me as to why I would contemplate retracting your invite?"

"Well, I probably won't be here much longer now that we've laid out the rebranding, and… I'm not your favorite person at the moment." Despite my effort to lock it down, I say that last part with sadness. It's useless telling him how I feel with his obvious aggression toward me. I don't need to hear his rejection to know it's there.

He looks at me for a moment with regret before it's gone too soon, making me question if I imagined it. "I will not repeat again what I've already said about you being done here. As for whether you're in my favor or not is of no significance. You are part of the staff and should go for no other reason than to support your team. And, Lily, you are not to attend the event with a coworker. Is that understood?"

"Yes, sir. Will there be anything else, Mr. Dubree?" All said with as much venom as I can muster because I want to murder him right now. He better let me go. The hurt from his callous words is squeezing my lungs in a vise. I'm this close to screaming my way out of here or bursting into tears. Either one won't be pretty.

"You're dismissed, Miss Thompson. Until tomorrow." He nods his head goodbye. I turn around as fast as possible and get out of there before he has time to change his mind.

"Are you okay?" Jordan asks in concern as I grab my computer from the table. He waited for me, probably worried about the scolding he imagined I received.

I try to compose myself before answering, taking a deep breath to calm my rapidly beating heart. "Definitely. He addressed the topic about me leaving the company. I guess I will be staying longer." I reveal the half-truth with way more enthusiasm than I feel.

"That's great. I'm glad we'll have more time together. To work, I mean. Well, and actually, do you have a plus-one to the party tomorrow, because if not, we could always go together?" You've got to be freaking kidding me right now.

What in the actual hell is going on with my life? Somehow, I must have developed a natural sign on my back that says, "Hot and ready to be bothered! This girl needs a boyfriend, so go ahead, make your move now!" Part of me is about to bust out laughing at the absurdity of this, especially right after the conversation with Sebastian. Still, the rational part of me doesn't, realizing that would hurt Jordan's feelings, so I respond in the nicest way possible instead.

"Sorry, Jordan, I'm seeing someone right now, but he already had plans tomorrow, so I'm bringing my best friend, Cici, with me." There, crisis avoided.

"Oh, great. Well, I didn't want to waste the opportunity. Hey, I'm glad you won't be going anywhere for a while. I like working with you." He smiles at me. "I'll see you tomorrow night then." He gets up and walks away.

And as I turn to do the same, I see Sebastian lurking in the shadows with a smirk that says, *I told you so.* The smug bastard.

Sebastian

I couldn't help myself; it was just too perfect to let her see me and rub it in that I was right. I literally couldn't have planned that better myself. The look Lily gives me is priceless as she leaves and well worth my sneaking around the corner listening while receiving odd looks from various employees.

Damn her for getting under my skin. Before I even entered the room, I saw her through the window in that tight-ass dress that hugged her cleavage, leaving no question to how delectable her tits are. Seeing her proximity to Jordan, my ire rose, frustrated it wasn't me who savored her presence but the man sitting next to her.

Now that I put an end to that issue, the only question I'm asking myself as I walk back to my office is who she was referring to that she was seeing already or was that just an excuse because I made it clear she couldn't attend with a coworker. I wish there was a way to prevent her from bringing Jackson. Every time I turn around, someone new tries to get her. How has she gone this long without a serious boyfriend? Could she really have been that busy or just goddamn oblivious to the attention?

I stop at Lucy's desk on the way into my office. "Is everything ready for tomorrow?"

"Yes sir, there should be no hiccups. I have everything under control. All you need to worry about is you and your companion for the evening," she says, fishing for information.

"Good. That's what I like to hear. I won't be having anyone accompany me. I don't need the distraction." Her shock is evident. I never attend an event without a woman on my arm.

"Oh? If it's a matter of finding someone suitable, I'd be happy to call some prospects."

"I'll be very distracted, and I have someone if I change my mind. Remember to begin the evening with only background music and continue to edge it up throughout the night. I may signal you at some point to increase the volume and get the party in full swing." This is all part of the plan I've been orchestrating.

"I'll be sure to give the DJ those instructions. Let me know if you think of anything else."

"Thank you, Lucy, see you tomorrow." I proceed to my office and shut the door.

Finally, behind closed doors, I take a deep breath to steady myself. Seeing Lily again reminded me how much I've longed to have her in my arms, hear her moans and feel her trembles. I keep reminding myself to look at the endgame and not give in to my desire to torture her all the way home this evening for her behavior this afternoon. I could see her reaction to me. I know she's as affected as I am. Giving her one more night to ruminate about it will work in my favor. Tomorrow is payday; I can wait. I have to.

I'm pouring my nightly glass of port when Eli barges in unannounced. Looking at my watch, I see it's just after five, which would explain. "Dude, could you be any more of an ass to that girl?"

"Would you like a glass?" I ask, instead of answering his question.

"Sure. So tell me how that behavior in there could possibly be part of your plan. Because if I were Lily, I'd take Jackson's hand and walk into the sunset if forced to choose between you two. I was there when you called her out in front of everyone, and I heard about your lovely entrance. I know you treat most people like a rock in your shoe, but I'm pretty sure that's not the way to win her over."

I hand him his glass, taking time to savor mine before I dignify his remark with an answer. "She brings out the beast in me, and I think she likes that part just as much as the other, so save me the lecture. As for today, I saw her with Jordan, and it flipped a switch. My intention was just to be near her, make her squirm and get a reaction. But seeing yet another guy try to move in on my territory? I may have acted less than amicable."

"You think? Just tell the girl you like her and get it over with already. I don't know why you even let her go in the first place." Does he not listen?

"There was no way I was getting involved with a girl who's hung up on someone else. I'm not breaking her in for another man to swoop in and have her. She needed to sort her shit out."

"Well, what if she sorted it and you're in the trash bin?"

"She won't have a choice after tomorrow. I'm making her mine. Don't you have something better to do than stand here lecturing me?"

Standing, he replies, "As a matter of fact, I do. I won't be around until tomorrow night, so I'll see you then. I hope you know what you're doing. You should try not to fuck it up anymore because I'd honestly like to see this work out for you," he says sincerely before setting his empty glass down and leaving. At least one of us is getting lucky these days.

22

YOU'RE MINE

Sebastian

THE PARTY IS GOING GREAT AND IN FULL SWING. EVERYONE SEEMS to be enjoying themselves and dancing to the music. I've made the rounds and talked to anyone important enough to have my attention. Although I haven't been able to keep my eyes off Lily, who looks sexier than should be allowed in her short-as-fuck skirt and silk blouse with one too many buttons undone.

I saw Brad standing too close to her, ogling the shit out of her chest, and even had the nerve to put his arm around her waist as he introduced her. It took everything in me not to go over there, break said arm and rip his eye sockets out. Luckily, Cici came to her rescue and dragged her away to the main area before I could make a spectacle of myself.

They've been near the DJ's station for a while now, just watching the room and talking. Eli has been suspiciously close to Lily all night, which is something I plan on addressing. And Jordan is lucky he found another piece of arm candy to occupy his attention, or I probably would have had to fire him next week.

We already made the presentation, which was well received, and ac-knowledged those who helped along the way. It didn't go unnoticed that

Brad wasn't paying attention to anything we said but focusing solely on Lily. It's time to have another talk with the guy—this time more direct.

I'm whispering something about the party into Lucy's ear, while keeping my eyes trained on Lily, studying her reaction. Standing across the room, her attention has been discreetly focused in my direction. She's still trying to fight against the draw she has to me. The jealousy in her eyes can be seen from here. I'm determined to prove it's me she burns for and not him. Tonight, I plan to enlighten her. It's time she stops denying it.

This last week was the longest in history pretending I was done with her. I'd hoped she'd come to her senses and realize she's been obsessing over the wrong guy. But apparently, it's going to take more than silent treatment.

From the corner of my eye, I notice Cici, who's standing next to her, whisper something in her ear, causing Lily's gaze to move toward the entry. I turn to look at what has their attention and seethe. It's him, Jackson Soloman, the object of her *misplaced* infatuation. I was relieved when Lily showed up with Cici tonight, so Eli must have invited him. I recognize his friend Braden walk in with him. Goddammit, Eli should know better. I will have words with my brother, especially if he did this purposefully, which I suspect is the case. But that can wait.

Seeing her priority shift and her focus turn to him solidifies my decision. It will have to be sooner rather than later that I prove to her who she really wants. I lean down, instructing Lucy to raise the volume as discussed. Then, without hesitation, I stalk with purpose in Lily's direction with a look of absolute determination. Heads turn my way as I pass, I'm sure noticing my aggressiveness. I reach Lily and stop directly before her, waiting for her eyes to meet mine.

Lily

While I stare at Jackson, shocked that he's here and wondering how this will all play out, a warm shadow moves in, blocking my view. I look up at Sebastian, standing mere inches away, his eyes boring into me. His body crowds my space, commanding attention. He was across the room, flirting with his secretary, a moment ago. How did he end up here? The proximity to him causes my body heat to rise. He raises his hand to my cheek not softly but demanding, sliding his thumb firmly across my bottom lip. "What are you doing?" I ask as the heat rises between my legs.

"Claiming what's mine," he states. I see his head tilt and immediately realize his intention.

My eyes go wide, and the room seems to hush as he moves in swiftly and sensually nips the same lip he just caressed. I gasp in shock, making my lips part. He uses the opportunity to absolutely invade my mouth, and in that moment, all propriety flies out the window. I'm lost in him as he grips my neck possessively and moves his arm around my waist, pulling me close, deepening the kiss with intention. God, I've missed him. And this—the feeling of need that seems to always take over when I'm in his arms. My fingers tangle in his hair, losing myself to desire. Pressing my body into him, I feel his rock-hard bulge against me, and wetness instantly coats my core.

"I'm going to have you begging for it," he whispers in my ear. "Can you feel how bad I want you, Lily?" Suddenly, I'm lifted onto his pelvis, my legs instinctively wrapping around his waist. If I thought I could feel him before… whoa, can I feel him now. The room blurs as I'm carried swiftly away in his strong embrace.

I should be embarrassed about what just happened. It should concern me that we just mauled each other in front of a roomful of people who watched me be carted off. And lastly, it should bother me that I just closed the door to Jackson in the worst way possible. But no, all that matters at this moment is the way I feel in Sebastian's arms as he whisks me upstairs and down a hallway. Anticipation of his next move is the only thing my mind is focused on.

I feel one arm leave my body briefly as a door opens and then shuts behind us. I'm suddenly up against a wall, still in Sebastian's arms, right where I want to be. It barely registers that he brought me to a bedroom, whether his or not, I'm unsure. The room is dark, with only dim light filtering in through the windows from a full moon. His mouth is possessive and brutal and hasn't let up at all, only now pausing to pull my shirt swiftly down my arms; I was obviously too distracted to notice him undoing my buttons. His mouth moves to my ear. "Did you think I didn't notice you eye fucking me from across the room?"

"I was not! And how would you? You were too busy flirting with your secretary," I protest and glare, breathing heavily. Then add, "I was looking at Jackson, not you."

He grabs my hair hard and pulls my head back to look up. "Repeat his name in my vicinity again and see what happens." I just continue glaring, not wanting to show that his aggression makes my body feel things I'm sure it shouldn't.

"Why are you doing this? You haven't talked to me in a week; you don't do relationships, remember?"

He scowls. "This week has been hell, and I'm done waiting around. You're mine. That's all that matters." He kisses down my neck, murmuring along the way, "I'm done with you pining over someone else when it's me you want." He moves back to my ear, licking, sucking and nipping, making me moan. "No more games, Lily. You won't remember his name after I get through with you."

I feel my bra unclasp right before he slides it off, baring my breasts while continuing to devour my neck. The sensation of his shirt rubbing against my exposed nipples is heavenly. He pulls back, and I see the look of absolute possessiveness as he penetrates my body with his eyes. While still holding me in his arms, his hands give each ass cheek a firm squeeze as he lifts me higher to bring his mouth to my hard nipple. My eyes close in ecstasy, and I drop my head back against the wall, making a guttural sound I didn't know was possible. I've craved this ever since he gave me a taste last week. I ache for something more. I'm consumed trying to absorb all my body's reactions when he swiftly turns, carrying me further into the room. I yelp as I'm tossed onto a bed. When I look up, it's to a devious grin on Sebastian's face.

He walks around to the other side of the bed, opposite where we entered from. Standing there, he unbuttons his dress shirt, taking it off, followed by the shirt underneath. A window behind him silhouettes his body, accentuating his powerful build. I am in pure and absolute lust. He takes his phone from his pants pocket, and a few seconds later, music plays, enough to drown out the sound of the party downstairs. He crawls over and lies on his side, body turned toward mine, braced on his elbow looking down at me. Silently, he roams over my body with his free hand, exploring, touching and grazing my skin like he's memorizing it. It feels incredible and leaves erotic shivers in its wake.

I notice his gaze flicker behind me right before he grabs my hair aggressively and wrenches my head toward him. "Are you done pretending you don't want me?" he asks seductively, and my core immediately clenches.

"What makes you think I want you?" I ask defiantly while trying to ignore that I just went up in flames from his aggression again. Something is holding me back from giving in to him too quickly. Resisting him seems to drive him wild. I think I like him that way.

His other hand swiftly reaches under my skirt, straight to my mound. I can't believe he just dove right in with no warning. But the relief from his touch, to have him where I've dreamt about all week, makes me moan in relief.

"Mmmm, that's what I thought. Your wetness is all the proof I need. You can't fool me, sweetheart. Your panties are soaked. You haven't let anyone touch this beautiful pussy other than me, have you?" he asks as his thumb softly rubs over my most sensitive spot, making my body jerk in reaction and another knowing smirk appear on his face.

My skin heats at his touch, his words and his stare, making me tremble. I shake my head, my rapid breathing making words impossible.

"That's good, baby, because this pussy is mine." His mouth slams down, his tongue searching for mine. He squeezes my core one last time before bringing his hand back up to knead my breast and pinch the nipple hard. I cry out and my body bucks.

"Does that feel good? I think you like it a little rough, huh?"

I whimper and moan uncontrollably and wonder what the heck is wrong with me? Why does my body react to this cruel torture? I'm torn between lust and disgust in myself as I try to process this onslaught of emotions. His lips leave mine and work their way down my jaw, moving on to explore my neck. I'm panting and desperate with want as he licks, sucks and bites while continuing to caress both my breasts and inflict nips of pain to my nipples.

His hand travels further down, grazing my stomach, until he reaches my skirt. I feel him push it down. "You ready for me to make you feel good?"

I'm lost to my traitorous body and drunk on his touch. Words fail me, and all I can manage to do is barely whimper a yes. I feel my skirt come off while he continues to ravish my neck, sucking and biting everywhere like he's marking me. Every nip of his teeth causes me to convulse in both pain and pleasure. My need is building to an unbearable level.

Sebastian

She responds so well. The sounds she makes to every touch, kiss and lick—and especially the ones that come out when I bite or pinch—make my cock pulse with need. I can't seem to get enough of her delicious body; the one thing repeating over and over in my mind is *mine*.

Seeing Jackson walk in after I laid down next to Lily didn't surprise or bother me. I don't know what he hoped to gain from following other than to stop this, but it doesn't matter; he's too damn late. I don't give a fuck about his feelings for her or what his intentions are, and there's no better way to prove that than to let him witness exactly who she wants. If he's pissed off at anyone, it should be at himself for waiting so long. For now, he may as well enjoy the show because this is the closest he'll ever get to Lily again. I'm more determined than ever to prove this innocent beauty belongs to me. I want to consume this body, these lips, her perfect fucking tits, but most of all, I am going to make her virgin pussy mine and mine alone.

As my hand travels further down, my head lowers to take her plump nipple in my mouth. I suck the whole thing in and flick my tongue over the tip repeatedly before biting it, making her head fall back as she moans. Her hand presses on my head, encouraging me to go harder.

I lift to look at her. "You're a needy little thing, aren't you? Am I the only one that's made you feel this good, baby?"

She nods her head aggressively with her eyes closed.

"My innocent Lily, you're wrecked for me. I've barely even begun."

I continue from one breast to the other, glancing at Jackson, who now occupies a chair in a darkened corner by the door, silently watching as I claim every part of her beautiful body. Knowing he's there intensifies the need to draw all the sounds I can from her and show him how she aches for my touch. It makes my dick that much harder anticipating her reaction to seeing him there. The reveal needs to be perfect, when she's so far gone in lust, it'll flood her senses, making this the best night of our lives. Hell, quite possibly his too.

With her skirt out of the way, my hand sneaks down again to cup her soft, wet mound. "Ah, my little vixen. Who knew you were such a filthy girl wearing this sexy strip of lace under your short skirt for anyone to glimpse?" She looks at me with longing.

I rub her clit with my thumb while putting pressure on her opening with my fingers, her panties providing the thinnest of barriers for now. Her body immediately bucks, her head goes back and her moans grow louder.

She mumbles my name. "Sebastian…," she pleads.

"That's right, baby, who makes you feel good?" I look up and smirk, seeing Jackson now with his hand on his crotch and a scowl on his face.

"Sebastian, please, I need more," she begs.

Music to my ears. "Be patient, baby girl. Greedy girls only come when I say. Is that what you want, huh? To come all over my fingers, or would you like to come while my tongue fucks your virgin pussy?"

"I don't know…" Her response is timid.

"You haven't had anyone's mouth down there, have you, baby?" I ask, still amazed by her lack of experience. She looks up shyly and shakes her head while biting her bottom lip. Fuck, she has no idea how sexy she is. I can't wait to show her how good I can make her feel with my tongue.

"Oh, baby, you're in for a treat tonight." I grab the delicate strings to her panties and slowly pull them down, moving my body with them. As soon as my face reaches her exquisite heat, I inhale. She smells divine. I pull her knees up and push them apart, sliding my hands down her inner thighs to her gorgeous center. I spread her lips and blow, making her squirm and pant aggressively.

"Sebastian…," she moans.

I grab under her ass, lifting slightly, and descend. She gasps in shock as I dive into her tight canal with my tongue. Her taste is fucking exquisite, and I can't get enough. My need to consume her overcomes me as I continue to suck, lick and fuck her with my tongue, shoving my mouth as hard as I can against her delectable pussy, eating her up. The sounds radiating from her make it so intense. My cock is pulsing so hard it hurts. I can feel the precum dripping from my shaft. God, this girl drives me wild, and knowing I'm the one to defile her makes me insane with desire. I want all of her.

Moving up to her sweet little nub, I suck on her clit while bringing my hand to her entrance, rimming her opening with the tip of my finger. She whimpers even more, begging for penetration. I slowly push my middle finger in. She's so fucking tight my dick is dying to be inside. It takes everything in me to go slow and get her ready for my cock, when all I want to do is plunge in. Not preparing her would make me an asshole, and I need to make this so damn good because this may be the first time I fuck her, but it certainly won't be the last.

"Oh God," she calls out, in equal parts pain and ecstasy once I add another finger. As I lick her clit and pump my fingers in and out, faster and harder, her pussy swallows them, and her cries grow louder. I feel her walls start to contract.

"That's it, baby, feel it. Squeeze my fingers just like that. I want your juices running down my chin. Come for me, now!" I command at the same time I add a third finger and suck her clit into my mouth.

She comes undone, screaming my name. Fucking beautiful. She was made for me. Her pussy clamps around my fingers like it's milking them, her muscles contracting, satisfying the craving I know she's had since last week. It's such a fucking gift that my tongue, hand, and fingers are the only ones to have felt her pleasure. Along with my dick, they'll also be the last. I'm wrecked for her.

After getting lost in her pussy and ensuring I lap up every drop of her pleasure, I glance over from between her legs at our voyeur. His eyes are glued to where my head meets her body with a seething, lustful look on his face and a death grip around his dick. All I can do not to taunt him, which would bring her attention to our guest, is to focus on my girl. My tongue grazes her sensitive clit one last time before I bring my body back up to hers.

Lily

The feelings just kept building and building. They became so intense, I started to panic that something was wrong. I was just about to stop him when his voice sounded, ordering my release, and it burst inside me, so much more intense than the others. It keeps getting better and better. My orgasm goes on forever, pulsing in tune with his fingers pumping in and out of me. The throbbing finally stops, and my breath calms, already missing the loss of his touch. But only for a second before he slides back up over me and demands I open my mouth.

He shoves two fingers in. Shock and confusion sweep over me. "Taste your pleasure, baby. Suck it off. All of it." Reluctantly, I do as he orders. While I suck, he grinds against me. And oh my God, once again, my body can't help but react, and I start moaning while sucking my juices from his fingers. How incredibly turned on I am by this insanely dirty act is frightening.

"That's right, suck them good, sweetheart, because the next thing you'll be sucking is my cock. You've never had a cock in that mouth of yours, have you?" he asks.

I shake my head, still shocked at what his filthy words do to my body. This is an entirely different side of him than last week. I'm embarrassed to say that I'm not sure which one I like better, but my body may have a preference by the way my eyes are closed in ecstasy while I'm sucking his fingers and meeting him thrust for thrust. My mind can't decide whether I want to push him away in humiliation or beg for more.

The decision is made for me when he takes his hand from my mouth. "I saved one for me." I can't believe he had three fingers inside me; I didn't even know that was possible. He wraps his lips around his third finger, sucking and licking as he slowly pulls it out before releasing it with a pop. "Best dessert ever," he states, looking at me lustfully. Holy hell, how did I end up catching the eye of an apparent sex god?

He pushes himself up to sit on me, and I can't help but ogle his chiseled chest and be in awe of his abs, which have four ripples on each side, if possible. My hands timidly make their way up and down, feeling his smooth skin and the hardness of his muscles. "I take it you like what you see?"

"Don't be cocky," I tease him even though he has every right to be. I may be naïve when it comes to the opposite sex, but I'm certainly not blind.

He chuckles. "Just stating the obvious, baby."

Our banter doesn't stop me from working my way down to the waistband of his jeans. Intrigue makes me want to see more since I've never seen one in real life. I've looked at porn just to see what they look like. Finding courage, I undo his belt, unbutton his jeans and start to lower his zipper, but he stops me before I get further by grabbing my hands in his.

"As much as I'd love to teach you how to handle my cock, it'll have to wait till next time. I need you, Lily. Now."

Stunned, my body stills, and panic sets in. The reality of what he said and what we're about to do hits me. The feelings of lust overtaking my body have made my mind go crazy. "Wait, no, we shouldn't do this," I say, pulling my hands out of his. My body begins to rise, but he doesn't let me.

Instead, he pulls his belt out from his pants, grabs both my wrists and somehow secures it

around them. He then laces his fingers in mine and pins them above my head as he lays his body back over me in a matter of seconds. Holy hotness, I cannot process what is happening with all the conflicting thoughts in my brain. "Not so fast, my little vixen. We *should* do this, and we *will*. You haven't had the main course yet."

An intense, dominant look appears as he lowers his head and kisses me passionately while grinding his pelvis into my heat. He knows my body wants this but needs my brain to catch up, and he's got my number because I'm meeting him thrust for thrust at this point. Right now, I want to be consumed by him and give in to the passion. I feel his pants come down while he continues to restrain me with one hand. With his legs between my own, he knees mine apart.

I feel his now unrestrained sex up against mine. "Sebastian…," I pant, finding myself willingly opening wider, ready and eager for what comes next.

23

NO GOING BACK

Sebastian

CAN'T WAIT ANY LONGER. MY DICK IS THROBBING, AND I NEED TO claim her. She panicked when I made my intentions clear, but only until I distracted her with my mouth again. It doesn't take much because deep down she wants this. Her innocence is invigorating, making all the easy women I've been pacifying myself with seem meager. Being with Lily and claiming all her firsts is like nothing I've experienced.

I rise up and look into her eyes. "Are you good now?" I ask while still holding her wrists above her head.

"Yes," she answers in a soft, breathless tone. It's all I need to hear in order to proceed.

I dip my head again and softly take her mouth while I fist my cock and tease it along her slit, coating it in her juices. There's no way I'm putting a barrier between us and since she's been so up in my head that I haven't been with anyone since my last test, we're in the clear. I've probably given myself carpal tunnel by now.

I break our kiss and rise to look at her while rubbing my cock up and down her pussy. "Baby, I'm tested regularly. Are you on birth control?"

Once again, she looks at me with her signature look of shock, making me stiffen more, if possible.

She nods.

"Good, because I need to feel you. Skin to skin, baby, only you, okay?" This will be a first for me too, but I can't imagine it any other way. This girl is all mine. I see the conflicting emotions on her face when she feels me pause at her entrance, but she nods nonetheless. Her fear produces purely animalistic thoughts in my mind. I'm glad I didn't allow her to get her eyes or hands on my dick earlier; then she'd really be scared. I'm not small. I feel her hips rise, begging for me to fill her while the awareness of what's about to happen sinks into her features.

"You like that, don't you, baby? The feel of my cock against your virgin hole. Think you can take it?" I push, giving the slightest pressure. I'm aching with need at this point. And she's mewling in response, nervous and wanting simultaneously.

"I know you can. You were made for me, sweetheart. Relax. Let me give you what you've been waiting for." I slowly start to penetrate, my eyes trained on hers. She tugs on her hands, squirming in reluctance and anticipation, and I can't help but reach my breaking point of patience. "Fuck, Lily, you feel so goddamn good."

"Ah," she grunts, feeling the bite of the initial intrusion. She feels like heaven.

"Do you feel your pussy sucking my cock in, wanting more? It's so slick for me." I push in a couple centimeters more. "God, woman, you are sooo... fucking... tight." I can see her tension, so I lean down to ravage her mouth and continue to push in and out with small movements, pulling her juices from her, spreading her tight channel by going further with each thrust. I'm lost in her until I realize I'm already halfway in and immediately stop. She whimpers in protest and tries to buck into me.

Choosing this moment, I grab her chin and force her head to the side, toward the dark corner I've been distracting her from. It's time for her to see our audience. I resume moving in and out at a slower pace, using all the willpower I can muster not to breach completely. Her eyes take seconds to focus, then immediately go wide, gasping as she identifies the shadow. He now sits with his legs resting leisurely apart, pants unbuttoned and pushed down enough to fist his dick, jerking off slowly.

"Jackson, what are you doing here?" she screeches as she tries unsuccessfully to wriggle free.

He smirks and stills his hand. "Enjoying the show of course. Don't stop on my account. It was just getting good," he says with humor.

She licks her lips, and I feel her squirm under me while her walls squeeze around my dick. It's an obvious sign she's turned on, whether she wants to be or not. I take this as my cue to pick up the pace again. Her eyes haven't left Jackson as he starts stroking himself while maintaining eye contact with Lily. I begin to move faster, still holding back from full penetration.

It's so fucking erotic seeing her watch him, eyes glued to where his hand moves up and down, gripping his cock tight and quickening his pace as he watches me fuck her. She's so turned on by the scene, breathing hard, making the sexiest cries of pleasure, while I'm soaking it all in. Never have I been this transfixed during sex. I've waited long enough. I want more.

The need to claim her and make sure she's mine is overpowering. I grab her jaw firmly and turn her focus back to me.

Lily

I never imagined I'd be losing my virginity with an audience, not to mention that audience being the guy I dreamed it would be with. But here I am having the most erotic experience I didn't even know existed, and I'm probably going to hell for it. Sebastian wrenches my face toward him, and I see the carnal look in his eyes. He's been thrusting in and out of me, working me into a frenzy, but I know he's holding back, and it's driving me crazy. I'm desperate to have him fill me completely. I look into his eyes, pleading with unspoken words. I want everything he has to give me.

"Are you ready, baby girl? It's time I make you mine. And, sweetheart, there's no going back." He withdraws gradually, leaving just the tip inside my entrance, then slowly pushes in again. Agonizingly slow.

It's killing me. I whimper from wanting more, needing more.

"What do you want, Lily?"

"Don't make me say it. Just do it. Please," I beg. Frustrated, I thrust up, trying to force him into me.

"You need to say it, Lily, so I know you want this."

I shake my head.

"Come on, baby, let me hear the words. I know you need it, sweet girl. Let me in. Let me claim you." His words stoke the fire even more. He continues his short thrusts in and out of me but quickens the pace, driving me wild, leaving that last little bit out of my reach.

Damn him. "Please, Sebastian, I need you so bad. I want it." I'm practically in tears.

"You want my cock deep inside your virgin pussy, huh? Are you sure?" He picks up speed even more.

"God, yes! Sebastian… please… now… I'm begging you, please just take me!" I am crying now. I'm so close to that amazing feeling again, spurred on by his dirty talk as much as everything else.

"Good girl. This may hurt a bit, sweetheart," Sebastian says gruffly, right before he forcefully plunges as deep as possible. "Mine!" he yells as he makes me his.

I cry out in pain, feeling like I was just ripped open. Oh my God, he still had a lot farther to go. My eyes squeeze shut, automatically shedding tears I didn't mean to have. His hand on my jaw squeezes as he growls quietly, "Eyes open. Look at me while I fuck you." I obey, immediately. He stares into my eyes for what seem like minutes, but I know only seconds pass before he leans down and kisses me tenderly.

"I'm going to move now," he whispers between kisses. I nod as I feel him slowly pull out. Just as I breathe a sigh of relief, he plunges in hard. I squeal loudly in surprise and see the fire in his eyes return as he hovers over me. There's barely a pause this time before he repeats the movement, and only a gasp releases with this one. He continues repeatedly, the deep guttural sounds emanating from him getting louder as he goes faster and more forcefully with each thrust. Before I know it, all pain disappears, replaced by a different sensation—one I'm now familiar with. I want more and I can't seem to get it. I pull on my wrists that he's still holding above my head.

"Please, I need…," I plead, not knowing what I'm asking for.

"I'll give you everything, Lily. Tell me what you want."

"You, Sebastian. I want you. Oh God, harder. Please, Sebastian, I need you to…," I cry. His strokes become faster and harder than I thought possible, banging the headboard into the wall. He brings my leg up to penetrate deeper still.

"Oh, you've got me, baby. Do you hear that, Jackson? I'm…" He thrusts hard. "What…" *Thrust.* "She…" *Thrust.* "Wants." *Thrust.* "Give it to me, Lily. Tell me you're mine. Now!"

And that's all it takes as I scream out his name and say the words while my muscles clench in the most intense moment of my life. Rather than let up, he seems to thrust harder, expanding with every push.

"You…" *Thrust.* "Are…" *Thrust.* "MINE." *Thrust.* He stops moving. "FUUUUCK!" he yells as he holds still deep inside me, and I feel him pulsing, filling me with his cum.

As soon as his body relaxes and our breathing slows, I hear the faint sound of a door closing. I can't believe I forgot he was here. I turn my head to confirm what I heard; sure enough, Jackson is gone. I close my eyes in shame.

"I think we just gave him the best night of his life, although I'm sure he would've rather been in my place." Sebastian chuckles, alerting me to the fact he's still inside me.

I turn my head back to him. He's looking down at me with contemplation. It makes me more nervous than I already am, wondering what he's thinking. What just happened? Did Jackson seriously just sit there and pleasure himself while watching me lose my virginity? Did Sebastian like it? Was I good enough for him? Is it always that intense?

"Penny for your thoughts?" he asks, still not moving.

"You're… still inside me," I point out as he smirks.

"You're cute." He kisses me on my nose. "And you better get used to it. It's my new favorite place to be." He stares into my eyes. "That was hands down the most amazing." *Kiss.* "Sexy." *Kiss.* "Hot." *Kiss.* "And satisfying sexual experience I've had. And Lily?" *Kiss.* "I've had a lot." Well, that answers that.

He kisses me deeply. I am lost to this man and his words.

"Uhhh, Sebastian." I pull away to look at him. "You're, um, getting bigger." I feel his shaft growing inside me.

He chuckles. "You're right. It's hard not to, pun intended." He winks at me. Ugh, he's so adorable. "Let me get something to clean you up with. I'll be right back. Don't move." He says the last part sternly before pulling out of me slowly and retreating toward a door I hadn't noticed before. All I can see is his back, and oh my is it delicious. He disappears through the door, and I see a light come on. Two minutes later he steps out, still completely naked, and I see everything as he walks toward me. Holy shit, he's not fully hard and it's big. I can't even imagine its size when it's ready for action. When he reaches the bed with a warm washcloth, he goes to push my legs open, which I quickly squeeze together.

"What are you doing?" I squeal. "I can do that myself!"

He grabs my legs firmly, pushing them apart. "Shh, I know you can, but I'm here to do it for you, so just relax." When he's finished, he tosses the cloth toward the bathroom, pulls the covers back and climbs in. "Now. Tell me what you're thinking," he commands.

I consider my answer before responding. He's patient, caressing my hair while waiting. "I'm not sure what just happened. I don't think I was supposed to lose my virginity while someone watched, let alone someone I have a relationship with."

He stills his hands, grips my chin and pulls my face toward him. "Lily, you don't have a relationship with anyone but the man lying next to you right now, and if you still have doubts about that, it's going to be a long night, sweetheart. As far as being watched, did you like it?"

"Yes. No. I don't know. I'm not supposed to like it. It feels wrong."

"Did you like everything else that happened?" His hand is roaming now, down my neck, my shoulder, my breasts. It's distracting, which is probably his goal, as always.

"Yes, and at the risk of inflating your ego, it was better than I imagined. It wasn't what I expected for my first time, but I loved everything about it."

"Then nothing was wrong about what we did. That only heightened your pleasure," he says while leisurely stroking my belly and around my hips.

"We'll have to agree to disagree on that point, but back to your comment about being in a relationship. What are you saying? I'm exclusively with you, but you're not in return. Wasn't that what you were trying to explain to me? I can't put myself in that position, Sebastian, even more so now that we've had sex. I need to protect myself."

"I already warned you, baby, there's no going back. You're mine now, whether you like it or not. I didn't say I wouldn't be exclusive, but I can't make a long-term commitment or promise romance. I don't do love, Lily. It's not in the cards for me. Right now, I want to spend time with you. You've captivated me, but I can't be your happily ever after."

I turn my body more to face him. "So you won't screw around while you and I are screwing around, but that's all this will be until you're done with me?"

He's visibly frustrated now. Not what I wanted after what we just did, but it can't be avoided forever. He sighs loudly, turns on his back and runs his hands through his hair. I instantly miss his touch.

"Damn it, Lily, I can't give you the answers you're looking for right now. Can we not just enjoy the moment and take it one day at a time?"

"Well, there's a party going on downstairs, and there's no way I'm showing my face in front of those people after being hauled away, so for now, I guess you're stuck with me. Or feel free to go back to your party." I flop onto my back in frustration and put my arm over my head, exasperated.

Sebastian

Her petulance is adorable. Every new side of her fascinates me. I turn toward her and stare down, taking her in. I know she's too vulnerable for me, which makes me a dick for taking her and an even bigger one for keeping her, but damn it, I can't seem to make myself walk away. It's not an option. I'm addicted. The problem is, I don't know how long this feeling will last. It's all new to me. I've never been with a woman for anything other than sex. One thing's for sure, she bumped into the wrong guy that night at the club. Then, meeting at her office again was a cruel twist of fate. Her future was sealed that day. She just didn't know it yet.

I can't refrain from touching her, so I don't as I pull her arm from her face and push her hair back. "You know, I kind of like you pouting. Maybe you should do it more often instead of fighting with me. I'd much rather kiss away your frustration than spank it out of you." I feel her body react to my words.

"Or maybe you like when I spank the insolence out of you,

hmmm?" She moans as I kiss her, confirming I'm spot on. I swear she was meant for me.

"Now tell me, why would I ever want to go back downstairs when my favorite form of entertainment is right here?" I say as I nuzzle her neck.

She pulls away. "Because you can't just abandon your own party. It's rude. They all know what's happening thanks to that show you put on down there, and now they're all probably wondering when you'll finish up and get back to the party."

"I thought you knew this already, but I don't give two shits what anyone thinks about me. Besides, that show was intentional, now everyone in that room knows who you belong to. And, Lily, I'm not even close to finished. In fact, should we continue your training? You seemed pretty interested in getting your hands down my pants earlier, and it just so happens I'm not wearing any…." I pull her flush against me and roll us so she's lying on top of me.

Immediately my dick is thick and ready. Even though I'm looking forward to fucking her mouth, I don't think I can wait for anything other than getting inside her again. My hands grab her face, holding her mouth to mine. I lose all control once again as I devour her, wrapping my hand around the back of her head, holding her tight as I draw the whimpers from her mouth. She's already grinding on me. It would be easy to slip right in.

"How are you feeling, baby? Are you sore?" Reluctantly, I break the kiss to ask before making the decision for her.

"Not sore enough, apparently. You drive me crazy. I want more." Her lips connect with mine.

"Shit, woman, I've unleashed a lion. Who knew what my prude little mouse would turn into." I kiss her into oblivion again. "Now sit up and ride me." Damn. She's gorgeous, her hair falling over her shoulders, tits on display and her perfect pink pussy ready for more. I grab her ass and give it a lift, encouraging her to rise up on her knees as I grab my cock and position it. I can feel how wet she is; she'll have no problem taking me in.

"C'mon, baby, drop down and take it. You're in control now. Go as fast or slow as you want." I rub her clit as she tentatively eases down and watch as she tips her head back, opening her mouth in ecstasy. She wants this. I see all hesitation disappear and pleasure take over.

"Oh wow, that's a lot," she says when her body is fully seated. "Give me a minute." She bites her lip.

"Take all the time you need, sweetheart, I'm enjoying the view," I say as I grab her breasts and rub my thumbs over each nipple. I feel her body tense while the sensations from my touch make her walls clench around my cock. Feeling a slight movement from her hips tells me she's ready to go, thank God.

"What do I do?" Her shyness is humbling. I don't deserve her innocence, that's for sure.

"Anything you want, sweetheart. You can move your hips front to back, lift yourself up and down—whatever feels good. Don't be afraid. You won't break me. Just move and see what you like." I thumb her clit some more, and she moans, thrusting her hips forward. Fuck that feels amazing. Her eyes glaze over, and she grinds on me, forward and backward, panting and creaming around my cock until I lose all reason and need to take control.

Grabbing her neck, I pull her down, taking her mouth savagely as I squeeze her ass and pump myself into her from below. My thrusts are hard and fast, and within a minute, we're both coming. She screams her orgasm into my neck as I release my seed into her for the second time tonight. I feel like a goddamn teenager.

"Wow, just wow," she says, making me chuckle at her reaction. She's lying limp on top of me.

"For not wanting to inflate my ego, you sure are doing wonders. But to be fair, I'd say you're pretty wow yourself." I kiss the top of her head.

After we lie in silence for a few minutes, she props herself onto her elbows and looks at me, concerned. "Is it normal to just stay like this after... you know... you're done? I thought people got up and did their thing or at least disentangled themselves. And um, I'm pretty sure there's a rule that I'm... supposed to go to the bathroom?"

I can't help smiling at her timidness, tucking her hair behind her ears as I respond. "I normally get up and leave right after, but like I said, I like it here." I give her a little thrust, making her giggle, adding to my list of favorite sounds. Right under her moans of course. "Although you're right. I should probably let you up at some point. Or we could always go for the record of filling you with the most cum in one night?"

She slaps my chest. "Eww, you're terrible! That is not a thing."

"It is. Google it. Although I think for your first night of sex, that might wreck you, so we'll have to try it some other time." This earns me an eye roll right before I flip us over. I pull out slowly to prevent my dick from getting the wrong impression and going hard again. Shit. Seeing her tense as I do shows me that she's more sore than she let on.

"Hey, let's get you cleaned up and relaxed. Come on," I say, standing up and reaching for her hand, "let's go soothe your pussy in a hot bath so I can use it again tomorrow." I love riling her up.

"You're so disgusting. How did I end up giving in to you?"

I nuzzle her in my arms as she stands. "Baby, you never had a choice. But if it makes you feel better, I'll let you keep thinking you did."

After a long soak in my never before used gigantic bathtub fit for an orgy, I tuck her into my side under the covers. Within seconds, her breathing deepens, and I feel her body relax into slumber. Holding her tight and listening to her breathe, I get lost in my thoughts.

It dawns on me that this is the only time I've had a woman in my bed. I've always gone elsewhere to satisfy my needs. It makes for an easy and fast exit on my terms, not allowing them the opportunity to plead for more. The significance of her lying in my arms isn't lost on me. I refuse to give it more acknowledgment other than the simple explanation that she needs more than I'm used to giving. I don't take lightly that I took her virginity. Just because she wasn't saving herself for marriage didn't make it any less of a big decision. Someone had to be her first; I'm honored it was me.

Now the question is, what am I going to do moving forward? I've been honest with her from the start about what this is and what it isn't. I won't end up in love and oblivious to everything else around me. There's too much responsibility with my company, and Eli has already commented on my absence and distraction. I refuse to abandon my brother like our dad did. It won't happen. Spending time with Lily is one thing, but I won't overhaul my life.

What I will do and look forward to is teaching her everything about her sexuality and opening her up to my world. Now that I've experienced her hunger for passion, the possibilities are endless. She could be the perfect companion. Someone to satisfy all my needs without expectations for more. Since she came into this with her eyes wide open, I won't have to worry about giving her the wrong impression. Hell, she's already in my bed; it can't get any more convoluted than that. I may as well have some fun for a while. And on that final contented thought, slumber finally takes hold.

24

NO REGRETS

A S I START TO WAKE, IT REGISTERS IMMEDIATELY THAT I'M roasting. What the…? *OH MY GOD!* My eyes are still closed as awareness sets in and I feel Sebastian flush against me, hence the reason for my overheating. I hear deep breathing, indicating he's still sleeping. Then, everything rushes back from the night before, jolting my eyes open. The daylight peeks in the window, telling me it's early dawn. I slowly ease away and turn around to take him in.

He's gorgeous. I cannot fathom how this sexy god of a man and master in the bedroom ended up going for someone like me, which leads me right back to where I started and wondering if this was all just a play to get my V-card. Although I suppose it's a little late to worry about that. What's done is done. And oh my was it done well. Remembering the unbelievable orgasms he gave me has my body heating up again. So, do I really care if he *was* just going for that? Deep down, I know I do, but I'm not letting myself go there. I have to keep a level head and remember this isn't anything more than two consenting adults finding pleasure. I can do this. At least, that's what I'm telling myself anyway.

I take stock of my surroundings. Looking around at what I assume is his bedroom, I'm taken back to last night, and my eyes land on the chair Jackson was in. I cringe in mortification. How will I ever face him again, and what the hell do I say? "Oh hey, hope it was as good for you as it was for me." Yeah, so not happening. The bigger question is, why didn't I stop it? I could've told him to leave, but admitting the truth, even to myself, feels humiliating. Sebastian was right, it did turn me on… a lot. Seconds after the shock wore off, I was glued to what he was doing. Rubbing himself while watching us was hot as hell to say the least.

Coming back from my thoughts, I focus on the room. It's immaculate. Well, minus our clothes that are strewn about. It's decorated with modern furniture in gray and ivory with black accents. The artwork adorning the walls are black-and-white photos of various scenes around San Diego. I notice the door to the bathroom and remember the end of the night. How he cared for me sure seemed like he was in this for more than one night. And he did say he planned on having more of me. However, nothing more was said or discussed before I passed out the minute he snuggled me into bed.

Careful not to wake him, I crawl out. I need a few moments before I can face Sebastian this morning. I tiptoe to the bathroom over the softest carpet ever and quietly close the door, not making a sound. A heavy sigh of relief comes out. I'm scared to look in the mirror, but I do. Oh hell, I'm a wreck. All my makeup from last night is shadowed around my eyes, and my hair is a mess. After relieving myself, I grab some tissues, then search for a brush. *Bingo!* It takes a while, but I manage to tame my hair into something tolerable.

Finding the toothpaste next, I dab some on my finger and use it to brush my teeth, at least to remove the film from sleeping. After rinsing, I glance into the mirror and smile. Do I look different? I can't believe I had sex. I might not look different, but I feel different. Speaking of, I'm a little sore. My inner thighs feel like they had quite the workout, and the sting between my legs is slightly unpleasant. I suppose it's a small price to pay for last night's pleasure.

I go to walk out and pause with my hand on the doorknob. I'm naked. Should I wrap a towel around me? It was dark in the room last night. What if he's awake and I have to walk across the room naked in front of him? *Ugh.* Maybe I'll just open the door and peek. Slowly, I turn the handle and pull the door open an inch, then realize I have to open it completely to see the bed from here. *Shoot.* Taking a deep breath, I open the door.

"Aaaah!" I scream. Sebastian stands in the doorway grinning at me—stark naked.

"Oh my God, don't do that! You scared the crap out of me."

"That's your fault for trying to be sneaky. What have you been doing in there?" he asks as he peruses me up and down. So much for modesty.

"I was freshening up so I wouldn't scare you. How long have you been up?" I ask him.

He smirks. "Since before I cracked my eyes open. Would you like to lend a hand?" He grabs his rock-hard self and strokes it slowly, making me gape.

He's huge. And crap if I'm not already turned on and ready for more. Damn it, I need separation. He's too much for me to handle. I need time to process without ending up under or over him again. Raising my eyes to his, I stammer, "Ummm, I think I should go."

I try to step around him, and he stops me with his hands on my shoulders. "Whoa, whoa, whoa, hang on there, mouse. What's going on?"

"Nothing. I just, I have to get home and… finish some homework and prepare for the week. Do laundry, clean. You know… stuff." I'm panicking now. I don't know how I'm supposed to act or what's supposed to happen next, but I do know I'm standing here naked, overwhelmed and confused. If I don't leave now, I'll be trapped in his web and eaten alive. God, where is this coming from? I'm freaking out; I need to go.

He looks at me with concern, contemplating. Moments later, his features harden. He releases me, straightening his posture.

"All right, let me get you some clothes, and I'll have my driver bring you home." Grabbing a few things from his drawers, he places a pair of shorts and a black shirt on the bed before dressing in joggers and a T-shirt and walking out without another word.

Finding my panties near the bed, I put those on before getting dressed. I can't resist bringing the shirt to my nose, breathing in. It's so Sebastian. Whether his detergent, his home or a combination of everything, it's distinctly his. Rounding up the rest of my things, I approach the door when he knocks softly, pushing it open.

"Blake is downstairs with the car. Are you ready to go?" he asks gruffly.

"Yep, sure am." He stares down to my bare feet, his eyebrows raised. "I think I'll carry my heels and go barefoot. I can always call Cici and have her meet me at the car with a pair of flip-flops for my walk of shame." I go for sarcasm, given the mood in the room. I'm winging it since this is all new to me. He shakes his head and ushers me out.

I follow him downstairs to an army of staff cleaning up after last night's party. *Speaking of a walk of shame.* I catch a few glances and cringe. Sebastian places his hand on my back and guides me out the door to the elevator. We don't speak on the way down, the tension building. The doors open directly into a parking garage where the car is waiting. Sebastian opens the door for me to get in, but I pause.

"Sebastian, I… I'm sorry. I'm confused. Thank you for last night, for being sweet, and the bath. And thank you for letting me stay. I… I'll see you tomorrow?" I pull his head down and stand on my tiptoes to kiss his cheek before quickly getting in the car.

Sebastian

"So, how was the rest of the party last night?" I ask Eli as I line up my target, finally bringing it up. We decided to go to the ranch and shoot our 22s today since the weather was nice. We've been shooting since we were old enough to pull the trigger. Dad was an avid marksman and took pride in teaching us. We discovered he kept every trophy we brought home when we went through the house before selling it. It's refreshing to be out here, distracting me from my thoughts, and away from my condo while it's put back together.

"Interesting, I can tell you that," he answers before firing off a few rounds.

"How so?" I ask, taking my next round of shots.

"Well, you made quite the scene for one thing. There were plenty of chins on the ground as you walked away with Lily wrapped around you. The look on her boss's face was priceless. Then there's the fact that Jackson disappeared shortly after, and when he returned a while later, something was off. You wouldn't know anything about that, would you?" I know he's been dying to get all the details, but for some reason, he refrained from bringing it up, leaving the decision to talk about it in my hands. I'm sure the wait was killing him.

"I got my point across to everyone in the room that Lily is off-limits, don't you think? As for her boss, that asshole can fuck off. And I don't give two shits about Jackson or anyone else there." I decide not to tell him about our voyeur yet. I'm not sure I'm ready for a lecture since he's been big on that lately. It sure would help to get his take on everything else, though.

"Come on, Seb, spill it. You're in a mood. I figured you'd get her out of your system once you finally popped her cherry, but there's obviously more going on. Or am I wrong in assuming you stole her virtue last night?" He's busy sighting his target or he would've seen the fury in my eyes at his crass words. Things I would have said myself only a few weeks ago, but now… it's unacceptable.

Struggling to remain calm, I take a deep breath before speaking. "Eli, I'm only going to say this once, and I never want to have to repeat myself. Don't talk about Lily or what I do with her disrespectfully. I won't tolerate it, is that clear?"

He turns toward me and steps back with his hands up in surrender. "Dude, yeah, I hear you loud and clear. Sorry, man, I'm not used to things being on the up-and-up with you, you know? It may take a while to adapt. Now tell me what the fuck is going on to make you look like you're ready to shoot your brother."

"I didn't steal her virtue, she gave it to me willingly. She was begging for it by the time I sank into her. It was easily the best fuck I've ever had, and you know that's saying a lot." Thinking about it has me growing hard already.

"So what's the catch? Let me guess, she didn't take too kindly to you sending her on her way after." He smirks.

"I did not send her on her way, asshole. She stayed the night." I ignore the shock on his face and keep going. "This morning, she came out of the bathroom after 'freshening up,' looked down at my cock like she wanted to eat it, giving me hope she was ready for round three. The very next breath, she tells me she needs to go—her list of reasons total bullshit. I stood there for all of five seconds, ready to talk her into staying, but then came to my senses and let her leave. Fuck if I'm going to beg a woman to stick around. She's lucky I even let her stay."

One minute I'm ready to teach her how to suck my cock, and the next, she's walking out the door. I'm beyond pissed at myself for the thoughts that ran through my mind when I initially stopped her. I almost begged her to stay. What the fuck is wrong with me? Her leaving is exactly what should've happened. So why do I feel like shit?

He sets his gun down and turns to face me, leaning against the table, crossing his arms over his chest, his full attention on me. "Dude, you are a walking contradiction. You bite my head off for disrespecting her, then turn around and do it yourself. You better figure your shit out and decide what you're doing."

What the fuck am I doing? I run my hand through my hair and let out a frustrated growl. "Fuck, I don't know. She's got me all wrapped up in my head. I've been candid about this not being permanent. I told her I expected exclusivity and guaranteed the same while sleeping together. I clearly don't do relationships, but I want to spend more time with her, and I've told her as much."

"And by spending time with her, you mean fucking?"

"Eli," I growl in warning.

"Hey, I'm just trying to get to the bottom of this. You want me to say 'making love' instead? You just told me no feelings are involved, although that's not what it sounds like, bro. Sounds to me like you have a shit ton of feelings about this, so what are you going to do about it?"

"You seem pretty good at dishing out advice lately, so you tell me. Do I give her space and pretend not to give a shit, or do I get her back in my bed pronto?"

"Again, such a double standard. I'm gonna go with option C. Ask her out on a date again. You know, those things you do when you have sex with the same woman more than once? Oh wait, that's right—you've never done that. Seriously, Sebastian, put some effort in. As crude as I sounded earlier, I know she's special, and I don't want to see either of you broken if this ends badly. It may be too late for Lily, which could be why she retreated this morning. Maybe she's trying to keep her distance. You're heading into uncharted territory, man. Tread lightly and be open to feeling something other than lust, yeah?"

Me: Did you finish everything today?

Lily: Pretty much.

Me: You sure left in a hurry this morning. I was hoping to continue your training.

Lily: I could see that. It's just that I'm trying to stay on page with the whole no relationship thing, and to do that, I needed some distance. It's difficult to shut my feelings off.

Me: Do you regret choosing me and not someone who could give you more?

I refuse to say his name. Asking this question kills me, but she may be more forthcoming through text. And I need to know, whether I like the answer or not. Although I'm not sure it would change my actions going forward. I crave more time with her, and if I have to fight for it, so be it. Seeing her dots on the screen appear and disappear is driving me mad.

Me: The truth, Lily, don't sugarcoat it.

Lily: I don't regret last night. What I regret is allowing myself to have last night. You scare me. Not in a violent way, but in a way that can break me. I like the way you make me feel, the passion you ignite. I even like the things I shouldn't, like your dominance. Then, the snippets of your true self I sometimes see make me want more, and that's what scares me. I can't afford to fall for you more than I may already have. You need to know this now, so if I have to push you away when it's too much, you'll understand.

Me: Go out with me tomorrow night.

Lily: Really? You went straight to asking me out after all that? You're certifiable. I'll think about it.

Me: You'll think about it? I must not have been as good as I thought.

Lily: Eye roll. At least I know what you meant by "go out." Good night, Sebastian.

Me: Good night and sweet dreams, baby. Oh and, Lily, don't touch yourself until I say you can.

Lily: Eye roll again. I already told you I don't do that. Maybe you should refrain as well.

Me: Eye roll me in person tomorrow and see what happens. And, baby, my hand is the only thing that keeps me from showing up at your place every night.

Lily: Eye roll....

25

DOMESTICATING

Lily

'M IN THE KITCHEN MONDAY MORNING WHEN I HEAR THE FRONT door open and turn to see Cici walking in, looking less than put together. She texted that she wouldn't be home again last night, but that's about it. My barefoot walk into the building yesterday was less than ideal, but I can at least thank my lucky stars for not running into Jackson on the way in, nor before or after my run. God finally answered a prayer.

"Good morning, sunshine. I take it you had a good rest of your weekend?" I ask as I pour her a cup of coffee and hand it over.

"Ridiculously good. And I assume from your text Saturday night that you had an equally amazing time?" she asks, eyebrows raised. Not having her here to talk to yesterday killed me. The run didn't help calm me down, and all I did was ruminate the entire day, getting nowhere other than feeling like a lunatic.

"Yes and no. But before I get into it, even though there's a lot to catch you up on, I have to get ready for school."

She pouts in response. "Dinner tonight and we can catch up? There's no way I can wait longer than that for a play-by-play. The fact that you landed such a hottie is delicious, and you better spill everything."

I'm supposed to tell Sebastian if I'll go out with him tonight. After briefly contemplating, I respond enthusiastically. "You know what, yeah, let's do it!" Maybe it's meant to be. Two can play the waiting game.

"Awesome. I'll be home around six. I'm working all day for the parents, which sucks, considering I worked yesterday afternoon. Think I can turn them in for violating child labor laws?" She may actually be serious.

Laughing, I answer, "Maybe if you were a child. At this point, I think you would just be cutting yourself out of your trust. How about I make an amazing dinner? I'll surprise you with something. Grab the wine on your way home; we'll need it."

"Sounds perfect! I can't wait."

"Yay! I haven't cooked for us in so long, and honestly, I really need some girl talk. Be ready with some shock absorbers in place and a hell of a lot of advice." I leave her on that note and head to my room.

I've had butterflies all morning in anticipation of seeing Sebastian this afternoon. I picked a short, flared skirt for today… just in case. God, I feel like a completely different person than last week. Thoughts like that never would've entered my mind, and now it's all I think about. Is it normal, or am I crazy? One of the many questions I need answered. And Cici's the perfect woman for the job since she's been around the block a few times. I made the right decision to have girls' night instead of date night. I need to get my head straight and safeguard myself. It's time to take the upper hand.

Leaving for school, I consider how lucky it is I've not run into Jackson yet. I was seeing him constantly for a while, but now he's disappeared. It's a good thing for now because I'm still nervous about what to say. I hope it's not awkward for the rest of our lives, especially since I'm his sister's best friend and we see each other on multiple occasions. So, as reluctant as I am to have a conversation, I know it's inevitable. I wonder if I should just bite the bullet and reach out to him.

I'm pondering this as I sit next to Kevin in Professor Milton's class. "Happy Monday! How was your weekend?" Oh boy, not even going near this with Kevin.

"Pretty good. I finally had time for a longer run yesterday. How was yours?" I'm getting good at this deflection thing.

"No complaints here. The surf was great this weekend. The weather's been epic. So, are you getting nervous for the gala this Friday? Going up in front of all those bigwigs to accept your award? No better way to get noticed than that, huh?" He bumps my shoulder with his.

"Wow, Kevin, thanks. I wasn't nervous, just excited, but when you put it that way..."

"I'm just messing. You'll rock it up there. Do you have to give a speech or just be handed the award and take a picture?"

Shit, why didn't I think of that? What if I have to speak? I wouldn't say public speaking is one of my strong suits. "I guess I better stop and talk to Professor Milton after class to find out. I'm glad you asked. That would've been terrible if I had to say something without being prepared."

"That's what I'm here for, babe. Hey, do you want to grab a drink before? To loosen up, you know?" Well, I guess I won't be avoiding it.

"That probably isn't a good idea. I'm seeing Sebastian exclusively now. Sorry, Kevin, I wasn't keeping it from you. It just became official over the weekend and I don't think he'd be okay with a pre-drink. I haven't told him about Friday yet." I cringe at the thought.

"Oh, I see how it is. You were holding out on me when I asked about your weekend. Well, I'm happy for you. If he hurts you in any way, though, I'll make him wish he were dead." That came out in a way I've never heard from Kevin before: disturbing.

"Thanks for that, but I'll be fine."

Kevin leans over as the professor starts his lecture. "Hey, let's grab coffee after you talk to Professor Milton. I'll buy." He winks and doesn't wait for an answer before turning his attention to the front.

Sebastian

Monday morning presents a handful of fires to put out from the weekend. I'm still knee-deep in shit by the time Blake sends a text to see if I'll be joining for Lily's transport this afternoon. I intended to. However, luck is not in my favor today. Unfortunately, I doubt I'll have time to see the lovely Miss Thompson before the end of the day.

"Where are we on the Ryker transaction?" I bark into the phone.

Eli sits on the other side of my desk while my phone is on speaker with the head of legal.

"No further than when you asked on Friday, sir. I'm pushing as hard as possible but can only do so much before receiving backlash. I'm on it, though."

"Not good enough. If I need to call myself, I will. I won't be ignored, Phil, which means if you're being ignored, I'm being ignored. Take care of it, or I'll find someone who can," I snap into the phone and end the call.

Eli raises his eyebrows. "You do know Phil is the longest and most respected member of our legal team, which means replacing him would be damn near impossible. I'd be careful who you choose to take your frustration out on, Seb. He's probably not the guy to piss all over. So… it's been one heck of a Monday, huh?"

"That's putting it mildly. I don't remember the last time we had this many issues in one day, and we still have hours to go. Fuck, this is certainly not what I planned on doing over my lunch hour. I can tell you that." I run a hand through my hair in frustration. I probably look like I just crawled out of bed with as many times as I've repeated the motion.

"Oh, I'm sure it's not what you planned on 'doing.' Isn't it Lily's afternoon in the office? Have you talked to her since she ran out on you?"

"Shit, don't remind me. I ended up texting her last night and took your advice again. Told her I wanted to take her out tonight. She hasn't given me an answer yet, though. Said she'd think about it, but I've been so busy I haven't had the chance to talk with her."

"Wow, this must be the only woman A, that you've asked out twice, and B, hasn't tripped over herself accepting. I think you've met your match, brother. Although maybe you're not as good in the sack as you think if she had to think about it." I want to wipe the smirk off his face with my fist.

"The three orgasms I gave her say otherwise. Seriously though, how did I end up chasing the most frustrating woman alive?"

"I'd say you were a goner from the minute she turned you down. You're not one to pass up a challenge. And have you ever actually been denied by a woman? I'm going to go with no. She's become your new favorite pastime, and I'll admit that it's prime entertainment seeing her rile you up." Eli is laughing as he makes his way to the door, enjoying this way too much.

"Shouldn't you be focusing more on your own exploits than mine? It's a sad day when you're so bored with your sex life that you invade your brother's," I call out as he starts to exit.

"Oh, don't worry about me. If you weren't so wrapped up with that feisty obsession of yours, you'd know I'm the farthest thing from bored. Later, bro." Turning around to wink at me, he shuts the door without further explanation.

Damn it, that's precisely the reason I can't let her get any more under my skin than she already has. He just called me out on being too preoccupied with a woman to care what he's been up to. We usually talk about our conquests and compare notes, yet here I am, so consumed with Lily that I haven't bothered to ask Eli what he's been doing, or rather who. This is a perfect example of why I refuse to be trapped by love. It makes you oblivious to everything around you, especially those who matter. As long as I keep reminding myself that, there's no reason I can't enjoy the sexual side of things. With that in mind and a break between meetings, I decide to check in with Miss Feisty herself.

Me:My Monday's been quite the struggle. Would you like to relieve some of my stress?

Lily:We're neck-deep in getting the new branding ready to roll out. Sorry.

Me: Not the answer I was looking for. Are you going out with me tonight?

Lily:I promised Cici a girls' night, so no. I'll make it up to you on the way home.

Me:Damn right you will.

Lily

"I have a favor to ask," I tell Sebastian as he gets in the car behind me.

"Anything, sweetheart," he says, grabbing my hand and kissing it. How do two words completely undo me? I'm ready to hop over the seat and ride him, and I can tell by the look in his eyes he'd be more than okay with that.

"I'm cooking dinner tonight and I need some groceries. I was hoping Blake could stop at the store on the way to my building." Feeling guilty, I quickly add, "You could always have him drop you off at your place, so you don't have to go with me." I'm pretty sure Sebastian doesn't shop for his groceries.

"Lily, did you forget that I live right by the office? I walk to work. I only go on these drives to spend time with you. If you need groceries, I'll go with you." I'm melting.

He pushes the intercom button. "Stop at any grocery store near Lily's place before bringing her home. And feel free to take the longer route," he tells Blake.

I blush at his words. "Thank you. I appreciate it."

"Now get your sexy ass over here and ride me. You damn near killed me with this easy-access skirt. You're wearing it to the office again soon since I didn't get to bend you over my desk and fuck you senseless. Had I the time, that would've happened today." I'm in his lap and straddling him before he even finishes talking.

This man can take me from zero to sixty with one sentence, one kiss—hell, one look is probably enough. I feel his shaft at my center, and when I roll my hips back just right, it presses onto my clit perfectly. I remember the last time I came like this. I moan into his mouth. Thanks to today's wardrobe choice, he's squeezing my bare ass while devouring me and matching my hip movement with his thrusts. He drives me mad.

"Please, Sebastian," I plead.

"Please what, Lily? Please touch you? Please taste you? Please fuck you? Tell me what you're asking for, sweetheart." He keeps talking in between kisses and licks to my throat.

"Please fuck me, Sebastian. I want you so bad." I feel him start to undo his pants.

"On one condition," he says sternly.

"Ugh, you and your conditions," I say, frustrated as I lay my head on his shoulder. Instinctively, I start to lick and kiss his neck. Wow, that feels good. I want to keep tasting him. I see why he does this. It's not just for my pleasure; I get it now. I hear him moan, which makes me feral.

"Fuck, Lily, you're amazing. My dick is going to revolt if I don't get it inside you soon. I want you to touch yourself. That's my condition, baby. Touch your pussy and feel how wet you are for me." Both his hands move down suddenly, and the next thing I know, my panties are ripped apart, and he's thumbing my sweet spot.

Holy fuck. Between his caveman actions and the filthy words flowing from his mouth, I'm a goner. I've never touched myself, though. I don't know what to do. Rising from his neck, I see the lust in his eyes that must rival mine. He grabs my hand and places it over his, letting me feel how he moves his fingers for a minute before slipping his hand out.

"Move your fingers, Lily. Do you feel how slick you are? Rub yourself, baby, do whatever feels good. Make yourself come, and I'll give you what you want. We both will." He undoes his pants as he gives me orders.

I cannot believe my hand is on my most intimate part. It feels… good. Like, really good. The sensitive spot that always brings me pleasure is so easy to manipulate when I can feel it myself. I think I could orgasm within seconds. Especially with Sebastian glued to what I'm doing while he does the same, squeezing his shaft tight and pumping his fist with one hand while the other kneads my breast. I'm so close.

Low husky words come from his lips. "Good girl, that's it. Make yourself come, so I can fuck the hell out of that tight little pussy." His words put me over the edge.

"Aaaah, Sebastian! Oh my Godddd." My head drops down on his shoulder as I feel the delicious pulses. Sebastian lifts my body with one arm and places his tip at my entrance. He releases me, forcing me to take him fast and deep. I cry out in shock, squeezing my eyes shut to bear the sting. He fills me completely, giving my body no time to adjust.

"Thank fuck! The only thing I thought about all day, baby, right here. Filling you and making you scream. I'll never get enough. Come on, Lily, ride my cock. You've got one minute before I take over."

I sit up and start rocking my hips back and forth, pushing past the pain toward pleasure. Both his hands are squeezing my breasts now, flicking and pinching my nipples.

"That's it, baby, you got it." He uses his hold on my chest to pull me closer and kisses me like his life depends on it. It's all just too much, I can't take any more.

"I can't, please, just take over. I need you in control, Sebastian." No truer words could have slipped from my mouth.

"That's what I like to hear, baby. Hold tight for me."

I do as he says, grabbing the seat behind him and tucking my head into his shoulder. Then, holy crap! He pounds into me hard and fast, thrusting up so furiously that I panic, remembering we're in a car and it's probably shaking like crazy. Before I have time to freak out, I feel his finger putting pressure on my forbidden back hole, and all rational thought flies out the window. Within seconds, I come undone for the second time today, crying out my release. Sebastian buries his head in my hair and grunts as I feel him release deep inside me. God, I love when he goes over the edge. It's empowering to know I have that effect on him. I make him lose control, and he does the same for me. We stay motionless as our pleasure fades and our breathing slows. Carefully, I move to sit up and look at him with a lazy smile of contentment.

"You're beautiful," he says, pushing my disheveled hair from my face. "And sexy." He rubs his thumb across my lower lip. "How did I end up the luckiest guy in the world?" He pulls me down and makes love to my mouth. Oh God, how am I ever going to survive this?

Sebastian

We're still cleaning up and putting ourselves back together when Blake pulls into a parking spot. Thankfully the car is stocked with personal care items, making it a heck of a lot easier. The only casualty was her panties. Knowing she's going bare under her skirt while walking through the store with me isn't going to help bring down my erection.

"I can't believe we just did that. I'm sure Blake felt and heard everything. I'm so embarrassed. And now I'll be walking through the store with nothing under my skirt thanks to you." She's so fucking sexy and has no clue.

"If it makes you feel any better, the privacy screen is soundproof. Although, if he wanted to listen in for his own enjoyment, he could easily turn the intercom on." I absolutely love getting her worked up. It's quickly becoming a habit.

"Oh my God, do you think he would? Ugh, this is humiliating. I can't believe I let myself get into another situation to do a walk of shame." I laugh as she hides her face in her hands.

"Sweetheart, Blake is not new to sexual activities happening back here. Driving Eli and I around for the last umpteen years has cured him of all propriety. What do you think the privacy screen is for?" I see her shoulders sag immediately, and it occurs to me that bringing up past sexual encounters was not the smoothest form of reassurance. *Shit.*

Pulling her into me, I kiss the top of her head and squeeze her ass. "Baby, knowing you have no panties on under that skirt puts me over the edge. And my dick? It's not going down anytime soon because of it. You'll have to walk in front of me the whole time so I don't scare anyone. Now come on, let's get your groceries." I pull her from the car and hold her hand in mine as we walk. Something about this moment makes me want to keep hold and not let go.

We're just approaching the front of the store, ready to grab a cart, when none other than Jackson walks out of the sliding doors, stopping dead in his tracks when he spots us. His gaze slides to our clasped hands. I can't imagine this is their first encounter since Saturday. They live in the same building for Christ's sake. But judging by the shocked look on Lily's face and the smoldering one on his, I'm assuming it is.

Closing the distance, we stop in front of him. There's a big part of me that would really like to have some fun with this fucker, but the wiser side of me knows that wouldn't make Lily happy. The fact that I'm altering my behavior based on a woman's feelings is entirely foreign to me. Rather than saying anything, I wait to see what happens.

"Hey" is all Lily manages to squeak out.

"Hey to you. I see you're jumping right into the domestication thing. Moving in already?" Oh, he's so butt hurt, I almost feel bad for him. Almost.

"No, Jackson, it's not like that. I'm cooking dinner for Cici tonight, and Sebastian was giving me a ride home from work." Hearing his name on her lips makes me cringe. But more importantly, what isn't it like, Lily? And really, 'just giving you a ride'? Well, I suppose she's right about that one.

Clearing my throat, I interject, "Actually, it is like that. Since she's pre-occupied this evening, we decided to thoroughly enjoy the 'ride' home. I'm sure you can use your imagination—oh wait, you don't need to." I smirk at him before continuing. "And if Lily agreed to spend every night in my bed, it still wouldn't be enough." Whoa, what the fuck did I just say? I quickly school my features to hide the chaos in my mind. I find myself squeezing Lily's hand in reassurance. Whether it's to reassure her or me, I don't know.

Both Jackson and Lily are speechless at this point. I'm fucking speechless at this point. After what feels like ages, Jackson clears his throat. "Well then, I guess I'll leave you guys to it. I'll just go use my imagination. On second thought, I think I'll use my memory. See you next time, Lily." He winks at her, salutes me and saunters off as if he hasn't a care in the world. *There won't be a next time, asshole.*

After a few stunned seconds, I decide to break the silence. "Are you okay, sweetheart?"

"Yeah, I'm fine." Simple answer to a simple question.

"Then why haven't you moved?" I point out the obvious. She's not fine, and at this moment, I'm glad she's having a girls' night. Feelings are way out of my wheelhouse.

She seems to snap out of it and pastes a fake smile on. "Oh my gosh, yeah, right. Let's go get this over with, shall we?" She leads the way, and twenty minutes later, we're climbing back into the car.

I'm helping set groceries on the kitchen counter as I look around. It's a nice place. Cici's parents own the building, so that makes sense. It's clean. I wonder which one of them is responsible or if it's both. Something tells me it's because of Lily. I don't know how I know; I just do.

"So do I get to see your room?" I move my eyebrows up and down and smirk.

"Probably not a good idea, considering Cici is due home any minute. How about we save that for next time?" she asks me in a flirty little voice.

I wrap my arms around her and rest my chin on her head. "The only thing I like about that answer is that you, once again, alluded to a next time, so I'll take it. Speaking of 'next times,' how about I take you to dinner tomorrow, and *if* the night goes well, you can stay at my place. No pressure. What do you say?" I don't remember the last time I was nervous waiting for an answer. Actually, I do. It was the last time I asked her out.

"I think I'd like that." She hugs me tightly with her response as I release the breath I was holding. Dipping down, I kiss her slowly, savoring the feel. But she pulls away, too soon. Meanwhile I'm trying to stop from picking her up and carrying her to her room.

"Cici really is going to walk in soon."

"All right, sweetheart, I'll leave you for now. But I'll be outside your office at five tomorrow." And on that note, before I change my mind, I walk away, which seems to be getting more difficult each time I do.

Lily

"I still can't believe you turned down a date with him to cook me dinner. Not only that, but you could have had at least two, maybe three more orgasms at the rate you're going." We giggle together and sip our wine. Ebony is between us while we're cozied up on the couch after dinner.

I've caught her up on everything. Even the bit about Jackson. Besides the yuck factor of it being her brother, she was enthusiastic about the scenario itself being incredibly hot. That's twice this week Cici has been jealous of my sex life. Never in a million years did I think that would happen. She's made me feel so much better about everything. Although the risk of falling for him and getting hurt in the end is something I can't resolve.

"You have no idea how much I needed this, Cici. I've been so tormented over what's normal. I'm in way over my head. I'm not sure I can separate sex and love like Sebastian can. God, he can be so cold and detached but then make a comment about every night not being enough, and you would think I meant the world to him. It's those moments that get to my head. I'm scared to keep going because I'll be ruined for anyone else by the time he's done with me." The tears are pooling.

"Oh, honey, I know. Especially since he's your first. That's always the hardest to get over. But why stress over something you can't control? Who knows, maybe you'll be the one to break through his shell and make him fall madly in love with you. From what you've told me, it's not far-fetched. But I don't want to get your hopes up. So bottom line? It doesn't matter. Have fun, enjoy the ride, and if worst-case scenario he breaks your heart, I'll be here to help you glue it back together. Right after I hire a hit man to take him out." Leave it to Cici to make me laugh.

"Thanks, Cici, but I also knew what I was getting into before I gave in, so it's not really Sebastian's fault if my heart gets broken in the end. I only have myself to blame for that."

"Fair enough. Now, when and how will you break the news about

Kevin being your date to the awards gala? I have a feeling that's not going to be an easy sell. Maybe you should just tell Kevin you're sorry, but he can't go." She and I both wince at the same time.

"He's not a date and that would be horrible of me. I can't do that. I'm going to have to tell Sebastian at dinner tomorrow. I was thinking of waiting until the end of the night, but it's probably better to have other people around, right? Then he can't completely come unglued without making a scene. I've given this a lot of thought," I say confidently.

"It seems like making a scene doesn't bother him, but good luck with that." She takes a sip of wine and moves on. "Speaking of tomorrow, what do you think Brad will say about the spectacle on Saturday? I saw him right after Sebastian carried you away, and he did not look happy."

Frustrated, I answer, "Frankly, it's none of his business. He's the one who wanted me to go out with Sebastian to begin with, so why the hell should he be pissed when it's exactly what he asked for? Ugh, I've been dreading tomorrow afternoon for that reason."

"I don't know. All I can say is happiness was not the emotion he displayed—that's for sure. You know what, who cares what Brad thinks? Let him fire you if he wants. You need to get out of there anyway, and then you could collect unemployment." She's so lucky she doesn't need to worry about money and jobs. If only I had the luxury to be as carefree as Cici.

"Yeah, but I also wouldn't have the reference from him that I'd like. It'd be terrible to have worked for a man I despise all these years for nothing. I know I have my degree and now the award under my belt, but I want all the advantages I can get to land a high-paying job."

"True that. Maybe we should get to work writing this one-minute speech you have to give in front of two hundred people, so you can dazzle the shit out of them."

"Cici, I don't think it's a good idea to do it while we're both half drunk." I always know when it's girls' night in, there won't just be one bottle of wine, but one for each of us and maybe a third to share. She and I always go overboard, but we have some of the best memories from nights like these.

"What are you talking about? That's the only time to do it." We both giggle as we get up for refills.

Sex God: Did you enjoy girls night?

Lily: Too much as always. I think my head is going to hurt tomorrow.

Sex God: LOL, that's what happens when you overindulge.

Lily: Thank you, Captain Obvious.

Sex God: I like it when you're sassy.

Lily: I like it when you're bossy.

Sex God: Hmmm, I'll keep that in mind. What else do you like?

Lily: OMG, I did NOT mean to send that! I'm drunk. I'm going to bed now.

Sex God: Maybe I'll have to ply you with alcohol tomorrow night to get more answers. Don't forget to pack for overnight.

Lily: I won't. Night, Sebastian.

Sex God: Good night, gorgeous. Sweet dreams.

Sex God: Take some aspirin and drink water.

Lily: Okay, Bossy....

Bossy: You haven't seen the half of it.

26

HOW SORRY ARE YOU

Lily

Oh God. My head is pounding. Coffee isn't working, and now I have to make it through class without falling asleep. Not only am I stressed about seeing Brad, but I'm miserable on top of it. When I unlock my phone to text Cici and see how she's feeling, it opens to the text thread with Sebastian. I scroll up. *Oh no, no, no.* I did not tell him that. What the hell was I thinking? That man needs no encouragement. And is that true? Do I like when he's bossy? That makes me sound cliché, like a weak pushover of a woman who needs a man to tell her what to do. That is not me.

But if I'm being honest, which apparently, I am when intoxicated, I like that side of Sebastian. It's sexy when he takes charge and I see his domineering side that comes so naturally. Plus, it's like taking a vacation from my mind when I don't have to think or let my nerves get in the way. However, knowing this to be true and admitting it are two different things. I just hope Sebastian ignores that little tidbit and chalks it up to drunk rambling.

Taking a deep cleansing breath and repeating my mantra, I walk into the office. I feel like it's been forever since I've been here. I love the arrangement with Dubree Enterprises. It's been nice not having to put up with Brad's crap so often. I barely make it to my desk before the Devil himself is rounding the corner. Oh boy, here we go.

"Good morning, Lily. Did you enjoy the rest of your weekend?" He's fishing. If he wants to know something, he can handle it like an adult and ask me directly.

"I did. How about you?" *Cut the crap, Brad.*

"It was great. That was quite the shindig at Sebastian Dubree's place, huh?" Well, we're getting closer.

"It was. I liked that they thanked your company. What did you think about the new branding reveal?" I can only distract him for so long, but it's worth a shot.

"It would've been an oversight on their part had they not acknowledged our years of dedication. The new brand seems more in line for today's market, and it's good timing for the company to make a change." He continues to stand in silence while I get situated. I decide not to say anything more, leaving the ball in his court.

"I saw Sebastian carry you upstairs during the party—in the most unprofessional manner, I might add. Were you planning on telling me that you two were together? Or were you just waiting to rip the rug out from under me?" Yep, here it is. I wasn't expecting this level of animosity though.

"I didn't think my dating life was any of your business, and honestly, I was just as surprised as everyone else at his actions. We hadn't made anything official or talked about it. I found out at the same time you did if it makes you feel any better." None of what I'm saying is untrue, so I feel good with my response.

"I would say it is my business when one of the largest accounts I hold is in limbo because of the man you're dating. So is this why he insisted you 'work' in their offices? To have you at his disposal?" *Oh no he did not.*

"I am not at his disposal, and dating him has nothing to do with the account. Your assumptions should be taken up with Mr. Dubree himself.

Do you have anything else to discuss, or can I get started?" *And please screw off now.*

"Don't be naïve. He wanted you the minute he walked into this office, and it's the only reason we're still involved. Just give me a little heads-up before something drastic happens, all right?" *He's not wrong.*

"I'll keep that in mind. You were going to give me a list of companies from my presentation you wanted me to contact for proposals. Do you have that list so I can get started?" *Then I can be done talking to you for the rest of the day.*

"I do. I'll email it over, and you can give me an update at the end of the day tomorrow on your progress. I hope you know what you're doing with a man like Sebastian Dubree, Lily. He's not the commitment type, if you know what I mean. I'd be careful if I were you." He abruptly turns and goes into his office without giving me a chance to respond. What really rubs me raw is that he's totally right, and I have no idea what I'm doing.

Sebastian

"The arrangements are made for the restaurant tonight, and the dress and shoes are already set to be delivered Friday. Will there be anything else, sir?" Lucy asks on my way out.

"That should do it. Thank you, Lucy." I head toward my brother's office. It's located kitty-corner from mine and mirrors my own, but the views are to the opposite side of the bay. We have a working lunch in his office today.

He catches my eye as I walk in and quickly ends his conversation, which I can't help but take notice of. "Sebastian just walked in. Talk later?" Someone familiar, who knows me, that he'll be speaking to again soon. *Hmmm.* I really haven't been paying enough attention.

"Who were you on the phone with?" I ask casually as I take a seat on the couch.

"Just a buddy of mine. So what's on the agenda for today? And more importantly, what did we order for lunch? I'm starved." I can tell he's deflecting. Instead of prodding, though, I decide to wait it out; he'll say something when he's ready.

"Whatever Lucy ordered for us. I'm sure it'll be one of your favorites, don't worry." I wink at him in jest. He hates coming to my office because of her infatuation with him. Hell, it makes me uncomfortable.

"You know you're early, right? Our call doesn't start for another thirty minutes. Did you run out of work to do 'cause I'd be happy to hand over some of mine."

"There's something I wanted to run by you." He joins me in the sitting area, waiting for me to proceed.

"Lily's going to be graduating in a couple months. I spoke with Bob Cooper, head of marketing, and apparently she's proven to be a great addition to the team. I was thinking we should offer her a full-time position upon graduation. We're always looking for fresh ideas, and she seems to fit in well here." Technically his approval isn't required, but I feel the need in this case.

"I bet she does." He laughs. "That was quite the pitch. Is there a reason you're not just hiring her without talking to me? You know you don't need my approval, so what's up?"

"Considering my connection to her, I didn't think it would be appropriate to decide without you. I'm already walking a fine line seeing her while she's in our employment. Offering full-time with a pay increase may cause some people to question my motives." I already know what's coming.

"So tell me, Seb, what are your motives? Is it to have an outstanding addition to our marketing department, or is it to keep Lily within your reach? You know I'll back you either way, bro. I'm just keeping it real." He knows me way too well.

"Keeping it real, huh? Both, I suppose. I do think she's amazing at her job. She pretty much runs Smith's office and originates half his campaigns herself. But I'd be lying if I said I didn't want to keep her close. By the way, I took your advice. I'm taking her to dinner tonight and asked her to stay over. I'm so out of my element here, man. She needs more than I can give, but I can't get enough of her. I can't stop, even though one of us will end up screwed in the end." I sigh in frustration but also relief. It feels good to confide in my brother.

"Sounds like you're getting in deep. That doesn't have to be a bad thing, Sebastian. Maybe just enjoy it and stop overthinking for once. Take it one day at a time and worry about the rest later. At least you're both getting screwed for now." He chuckles. Leave it to Eli to give sound advice these days, but regardless of how good it is, it's always easier said than done.

"If only it were that easy. I wish I could go back to simple meaningless fucks—now that was easy." Easy and boring.

"Do you? Because if that's what you'd prefer, you should do it now before you string her along and end up breaking her heart." Eli barely even knows Lily and defends the shit out of her every time. That's the effect she has on people. Something about her captivates those around her. I bet there's not a man out there able to resist her charm.

"Dude, we're so fucking good together that I can't even look at another woman. I'm wrecked for anyone else, I swear. She's so goddamn pliable and receptive. And to top it all off, she's submissive as hell in the bedroom." I see the look of shock on Eli's face.

"I certainly didn't see that one coming," Eli says skeptically.

"Outside of the bedroom, she's a fucking force to be reckoned with—I can tell you that. But the minute things turn sexual, she releases all control and doesn't even realize it. She's every wet dream come true." Dammit, I can't let her go.

"Sounds like a keeper to me. My advice? Don't fuck it up. I'll back whatever decision you make regarding hiring her full-time. And one last piece of advice, if she works here and something blows up between you two, that's gonna be a bitch to deal with. I'll give you that one for free, and if you pour us a drink, I'll consider that payment for the first." Goddamn voice of reason.

Upon returning to my own office after our call, Lucy hands me an envelope. "Justin dropped it by, sir."

"Justin?" I ask cluelessly.

She blushes. "Oh, sorry, Mr. Burns. Your security officer, sir. He also said to call and discuss it when you have time." I really haven't been paying attention to things if Lucy is banging my security detail unbeknownst to me. Crap, I've got to get my head out of my ass. Eli will be happy to hear she's moved on, although I may keep it in my back pocket for now. I can't give up my fun just yet.

Bewildered, I walk into my office without another word, sit down and open the envelope. I see red immediately. Why the hell are there pictures of Lily with Surfer Boy? It looks like they're in a coffee shop, probably on campus. I look at the date. It was yesterday. What the fuck? She didn't mention it. Is she intentionally keeping this from me? I pick up the phone.

"What have you got for me?"

"She met with a man for coffee yesterday, and something about the guy unnerved me. Rather than continue in the opposite direction he started in when they parted ways, he stopped, turned around and watched her go until she was out of sight. It seemed unusual. Thought I should run it by you, see if you want me to check into this guy at all."

I knew he had a crush on her; it was painfully obvious that night at the club. "I recognize him, and there's no need to investigate further. He's just a kid from college who's infatuated with her. I'm sure the only way he can check her out is behind her back. Have there been more occurrences with the stalker?" Knowing he's that into her annoys the shit out of me.

"No, I'm starting to wonder if it might've been someone watching the guy she was on the date with, but I'll continue to keep an eye out."

"Good. While I have you, Miss Thompson and I will be spending this evening together. I'll be taking her to dinner in the limo and would like additional security to ensure no photos are taken. I'll text you details after we hang up." I haven't explained to Lily yet that assumptions will be made and could become news if she's seen with me multiple times. I want her to be prepared if that happens, before it happens.

"Sounds good, sir. Let me know if you change your mind about the boy. Otherwise, I'll be in touch." He ends the call. Straight and to the point.

As angry as I am with Lily for not telling me about meeting with Kevin, I'm more excited for the lesson I'm going to give her. Thinking about it makes the bulge in my pants uncomfortable, so I table those thoughts for now. I'll have plenty of time to plan her punishment on the way to get her.

Lily

This day has been brutal. Not only because of my hangover this morning or the shit I had to put up with from Brad because of the sexy dress I'm wearing. But the anticipation for tonight with Sebastian is killing me. I've been wet all day.

It's finally time, and as I get up from my desk, I see a black car pull up to the curb out front. Except that instead of the regular sedan I'm used to, it's a stretch limo. Excitedly, I grab my bags, one from school and one for overnight, then head toward the entrance. "See you tomorrow, Brad," I yell as I walk out the door.

Blake holds the door open and takes my bags as I approach. Sebastian is seated on the bench between the two back doors, and I climb in next to him. When I make eye contact, I notice something isn't right. He didn't greet me immediately like normal or make one move to touch me. I'm not sure if I should say something or wait for him to make the first move.

Once the car starts rolling, he finally speaks in a low, menacing voice. "Did you forget to tell me anything yesterday?" *Did I?*

"Umm, no… not that I can think of." There's no way he knows about Kevin going with me to the gala. Only Kevin, Cici and I know that, and neither of them would tell Sebastian. Shoot, I did have to give Kevin's name to the coordinators for seating arrangements, but how could Sebastian have gotten that information? *Shit.*

"No plans other than girls' night? No one else you saw yesterday?" What is he getting at? This is weird.

"No, I went to school and then your office, and you took me home yourself, so you know I didn't go anywhere… oh wait, I did have coffee with Kevin in between classes. But that was just on campus." It can't be about that; how would he have known?

"You had coffee with Kevin. Did you not think it mattered enough to tell me because it was 'just on campus,' or did you not think going on a coffee date with a boy who obviously wants to fuck you was something you should tell me?" Okay then, there's my answer. But how in the hell does he even know?

"Wait a minute. It wasn't a date—we're always getting coffee after class. But how the heck do you even know?" I hate that he can remain so calm, but I start raising my voice the minute I get upset.

"How I know is not important. What *is*, though, is that you felt it was okay to indulge in another man's fantasy of being with you and even more so is the fact you didn't think it was important enough to tell me. Let me ask you this. If I went out to coffee with Gretta yesterday, the woman who ran into us at the restaurant the other night, and today our picture appeared in the society column, which you happened to have seen, would that be okay?" Why does he have to make such a good point, damn it. Now I feel bad.

"Well when you put it that way, it makes sense. I honestly thought nothing of it, so I didn't think to mention it. But from your perspective, you're right. I should have said something. I'm sorry, Sebastian."

"How sorry are you?" His voice sounds sultry this time, instantly making my insides clench with desire.

"How sorry do you want me to be?" I say seductively. Two can play that game.

"Get on your knees and wrap that sassy mouth around my cock." He widens his feet, making room to kneel between his legs. Okay, maybe two can't play that game. I stare at him in shock.

"Now," he demands.

Instantly my core clenches. His dominance and filthy words ignite me. I would never expect this kind of reaction from someone talking to me like that, but with Sebastian, it just does.

The problem is, I've never touched a man down there, let alone with my mouth. What if I'm terrible and he hates it? Knowing it's too late to worry about, I sink to my knees between his thighs and wait for instructions.

"It's not going to take itself out, sweetheart."

Reaching for his belt, I clumsily undo it, then fumble with the button. Once I manage that, I slide his zipper down slowly, prolonging the inevitable. Grabbing the waistband of both his pants and boxers, I tug as he slightly lifts helping me pull them down until his massive length springs free. And there it is, as giant as I remember—maybe even more so. I'm frozen, scared to make a wrong move.

"Touch it, Lily. Show me how sorry you are and make it good, baby."

He's not giving me much to go on. I tentatively reach out and only graze it with my fingers. *Oh, wow*. It's so soft, like silk. I curl my fingers around it and feel the ridge at the top. I can't help but run my thumb over the tip just to see what it feels like. He lets out a growl as it jerks in my hand. So I do it again, getting the same response.

"Damn, baby, you're torture. Wrap your hand around it now and squeeze. That's it… move up and down, baby… fuck yeah, just like that." He's watching me as I obey his commands with a carnal look on his face.

I think I like this.

After doing that a few more times, I can't resist leaning down to run my tongue over the tip to taste the bead of liquid there. Well that certainly got a reaction.

"Fuck, Lily, you're killing me. If you don't put my cock in that mouth of yours right the fuck now, I'm doing it for you." This is supposed to be for his pleasure, but I'm pretty sure I just drenched my panties.

Circling the tip with my tongue a few more times, my saliva starts dripping down his shaft. I lick my lips and wrap them around the head, slowly sliding down, taking him in as far as possible. He moans loudly as his hips thrust.

"Oh, fuck yeah. Now suck it. Good girl, just like that." He's watching me with a look of pure lust.

"Take it deeper. You got it, baby." He's panting between each command, losing himself more and more.

I wasn't sure I'd like doing this, but I'm so turned on I feel like I could climax myself.

"Fuck, Lily, your mouth feels so good around my cock." His head is tipped back on the seat, his eyes closed in ecstasy.

Seeing his reaction encourages me to go further, stretching, trying to take more each time. When I feel a slight thrust, I moan, so turned on that I'm responsible for his pleasure.

He brings his hand to my cheek. "All right, sweetheart, stay right there and don't move. I'm taking over, okay?" I look at him and nod.

"Good girl. You've got this, just relax." With a hand on each side of my head, he grips firmly and moves my head up and down, grunting out sounds of pleasure as he chooses the pace. "Fuck, baby, your mouth feels fucking amazing." I squeeze his thighs, trying to take it while he continues forcing my head further down each time. I'm starting to ache with my own need.

Then I grab on even tighter when he holds me still and, instead of moving my head, he starts thrusting into my mouth. "Take it, Lily. Relax your throat for me and open. Swallow me down." He plunges in, fucking my mouth, making me gag. He pulls out to let me breathe, only to plunge in deep and hold me there until I gag again, repeating the movement.

"Fuck, you're taking me so good. I could fuck your sweet mouth all night. You got it, baby. Yeah, choke on me." He holds me tight and pummels me relentlessly.

"I'm gonna come. Oh fuck… swallow it… take it all… fuck yeah… drink it up, baby." He stills as his dick pulses inside my mouth while his cum shoots down my throat.

"FUUUUUCK!" he shouts at the final release. I swallow as much as I can, the rest spilling out around his cock as he pulls me up.

I slowly gaze up to see him looking at me in amazement. He wipes the cum from my chin with his thumb and puts it in my mouth. I suck it off, and he groans. I feel myself clench down there. He pulls me onto his lap and devours my mouth, and I wonder if he can taste himself.

"Goddamn, baby, that was amazing. It's your turn now, sweetheart. You deserve it after that stellar performance. Don't think you're getting out of your punishment, but I'll save it for later." *Oh. My. God.* I'm twisted if that's the part that turns me on.

"Why don't you go lie down on that seat over there and let me see how wet you are from sucking my cock."

I think I could get off from his words alone. Slowly, I start to make my way, and he swats my ass. "You better hurry, babe. We only have so much time, and I want to make sure you're satisfied, hm?" I quicken my pace and lie face up on the long bench seat under the windows.

He pushes my dress up all the way so my breasts are on display, making my nipples pebble from the cool air. I figured going braless today would be one less item of clothing to worry about. What has become of me? After removing my panties, he props my leg up on the top of the seat back and pushes my other one out as far as it'll go, spreading me wide open as he stares down. My body lights up from his gaze.

"Fuck, baby, your pussy's a thing of worship. It's so wet for me. What do you want, Lily? Are you going to beg me to taste it?"

I'd do anything at this point. "Please taste me, Sebastian. I need it so bad."

And taste he does. *Oh God.* He licks me slowly from the bottom to the top until he flicks my clit with his tongue, then repeats the motion. The third time's a charm when he spears me with his tongue and laps up my juices like it's his favorite meal. I'm going insane with pleasure, trying to buck my hips but unable as he holds me down. His mouth travels back up, and I can't help but beg now.

"Please, Sebastian. Please."

I feel his finger circling my entrance. "Is this what you want, Lily?"

"Yes."

He plunges into me, thrusting deep while he flicks my clit with his tongue. The moment his fingers curl inside me, I'm lost. My orgasm hits me hard. Probably the buildup from going down on him. I scream out in pleasure, but he doesn't quit, dragging it on and on, and just when I think it's over, it's not.

"Come on, baby, give it to me. I know you have one more in you. Let me have it. Come for me."

I cry out at the intensity as he sends me over again, immediately removing his fingers and shoving his tongue deep inside as I pulse around it.

Hearing him groan, I raise my head to look at him. He's furiously rubbing his cock at the same time. Suddenly he rises, stroking hard as his head whips back, grunting loudly while shooting his climax where his mouth was. And if I hadn't just orgasmed a moment ago, that surely would have done me in.

"Wow, if that's what happens when you're mad at me, I'm making you mad more often." I mean, seriously, that was hot. He chuckles in response.

"Oh, baby, you don't know what you're in for. You may be eating your words later. I'm not even close to being done with you."

"Good. I don't ever want you to be done with me." Oh crap, I didn't mean to say that. He's going to take it the wrong way. Except that may be the exact way I mean it. Unfortunately, I think I've already fallen.

After a long pause, Sebastian breaks the silence, choosing a distraction. "We have a lot of cleaning up to do, and it looks like we're getting close. Wait there and I'll grab supplies." He's back within seconds.

"Are you going to let me clean myself up this time?" I ask him.

"Now why would I allow that?"

"Because I'm more than capable of taking care of myself, and then we could both clean up at the same time. Makes sense to me." Something tells me he's not going to see it that way.

"Lily, it's my job to care for you. Now let me, okay, sweetheart?"
How can I resist that?

"Okay." *Definitely fallen.*

Sebastian

"So where are we going? This is a long way to go for dinner." I'm surprised she's just now asking.

"I'm taking you to a fantastic restaurant in La Jolla, where we have a family ranch nearby. We're stopping there, and I'm teaching you how to shoot a gun. Or do you already know how?" She looks at me and giggles for some reason.

"No, I've never been around guns. So I definitely don't know how to shoot one."

The car makes the turn into the long driveway up to the house. I've never brought a woman here before—yet another thing I was compelled to do with her.

"Good, so we can add it to the list of firsts. Your list is getting pretty long by now, huh?" I laugh. "Don't worry, I've had a few added to mine as well," I say reassuringly.

She gets a curious look on her face. "Like what? Mine are pretty much all sexual, but what could yours be?"

"Having sex with the same woman more than once. Having a woman in my bed. Grocery shopping with a woman." I smirk. "And I bet you thought I was going to say grocery shopping period, didn't you?" I pull her against me and tickle her, making her laugh like crazy. I stop as the car pulls up to the front.

"*This* is the ranch you were talking about? Is that slang for castle?" Her eyes are wide, taking it all in.

"The ranch part refers to the land around the house," I explain.

"Sebastian, that isn't a house. At minimum I would call it a mansion. And I'm not sure that does it justice. Is this where you grew up?" she asks as we exit the limo.

"No, but we spent most holidays here. With it being so close, my brother and I still visit often and use it as an escape. You're the first person other than Eli who's been here. One more first for my side." I want her to know there's more to meaningful firsts than sex.

"I think your list might rival mine," she teases.

"We better add some more to yours then. I have plenty of things in mind." I smirk at her, and she blushes. Her sexual shyness is endearing and contradicts her appetite for more. I love how eager she is in the bedroom, but what really gets me is how happy she is being with me out of the bedroom. She's easy to be around. Moments like this are why I need to be careful. If I get too comfortable, I could lose myself.

"It's beautiful, Sebastian. I'm glad you brought me here. I can't believe there's something this magnificent right in our backyard. If I were you, I'd be here all the time." Her smile is contagious.

I take her around back where the shooting range is instead of going inside. "Well, responsibilities take priority, but we do come out here our fair share, especially because we like outdoor target practice. Come on, I'll show you. We'll see how good you are at following directions." *Because after this, you'll need to be exceptional at it. I can't wait.*

27

THE CONVERSATION IS OVER

Sebastian

"THAT'S NOT FAIR. YOU DIDN'T TELL ME YOU WERE AN EXPERT! And you made it seem like I was doing so good. You cheated!" She's still arguing about losing the bet we made as we head up the back porch into the house. We have an hour before dinner, and I have plenty on the agenda before then.

"You were doing good. I just didn't mention that your target was much closer for practice. During competition, we need equal playing fields." I wink and lead her into the house.

"Whoa. You're lucky I'm distracted by this… I don't even have words." I watch her take it all in. "This is insane. It's like something you'd see in a castle. It's gorgeous, Sebastian." She's turning her head this way and that as I lead her further toward the stairs.

"Just wait until you see the bedroom. That's where it really shows itself." I lead her up the vast winding staircase, and we pause on the landing so she can take in the view of the back property stretching as far as the eye can see.

"Okay, this definitely puts things in perspective. You are seriously so far out of my league, it's not even funny. I've never seen anything like this. I guess this is the difference between the haves and the have-nots." She brings her hand up to cover her mouth, her eyes wide. "Oh my gosh, I'm sorry. That was rude. I'm just…. Crap, that really wasn't nice. I'm kind of making a mess of this." She buries her face in her hands, and I'm having so much fun watching her backpedal, I almost don't want to put her out of her misery, but I can't hold it in anymore and start laughing.

She whacks me on my arm. "Sorry, it's just watching your face go from awe to horror to apologetic was just priceless. I'm not offended. I can't help that I grew up with money, and I'm certainly not apologizing for it. It is what it is. It's refreshing to see your take on things though. I like it." I lean over and kiss the top of her head. "Now come on, the bedroom is next on the tour."

We go down the right hallway to the last door on the left. It's one of two master rooms, the other belonging to Eli at the opposite end of the house. We walk in, and I see her overnight bag has been brought in so she can freshen up for dinner. We're not staying here tonight; I'm taking her back to my place in the city so we don't have such a long commute for work in the morning.

"Oh my God."

It's the reaction I expected. I didn't furnish the room; it's always been like this. Opulent to the extreme. An oversized four-poster bed fit for a king, with drapes and all. Then there's the larger-than-life fireplace with huge armchairs in front. There's also a seating area to the right as you walk in with a love seat and more chairs. It's all styled in the fashions of the Victorian era, which does give it the impression of being in a castle.

"Yeah, well I did tell you it was the best part. Now. Do you remember what I said about saving your punishment for later?" This time it's a real punishment so I'll need to walk her through it.

"Um, yes."

"Yes what?"

"Yes, sir?" Damn she goes into being submissive effortlessly.

"Good girl. Now let's pick a safe word for you. Do you know what that is?" My dick is getting hard in anticipation. And if my instincts are correct, I bet she's already slick with desire.

"Yes." She quickly adds, "Sir."

"Good. Would you like to pick one or should I decide for you? It can be as simple as stop or a color or any word that you can say quickly and remember easily." The word should be her choice, but she might not be able to think, being put on the spot like this.

"I'll go with stop, sir." I can tell she's nervous now. As she should be. I'd be concerned if she wasn't.

"Good choice. I want you to understand that I only want you to use that word as a last resort, not just because you're uncomfortable or something is painful. There will be pain, but I won't do anything you can't handle or that will leave any lasting effects. The word should only be used when you feel you have reached your tolerance level or are afraid outside the normal parameters of this scenario. Do you understand?" If we were just playing and this wasn't a punishment, I wouldn't have to be quite so detailed, but I plan on pushing her limits today.

"Yes, I understand, sir. Are you going to hurt me? Sir." She's shaking at this point, and I know she's nervous, but I also hear the intrigue. She's curious.

"Today I'm going to spank you. It's not foreplay though. It will hurt and you won't like it. But you'll remember why you shouldn't be having coffee with another man after this unless you talk to me. Is that clear?"

"Yes, but I'm nervous, sir." She's ready. I'm not going to prolong this anymore; the anticipation is worse than the actual punishment sometimes.

"You should be. That's normal. Now, I'm going to sit on that love seat. You're going to stay right where you are and undress while I watch. I'll instruct you from there." It didn't go unnoticed when her legs clenched. She is definitely receptive to this so far.

I walk over and sit down casually. She waits for me to be situated before she slowly begins to peel her clothes off. Seeing her standing there, naked and waiting, is absolutely mouthwatering. She's an angel.

"You're so fucking beautiful. You were made for me." I see her slight smile and blush at my words. "Now, I want you to come and kneel down right here." I point to the ground on the right side of my legs. "Good girl." I run my hand through her hair, and she leans into me. My dick jerks at her subtle reaction. "Now, lay yourself over my legs, face down with your ass up for me."

Lily

Oh my God, this is really happening. Why do I feel the clench in my core whenever I hear the words "good girl" out of his mouth? I am so messed up. I'm trembling now, nervous for what comes next. Following his instruction, I bend over to lay my torso on his legs. It's not the most comfortable position to be in, but I manage to maneuver myself enough to find a spot that works and settle. He runs his hand down my back and over my butt cheeks, caressing them. It feels so good, but my whole body is stiff in fear of what's to come.

"So, Lily, I've spanked you before, and yes, those were for being naughty, but this is different. I pleasured you after those spankings. This time, there won't be any pleasure. When I'm done, I'm going to feel how wet this makes you and bring you so close to climax you'll be begging for release. But you're not going to get it. You're going to sit through dinner in your state of need and wait for your pleasure like a good girl. Is that understood?"

"Yes, sir." I'm shaking with need already. He's been caressing my backside this whole time, getting close to my opening but not touching it. Not only am I nervous as hell, but I'm so turned on. I don't know if I can handle what he was explaining about bringing me close and then not letting me climax. It sounds worse than the spanking itself.

"Good, Lily. I'm going to give you ten slaps since this is new, and then I'm going to edge you. Are you ready?"

"Yes, sir." So that's what it's called. Hmmm. *OUCH!* Holy crap, that was way harder than last time, and that was only the first one. *AHHH!* Number two was the same but on the other cheek. He caresses both cheeks, giving me a reprieve. I'm going crazy with desire right now. There's a part of me that feels like this is so wrong, but that's also what turns me on.

AHHHH! Okay, that was two in a row. That hurt more with the sting still there from the last ones. It makes my face scrunch up in pain, but I haven't made a noise yet other than the panting I can't seem to control.

"Fuck, your ass is gorgeous. You look so good with a shade of pink on your cheeks, baby. You know I'd rather be playing than punishing, so I could sink my dick inside after. I hope you learn your lesson, Lily."

"Ahhhh," I cry out this time. *OH MY GOD!* Two more hard slaps.

They bring tears to my eyes. I can feel liquid pooling at my entrance. God, I want him to take me so bad.

"That's it, baby. You're doing so good. Only four more to go, and you're done. Then I'm going to feel how drenched your pussy is for me."

I literally scream during the last four delivered in succession with no break in between. Tears are falling for sure at this point. I try to wriggle free, but he holds me down firmly with his hand on my back. Oh my God, that hurt. The sting is brutal and probably not going away anytime soon.

"Good girl. You took it so well, sweetheart. Should I feel how wet you are now?" His hand skims down my butt, his fingers skimming my forbidden hole and then lower until he's circling my wetness.

"Christ, Lily, you're sopping. I want to fuck you so bad right now. But this would all have been for nothing if I did that, huh, baby?"

"Sebastian, please. I'm sorry. I'll promise I'll tell you next time." I'm pleading I need it so bad.

He plunges in, and I moan in ecstasy. I'm close to bursting as he goes in and out, but then suddenly he's gone. His hand is on my ass again, caressing my stinging cheeks.

"So close already, huh? I'd say you enjoyed your spanking a little too much. I'll have to remember that. Oh, baby, you're going to be so ready for dinner to be over tonight."

I'm already wanting dinner to be over. Oh God, he's back at my entrance, touching me, teasing me. I'm panting with need. He sinks into me slowly this time. Excruciatingly slow. He does this a few more times before adding a third finger and going deeper. *Aaaaah*, I'm seriously right there, just a couple more seconds… he's gone.

I moan in misery.

"How does it feel, Lily, to have it taken away? It doesn't feel good, does it? This is your real punishment, baby. You can think of this every time you consider letting someone take you away from me." *Oh God.*

"Sebastian, I'm sorry. I won't do it again. Please just let me finish. Please." This is torture.

He rims my opening again and penetrates me once more, flicking his fingers inside me, until he feels my pending release and withdraws.

"Please, sir, I'm begging. Anything you want. Please don't do it again. I can't take any more." I'm crying now, my need is so bad.

"I know you're sorry, baby. You have a safe word, use it. Otherwise, I know you can take it. Just one more and you're done."

His hand returns, and I jump this time. I'm so sensitive. It won't take long at all; if he just stays a few seconds longer, I'm there. He dips into me, and I moan. Damn, it's close; just a little harder, and I've got it. I thrust my butt back, trying to finish, but he moves too quickly.

"AHHHH!" His hand comes down hard on my ass once more, and crap does it sting after already being sore.

"Uh-uh-uh, Lily. That wasn't very smart of you. Let's try this last one again and see if you can behave this time."

I take him in again, and right away I'm feeling the pull. He's plunging into me so deep, and I start to feel my climax come on only to get it yanked back as he removes his hand abruptly. I'm so frustrated that tears are falling. This sucks. This is the worst punishment ever. Pure torture.

He slowly helps me onto my knees after caressing my ass one last time and wipes the tears from under my eyes. Spreading his knees apart, he motions for me to move between his legs. He continues to caress my face and brush the tears away. "It's okay, baby. It's over now. That's the worst of it, I promise. I do have one other surprise for you though. You've given me no choice being this delectable. You don't get your release, but you'll sit there and watch while I have mine."

What? He thinks the worst is over? This is going to kill me. I'm going to combust if I watch him while he rubs himself off. Oh God, my core is aching. He undoes his pants and brings them down enough to release his engorged member. He grabs it, squeezes it hard and groans. His hand moves up and down slowly.

"Fuck me. This won't take long, sweetheart. You've got me so worked up, baby. Watching you submit to me is the sexiest fucking thing I've ever seen. Seeing your ass red for me. Knowing you're going to feel that every time you sit tomorrow. Fuck!"

He's pumping his hand up and down. I can tell from the veins popping out on his forearm how tight he's squeezing. Holy shit it's sexy. His eyes are on me, my body, my breasts, my eyes. His hand is pumping furiously now, his face tense as he gets closer to climax. He leans his head back and closes his eyes shut for a moment before he orders me up on my knees, off my heels.

I straighten up, and after he pumps his cock a few more times, he grunts loudly and comes, shooting out all over my front, marking me. And I swear it's the hottest thing I've ever seen in my life. After the last pulse, he pulls my head down so my mouth is at his tip.

"Clean it off. Now. Every last drop." And I do. I lick what's left on the tip and then close my mouth around him to suck off any remaining. I moan around his cock, before he yanks me off. "Fuck, Lily. You make it so goddamn hard to resist you, woman. I want to fuck you so hard right now. And just think, if you hadn't been a bad girl, I would be." With that, he leans over, takes my head in his hands and kisses me passionately while I'm throbbing with need. But I know there's no satisfaction for me until later.

Sebastian

I really hadn't planned that last part when I jerked off in front of her, but fuck if that wasn't the sexiest thing ever. Seeing the lust in her eyes as she watched while on her knees in front of me. *Shit.* The urge to mark her. *Fuuuck.* I couldn't resist. Not taking her after took all my willpower.

I'm still hard as we head into the restaurant. I imagine it probably won't go down until I finish inside her later. I booked the limo intentionally for the long drive time today. I figured we'd make full use of the extra space. I may have to give in before we get to my place and fuck the orgasm out of her on the drive back; I don't think I have it in me to wait.

"Where is everybody?" she asks as the maître d' seats us at a table in front of the window. I brought her to the Marine Room. It sits right at the ocean's edge, and when the tide comes up, it hits against the glass. It's a great place but has no privacy. Not unless you book the entire restaurant for the evening.

"I reserved the whole place tonight. I want you all to myself. If you haven't realized by now, I don't like to share." I notice a distressed look on her face at my words and wonder why. "I also thought we'd enjoy dinner without the possibility of running into someone I may know like last time." At that, she smiles.

"You don't have to do that, Sebastian. I realize you have a past. I try not to dwell on that fact, but I know it's there." Crap, I really should say something about my idiotic comment before. I knew it bothered her right when it came out.

"Yeah, and sorry about bringing that up yesterday. I wasn't thinking straight in my postcoital bliss. I apologize if I upset you, and it won't happen again. I'm being truthful when I say that any sexual encounters from my past don't hold a candle to ours. You have absolutely no reason to be jealous of anyone before you." I reach for her hand, and she blushes. I hope she believes me, because it's the honest to God truth. I'm unsure how long I can hold on to her without the promise of more that she's looking for, but I'll try for as long as possible because I'm wrecked for anyone else.

"Thank you. It was uncomfortable to hear, not to mention bad timing. But like I said, I'm not stupid. I know you're very 'well traveled.' I'll remember your words and try not to let it get to me again."

"Good." She makes things so easy. How is she so perfect?

The waiter arrives to take our drink order, and I choose a bottle of wine to share. He leaves us to review the menu.

"Would you like me to order for you, or do you know what you want?" I remember her sticker shock at the prices from our last date, so I took matters into my own hands, but now I think she's starting to understand that this is my lifestyle and accepting the cost that goes with it.

"I'd be fine either way, but I loved what you ordered last time, so why don't you pick." I fucking love that she gives me control so much. There couldn't be a woman more suited for me. Damn, I need to stop thinking that way.

"Sounds good. I'll get a few things, and we can try a little bit of each. I'll leave the dessert up to you, as you seem quite good at that."

"Oh, but yours was so much better," she says seductively. My little vixen. She's come out of her shell so much and I love knowing it was me who brought her out of it.

I give our order to the waiter after he serves the wine, and once we're alone, I pick up the glass to toast. "Here's to another lovely evening with the sexiest woman alive and currently the most sexually frustrated." I wink as we toast.

"I'm doing okay at the moment, but I was pretty much ready to jump you earlier, or at least die trying. That was torture!" I burst out laughing. I love how often I laugh with her.

"I'd have liked to see you try. It was *meant* to be torturous. And you know if it got to be too much you could've used your safe word. How do you feel about the punishment thing altogether? Is it something you would be okay with happening in the future? Was it tolerable? Did it turn you on?"

"That's a lot of questions at once. It was barely tolerable. One more time and I probably would've had to stop you. I was embarrassed and honestly a little humiliated, like I was just letting you do it for no good reason, and that frustrated me. But at the same time, it obviously turned me on. The things you said. And what you did at the end." She looks down, blushing, and picks up her wine.

"That's why they call it being submissive—you're giving in to me, and it's sexy as hell. It also shows you're putting your trust in me not to truly hurt you. You should also understand that I'm not trying to humiliate you. I like control, Lily, in all things, and you giving it to me means the world. I won't steer you wrong, sweetheart, and if it ever gets to be too much, you can always stop with your safe word. I promise, there's a lot more pleasure to be had than pain. You've only seen a small portion of it." I've had my hands on some part of her body this whole evening, but now I slide my hand up her leg and graze my hand in between. She clenches tight.

"Sebastian, you can't. Don't tease me. I can't take it at this point." She looks at me apologetically.

"We better change the subject then. How about this, you ask me something you want to know, and then it's my turn and so on."

She doesn't hesitate. "Why are you against relationships and love?" *Really, that's what she starts with?* I assumed this would come up eventually.

"Way to dive right in. Well, quick answer, relationships lead to love, and I've seen love destroy people, make them lose focus and forget about other important things in their life. My turn." An answer without *the answer*. I'm not ready for that yet.

"What are your plans after you graduate in a couple months?"

"I'm going to apply for employment at all the top marketing firms until I land a high-paying job and can stand on my own two feet. I've been living off other people's generosity for too long, and I want to be able to support myself fully. Not working for Brad will be the icing on the cake. My turn." Her smile is beautiful.

Perfect answer and just what I was hoping for. We may not be a marketing firm, but we employ a top-tier team for our organization and pay well. It's perfect.

Before she gets to ask her question, our food is delivered, and I'm already ordering a second bottle of wine. Lily ends up loving what I ordered, and we eat off each other's plates like we've been doing this for ages. We went back and forth with questions throughout the meal, getting to know each other, and the more I learn about this woman, the more I want to know. The more time I spend with her, the more time I want. Speaking of…

"Before I forget, there's an event on Friday I'd like you to join me for. It's an advertising awards gala. I'd love to have you by my side and it could be beneficial with some great networking opportunities for you." Her eyes go wide with panic. *What the fuck?*

Lily

Seriously, this is the worst timing. I'm pretty sure there isn't more than one advertising gala happening on Friday, so it must be the same thing. I'd decided to wait to bring it up since there were no people around us and I was already fricking punished once today. I don't think my ass can handle any more. Not to mention, we're having a fantastic time.

"Uhhh, I already have plans on Friday. I actually have to attend the gala to accept an award." I quickly grab my glass as an excuse to look away.

"Wow, that's great, Lily. We can go together then. What award did you win?" Oh boy, this is not going to end well.

"I won the student overall campaign award. It's a huge accomplishment. When the professor announced it in class, he said I'd have to attend the gala to accept the award and could bring someone. Kevin was right next to me." I see his whole demeanor change and his look darken. "It was while you weren't talking to me, or I would've asked you to go. Since Kevin was there throughout the project, listening to my ideas and hearing me stress, it made total sense at the time to include him. It was a complete spur-of-the-moment decision when I asked. But not as a date. He knows I don't want to be anything more than friends because I've made that clear to him numerous times, so I figured it was okay to bring him as just a friend. And now he knows you and I are together, and I even told him we couldn't meet for a drink before the event because that wouldn't be okay with you, or even okay period. Sebastian? Will you please say something?"

He's been completely stoic during my rambling. I figured he'd either yell at me, which of course he doesn't do, or say he'd be dealing with me later. I expected some sort of reaction.

"When were you going to tell me?" he calmly asks. I can hear the menace behind his words. God, it's unnerving; I'd rather him raise his voice.

"Tonight actually. During dinner. With people around. But then we got here, and there were no people, and I chickened out. I only asked him as a friend, Sebastian. You have to know that. I've had four years to date him and haven't—he's just not my type." He must know that.

"So answer me this, why have you needed to make that clear to him numerous times?" Damn this guy is good. I can't ever win an argument with him.

"Fine, because he *has* told me he'd like more. But I gave him the chance not to be friends if he couldn't handle ONLY being friends. He knows that's all we are or will ever be. He's good, I swear. And I only didn't want to tell you because of your reaction to the coffee thing. I wasn't not telling you. I just didn't think about it. And by the time I did, it was too late." Shit. I don't think I'm doing very good damage control. This all just sounds like crap. I should have told him the minute we started something back up. It's not like I didn't know how possessive he was. He carried me out of his own damn party to make a statement for Christ's sake. Clue number one right there.

"I think it's time we head back. We both have work early tomorrow. I'll pay the check and we can go." He signals the waiter for the check and hands a credit card over without even a glance.

Seriously? He's really that mad. So what, he's not going to finish the conversation?

"What does that mean? Are we going to talk about this on the way or go to your place to talk?"

"The conversation is over, Lily. You've had plenty of opportunities to talk. You chose not to. It's simple really—if I can't trust you, there's no point in allowing myself to be captivated by you anymore than I already am. It's called communication—something you clearly have issues with. I have enough issues of my own. I can't deal with someone else's."

The car ride home is silent. We sit in the back of the limo, staring out opposite windows so we don't have to look at one another. I can't believe this went so wrong. I should have told him when he confronted me about the coffee thing, but I was too scared. In hindsight, it probably would have gone so much better. I'm pretty sure when he said the conversation was over, he also meant us.

I'm so frustrated with myself for so many reasons. That I let myself get sucked in again. That I didn't take the chance earlier to tell him about the gala. That I'm sitting here shedding tears in front of him. But most importantly, because I let myself fall in love with a man who can't love me back.

28

LOVE TRIANGLE

Sebastian

"WHAT THE HELL HAPPENED? I THOUGHT YOU GOT THE PICTURES from the camera?" I'm yelling over the phone to security, trying to figure out how I woke up to a gossip magazine publishing pictures of Lily. Not only with me, but with Jackson from their date along with the three of us while in the parking lot at the grocery store. What the fuck?

The article "Real Life 'Why Choose' Romance?" speculates many possibilities. Still, the gist of the article is about "capturing the attention of playboy Sebastian Dubree." I knew this would happen, damn it, and I didn't even warn her about it. I planned to have that talk last night, but something interrupted.

"I'm not sure, but the pictures in the article aren't the ones I deleted from the camera. They're cell phone pictures. The guy in the corner that night must have taken some of his own. How he managed to get the others, I don't know. We haven't seen anyone suspicious around her, and we kept an eye out the entire time last night. There was no one." He's as frustrated as I am, I can tell. I know this isn't his fault; I'm simply blaming the only person around.

The picture of us was from our first date when I picked her up. Dammit. I kissed her on purpose that afternoon, I remember. I didn't even consider the consequences. This is my fault. The question is how to put this fire out and keep it from growing. I'm so pissed and have no one to blame but myself. "What's your plan of action?"

"I'll try to find the source, but they're usually strict about it, so that's probably a dead end. With this being a gossip piece and no privacy laws violated, I don't have any solid ammunition to press them to release the info. I already tightened up security around Miss Thompson this morning, so we should be able to prevent any more pictures."

"Good. It's integral you're there when she arrives at the gala this Friday. I don't want her bombarded by someone looking to further the story. In the meantime, ensure no one is lurking, and absolutely no one is to approach her from the media."

"Got it, sir. I'll instruct my staff immediately."

I make one last request. "Be sure you're not obvious. I don't want Lily knowing she's being watched. I want her to feel normal. Make interceptions before they happen and only reveal yourself if necessary."

"Yes, sir."

I slam the phone down in frustration. Damn it all to hell. How did I let this happen? I usually only worry about the media at large events or celebrity hot spots. I wasn't thinking, too wrapped up in feeling. And now here I am, without the girl who the media thinks captured my attention. Little do they know I was the one to capture her.

Dropping Lily off last night was brutal. I was so angry at her for not telling me her plans and keeping me in the dark. Would I have reacted differently if she'd told me earlier? I don't fucking know. I get it, we weren't talking then, but dammit, when we were, she had plenty of time to clue me in. What am I supposed to do, stand by while she has another man on her arm? That's not how I work. Fuck the article and it's "why choose" bullshit. I don't share.

Lily

There was no way in hell I was making it out of bed this morning for school. It's the first day I've missed all year. Unfortunately, I can't afford to miss work. My eyes are red and puffy, and I look like hell, but who cares? It's just Brad, and I don't give a crap what he thinks of me. I'm pretty sure there was nothing on the calendar today, relieving me from greeting clients and having to paste on a fake smile.

I cried for hours last night before I fell asleep. Cici was out again, so it was easy to wallow in my sorrow. I'm so angry at myself for getting into this situation. And I'm angry at Sebastian for being persistent and winning me over. I was doing fine before he showed up. My life was normal, uncomplicated… boring even. Now I have multiple men in pursuit of me, when all I want is one of them.

I've done as much as I can to cover up the blotchiness, but not good enough according to the look on Brad's face when he sees me. Great, I don't want to have to explain what happened. Maybe I'll tell him my cat died. Oh God, that's morbid; I can't.

"I take it you already saw the article then?"

"Uh, what?" I'm completely lost.

"Oh. I assumed that's why you look upset. So you haven't seen it?"

"Brad, what are you talking about?" I'm getting frustrated now.

"You might want to Google your name this morning. You're the star feature of the gossip column today. Sebastian Dubree is a high-profile man, Lily. Who he's dating is news, and that seems to be you. I'll give you some time to catch up on that end, but then come see me to go over the rest of the week." He walks away.

What the hell? I type in my name; sure enough there's a news article from today. Oh. My. God. I read through it and cringe. The article is all speculation from the pictures they have. There are no facts. It ends with: "Is Lily the heroine in her real life 'why choose' romance, or are two men fighting to the end? Stay tuned as we uncover the details of this steamy love triangle." What the actual? There's a picture of me kissing Sebastian on the sidewalk, one of me kissing Jackson on our date, and one with all three of us talking in the parking lot. This looks awful. If I thought things couldn't get worse, I was wrong.

I'm sure Sebastian is livid. There's no way he'll want to give me another chance after this, dashing my last hope. I've made a fool out of him. This article makes me look like a complete player. God, I feel terrible, knowing this is all my fault. Why did I fight my feelings for Sebastian?

And what was I thinking going out with Jackson after deciding to date Sebastian? Even though it's too late for any of these questions, I can't help but berate myself for my actions. There's no way I can fix this.

I enter Brad's office determined not to let him make this worse. "Brad, I'd rather not talk about the article. I read it, and it's all crap. I'm dealing with some personal issues, and I don't want to add to them. I'd like to dive right into work if that's okay?" The best thing I can do right now is distract myself.

"I'll leave it be for now. But I'd like to know if I should be worried about this affecting my business. I trust you'll bring it to my attention if anything changes regarding the arrangement with Dubree Enterprises?" he says with raised eyebrows.

"I will. So, do you want me to continue putting pitches together for the clients we outlined the other day using your suggestions?"

"Sure, I'll give you through tomorrow, and we'll proceed next week with the following steps." Situation avoided. I can't believe he conceded and isn't pressuring me for information. I must really look a mess if he's going easy on me.

After making it through the rest of the day focused on work and managing not to cry, I enter our building only to run into Jackson in the lobby. *Why, God, why?* "Hey, Jackson. So… did you happen to see the article today?" I may as well get it over with.

"Yeah, crazy, huh? Amazing they have nothing better to do than talk about other people's lives." He runs a hand through his hair. I would've gone crazy over that a few weeks ago, drooling, and now nothing.

"I'm sorry I pulled you into this. I'm also sorry if I led you on. I'm just sorry for everything." Once again I lose it, breaking down in tears.

Jackson pulls me into his arms. "Hey now, shh. It's not your fault, Lily. We're all adults. We make our own decisions. If anything, it's my fault. I was the asshole who made a move when I knew you started seeing someone. It was a dickhead thing to do. I'm the one that should be apologizing, not you. And I am sorry, Lily. I'm sorry you're being gossiped about and I'm sorry if I added to your stress." He continues to hold me and stroke my hair.

"No, I should've made better decisions. And you didn't do anything wrong. Are we good? Are we still friends?" I pull away and look up at him, wiping my tears.

"Lily, you mean the world to me. I want you to be happy, and no matter what, I'll always be here for you as your friend."

I lean in to hug him again, glad that we had this talk. At least something good came out of today.

"Thanks, Jackson. You don't know how relieved I am to hear that. I better get upstairs. Cici's waiting for me. I'll see you later." I wave and head into the elevator.

Cici's been blowing up my phone the whole time I was talking to Jackson, asking where I was. I texted earlier that I'd come right home to fill her in after she reached out frantic about the article.

"What took you so long? I've been texting you!" she bursts out as soon as I have the door open.

"I ran into Jackson in the lobby. We were talking," I tell her.

"Oh wow, how did that go? Had he seen the article?"

"Yeah. We both said sorry. He said he's there for me if I need him, and we'll always be friends. It was actually perfect timing. I needed that. I'm just glad one thing ended up going well today."

"So, what does Sebastian have to say about it? Is he pissed? Did he even know about you and Jackson kissing? I'm sure that was quite the shock for him to see." She wasn't home last night to hear how he broke things off. She has no idea.

"I didn't want to interfere with your date, but Sebastian cut things off last night, before the article came out. When he found out I asked Kevin to the gala and didn't tell him about it, he was livid. Said I obviously didn't know how communication worked and that he can't be with someone like that. He said he had enough issues of his own to deal with." The tears are pooling in my eyes from recounting our argument.

"Oh, honey, come here. I'm so sorry." She pulls me in for a hug, and again, I'm a blubbering fool.

"I don't know what to do, Cici. I think I'm in love with him, and I've royally screwed up. After some time to cool down, I thought he might come around, and we could talk. But now, with this article, I don't think he'll ever give me another chance. I've humiliated him. There I was kissing someone else while dating him. What was I thinking, Cici?" I just want to crawl in a hole and escape for a while.

"You were thinking you wanted no regrets in your new relationship. If you hadn't gone out with Jackson, would you have ever fully gotten over him? So, yeah, it looks bad, but you did nothing wrong. You were up front with Sebastian about seeing Jackson. He knew, and he still pursued you. That's on him. You're not the woman they're portraying in that article, Lily. Don't let them make you doubt yourself."

"This is such a mess. I just wish I could fix everything. Maybe I just need to sleep it off… for a week maybe?" I give her half a smile and one more hug before I trudge to my room.

I decide to bite the bullet and send a text to Sebastian. It's killing me that I've put him in this position, and I want to apologize.

> Lily: Hey, I'm sorry about the article. I don't know how they got all those pictures. I'm sorry I made you look bad, and most of all, I'm sorry I didn't tell you about the gala.

> Heartbreak: The article is in no way your fault. I'm getting to the bottom of it. They won't write anything else about you—I'll make sure of it. We ran our course, Lily, don't worry about it.

Is there really anything to say after that? I don't know what I expected, but I had a slight hope he'd say he missed me. It certainly wasn't that we'd "run our course." I'm glad I didn't give in and type that I missed him, because we're obviously not on the same page. I finally manage to cry myself into a miserable night's sleep.

29

WEAR IT

Lily

FEEL LIKE ABSOLUTE CRAP WHEN I OPEN MY EYES FRIDAY MORNING. They're puffy and practically swollen shut from crying myself to sleep for the past three nights. I probably shouldn't even be going to the gala this evening, but it's an opportunity I can't pass up. Seeing Sebastian is going to be agonizing. It'll be a feat if I manage to keep it together.

Funny, we weren't even *together*, together. Now that I think about it, I don't think it's considered a breakup. That's what it feels like though. Eventually we could have been something more had I only been up front. Or maybe it was inevitable. It's not like I have the best track record of people I love staying in my life. First, Mom, then Dad. Now Sebastian. Maybe I'm the problem. Maybe I'm being punished for something I did in a past life.

How awkward is it going to be with Kevin beside me all night, the very reason we broke up. Now the paparazzi will have one more guy to picture me with. Great, I'll go from heroine to whore. Damn it that I asked him to go. It was an impulsive decision, and if I'd just taken a few seconds to think first, I would've realized what a bad idea it was. Not because of Sebastian, since we weren't even talking, but because it could give Kevin false hope. I was scared to lose him as a friend and wanted to smooth things over. Our friendship means a lot. I don't have many, so the ones I have are important. Now, I may have saved a friendship, only to lose the man I love.

Frustrated, I get out of bed and go to the kitchen. Cici is there with the same look of sympathy I've seen for the last couple days now and hands me a cup of coffee.

"How are you this morning? You cried yourself to sleep again last night, didn't you?" she asks carefully.

"It's that obvious, huh? I'm a mess. I can't go tonight, Cici. I can't face him—especially with Kevin there. I wish I could go back in time and do things differently." I plop on the barstool and sip my coffee.

"I know, Lily, but you have to go. You'll just need to focus on networking and nothing else. Ignore Sebastian, ignore Brad, and don't let Kevin continue to make you feel bad for only wanting to be friends. You've made your feelings clear, and either he needs to accept it or walk away." Everything she says is true; if only I were strong enough to follow through.

"You're right and I'll try. I just need to make it through today until you can give me another pep talk when I get home. You'll be here to help me get ready, right?" I can't do it without her.

"Definitely. Mostly because I know if I'm not, you'll chicken out and stay home." She smiles knowingly.

"Ugh. I better get ready for work. Cross your fingers for me that I make it through the day with no encounters," I say as I trudge back into my room.

Deciding what to wear, I choose a boring pantsuit that won't stand out. I'm praying I don't run into him so I don't lose it at the office. Although what if that's what happens tonight? This seriously sucks. Maybe I should have been more like Sebastian and vowed not to get suckered into feelings, because this blows.

Sebastian

I know I'm being a chicken shit, but scheduling myself out of the office today was the only way I knew I could keep my distance from Lily. Being in the same building would have been too tempting. I hated sending that text last night, but ending things was the right decision. There can't be a relationship without trust, and damn it, I didn't want a relationship anyway. I already let myself get far too invested. Her omission was the sign I needed to bring clarity, and it came at the perfect time, before my feelings got any more out of control. It's unfortunate she had to be hurt in the process.

My phone buzzes, and I pull it out of my pocket. No surprise it's Eli. "Hey, what's up?" I answer.

"Where are you? Lucy told me you're out for the day?"

"Yeah, I thought it would be good to do some drop-ins at a few of our local subsidiaries and see how they're doing." I know he won't buy it, but it's the best I came up with.

"Sure, you did. Perhaps to avoid someone?" he asks smugly.

"I don't think it's wise to see her yet. And not just for my sake but hers. She'll be more comfortable knowing I'm not there today."

"Sebastian, look, I know she should have told you about the gala, and I'm not saying what she did was right, but don't you think you're looking for any excuse to pull away? You've been trying to keep her at arm's length the entire time, and now you're just using this as your way out. Why? Because you know you have feelings for her, and you're being a coward."

"How much do I owe, Doctor Dubree? Jesus Christ, Eli, give it a rest, would you? It's not like I was going to marry the damn girl. It was sex."

"Sure, whatever makes you sleep better. I'll call you if I need anything. Otherwise, I'll see you tonight." He ends the call abruptly, clearly unhappy with me.

He's my date this evening since my first choice already had one. I can't bring myself to pull my regular crap and find a one-off. I can already tell Eli's going to be a bundle of joy. Fuck, maybe he's right and I am being a coward.

These last couple days have been hell. I've snapped at everyone who gets within earshot for no reason. On Wednesday night, I drank myself into a stupor in order to pass out and stop thinking about her, which didn't even fucking work since she starred in my dreams. Then my hangover was so bad, I couldn't bring myself to do a repeat so I sat deliberating all night. While doing so, I realized she is everything I could ever want in a woman... *if* I wanted one. The problem is she compels me to want her. I find myself longing for more with her, and that scares the hell out of me. Honestly, I'm already too far gone, and if I'm already neglecting the people in my inner circle as much as I have at this point, imagine how bad it would be if I fell in love with her. Is that a risk I'm willing to take?

Lily

So far so good. I caught wind that Sebastian is out for the day, lucky me. No one has said anything about Friday still, and everyone's behaving pleasantly enough. Only two coworkers that I've noticed are less than enthused about me being the boss's… whatever. Little do they know I'm not anymore.

Outside my office I overhear Bob, the head of marketing, talking to someone about tonight's gala. This is a perfect opportunity to get some information. Stepping around the corner, I interject into the conversation. "Hey, Bob, I was just curious about the gala tonight. Does everyone go? Did any of your projects win?" I hope that sounded innocent enough.

"No, not everyone. Eli, Sebastian, and whoever is responsible for a winning submission. Tonight, we have quite a few categories we picked up an award in, so they're having me attend to represent the entire group. Eli and Sebastian have done a great job hiring a stellar team for this department. We rival the top firms out there. You should consider going full-time after you graduate. I think you'd be a great addition, and I'd be happy to put in a recommendation."

"Wow, thank you, Bob, that means a lot to me. I'll keep it in mind. Anyway, I was asking because I'll be at the gala tonight. I won the student category for best campaign."

"That's fantastic and not at all surprising. I look forward to seeing you there and introducing you to my wife Natalie." He probably thinks I'll be there with Sebastian.

"Sounds great, Bob. I'll see you there." Smiling, I walk away and retreat back to my office.

As soon as five o'clock hits, I make my way to the elevator. After stepping inside, I see Eli in the back and smile in acknowledgement. When I exit into the lobby he catches up to me.

"Lily, hey, can I talk to you for a minute?" He looks sheepish.

"Sure, Eli, what's up?" I ask as he motions for me to follow him to the side for more privacy.

"I want to apologize for my brother. He can be difficult to handle sometimes to say the least. How are you doing?" he asks nervously.

"I appreciate that, Eli, but it's not your responsibility to apologize for Sebastian. And regardless, he has every right to be upset. I should have been upfront with him. And thank you for asking. I'm doing the best I can, just taking it day by day. Tonight may be uncomfortable." I smile to make light of a crappy situation. Just talking about it makes my eyes water. I hope I'm concealing it well enough.

"Do you still have feelings for him, or is it too late? Sorry if that's none of my business," he quickly adds. "I just care a lot for the guy, and I know how torn up he is." He looks conflicted. I can tell he loves his brother.

"I've never been in love before now, but I'm pretty sure it takes more than a couple days to fade. As for being too late, you're asking the wrong person."

"You love Sebastian?" he asks incredulously.

"Unfortunately. I didn't mean to, and I wasn't going to tell him. He made it clear from the beginning what this was. It's certainly not his fault I'm in this situation when I knew exactly what I was getting into. I'm a big girl, I'll be fine. But thanks again for checking in with me. Sebastian's lucky to have you." With that, I turn and walk away, hoping I really will be okay.

I'm still going over the conversation with Eli in my head when I walk in our front door. After greeting the needy Miss Ebony, I set my stuff down and head into the kitchen with her in my arms. I've been the more needy one between us over the last couple days, that's for sure.

Cici has a glass of wine for me with an interesting look on her face. "You got a delivery today. Two boxes arrived about an hour ago. Are you expecting anything?"

"No. Is that them?" I ask, pointing to two boxes sitting on the living room table.

"Yeah, it doesn't say who they're from, just the store name. Hurry up and open them. It's killing me. I considered peeking inside and not telling you, but I didn't. I was this close." She shows me a tiny gap in between her thumb and pointer finger.

"Cici, you're terrible," I say, smiling.

I open up the smaller one to a pair of shoes. There's no indication of who they came from. They're expensive, I can tell.

"Oh my God, Lily, those are like the most-wanted shoes of the season right now. Holy shit, girl, open the other one. I'm dying here."

I take the lid off the other box and stare down at the most beautiful designer dress. It matches the shoes perfectly. Again, no message.

"Wow, I guess you know what you're wearing tonight, huh?" She's taking the dress out and holding it up.

"Cici, stop! I'm not keeping them. It doesn't even say who it's from. What if they got delivered to the wrong address?" There, that makes total sense.

"Good call, except the delivery person said it was for Lily Thompson. He wouldn't even leave them until I showed him something with your name on it. What if it's from Sebastian and he wants to make up?"

"Please don't talk like that. I can't get my hopes up. Let's call the store and ask who bought it. Will you do it? Pleassssse?"

"Yeah, okay. Let me get my phone."

Five minutes later, we still don't know who they're from—privacy crap apparently. We at least found out they were purchased on Monday. That means it could have been Sebastian right before our falling out.

"Listen, I'm still not wearing them. He probably forgot he even bought them for me. I'm returning both tomorrow. And if they're from someone else, that's even worse because they shouldn't be. I'm not wearing it. End of discussion." Damn these setbacks with my emotions—the conversation with Eli and now this.

Cici doesn't let it rest. "I have an idea. Why don't you text Sebastian and ask if it was an accident or if it's even from him. Then at least you'll know someone else isn't being creepy. I see that look. Come on, Lily, stop thinking and just do it." She has a good point about making sure it wasn't anyone else.

"Ugh, fine." I give in and grab my phone.

> Lily: Hey, I just want to see if a dress and shoes that got delivered today are from you by chance? If so, I can return them to the store tomorrow.
>
> Heartbreak: WEAR THEM.

"Uh, mystery solved and his only response was 'wear them' in all caps," I inform her.

"*Eeeeee!*" she squeals and claps her hands like a kid at a carnival. "I knew it! He does want to get back together."

"Cici, that's not what this means. He only wants me to wear the items that were already purchased anyway. It means nothing. I'm not going to give it any more thought, and you shouldn't either."

"Fine, but I'm allowed to think what I want." She sticks her tongue out, and I give her a shove in return.

"C'mon, help me get ready for this damn thing," I say and she happily carries the dress while I grab the shoes and head back to my room.

Forty-five minutes later, I look like a million bucks. Cici is unbelievably talented at hair and makeup. This will give me the boost I need to make it through the night.

"God, Cici, thank you so much. You always make me look so… amazing. Seriously, we may have to try that sister-wife thing someday, I don't know if I can survive without you." I grab my clutch and say goodbye before heading out.

Sebastian

Why did I even come tonight? Seeing Lily is going to be the death of me. But not seeing her would be worse. What the fuck was I thinking ordering her to wear the dress I sent. I was fuming after she offered to return it. I had plenty of time to cancel the order, which after briefly considering, chose not to do. I want her to shine in her moment. But now she's going to capture the eye of every man here. Although she probably would have done that without the dress. She just draws people in, and no one more so than me.

"Fancy seeing you here," Eli says, finding me at the bar.

"Fuck off." I've been ruminating all day over Eli's words earlier. I'm pissed they had such an impact on me. Who is he to question my actions? I'm only trying to prevent going down the same path as our father. If I make a sacrifice to protect our future, then so be it. His memory seems to have short-circuited if he can't put two and two together.

"Anyone here catch your fancy? How about that blonde over there with her tits halfway out of her dress—her nipples just might be peeking. I bet you could take her home." *Asshole.*

"Shut the fuck up, Eli. I know you're not stupid. Yeah, I got in too deep with Lily. I said it. Now will you stop egging me on?"

"No, not until you stop being an idiot. By the way, I had a nice chat with her today." He stops at that. Damn it, I knew having him here would haunt me.

"Go on then. I know you're dying to tell me."

"It was interesting to say the least. Not surprisingly, Lily takes all the blame. Said she should have been up front with you. Very admirable, although I think it's total shit. You're a prick and we all know it. She's unfortunately in love with you. Didn't say I couldn't tell you, only that *she* hadn't told you. I feel sorry for her since you could never reciprocate those feelings. She ended the conversation with glistening eyes, saying she's a big girl and knew exactly what she was getting into, so she'd be fine. You, however, I'm not so sure about. If you get any burlier, I'm going to pull your head out of your ass for you." With a smug look, he sips his drink, apparently done with his speech. I seriously want to knock my brother upside the head. He's always been the one person who got me, and now he's acting like a little prick. How did one woman turn him against me?

Wait, did he just say she loved me? That's not possible. I'm controlling, possessive, and I refused the possibility of more. There's no way she could love someone like that. He had to have misunderstood. She may love certain things about me but certainly not *me*. She deserves better; someone more suited for her. But when I think about her with anyone else, it's like a knife in my gut.

I'm still stewing when Lily appears at the entrance. We're both speechless. I instructed Lucy on what I wanted, but holy shit, this is next level. It looks like she just stepped out of a magazine. Sleek, sophisticated, sexy. Fuck, I should have let her return it. I wouldn't have ordered her to wear it had I known it would make her a male magnet. *Fuck me.* There's barely a man in the room without his eyes on her.

"Well, brother, I guess it's a good thing you're not together, because she's about to be hit on by every guy in the building and now you won't have to fight anyone." He whistles quietly. "You sure know how to pick 'em." I'm seriously going to murder him by night's end.

"I need another drink." *An endless supply.*

Luckily, Eli decides he's had enough of me and leaves for better company. My eyes stay glued to her as she works the room, and mine aren't the only ones. No man can resist. I see Bob introduce his wife and I watch Lily as they converse. She is perfect in every way. From her greeting to her goodbye, she is the epitome of class. The only thing wrong with the picture is she should be by my side, not standing beside that boy all night. His obsession is evident from here, making me sick to my stomach.

Cringing, I see Brad approach, not bothering to hide the absolute lust in his eyes. When he goes in for a hug, her distaste is apparent as her body stiffens. He has the nerve to place his hand much lower than acceptable. I'm two seconds from making my way over when he releases her. Watching him introduce her pushes me to the brink of my tolerance. I should be the one making introductions for Lily, escorting her throughout the room. And it's no one's fault but my own that I'm not.

I've come to the complete realization that I fucked up. It hit me the minute she walked in the room. Watching her all evening has only confirmed it. As much as I wish it possible, I can't change the past. In hindsight, I should have simply agreed to the boy's attendance while insisting she be at my side. Instead, my anger got the best of me. It's time to fix this and make her mine once and for all; hopefully I'm not too late. With my decision made, I start toward her. Before I make it five feet we're called to our seats for the main event. For now, it will have to wait.

Lily's table is three down from mine on the left. I've avoided making eye contact thus far, not wanting to see the hurt I caused. Making small talk during dinner is daunting with my preoccupation, and Eli takes over, keeping the focus on himself. Her category is about to be called, and my anticipation grows. It's finally announced, and I get lost in the sight of her as she makes her way across the stage. With the award in hand, she approaches the microphone. Simply stunning. The entire room is captivated.

Lily

I'm a nervous wreck as I walk to the podium. You can have the best dress, the shoes to go with it, incredible hair and makeup, and it still doesn't take the jitters away. The room claps as I accept the award and approach the podium.

"Thank you so much to the American Advertising Awards panel for choosing my project. This is truly an honor. I want to thank Professor Milton for believing my work worthy of submission and for the wonderful teaching and guidance you've provided me over the last four years. I look forward to creating more amazing work through my future career in marketing. Again, thank you so much."

The crowd gives a round of applause as I leave the stage. I caught sight of Sebastian once during my speech and was shocked by the intensity of his gaze. I had to look away immediately or I would've botched the rest. We haven't spoken at all this evening and, until that moment, hadn't even made eye contact. I've tried to keep from looking at him, as impossible as it was, but I did catch a couple glimpses and he looks amazing, of course. I was relieved to notice that there wasn't a woman on his arm. I think that would have broken me. Just being in the same room without his acknowledgment is already breaking my heart. I had the slightest hope from his insistence to wear the dress that he had a change of heart, but that's obviously not the case.

My nerves are shot, so instead of returning to my seat, I go for the bar instead, mouthing an apology to Kevin on the way. Luckily, the bartender takes my order immediately. What a night. I got peppered with questions about Sebastian and I on the way in by some reporter. Thank goodness there was security around to intervene as I stood there stunned. Then being paraded around by Brad was maddening. I'm glad I was able to meet so many people, but the way he was introducing me just gave me the creeps for some reason. I thought Kevin would be a buffer, but he stayed behind us the whole night. It was all around awkward.

"Make that two of whatever the lady ordered," Brad says, appearing out of nowhere. Great, more socializing with Douchebag. "Lily, great job on your acceptance speech. Seeing you blossom over the last few years has been quite the privilege. I always knew you would be one of the best in the field, and can I just say again how stunning you look tonight."

"I'll get that." I hear Kevin say from behind me as he steps up to the bar, handing his credit card over at the same time the waiter places my drink down.

"Kevin, you don't have to do that," I insist.

"I want to. Now I can have the first drink," he says jokingly and winks as he picks it up.

"I would have let you regardless but thank you." I turn back toward Brad as he continues the conversation. I was hoping Kevin would be able to save me, but he's not much help.

"So, Lily, have you thought about what you're going to do after you graduate?" Brad asks.

"I want to start applying to some big marketing firms as it gets closer. You knew I wasn't going to stick around forever, right?" I smile in jest, hoping this doesn't go in the wrong direction.

He takes a sip of his drink, reminding me how much I needed mine. I turn to Kevin, and he hands it over with a smile. I smile back and almost down the whole thing.

"You know, Lily, you could come in as a partner, and we could grow the firm to become one of those powerhouses you dream of. With my years of experience and your fresh ideas, we'd be a great team." Crap, I really hate that he's springing this on me now, but maybe it's a good thing considering we're surrounded by people.

"I'm sure we would, but I really want to get my feet wet and see what it's like working for one of the big guys. I appreciate the offer and am flattered that you'd consider me, but I think I'll stick to my plan."

"Well, that's too bad. I really saw a future with you… in marketing that is," he adds with a smirk on his face.

This is getting uncomfortable, and maybe now would be a good time to make my exit. "Well, boys, I think it's time for a trip to the ladies' room. If you'll excuse me," I say, finishing my drink. Unfortunately, things don't always go as planned.

Brad takes the opportunity. "You know what, I'll escort you. I need to use the men's room myself."

"All right then. Kevin, I'll be back in just a bit."

"I'll be here," Kevin says in return.

As we head toward the restrooms, Brad takes it upon himself to place his hand on my back as if he's truly escorting me. Seriously, the nerve of this guy. Luckily, I see the bathroom just ahead.

"Thanks, Brad, I think I got it from here." I immediately pick up my pace and escape inside.

As I'm reapplying my lipstick, I start to feel woozy. Must've downed my drink too fast. It really seems to be hitting me more than usual. My nerves have been shot all night; maybe I forgot to eat as much as I should've. Crap, I'm really not feeling well all of a sudden. I better get Kevin and let him know I need to go home and cut the night short. The room spins as I turn around, and I realize it's probably not a good idea to go back in. Instead I head toward the exit to grab one of the taxis waiting outside. I'll just text Kevin to apologize.

30

NEVER LET YOU GO

Sebastian

'M FINALLY READY TO GET A HANDLE ON MY SHIT THIS MORNING. Hitting the gym to release some aggression seemed like a good idea before moving forward with my plan. After three hours of sweating, I'm prepared to talk it out with Lily and convince her to give me a chance.

I felt defeated after realizing she'd left the gala last night. Seeing her at the bar flanked by Kevin and Brad after her speech made my blood boil, deciding then and there it was time to set things straight. But as I stood to head over, Bob and his wife Natalie approached and by the time I turned around, she was gone. I tried looking for her at the bathrooms, even barging in, only to realize I was too late.

Eli distracted me from my frustration by taking us to the club, pushing me to catch up on some of the duties I'd been neglecting as of late. It worked, keeping me busy until midnight, with no time to ponder my situation or ruminate on what Lily could be doing or who she could be with.

Although once I made it home, all rationality left, and my thoughts took a nosedive. Before closing my eyes, I couldn't refrain from sending her one last text telling her how beautiful she looked, how wonderful she spoke and how sorry I was. All unanswered. Which in turn, only made me more anxious about who she may have left with.

Having had time to work out my thoughts at the gym, I feel confident knocking on Lily's door with flowers in hand. I gave her no warning I was coming. Cici opens the door and looks at me skeptically. "What are you doing here? Where's Lily?" she asks in confusion.

"I'm here to see her. We need to talk. I take it she's not in?" The thought makes me seethe. The possibility that she stayed the night with another man has me in knots.

She motions me inside and closes the door, turning on me with concern in her eyes. "I don't know what's going on, but she sent a text last night saying she was with you and wouldn't be home for the weekend. Did you not leave with her?"

"I don't know who she left with. One minute I was on my way to talk to her, and the next I turned around and she was gone. I assumed she went home, or at least that's what I was hoping. Maybe she didn't want to say who she was really with." I set the flowers on the counter and run my hand through my hair in frustration.

"I know Lily. She wouldn't lie to me like that," she insists.

"Well, I don't know what to tell you because she isn't with me, so where the hell is she?" Cici doesn't answer.

"You know what? Call your brother. Maybe she had a change of heart." A possibility I hadn't contemplated, but it makes total sense. He was the reason she couldn't commit to begin with. One fuckup from me, and there's no reason not to turn back to him. Goddammit.

"She wouldn't have. Her mind was made up, and it wasn't Jackson she wanted—it was you. You went and fucked that up." Did she just call me out? I don't have time for this bullshit.

"Just call your brother. Now," I demand.

"Fine, but I know she's not there." I hear the one-sided exchange, and I can already tell Cici's right. Lily hasn't been there. The relief I feel is indescribable. However short-lived, because that still leaves the question, where the hell is she?

"The last two people I saw her talking to at the party were Kevin and her boss, Brad. One of them had to have seen her leave or know where she is." I'm interrupted by a pounding on the front door.

Cici opens it to a frantic Jackson barging into the room.

"What do you mean you don't know where Lily is? What's going on?" Jackson demands.

"This doesn't concern you. You should leave and mind your own business," I reply angrily.

"Listen, asshole, she might not have chosen me, but she's still my goddamn friend and somebody I care about, so I'm making it my business. Now what the hell is going on?" I can tell he's not going to back down.

"You know what? Never mind, I'll find her myself. I'm out of here." I turn to leave, but Cici calls out.

"Sebastian, wait. We're all concerned here. Let's stick together and help each other figure this out. I can get ahold of Kevin while you call her boss. Then we'll decide where to go from there. It'll be faster this way. Lily gave me Kevin's number after we met at the club." She doesn't wait for a response and makes the call. Frustrated, I do the same because she's right; the more hands on deck, the quicker we find Lily.

We hang up with no more answers than before. Brad insists he didn't see her after walking her to the restroom, admitting he didn't make it out for a while due to an upset stomach and assumed she had left already. Kevin said he got a text from her that she was going home in a taxi with an apology saying she wasn't feeling well. That leaves us nowhere.

"So what, she just disappeared?" Jackson pipes in.

"It appears that way. The more important question is, why would she send a text telling Cici she was with me for the weekend? It makes no sense. And honestly, I don't trust either of those two as far as I can throw them. There's got to be something we're missing. Did Kevin say where he went after the event?" I ask Cici.

"Well, no, but I didn't ask him." Seeing the look of disapproval on my face, she continues, "He wasn't my concern, Lily is. Did you ask Brad where he went?"

I let out a frustrated sigh. "No, I didn't." A satisfied look crosses her face.

"All right then. What do we do now?" Cici contemplates. "Why don't I try texting her again?" She reads out her text as she types. "'Hey, Lily, Sebastian is here looking for you. He said you weren't with him last night.

Is everything okay? We're worried about you.' Okay, now what?" she asks, waiting for someone to come up with an idea.

"I'm going to call my security team and see if I can't dig up any of the front entrance camera footage from the venue."

Lily

My head is pounding. *Crap.* I don't remember how I got home last night. Did I let myself get that out of control? Reluctantly, I peel my eyes open and immediately notice this isn't my bed. I have no idea where I am. When I move to sit up, I'm stopped by a tug on my ankle. I lift the covers to see a rope around it. *What the hell is going on?* Questions flood my mind as I start to panic.

"Good morning, sleepyhead" comes a voice from the doorway. *Wait…* I recognize that voice. He enters completely. *Oh my God.* "You should learn to control your drinking, Lily. It's a terrible habit. However, you're not entirely at fault. There may have been a little something slipped into your drink last night," he mockingly says as he sits in a chair by the bed.

"Why am I here and tied to the bed? What's going on? What happened?" I'm so confused. I have no idea how I got here or why he's doing this.

"I'm sure you have a lot of questions. All in due time, which we have plenty of now that we're finally together."

"You're scaring me. Will you please tell me what's happening? What do you want?" Panic has officially set in.

"I want it all, Lily. I want what's mine."

"What do you mean? Seriously, you can't just take me, this is crazy." I don't know his plan for me, but I need to keep him talking and hopefully distracted enough from doing anything rash. Trying to figure a way out of this is all that's running through my mind.

"The only crazy thing is that I can't get you out of my mind. I've tried. Now I'm trying a different tactic. This can work. You just need a little persuasion is all," he says in a seductive voice.

Crap, that is not the direction I want this to go. *Please no.* "I can't be persuaded. It doesn't work like that. Please just let me go. People are going to be looking for me. You could get in trouble for this." There. Maybe common sense will get through. He can't assume that no one is going to question where I disappeared to.

"We won't have to worry about that. Nobody important saw us leave, and those who did only thought I was helping my date, who had too much to drink. Cici also received a text from you last night telling her you wouldn't be home for the weekend because you had some making up to do with Sebastian."

"Okay, then what? That only covers the weekend, and then Cici will figure it out. There are other people who will be worried if they don't hear from me." There actually aren't, but he doesn't need to know that. "You're delusional if you think there's anything you can do or say to make me want you at this point." He stands up and walks toward the bed.

"That's where you're wrong." Reaching his hand toward me, I immediately flinch away.

He grabs my hair and pulls me toward him roughly while his other hand strokes my cheek. Tears pool in my eyes and make their way down.

"Now, now, Lily, please don't make me hurt you. Things will go much smoother if you accept the inevitable. This doesn't have to be difficult. Just let me show you what I can offer."

"I don't want anything from you. Please don't, I'm begging. I don't need you to show me anything. Just let me go before it's too late." I'm starting to lose hope. The tears are flowing now, and I don't know what direction to take; nothing seems to be working.

"I know what you need, Lily. Don't worry, I can give you that and so much more. I promise."

He continues to hold my head firmly while his other hand goes downward as he leans in to kiss me. My instincts set in and I fight him, using all my strength to push him away. I succeed in keeping his lips off me, but I'm no match for his strength. He reaches in his back pocket as he pins me down and brings out a pair of handcuffs. I continue to struggle. I'm not going down without a fight. He manages to get my hands secured to the bedpost above my head. Now I only have one free limb, and I'm sure if I start trying to kick him, he'll secure that next. Better to save it for later if things get really bad.

"I didn't want to do that, but you gave me no choice. I told you this could be easy if you just give in. Although maybe you like this better, huh?" The look in his eyes tells me he likes it better.

His hand touches my stomach, and I have no way to stop it. He grazes my skin while pushing my shirt up. It didn't even register that I'm not in my dress until now. That means he had me undressed while I was passed out. What has he already done when I couldn't defend myself? The thought makes me sick. His hand skims the underside of my breast, and I squirm, trying to keep him off me, but he's not deterred. *Oh God, please don't let this happen.*

Sebastian

I dial security while Cici stares at her phone, waiting to hear back from Lily, and Jackson continues to pace.

"Good morning, sir." He picks up immediately.

"Did anyone have eyes on Lily last night?" I ask. Maybe they happened to catch her leaving.

"Not after she entered the gala. We intervened when a reporter approached her at the entrance and then called it a night." Fuck. That's my fault. I should have instructed them to stay until she made it home. I didn't know the situation was this fucked up.

"She appears to be missing. Apparently, no one saw her leave the gala or has any idea where she could be. Kevin claims she wasn't feeling well and left in a taxi. Her best friend received a text from Lily last night saying she would be with me all weekend, but I haven't seen her. She's not answering any texts or calls. Can you retrieve the security footage from the front of the venue around nine o'clock last night onward? Also, get me Kevin's address, the guy from coffee on campus, as well as the home address of Brad Smith, her boss. Get them by any means necessary."

"I already have Kevin's address. Even though you told me not to bother looking into him, I followed a hunch and did it anyway. You mentioned he was just a friend from college, however, in my search it came up that he went to high school with Lily as well. More suspicious is that he happens to live two blocks from her. A full report was going to be on your desk Monday morning. I'm sorry I didn't have the information to you sooner."

"Dammit. It's not your fault and I'm glad you followed your instincts. We need to use this to our advantage and get to her before it's too late. Text me the address immediately. I happen to be at Lily's place right now."

"I don't know if it's the best idea for you to go barging in there if he does have her. He could be deranged enough to do something drastic," he warns.

"Let me worry about that. In the meantime, have a file ready to hand over to the police in case. I'll keep you posted." I end the call. Fuck, I'm sure he has her. I should have been paying more attention to him last night, but I couldn't seem to keep my focus off Lily. I should've caught something in his behavior. This is my fault. If anything happens to her, I have no one else to blame. Here I was trying to protect everyone else in my life by keeping my distance, yet I failed the one person who needed me most.

"Did either of you know Kevin in high school?" They both appear confused and insist he didn't go to high school with them.

"Well apparently he did. His infatuation with Lily obviously goes further back than we thought. Even more disturbing is that he also happens to reside a couple blocks over. Jackson, how about you and I head over and confront this son of a bitch?" A little backup would be nice, especially if the guy is unhinged.

Cici chimes in. "Don't even think about going over there without me. If you go, I go." Both Jackson and I bark out no at the same time. I decide to reason with her.

"Cici, we need you here in case we're wrong on this, and she shows up. I promise we'll let you know as soon as we have any answers," I assure her and thankfully, she agrees.

Jackson and I are out the door in two seconds. He tells me he'll meet me in the lobby after he stops at his apartment to grab something. I hope that something is a loaded gun. Minutes later, we're walking out the front doors with the address in hand, hurrying down the street. I'm trying not to imagine what we may find when we get there. Right now, the only thing I need to focus on is getting her back, not the possibility that I may be too late once again.

31

YOU DESERVE TO KNOW

Lily

"YOU KNOW, CICI ISN'T THE ONLY ONE YOU SHOULD WORRY ABOUT. Sebastian is going to wonder where I am when he doesn't hear from me," I say, trying to distract him before he goes further than my breast.

"Lily, I'm not stupid. I saw you avoid each other like the plague last night, but nice try. I was two steps ahead of you the entire time. How do you think they got those pictures of you in the paper? I figured painting you as the slut you are, Sebastian would have nothing to do with you. The one guy you gave no mind to was able to tear you apart. That'll teach you, Lily. Don't be blind to what's right in front of you. But don't worry, doll, you have plenty of time to make it up to me."

My tears won't stop now. He has no idea how right he is, considering he is the reason Sebastian stopped seeing me. I panic as his hand lowers toward my underwear, and just as I'm about to bring my free leg up to knee him, there's a loud knock from somewhere in the house. Has someone come for me? Please, let that be it.

"Good things come to those who wait, darling. I won't be long." He leans down and ends up kissing my cheek as I turn my head away from him.

Before getting up, he grabs something from the floor, and when I see the duct tape, I beg immediately. "No, please, Kevin, don't do that. I'll be quiet, I swear." I'm so afraid. What if I panic and can't breathe through the tape? What if he comes back and leaves it on while he finishes what he started? Oh God, I can't handle this.

"Better to be safe than sorry. Wouldn't want you calling out for help now, would we? *Shh*, Lily. *Shh*. It's okay. I'll be right back." He's seriously trying to console me as he covers my mouth with duct tape. He's sick in the head. Running his hand over my hair, he stares down at me with longing.

The knock sounds again, louder this time. Making his way to the door, he turns and looks at me with some kind of sick satisfaction on his face before leaving. I hear the door lock behind him. I sigh in relief, thankful he's gone... for now. I know he'll be back, and next time there won't be anyone to interrupt whatever his plan is. I struggle but fail to hear anything; the walls are too thick. There must be something I can do.

If I could just figure out how to make noise, I could draw their attention and at least cause whoever's at the door to question the sounds coming from inside. Trying to yell past the tape does no good and barely makes me louder than a cat's meow. I pull against the restraints to see if they budge but only dig the cuffs into my skin. I jerk my body to move the bed and make noise that way, but I have too little leverage to create enough force. I'm about to give in to my frustration and admit defeat when it registers that I still have one leg free.

Sebastian

Jackson and I stop in front of the building matching the address I was given. It's like theirs with a lobby in front. "How do you want to do this? I've met him, so he knows what I look like and might not open the door if he sees me," I tell him. All I want to do is kick the door down and barge in, but I don't want to jeopardize Lily. If he hurts her...

"Yeah, well thanks to that article, he probably knows what I look like too. I haven't met him though, so maybe he won't recognize me right away. Why don't I knock, and you stand to the side." He sees the look of defiance in my face and holds his hand up. "Only until he opens the door.

Once he does that, he can't keep us out. I brought some incentive with me." He lifts his shirt and shows me the gun in the waistband of his pants.

"All right, let's go then. If he tries to slam the door in your face, stick your foot in the jamb. He's obviously not going to fess up, so we'll have to make it inside and search the place. He may not even have her here." Fuck, this is killing me.

"Don't worry, he won't have a chance to shut me out, I'll play it cool. Let's read his reaction. If he's afraid to let me in, then chances are she's there." I fucking hope so.

We reach the hallway, and I stop two doors down, while Jackson goes to knock. It's the longest few seconds of my life. There's no answer. We make eye contact, and Jackson knocks again, with more force this time. We wait another minute, and right as he raises his hand again, the door opens.

"Hi, can I help you?" Forcing myself to remain in position is excruciating. All I want to do is strangle the motherfucker.

"Yeah, hey, you're a friend of Lily's, right?" Jackson asks him.

"I am. We go to college together. Who are you? Is she okay?" The lying little fucker; I can hear it from here.

"I'm Jackson, Lily's friend. I was wondering if you'd seen her by chance. No one can get ahold of her, and she mentioned she was going to some event with you last night?" Smooth one, Jackson.

"Yeah, we went to her award dinner, but she said she was sick and went home. Have you checked there?" I'm done with this charade. He has thirty more seconds to make a move, or I will.

"See, that's the thing, she didn't go home. Do you mind if I come in and we can brainstorm about where she might be?" Jackson's poised and ready, I can tell. Kevin's answer determines whether we go in nicely or by force.

"Now isn't a good time. I'd like to help, but I was getting ready to head out. I've got somewhere I need to be."

I step forward. "That's not going to work for us," I say menacingly. I spot Jackson reach for the gun and pull it out.

Kevin raises his hands in defense. "Christ, all right, come in." Wise choice, asshole.

We walk in, and I notice music playing. Is he trying to cover up noise in the background? He walks us to the kitchen and tries to play it cool.

"I really wish I had any information for you, but I didn't see Lily after she went to the bathroom with her boss. Maybe you should talk to him." He's standing behind the counter opening and closing drawers, like he's looking for something.

"Well, we're here now. You wouldn't mind us taking a peek around, would you?" Jackson says. I'm too pissed to speak. The only thing I want to do is punch this guy's lights out and find Lily.

"Actually I do. You can't just barge in here and invade my privacy—" All at once we hear a faint thumping. Like someone's banging on the wall. Kevin's eyes widen as he registers the murderous look on our faces.

Jackson and I immediately move toward the sound coming from down the hallway. I hear Kevin behind us and turn around in time to see him lunge for Jackson with a knife in his hand. I warn Jackson, who moves to the side, and watch as he body slams Kevin to the ground, the knife falling to the floor.

"Go find Lily. I'll keep watch on this fucker and call the cops," Jackson pants out as he straddles Kevin.

Lily

Please, God, let whoever is at the door still be there. I pound and pound until my body aches from the awkward position I'm twisted in and the sheer force behind my effort. I'm midkick when I hear a ruckus on the other side of the door. It sounds like fighting. I kick with all my might knowing someone's out there. I hear a familiar voice shouting my name before the door bursts open. Sebastian takes one look at the bed in horror and rushes over, gripping my head in his hands. All at once, I can see the relief and anger and another emotion I'm scared to think too much about in his eyes, and I burst into tears.

"Fuck, Lily, I'm so sorry. God, I'm so sorry, baby. Let me get this tape off, okay?" I nod.

He starts to pull it off slowly. *Ouch.* I shake my head and try to tell him go faster, but it's garbled. Instead, I flick my head quickly to the side, and he understands.

"I don't want to hurt you, sweetheart." I do it again. "Fuck, okay, on the count of three. One, two, three…" He rips halfway, giving me one second to breathe before finishing the job.

My eyes pool with more tears from the pain, and immediately Sebastian's lips are on mine, his thumbs wiping my tears as he murmurs between kisses.

"I'm so damn sorry, baby. You're safe now. I'm going to get you out of here. Are you okay? Did he hurt you? I'll kill that motherfucker here and now if he did." He goes to work untying my foot.

"No, not yet. He was about to, but you got here right in time." The key to the handcuffs is on the side table. Kevin wasn't worried about me reaching it. Once free, I throw my arms around Sebastian and lose myself. "I'm so glad you're here. If you hadn't gotten here when you did, it would have been so much worse. Thank you for finding me. How did you?" I ask between sobs.

Pulling me onto his lap, he holds me tight to his chest and kisses the top of my head, consoling me. "I'll tell you all about it, but right now let's get you out of here. Fuck, I was so worried about you, baby, praying I wasn't too late. Thank God we made it in time. I got you, sweetheart. I'm not ever letting go." He cradles my body and lifts me as he stands. I lay my head on his shoulder, so relieved, and let myself relax in the safety of his arms.

"Who's we? Who else is here?" I ask, his words sinking in.

"You'll see." We reach the end of the hallway, and there's Jackson, his face etched with worry while keeping an eye on an unconscious Kevin.

Sebastian addresses him. "She's okay. We got here just in time it sounds like. Here, he was generous enough to provide these." Sebastian hands him the handcuffs that were moments ago around my wrists.

Jackson secures Kevin's hands behind his back and stands facing us. "I knocked him out. Fucker had it coming. You gave us quite the scare, Lily. Be real with me, did he hurt you? Say the word, and I'll make sure he can't do anything like this ever again. I mean it," Jackson says with a gun in his hand.

"No, Jackson, I swear. He was about to, but really, you got here just in time. Thank you." He nods his head and my tears start to flow again.

"I'll stay and watch over him while you take Lily back to her place. I already texted Cici. She's frantic. The cops are on their way. Go, I got this." He nods to Sebastian and smiles at me sadly.

"Thank you, Jackson. This wouldn't have been easy without you. I appreciate your help, even though it wasn't for me." On that final note, Sebastian walks out the door. I realize where we are as he steps outside. We're only two blocks from my building. *What the hell?*

"I can walk now, Sebastian. It's not far." I feel silly being carried down the street.

He looks at me fiercely. "I told you I was never letting you go, and I meant it. I almost lost you, Lily. Twice. First from my own behavior and then because of some psychopath. This could've been prevented had I handled things differently. I'm so sorry. Can you ever forgive me?" The remorse on his face is almost too much to bear.

Before I can respond, though, Cici yells my name and runs toward us. Immediately she throws her arms around me, crying. "I was so worried about you. I can't believe he took you. God, I should've called to make sure. Oh, Lily, I'm so sorry."

"You all need to quit saying you're sorry and blaming yourselves. This is no one's fault but Kevin's. I know he texted you, Cici. There was no reason for you to call me. I was the idiot who let him slip something into my drink." How did I let that happen?

"Come on, let's get her inside so she can relax before the police arrive. I'm sure they'll want a full statement, and then we can all hear the details together. Jackson probably wants to be clued in as well, so let's just rest and regroup for now." Wow. I never thought Sebastian would consider Jackson's feelings or that things may be normal between us three, but apparently something good did come out of this.

Sebastian

I can't get enough of her, can't stop touching her, afraid she'll disappear. She may get annoyed with my hovering, but I can't seem to help it. The thoughts that went through my mind from the moment I knew she was in trouble until having her in my arms are too fresh for me to give her an ounce of space. I don't know how it happened or when exactly, but I fell in love with Lily somewhere along the way, and now that it's hit me, I refuse to let her go. It kills me that it took something so drastic to make me realize it.

We haven't had a moment to talk about us or where we stand, but I can't go any longer without making my feelings known. The police arrived minutes after returning to her place with Jackson not far behind, assuring us that Kevin was in custody. After the questioning she had to endure and each of us having to give our statements, she was exhausted. By the time I carried her to my bed upon bringing her to my place, she was practically passed out. I texted Eli on the way home and filled him in briefly, letting him know I wouldn't be in the office for a day or two. He was shocked, of course, and I assured him I'd share details soon.

She didn't protest when I announced we were leaving her apartment. No question as to where we were going. She sagged with relief when I said it was time for us to go, assuring me it was what she needed. I held her to me the whole way here and couldn't stop staring just to assure myself she was okay. Now my body refuses to give her an inch of space as I gaze down at her while she sleeps. There's no question she belongs here with me.

Hearing the words that asshole said to her and what he was about to do before we arrived made my blood boil. Thanks to Cici's insistence that I stay and my security officer's instincts, we made it to her in time but not soon enough to keep his hands off her completely. Yet again, my own stubbornness almost got in the way. I won't make that mistake again.

There will be no doubt after tonight how I feel about her, and if I'm lucky, she'll give me the chance to prove it.

It looks like I'm about to find out. Judging by her movements, she's scared as she starts to wake.

"Lily, you're okay. I'm here. I've got you," I say soothingly, pulling her in tight and rubbing her back.

Blinking her eyes open, she looks up at me in relief, then nuzzles into my chest. I'm the luckiest man in the world right now. I don't think I deserve her in any way, but I vow to work on becoming the kind of man that does.

"How are you feeling, sweetheart? What's happening in that mind of yours?" I can't imagine the fear she must have gone through and the effect it will have. I want to be here for her and help her through this.

"I'm trying to figure out what I'm doing here and why you were even looking for me. The last time we were together you said we were done. I'm confused." Her head is on my chest, and she's running her fingers lightly over my skin as she lies there.

"That's not where I thought you'd start, and trust me, I do want to get to that, but can you tell me how you're doing right now? That was a lot to go through, and I'm worried about you, baby." I don't want her to hold anything in only to have it come back and haunt her. I want no distractions when we discuss our relationship.

"I just feel so stupid. I keep wondering if there were signs I missed along the way. To be completely blindsided like that is just crazy. How could the fact that he was mentally disturbed not register at some point over the years, or was I just that oblivious? I'm mad I let myself fall into that situation. And honestly, the worst part is I can't stop thinking about what was about to happen when you got there and if you hadn't... I was so helpless. I wouldn't have been able to stop him." After unloading it all, her sobs take over.

I hold her tight and let the tears flow. She needs this release. I knew it was there somewhere, waiting to come out, and I'm glad to be the one to comfort her while she lets go. Only when her breathing slows and her tears become a trickle do I speak.

"There's no telling how long he may have been like that, Lily. He may have been perfectly normal until something triggered a psychotic episode. Chances are, there were no signs, nothing you missed or would have picked up on. Don't rack your brain thinking back, and don't blame yourself for any part of this. You were the victim of a calculated attack. You trusted a friend who gave you no reason otherwise. As far as what could've happened... I can't say my mind is functioning any better than yours on that topic. We did get there in time, though, and what could have happened didn't. To imagine a different outcome does neither of us any good. You're here now, safe in my arms, and I swear I won't let anybody hurt you again." I hold her tight, never wanting to let go.

She rises slightly and leans on her elbow, looking at me. I wipe her tears as she speaks. "Thank you for coming for me. You still need to explain how you ended up on my doorstep, but I need to say something first. When I was in that room, not knowing what the future looked like or how it would end, I had one regret over all others... I never told you how I felt. I was afraid to scare you away. But you deserve to know. Sebastian, I love you. And it's okay if—"

I cut her off with a kiss. God, how I've missed her. She just made me the happiest fucking bastard in the world, and she has no idea I feel the same. Pulling back, I smile for the first time in days.

"God, you have no idea how happy it makes me to hear you say that. I was so afraid you were done dealing with my bullshit. The feelings I have for you scare the hell out of me, Lily, and rather than give in to them I kept trying to push you away. My dad took his own life. He left my brother and me because he was too in love with my mom and deep down it wrecked me. He chose his love for her over his love for us and I never got over it. I told myself I would never lose myself to love like he did." She wraps around me and buries her head in my chest.

"I'm so sorry, Sebastian. That wasn't fair to you and I'm sure it hurts." I pull back and lift her chin to look at me.

"I was on your doorstep this morning to tell you you're mine whether you liked it or not. I wasn't taking no for an answer, because, Lily, I get it now. I'm so fucking in love with you, it hurts. I'm sorry it took something like this to make me realize it for what it was. I fucked up." I cup her cheeks in my hands and pull her in close. "I love you, Lily Thompson, and I'll do whatever it takes to make it up to you from this moment on." The tears are rolling down her face as I kiss them away, before kissing her deeply, putting all the love so desperately trying to get out into this one kiss.

She pulls back a minute later to look at me. "Sebastian, I feel like I'm in a dream. I went from my worst nightmare to never wanting to wake up."

"Sweetheart, you don't ever have to wake up, because this is forever."

Epilogue

Five months later
Lily

"Lily, Mr. Dubree requested you in his office." Jackie, the marketing department's secretary, announces through the intercom.

"Sounds good. I'll head up shortly."

"Um, he said it was important and to drop whatever you're doing. Sorry," she says hesitantly.

"That's okay, Jackie. You're just the messenger. Thanks." I hang up and roll my eyes. Sebastian will only communicate through our secretaries at work these days. He's being stubborn because I won't move to the executive level with him. I admit, it would be a heck of a lot easier for us, but I refuse to be treated differently than other employees. Well, I am treated very differently, just not in regard to work.

The day he rescued me, my life changed drastically. After we both admitted our feelings, Sebastian tried demanding a few things. He wanted me to quit working for Brad and take on a permanent role at Dubree Enterprises. That one was easy, especially since the pay was worth it, and after my last conversation with Brad the night of the gala, I wasn't looking forward to returning. Now that I've graduated, I have a full-time position in the marketing department with a team of people I love and more than enough creative work to keep me busy.

The next thing he insisted on ended up being our first point of contention in our newly established relationship. He wanted me to move in with him, saying it was the only way he could rest, knowing I'd be safe. Part of me, the one that was still shaken up over my abduction, wanted to cave immediately. Even though Kevin was safely locked inside a psychiatric facility, the fear remained. The more independent side, however, rebelled. I wasn't ready to give up my own space, even though most nights I was at his place, or he was at mine. Needless to say, Sebastian doesn't do well with defiance, and after a grueling two months, I relented.

Cici was moving right after graduation anyway. She decided the only way to get her parents off her back was to take a job in another state, and *not* in property management. She put her people skills to good use and became a real estate agent in some booming town in Montana. She said it was far enough away but not the other side of the country so we could see each other easier. I haven't made it to Bozeman yet, and she's doing so well with her new job, she hasn't had time to visit either. I miss her like crazy, but at least I have Ebony. Cici was sad to leave her but refused to take her from me after the whole kidnapping episode. Ebony was glued to me after the whole ordeal, like she knew I needed comfort.

Since living together for the last three months, I've had time to reflect. I love Sebastian with all my heart, and I know he feels the same. But more than that, to feel truly cared for, for the first time in over seven years is humbling. He makes me want for nothing and treats me like the most precious thing in the world. It's a good feeling and made me realize how truly abandoned I'd felt since my dad left all those years ago. To have that weight lifted from my shoulders has made me breathe easier, smile more and enjoy life from a different perspective.

Lucy and I give each other knowing smirks as I pass by to open the door to his office, closing it behind me.

"Jackie said you needed to see me right away? I was right in the middle of something, you know." I love riling *him* up.

"You're going to be right in the middle of something else in a minute. Now get your ass over here and explain why Blake is the one telling me that you're not going home after work instead of hearing it from you." He scoots his chair back for me to come around and stand in front of him.

"Geez, he's fast. I just made plans an hour ago, and like I said, I was in the middle of something. If you'd been patient, you would've found out at lunch." I'm now leaning back against Sebastian's desk, facing him with my arms crossed over my chest.

"You had time to let Blake know, just not me?"

"That's because his day revolves around our schedules, and I wanted to give him ample time to make other plans. I know it's your night with Eli, so it wasn't time sensitive to tell you. You good now?" He's been very protective of me since that day five months ago. I'm lucky to have an ounce of freedom, but in all honesty, I love it. He makes me feel safe, and other than Cici, and now Lucy and Natalie since Cici up and moved away, there's no one else I care to be around anyway.

"You forgot to mention why it is you're not going home. And you've rolled your eyes twice now. Make it a third and you know what'll happen."

Make it a third…. *Hmmm, tempting.* "Cici texted me. She booked a last-minute flight to finally come visit and asked if I could meet for dinner. I probably won't be out late. It's just… she knows about your weekly nights out with Eli and figured it was perfect timing. It's not like I won't have security with me." Oops, that eye roll just slipped out. He grins knowingly.

Sebastian

I lunge forward and flip her around, bending her over my desk. Her delectable ass on display is mouthwatering. "You like to play with fire, don't you, Lily? You should know by now that I'm more tense on days I'll be away from you. I think you like to push my buttons." My little mouse has become quite the lion of late. She's almost as insatiable as me. "Your ass is begging for it, isn't it?"

"It wasn't intentional that time, just habit. And Sebastian, you act like this every Wednesday. You know you'll have to get used to it at some point and relax."

"Let me show you what I do to relax, Lily." Her skirt is pulled up, and I feel her smooth and silky skin.

"Grab the edge of my desk with both hands and don't move them. Understand?"

"Yes, sir." She grabs on while I pull back my hand and bring it down hard on her ass. The sound makes my dick jerk. She moans, and I bet she's already slick for me. I decide to find out.

"Is your pussy wet for me?" Plunging two fingers in, she cries out.

"Yes, Sebastian."

Fuck, she's always so ready. She probably started dripping on her way to my office. I remove my hand and smack her ass again, harder this time. She calls out my name, making my cock strain even more inside my slacks.

This time, after I dip into her soaking entrance, I bring my thumb up and rim her tight pucker above. I reach my other hand around to her front and rub her sweet spot as I slide into her tightness.

"Sebastian…" she moans.

"You like that, don't you, baby? Do you want me to fuck you here? Claim your last virgin hole?" Ever so slowly I move in and out while I rub her clit. I can feel her channel tightening, and I know she's close.

"Please, yes, I need it." She's right there, but I pull back.

"Don't worry, baby. It'll be mine soon, but we'll be in our bed for that. Right now, I'm going to fuck you so hard you're going to feel me all night." I unzip and guide the head to her entrance, rubbing it up and down, slathering it in her slickness. "You ready to come around my cock, baby?"

"Yes, please give it to me, Sebastian."

"Hold on tight, sweetheart. This won't be gentle." Pressing my hand onto her back, I push down firmly as I plunge in deep with one quick thrust. I don't pause before pulling back and pounding into her relentlessly. Using her body as leverage, I grab her shoulder with one hand and drive into her as hard as I can.

"Fuck, baby, you feel so tight like this. You're taking me so good." Over and over, I thrust, fucking her harder than ever before. I grunt in exertion. The feel of her round ass slapping up against me feels like sin and the noise is music to my ears. Bending her over my desk gets me so much deeper. She's screaming my name, begging me not to stop. With her climax closing in, I reach for her clit to bring it home.

"Good girl. You've got it." Her walls are clenching. "Scream for me, Lily. Give it to me, now." She comes undone, forcing my own climax to follow.

"Fuck, yes. Ahhh… God." I grunt out the rest of my release, filling her with my seed while I milk her climax as long as I can. Fuck, bringing her over the edge is one of my favorite things in life. I love pushing her to the limit of what she can take and even past it sometimes. What's surprising is how high her limits seem to be. Collapsing over her, I shower her back with kisses. God, I'll never tire of this. We lie there in silence for a moment, catching our breath.

I lift myself off, helping her up as I go. "Wow, Sebastian, that was… just wow. You've ruined me for life, I swear. There's no way you can top that."

"That sounds like a challenge, sweetheart. One I am certainly looking forward to. Luckily, we have our whole lives to complete it." I kiss her before she walks to the bathroom.

That's the hardest I've let her have it, she'll definitely be feeling that all night. It might not be a fair excuse, but I can't put her kidnapping to rest. It plagues my mind every time I'm without her, making the beast come out in me. My worry takes over, and it becomes difficult to keep myself in check. As important as it is that Eli and I have these weekly nights out, it still takes a toll on me. Which is precisely why I need them, to maintain some sort of sanity when it comes to my love for Lily. Falling hard for the woman in our life must run in the family. I can't wait until Eli finds his.

When she walks back in, I motion her over and pull her onto my lap, continuing our conversation from earlier. "I'm glad to hear Cici is coming to visit, but next time will you tell me your plans before I hear them from someone else? A text message at least?" She's laying her head on my shoulder, cuddled into me. My favorite place to have her—when she's not under me.

"That's the problem. It wouldn't have been a quick text. You would've wanted to know when, where and with who, then discuss which security guard was on shift. That's why I was waiting until lunch, so we had time for all your questions." I can't see them, but I know her eyes just rolled. I really need to break her of that habit one of these days. Or maybe not.

"You know, it would be easier if you had an office next to me and could just walk over." She's the most stubborn woman I've ever met and refuses to budge on this.

"Don't start, Sebastian. You know it's not going to happen. What do you and Eli have planned for tonight?" she asks, changing the subject and sitting up.

"Oh, you know, another wild night on the town." I lean in to kiss the tip of her nose. "No, we're just going to grab dinner at some restaurant Eli wants to try. Who knows, maybe we'll end up at the same place," I tease, knowing she has no idea what's in store.

"I wouldn't be surprised. You're lucky I love you and all your crazy." She leans in to kiss me goodbye.

Holding her tight, I deepen the kiss until her hands are tangled in my hair. Smiling, I pull away. "Damn right I am. I love you too, my little sex fiend. Have fun tonight and make good decisions," I say subtly as I slap her on the ass before she walks away.

"Always," she says, blowing me a kiss as she exits. *Thank God for soundproofing,* I think as I see Lucy at her desk, oblivious to what just happened.

Lily

"I still can't believe you get to have sex with your boyfriend in the office all the time. I'm so jealous. I never thought the day would come when you would be getting lucky more than me." Cici sighs dramatically.

"The best part is knowing I can't get in trouble with the boss." We both giggle as we walk into the club. I reluctantly let her talk me into stopping for one drink before heading home. She begged me, saying it's been too long and she missed me. She still knows how to pull my strings. Although it wasn't hard, I've really missed her too; FaceTime just isn't the same.

The bouncers know us, of course, being one of the owners' girlfriends and all, so we're escorted directly to the VIP. It's weird saying girlfriend or boyfriend. Living and working together has caused Sebastian and I to become closer in such a short amount of time. It's surreal and feels like so much more than just those simple labels already.

"Oh shoot. I forgot to text Sebastian that we were stopping here. Let me do that real quick." Reaching for my phone while Cici orders us each a cosmo, I immediately see a text from Sebastian. Shit.

Love of my life: Having fun?

Oh good, it was only five minutes ago. It must've been as we were walking in.

> Me: It's been great. She talked me into having one drink at the club. We just walked in.
>
> Love of my life: I know, Lily. I see you.
>
> Me: What?! You're here? Where are you?

I look around, trying to spot him, but I don't see him anywhere. This is so weird. Crap, he's probably pissed.

"Apparently he's here somewhere. I'm sure he's simmering over the fact that I didn't text him before we came," I tell her, continuing to look around.

"What? That's so weird. I thought he was going to dinner with Eli. He can't be mad at you since he didn't mention coming here either." She makes a good point.

> Love of my life: I'm disappointed you didn't inform me of your change of plans. You know I worry. That's twice today. What am I going to do with you?
>
> Me: Let it slide since you didn't tell me you were coming here either?
>
> Love of my life: The club is my job and I'm not worried about someone harming me. Enjoy your drink, Lily. I'll see you at home. Your punishment will be waiting.
>
> Me: Please, Sebastian, don't leave. I texted you the minute we sat down.

He doesn't respond.

"Well that sucks. He's upset I didn't tell him before we came and said he'd see me at home. Ugh, he's so frustrating sometimes." I sip my drink, still trying to spot him. I wouldn't put it past him to stay and keep an eye on me.

"I don't know how you put up with it, honestly. Are you sure it's not too much?" she asks with concern.

"It's weird, but I sort of like it. Some women might feel smothered, but I just feel cared for. I know he worries about me, and I don't blame him after what happened. We never argue because he concedes to anything not related to my safety. And honestly, Cici, sometimes I piss him off just to get what I want in the bedroom. I feel terrible admitting it, but I'd say it's a win-win." I giggle and sip my drink.

"Well in that case, go to the bathroom and freshen up. Then we'll get you home to your man so he can reprimand you." She winks at me knowingly.

I grab my clutch and head back. Once I'm finished and walking out from the ladies' room, someone grabs me from behind with a strong arm around my waist and a hand over my mouth, pulling me around the corner. I panic but immediately relax when I hear the soothing sound of Sebastian's voice.

"Do you remember the first test I gave you six months ago in this very spot? You passed with flying colors if I remember right, even though you wouldn't admit it," he says seductively as he removes his hand from my mouth and caresses down my neck.

"Yes, how could I forget?" I say, breathless.

"Well, you just passed your last test, Lily." I have no idea what he's talking about. Last test? Is he that mad about me not texting and telling me we're over? Wait, but he said I passed.

He flips us around, so I'm pinned with my chest against the wall. He's pressing into me from behind. I don't know what he's aiming for, but I'm so incredibly turned on right now it's sickening.

"Sebastian, what are you doing? I'm sorry I didn't text right away. I know you worry. I love you."

"Shh. It's okay, sweetheart. I had to make sure you understood exactly who I am and what you're getting into by being with me, that you're okay with it. I heard the whole conversation with Cici. I planned it with her. I need to know you can handle me, baby." He's whispering in my ear, still pressing me into the wall, while pushing his groin into me. Holy Christ.

"What… why?" I ask in confusion. He turns me around and steps back a foot, lowering to one knee as he reaches into his pocket and pulls something out. *Oh my God!*

"Because I love you, Lily Thompson, and I want you in my life now and forever. It may seem too soon to some, but I don't need any more time to be sure that you're the only woman for me. I know I'm possessive, but it's because I care for you. I know I'm strict, but it's because I worry about you. I know I'm domineering, but it's because I want you. And I know I smother the hell out of you, but it's because I love you more than I ever thought possible. Please say yes to being mine forever. Let's add another first to both our lists. Lily, will you marry me and allow me to take care of you for the rest of our lives?" The tears are streaming down my face as he finishes. I catch the slightest movement in the corner of my eye and look over to Cici and Eli standing nearby, waiting for my response.

I turn back to Sebastian and see the love in his eyes along with the nervous anticipation for my answer. "Yes! Yes, I'll marry you. I want forever with you too. I love you so much, Sebastian!" I'm crying tears of joy as he slides the ring on my finger and stands to pull me into his embrace.

"Lily, you've made me the happiest man in the world more times than I can count, and I vow to spend the rest of my life doing the same for you."

Ready for Jackson's story in *Dangerous Pursuit?*

Mia Nightingale Marcos is more nightmare than nightingale.

I'm handed the reins to the family business along with an inexperienced assistant barely out of high school. Not to mention, she's distractingly beautiful and completely off-limits. I plan to be so unbearable she'll quit, but she's tougher than she looks. Now she appears to be hiding something and the deeper I dig, the more invested I become, causing my world to spin.

Just when I think I've got her figured out, she vanishes, leaving a trail of unanswered questions, sending me on a dangerous pursuit.

Jackson Soloman is the boss from hell.

But I can handle him. Balancing work by day and poker by night was a breeze until Jackson stepped in. It was easier when he was making my life hell, not trying to play hero. Now, I can't shake him off, and with the growing attraction between us, I'm not sure I want to.
Just when I think I've hit the jackpot, I'm forced to fold, leaving everything behind for a chance at salvation.

Will Mia and Jackson survive the trials of deceit and danger that lie ahead? In a heart-wrenching climax that tests their love and commitment, every decision could be their last bet.

Scan the barcode below to explore book three, Dangerous Pursuit, in the unbelievably hot ***Pursuit Series.***

Don't miss Lucy and Justin's story in *Holidate Pursuit,*
a holiday novella in The Pursuit Series

**Do I have a sign on my back that says,
'Love her and leave her'?
Because that's what it feels like these days.**

I thought I'd never see Justin again when he ghosted me after the best night of my life. But guess who shows up at the company Christmas party months later wanting to talk? I don't think so Mr. Burns. Burn me once, shame on you. Burn me twice, shame on me. That's sober Lucy talking. Drunk Lucy has a different idea—she asks him to stand in as my fake fiancé this Christmas. Thank God he's smart enough to say no… or is he?

One week. One bed. How could I resist?

I had my reasons for disappearing on Lucy, and I've regretted it ever since. So, when the opportunity presents itself, I can't refuse my shot at redemption. Just as it starts to feel like a second chance, the tree comes crashing down.

**Filled with humor, heart, and holiday magic,
Holidate Pursuit is a fun, steamy romance about
second chances and choosing love over all else.**

To Purchase *Holidate Pursuit,* visit www.bethanyrosa.com
Or scan below:

If you'd like to purchase other books in the Pursuit Series or keep up with upcoming releases and learn more about author Bethany Rosa, visit www.BethanyRosa.com

Or scan below: